BROKEN BLADES

NOVELS BY **LIZ SAUCO**
available from Dark Waters Publishing:

BLADES OF THE GODDESS

LOST BLADES
BROKEN BLADES
BLADES REFORGED

COLORS OF MAGIC

Broken Blades

Blades of the Goddess Book 2

Liz Sauco

Dark Waters Publishing

Broken Blades

Hardcover ISBN: 978-1-960723-06-2

Paperback ISBN: 978-1-960723-05-5

E-book ISBN: 978-1-960723-04-8

Audiobook ISBN: 978-1-960723-07-9

Published by Dark Waters Publishing

5600 Post Rd

Suite 114-PMB#307

East Greenwich RI 02818

First edition: January 2024

10 9 8 7 6 5 4 3 2

Cover design by Liz Sauco

lizsauco.com

To Jessy and Jen.

WORLD MAP
GAIA
COUNTRIES - 2026 AG

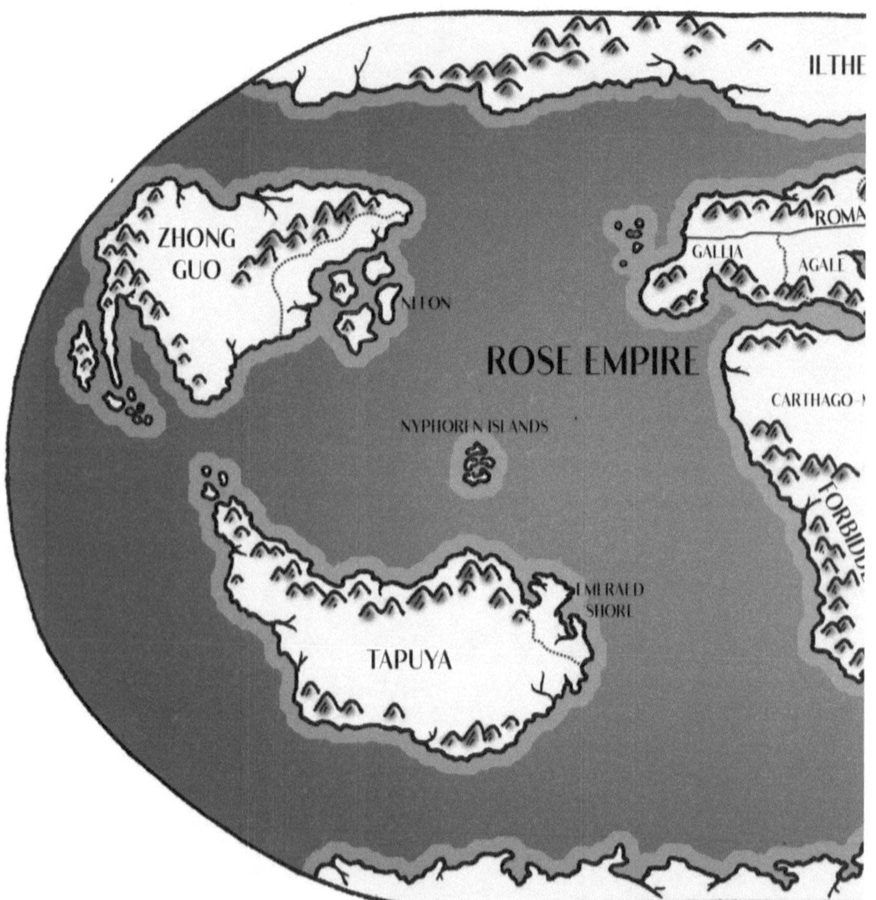

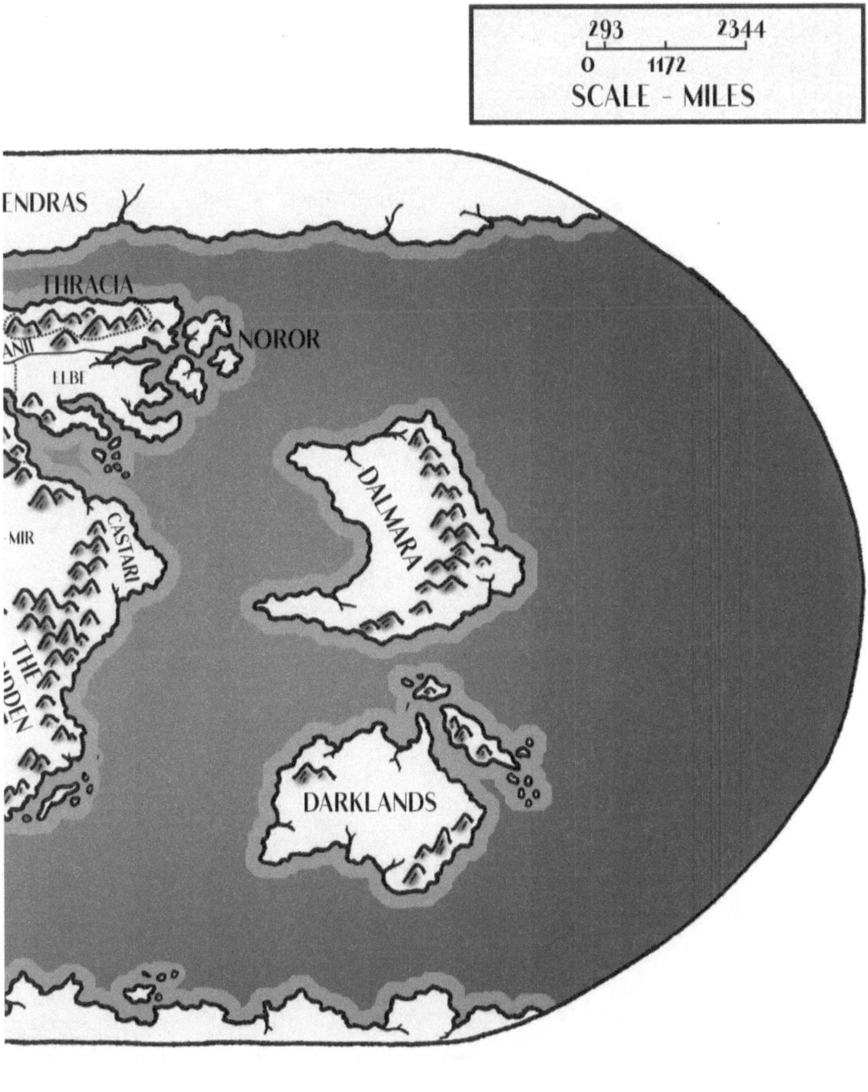

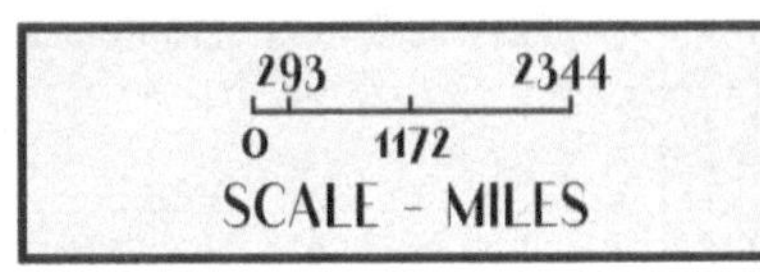
293
2344
0
1172
SCALE - MILES

ENDRAS
THRACIA
NOROR
ELBE
MIR
CASTARI
DALMARA
THE
DEN
DARKLANDS

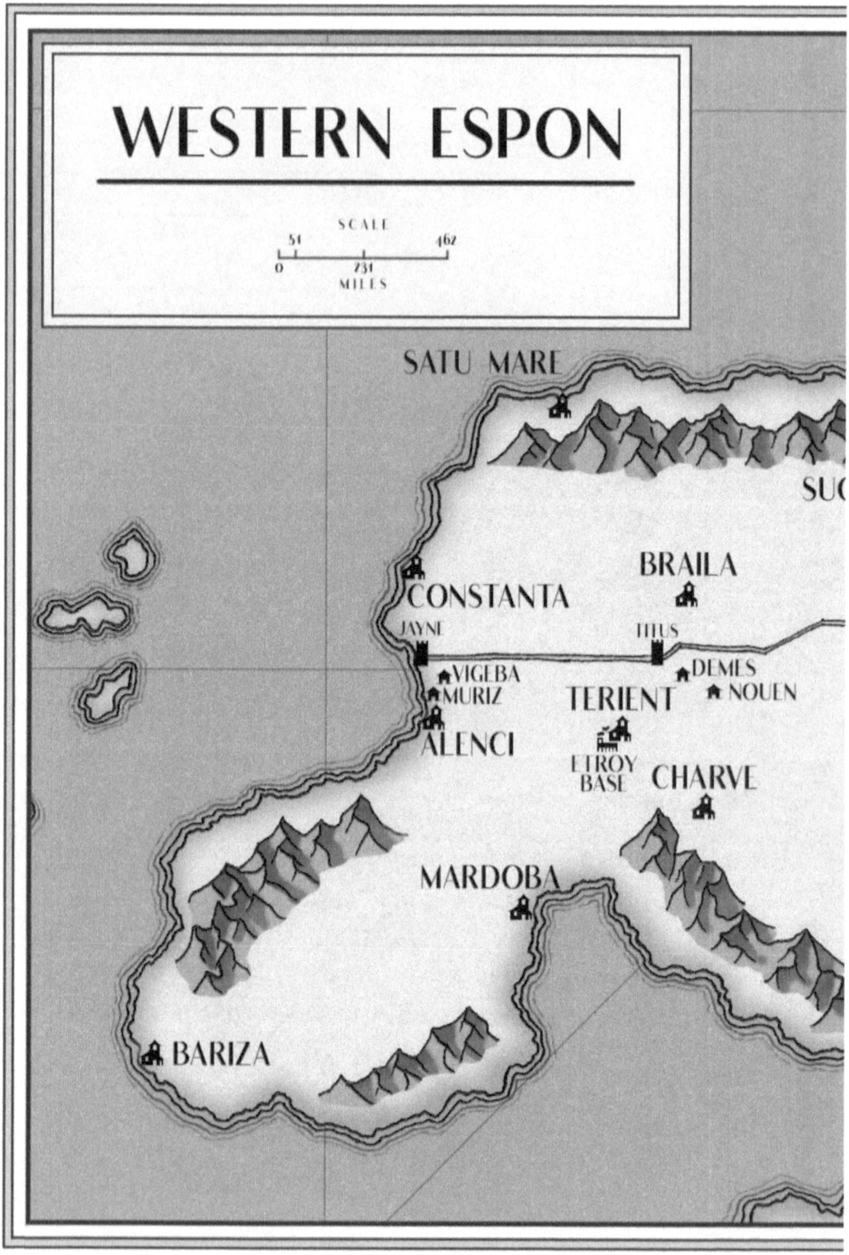

WESTERN ESPON
SCALE
51
462
0
231
MILES
SATU MARE
SUC
BRAILA
CONSTANTA
JAYNE
TITUS
VIGEBA
DEMES
MURIZ
TERIENT
NOUEN
ALENCI
ETROY
BASE
CHARVE
MARDOBA
BARIZA

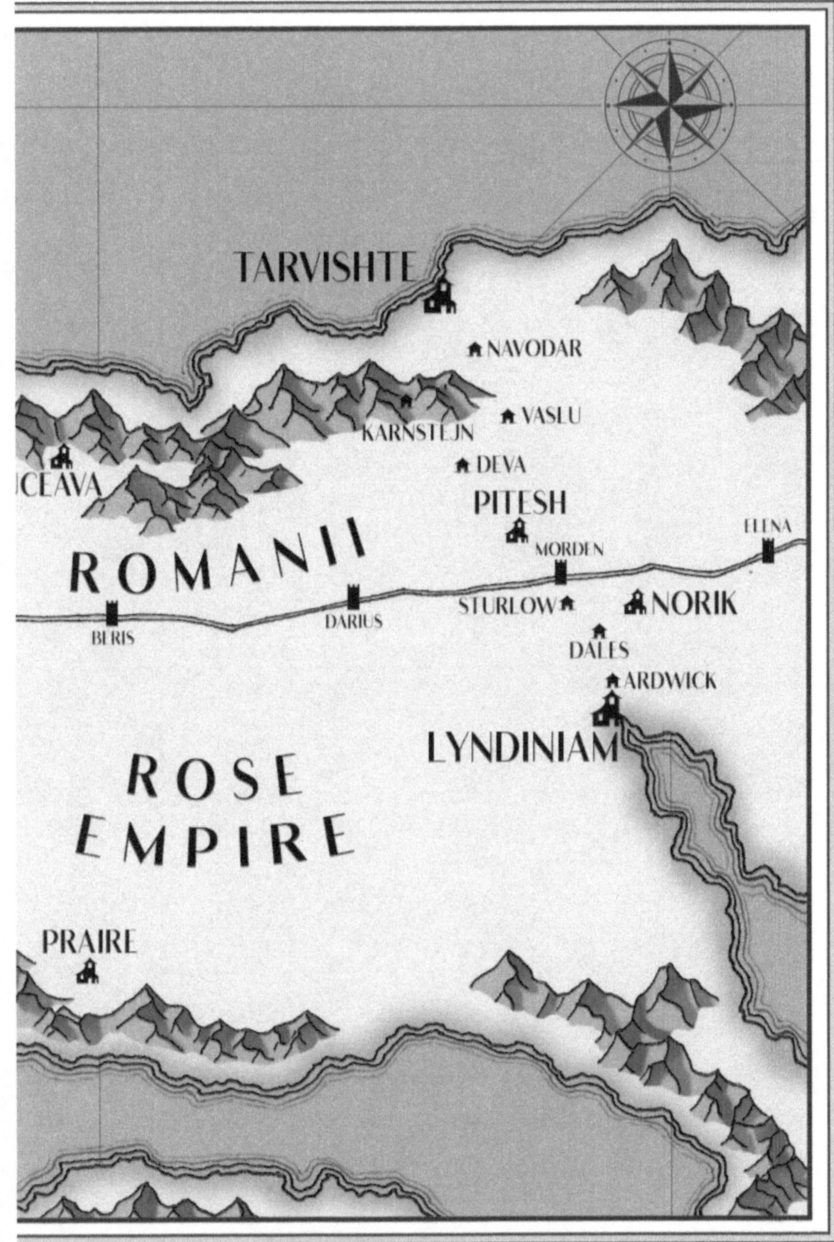

TARVISHTE
NAVODAR
VASLU
KARNSTEJN
DEVA
PITESH
ELENA
MORDEN
ROMANII
STURLOW
NORIK
UCEAVA
DARIUS
DALES
BERIS
ARDWICK
LYNDINIAM
ROSE
EMPIRE
PRAIRE

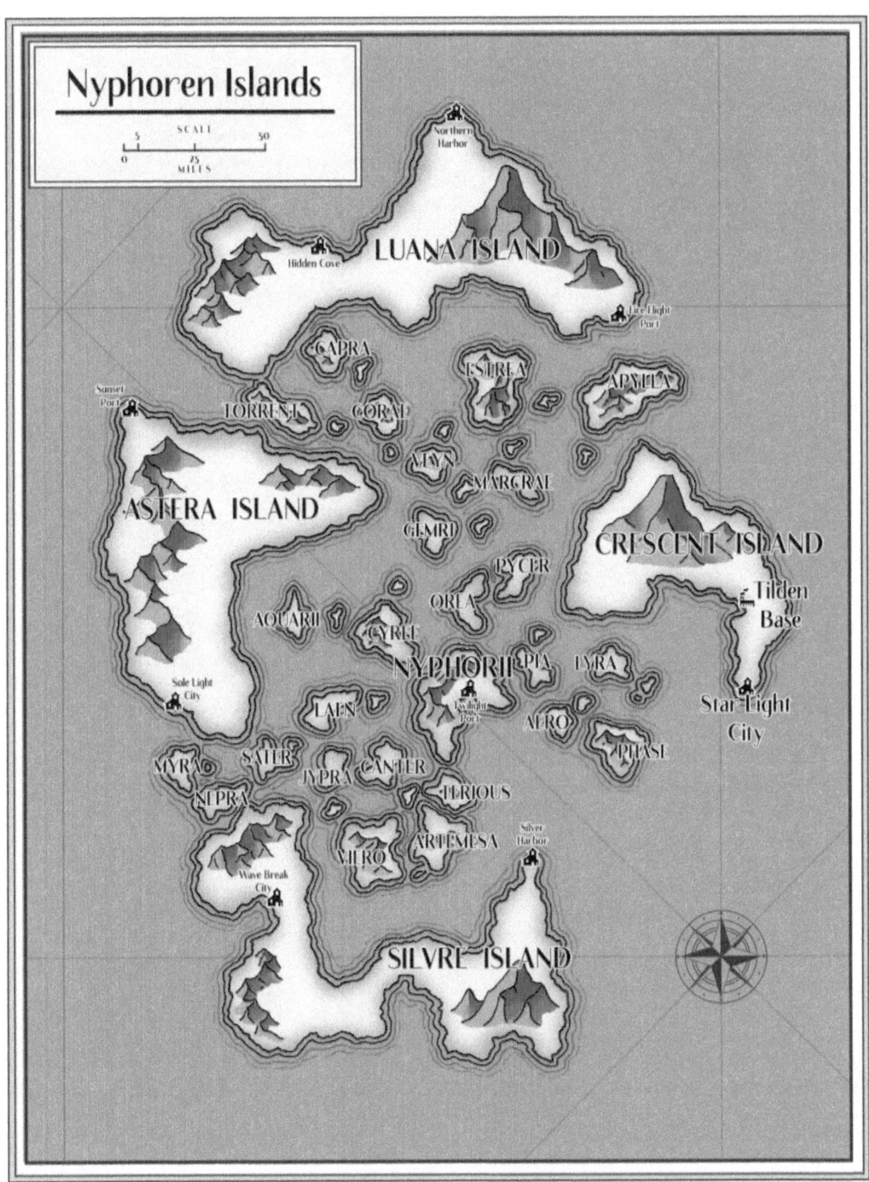

Nyphoren Islands
SCALE
5
50
0
25
MILES
Northern Harbor
LUANA ISLAND
Hidden Cove
Fire Flight Port
CAPRA
ESTREA
APYLLA
Sunset Port
TORRENT
CORAL
MEYN
MARGRAE
ASTERA ISLAND
GEMRI
CRESCENT ISLAND
RYCER
Tilden Base
OREA
AQUARII
CYRIE
NYPHORII
PIA
LYRA
Star Light City
Sole Light City
LAEN
Twilight Port
AERO
MYRA
SATER
CANTER
PHASE
JYPRA
NEPRA
TERIOUS
ARTEMESA
Silver Harbor
VIERO
Wave Break City
SILVRE ISLAND

November 21, 2026 A.G.

Final Notes – Corpse of Abomination

Magic is life.

Life, and a will. The ability to affect and change the world around us. Even those who do not have what we consider to be magic ability are, technically, magical; they just lack the more dramatic application of their will that "magical" people are capable of. The terminology we use is quite imprecise, but this is a digression.

Why then does *technology* affect magic so? What about tech prevents or impedes that application of will? I imagine that if I knew the answer to that many more things would become clear to me. If the gods know, they do not speak of it, but by their very nature they are perhaps incapable of understanding the interaction in the first place. All living things are magical, but they *are* magic. Magic, and a will. Thus are Hades and Her siblings.

Another digression.

I have dissected the specimen of Abomination that delivered itself to us.

*Note: I shall have to come up with a better system of classification for them; demons are also Abomination, but these are certainly not demons. Jamirh calls them "bionics," but I'm not sure that is as precise as it could be either.

~~Cyborgs?~~

~~Anathema of Reality?~~

No, that doesn't roll off the tongue. Doesn't roll on it, either.

*Workshop later.

Tech has been integrated into an Avari's nervous system in a way I would not have thought possible had I not seen the results. The Avari had magic potential at one point, but the channels by which they might have manifested their will on the world have all been burnt out. Because of the integration of the tech, or was it something necessary to get the tech to integrate? Or did it happen before – a requirement of being chosen as a subject in the first place?

I can state this was definitely done to the Avari. There is not enough of their original body left for them to have done it to themselves.

Remaining organic matter: the brain, most of the head, left eye, nerves in the spinal column, upper chest, right shoulder and upper arm.

Everything else has been replaced by metal and tech. Even the spine itself has been replaced around the nerves with a metal casing (see notes from Nov 20).

I'm not familiar with the metal. It is very strong, and it is resistant to magic on its own. Perhaps a specially crafted alloy – steel and... I shall have to do more research.

*Note: Research magic-resistant alloys.

*Note: Come up with a better name.

A thought – did the subject still have any of its own will remaining by the time the transformation was complete? If not, why use a living being at all? It seems the most important part to save was the nervous system. In some ways, the brain of a person is like a very complex computer. Perhaps they were unable to build an actual computer complex enough to run the programming they wanted the end result to run on, and so co-opted an Avari brain to somehow run it instead?

Does the species matter? If so, why? Could the process be replicated on a Human? What about a dog? Or a Lorn? Is it just easy for them to acquire Avari subjects? How important is it that the subject have magic potential?

Magic is life, and a will. Every living thing is magical. Technically, the specimen lived when it attacked Jamirh in the palace. But I'm not sure it had a will anymore. Perhaps that is what makes it "Abomination" – the fundamental denial of a law of the universe, a sin against the world itself. The rare case of a mortal losing their will usually results in their death soon after, righting the sin done to them or by them. This is Hades' gift to mortals. But if She cannot reach these constructs, then the sin persists. And the world starts to warp as a result?

~~*Note: Ask Hades about the~~

Fact: Hades confirms She cannot reach the Avari who have become Abomination, and She struggles to perceive them. Ostensibly this is due to interference from the tech. Above hypothesis seems likely as a result.

They gave it an extra pair of arms. How necessary was that? The end result is still mostly Avari in form, even if most parts were replaced, but does it have to be? Could they build a casing for the nervous system with the shape of a vehicle or an animal? Is there a size restriction?

Many questions are still outstanding, far more than have been covered here. I will be unable to answer them without more data.

-Ander 11/21/26

Chapter One

"Jamirh! Are you okay?!"

Jamirh looked up from the white warg whose ears he was scratching to see Jeri practically fly into the courtyard, her dark uniform and long pale braid a sight he had sorely missed the past few days. He was surprised by how tired and frazzled she looked, as though she had rushed straight here from Pitesh as soon as she heard the news.

"I'm fine," he reassured, his long, pointed ears twitching upward. He gave the warg one last scratch before straightening up. "Welcome back. How was your trip?"

"What happened?" she exclaimed, stopping short and looking him up and down, clearly trying to determine if he had been injured. He guessed that was fair; she had spent quite some time and effort to ensure his safety in Tarvishte only for him to be attacked as soon as she was gone. "Are you sure you're okay?"

He ran a hand over his head self-consciously, checking that his ruby-colored hair was still in its ponytail. "Well... a lot happened, actually," he began, considering how best to explain in a way that wouldn't panic her more.

The warg whined, trying to push its head under his other hand for more attention as it ignored his attempt to straighten his vest.

"Things have changed a little around here since you left," he added, waving a hand at Frir, who was lounging on the other side of the courtyard on a marble bench. Frir waved back.

Jeri's green eyes narrowed as she took in the other Vampire. "Yes, I was told the Black Watch has been keeping a close eye on you," she said, her voice cooling. Jamirh wondered if she was remembering how Frir had accidentally revealed to Jamirh the Vampire belief that he was Ebryn Stormlight, the famous Avari Hero reborn.

Jamirh still didn't know what he thought of that. It was complicated. On one hand, they had good reasons to think what they did – he shared looks and abilities with the long-dead Avari, and their goddess had told them he was Ebryn reborn. On the other hand, he hated Ebryn and everything he stood for. But then, there was also the other thing...

"We need to move, or we die. Again."

Jamirh repressed a shudder at the memory and a voice that was his, but also not. Had it been Ebryn, or his imagination kicking into overdrive as a result of stress? He wasn't sure. No one seemed one hundred percent sure, not even the goddess herself. He still, after everything, had more questions than answers.

He could leave that part out.

"I was attacked by an Abomination, which turned out to be one of the super-secret bionics the Empire has been rumored to be creating, but Ander and Vlad killed it pretty handily after I spent several minutes flailing about in the dark with it. Then I found out

Hel is Hades – and that was a surprise, let me tell you – and then we had a conversation and I currently have possession of the Crystal Light Blade because of it. Everything has been in a sort of lockdown since, and there is always a member of the Black Watch in visual range of me." The warg made a quiet woof. "And I've been hanging around the wargs more, on Ander's recommendation."

Jeri stared at him like he had grown a second head. "What?"

Had he cut too much out of that explanation? Maybe, though he thought that covered all the high points. It had been a rough couple of days. Jamirh had thought about the attack so much that everything was starting to blur together. He really needed to stop thinking about it for a while, but how could he?

The warg gave a slightly annoyed huff and pushed its head under his hand again. He automatically started scratching behind its ears.

"The Abominations are being manufactured by the Empire, from what we can tell. They are combining Avari with tech." Jamirh sighed. "Avari have been going missing for years. I guess we sort of found them. Or... what's left of them. Ander could probably tell you more; he's been studying the corpse."

Jeri winced. "And it was the Abomination that somehow knocked out power in Pitesh and Tarvishte? I found evidence of one being in Pitesh, but not what it did."

Jamirh nodded. "According to Ander, yes, though he's not sure how yet. Apparently Hel saw something similar happen shortly before she lost her avatar. She says it also disrupts magic at short range, and they use a UV weapon against Vampires so there's a whole bunch of problems they can cause."

"It would have been too much to hope that they would be easily dealt with." Jeri turned another glare on Frir that Jamirh wasn't sure he deserved. The other Vampire wilted, then disappeared into a shadow. "Why the wargs, though?"

Jamirh shrugged. "Ander thinks they'll act as extra protection, or at least a warning. They were all very agitated while the Abomination was on the grounds; it's possible they sensed it before it revealed itself."

The warg blinked up at him in contentment as it leaned into him, its considerable weight almost knocking him over.

"Interesting," Jeri responded slowly, eyeing the warg with a frown.

The warg wagged its ridiculously large tail.

She grinned suddenly. "Remember when you were terrified of them?"

His ears flicked down in annoyance. "You mean when you showed up as a four-foot-tall wolf-creature after spending the previous couple of nights howling at us? You're right, I have no idea why *that* would have been terrifying."

Her grin turned sheepish. "I was howling *for* you, not at you, for what it's worth."

An even larger gray warg wandered into the courtyard. It padded over, sitting next to Jamirh and looking at him hopefully.

Jeri shook her head. "They are attention hogs, that's for sure," she drawled as Jamirh shifted so he could pet both at once.

"They kind of remind me of the pigeons in Lyndiniam. I mean, they're a lot bigger, and furrier, and more interested in people than the stuff they find on the ground, but they're everywhere to the point where you just get used to their presence," Jamirh explained. "And sometimes they look at people the way the pigeons looked at the shiny things they found," he added with a laugh.

Jeri rolled her eyes. "They can also be very interested in shiny things on the ground, so I wouldn't discount that as a similarity."

Suddenly, both wargs looked off into the distance for a moment before getting up and trotting away without so much as a single glance back.

"And there they go." Jeri sighed. "They definitely have minds of their own. Very appropriate creatures to be associated with the Lady." Her eyes slid towards him. "You said Hel lost her avatar?"

Jamirh gazed after the wargs as they wandered off. "Yeah."

Several moments passed.

Jeri coughed. "You said *Hel* lost *Her* avatar?" she tried again. "I thought you said–"

"Yeah, but I'm still calling her Hel," he interrupted. "She said it was okay."

Jeri's mouth formed a small "o." There was another minute of silence as she processed that. "How did you find out? Did She tell you? She wanted it to come from Her."

"Yeah, no, it didn't quite work out that way." He looked down, trying to brush the warg fur off his clothes.

The Vampire winced. "And you said you have the Blade now, too?" she asked hesitantly.

"Yup," he drawled, popping the "p." "Like I said, things have happened around here." He turned, beginning to walk back to the palace. "Though I have to say I'm impressed that the government didn't lie to the citizens about what happened."

"Why would it?" Jeri asked, sounding baffled as she followed.

Jamirh shrugged. "If something like that attack happened in the Empire, there is no way the truth would be reported. They would release some cover story, like 'a gas line exploded' or 'this very important part failed and exploded'. Reassurances that it wouldn't happen again would be given, and that would be the end of it."

Jeri stared. "People died."

"And?" he asked wryly as they entered the Palace of Dusk. The grand entryway and architecture of the building always made him feel small. "That wouldn't stop them. 'Those people died when the gas line exploded.' See? Logical conclusion."

The look of horror on her face was almost funny. "And people would believe that?"

Jamirh snorted. "Oh hell no. We'd know it was a coverup; we just wouldn't know what for. I don't know how much gas lines are even used in the Empire anymore." He considered that for a minute. "Actually, theories about bionic super-soldiers were pretty popular when we left Lyndiniam; it's very possible that the real explanation would have accidentally been floated around. People really like their conspiracy theories." He hummed. "I actually thought Hel was bionic when I first met her. Her magic was easier to accept as very advanced tech instead of, well, magic."

"That's a little ironic, all things considered," Jeri snorted. "She is so, so very terrible when it comes to anything even remotely tech-based. She doesn't seem to understand it at all, and it doesn't seem to like Her, either."

"I also had no idea that they looked like the monstrosity that attacked me, or I would have never made that mistake," Jamirh added with a shudder as they approached the quarters he had been staying in since Jeri had brought him to Tarvishte. "There was so little of the original Avari left. So much metal, and just... the strangest feeling of wrongness."

"Demons can cause that feeling too," Jeri mused. "I wonder why, if these Abominations are artificially made, they have the same effect, or something very similar. At least it makes it easier to determine if they've been through a place recently."

Jamirh blinked. "That's what you were tracking, when you went to Pitesh? You were looking for that... feeling, specifically?"

Jeri nodded. "The Lady and I both sensed it on the border of the Waste when we were coming north, so I know what the current problem 'feels' like. Such things can sometimes leave a residue of sorts in places it has been, if you know what you are looking for. So I was sent to Pitesh to look for it."

"I thought you were..." He stopped, thinking about it. "Never mind, I have no idea what I thought you were doing. Something magical, I guess, but that doesn't really make sense, does it? You don't have that kind of magic."

"No, I do not," she laughed. "Just a Vampire's better sense of the metaphysical. And occasionally the senses of a warg." She paused. "Very occasionally the senses of a cloud of bats."

"A cloud of bats?" Jamirh hadn't seen that one yet. "As in a whole group of bats? One person becoming multiple... how does that work?"

"It's hard to explain, but it does make perfect sense when you are a cloud of bats," Jeri said thoughtfully. "It's not a form I choose very often, but it is popular among some of the other Vampires."

"But are you controlling each bat separately? Or collectively? Does your mind become many minds that all sort of work together?" They came to a stop by his door.

"Sometimes, it is best not to think too hard about how something works," she suggested gently. "Especially when magic is concerned."

"Don't *you* need to know how it works?"

She shook her head. "No. In fact, sometimes things will... sort of break, if you think about them too hard."

Jamirh rolled his eyes as he opened the door. "Tech is simpler to understand than magic. At least it works the way it's supposed to."

Jeri hummed softly. "Does it, though?" She stopped as she entered the room, staring. "That's new."

"Like I said, there have been some changes around here." He walked over to stand next to the new television. Though it wasn't nearly as sleek as the vid screens he was used to seeing in Lyndiniam, it still got the job done. "Vlad basically declared that since I am going to be here for a while, my rooms might as well be set up for it, so I got a few new things. Apparently Vlad and a few other people around here like to be able to get news and other programs from the Empire, so they set mine up to be able to do the same, which is cool. And I somehow got a whole small kitchen, which I can only assume was through palace shenanigans, since that doorway wasn't there before." He gestured to the small space visible through the new opening. "I don't know that I'll ever really use it, but it's nice I guess."

"Uh huh." Jeri poked her head into the new room before turning back to Jamirh. "This feels more like an apartment now. Anything else new?"

"A few random things…" He trailed off, seeing her gaze land on the object on the long side table. "And yeah, that."

"So you did take it," she murmured, eyes glued to the Blade. "I wasn't sure anything would convince you to do so."

He shrugged awkwardly, eyeing it with distaste. "I don't know how helpful me having it will be, but…"

"Yes, a weapon, a sword? We are good with swords."

"…after having been trapped in a hallway with one of those things and *no* weapon, I figure any help I can get will be good, and Hel said the Blade will even destroy them on contact," he finished, shaking off the memory of the voice that was almost his. "Even if I don't know how to use it, I should at least be able to make contact, right?"

Jeri was silent for a long time, eyes never moving. "It is more than that," she finally began. "It's symbolic in ways I don't quite think you understand. Whether or not you believe you are the Hero reborn, others will, and seeing the Hero with the Crystal Light Blade sends a message. What that message is will be interpreted differently by different people." Her mouth twisted into a grimace. "Some will see it as a message of hope, since they will see you as their defender, and others of despair, because there must be something awful for you to defend them from. The Empire will certainly see it as a threat when they find out, and they will probably try even harder to kill you. Other political powers may start trying to position themselves to aid you or impede you, depending on what they think will benefit them the most."

"You paint such a pretty picture," Jamirh muttered, his ears drooping.

She shrugged. "What is done is done; it will be what it will be at this point. As far as actually wielding the Blade goes, however, I don't think we need to worry too much – if Miravu is right, we just need to show you how to use it, and as a Master of Blades you should be able to pick it up fairly quickly."

Jamirh fought back a wince, since the one thing he had not done in her absence was practice. "I still need to figure out how to use that ability properly. It helped keep me alive against that bionic monstrosity, but I don't think I'm using it in any way like how Miravu described."

"Thinking about it as 'using it properly' is probably not going to help you do so." Jeri laughed. "It is an innate magic; this is one of those things thinking too hard about doesn't help with."

"Well, I can't just *not* think about it," he protested. "That's not going to get me anywhere either."

Jeri's lips twitched. "And yet... well, we'll work on it."

"You can help me learn how to use it, right?" Jamirh asked. "Since you use swords?"

Her eyebrows raised. "You really want to learn how to use it? Properly, I mean?"

"I think I kind of have to at this point," he admitted, picking the thing up. It was heavier than it looked. "I still don't like Ebryn, and I definitely don't like being associated with him, but..." His stomach twisted, the words tasting like ash.

"I understand," Jeri said, sparing him from having to continue the thought.

"And definitely not Ander," he inserted quickly, remembering the one bout between the two of them. It hadn't been a fun experience, and he didn't much feel like revisiting it.

"Well, Ander could teach you, in that he does know how to use a longsword, but I think he is a poor choice for a teacher in general." Jeri winced slightly. "As we saw."

"Yeah, I'd like to try to avoid that." At least he had managed to get the better of the priest in the last exchange. "What *is* his deal, anyway? Sometimes he seems like he's trying to be helpful, and then..."

Jeri settled herself down on one of the couches with a sigh. "Ander is... well, something of a mystery, for all that he's been here for three hundred years. He never talks about himself. He's one of the Lady's own, so he's trusted, but... he's weird. We've never quite figured him out. And he never goes far from the Temple."

Jamirh blinked, not sure what to think of that.

The Vampire shook her head. "But on the topic of training, of course I'll help you. If the Abomination can reach you here, then we should try to give you every possible advantage you can get." She tilted her head as she studied the Blade in Jamirh's hands. "If Ebryn was also a Master of Blades, then what a waste of potential. He did have a reputation for being extremely stubborn though, so it seems pretty in character for him to pick one weapon and then refuse to try anything else. Try to think of it that way – you'll be *better* than Ebryn by the time we're done."

"Extremely stubborn" did sound like Ebryn, from the little he had heard about the long-dead Avari from people who had known him. It didn't sound like the voice he had heard while trying to survive his encounter with the bionic Abomination. That voice had been trying to be helpful, had sounded like it cared about his survival. Ebryn didn't fit that picture. Jamirh wasn't even sure Ebryn had cared about his *own* survival. And he thought he'd seen an image of something very much like the bionic attacking him, but Ebryn had never fought bionics. Ebryn had fought demons.

So then, what was it? Who was it? Had it just been his imagination? The more time that passed, the more difficult it was to remember.

Jamirh hated not knowing things. But if even a goddess wasn't sure, how was he going to find out? He had no interest in putting himself in that sort of situation again, Blade or no Blade. If he had to face the Abominations again, it would be on his terms, and he wouldn't need a voice in his mind to save him. He would save himself.

"Everything okay?" Jeri's voice was concerned as she studied him. He realized he had just been standing there, staring off into space, for probably longer than was normal.

"Yeah, fine," he responded quickly, trying to hide his embarrassment. "Just spaced out for a minute, sorry." He returned the Blade to its new home on his side table.

She eyed him for a moment longer before turning to the television. "Have you found anything fun to watch yet? Does it also get our channels, or just the Empire's?"

"Both." Jamirh turned on the television and sat down in one of the chairs. A pair of Human women were sitting behind a news desk, images of a mostly destroyed compound of sorts cycling to the side of them. He was about to change the channel to find something more entertaining when he saw the ticker at the bottom read "Aftermath of the Charve Military Base Explosion."

Jamirh blinked. "Hey, that's where Ander said Hel was being held, isn't it?"

Jeri studied the images. "That sounds correct. Wow, She did *not* go down quietly."

"You think she did all that?" Jamirh asked, aghast as he stared at the damage. Multiple buildings had been condemned, whole sections of them having been destroyed. "It looks like there were multiple explosions all across the base."

"Well, She *is* a goddess," Jeri said slowly as the anchors discussed rescue efforts. "And destruction is one of Her domains, so I wouldn't say it's beyond Her abilities, even if She was in a form that limited what She could do." Her voice sounded troubled, almost as though she were trying to convince both of them that that was the case.

"I guess we could ask Ander?" Jamirh suggested hesitantly. "Would he be able to ask her?"

"Anyone can ask Her; Ander's just more likely to hear the answer." She shrugged. "And then he might or might not relay that answer. It honestly might be better to go to the Temple and try to ask Her yourself. He doesn't like to be treated like a phone."

"Maybe that Human did some of it," he theorized, looking at the debris. "Wasn't he supposed to be helping her escape?"

"True," she agreed. "I guess we would have to ask to be sure, though."

"I wonder what happened to him," Jamirh mused. "Did he die with Hel's body? Or did he escape? I didn't think to ask her when we talked about it."

Jeri hesitated. "It doesn't look good from these pictures, but maybe he made it out?"

"...and hundreds of people found themselves trying to get onto the base just after the explosion, but when questioned, none seem to remember why," one of the anchors was saying. "The military is still looking into the strange phenomenon."

Jamirh looked at Jeri, who shrugged. "Could be any number of things, honestly, though it sounds like a Queen's Challenge."

He cocked his head to the side. "That shriek-thing she did to the door when we broke out of jail?"

Jeri winced. "Yes. Please don't remind me."

"I would say when you have a hammer, everything looks like a nail, but as a goddess, isn't she technically the hammer?" he mused thoughtfully.

The Vampire twitched. "There's no excuse for using that sort of magic on a door."

The first anchor cut herself off mid-sentence, looking as though she were listening to something through her earpiece. "This is breaking news; we have just been informed that the massive amount of destruction at the Charve Military Base was caused by a gas line explosion," she explained. "One of the old lines runs under the base and exploded at various points due to corrosion..."

Jeri turned very slowly to look at Jamirh, who just shrugged. "What can I say? A lot of our gas lines are apparently faulty."

Chapter Two

Takeshi looked up at the large stone tower lit by the waxing moon above. Magic traveled across its surface, powerful enough that it was visible to the naked eye, lines of power fading in and out of the gray brick. The Wall stretched in either direction as far as the eye could see, its smooth surface unbroken, a testament to the ultimate defense – an aegis cast over a whole country.

It was extremely impressive. Based on the colors threading through the stone he guessed nine people had been involved in the casting, which was an amazing display of skill and coordination. An aegis was the most difficult defense magic to cast that he knew of, though he had never heard of it being tied to an actual wall before. Unfortunately he had no idea how to get past it. He had found one of the towers, but it lacked any sort of entrance, and an aegis was notoriously impossible to break through without the caster's permission. He could throw everything he had at it and he would be drained of strength long before the aegis even noticed. No wonder no one had heard from Romanii in centuries.

The shinobi stepped back to consider, shivering as the wind cut through him. The temperature had done nothing but drop the farther north he got, and the utter desolation of the Waste hadn't provided any sort of cover or break from the weather. He was also exhausted; by his best estimate it had been around twenty-eight hours since he had last truly slept, though he wasn't completely sure. Time seemed to be jumping in strange spurts.

That was almost certainly a bad sign.

"Agreed."

And the memories of the voices of the women he had failed continued to follow him, adding to a steadily growing list of things that were tipping the mission inevitably towards failure. Taken in aggregate, everything that had happened since he had left Ni Fon indicated that he was not going to succeed, either through design or circumstance. Too many things had failed to add up, and he was losing hope. Where did that leave him?

No, he couldn't abandon his mission. He had to keep going.

"Do you?"

He tried to shut out the voices of doubt that were creeping in, Hel's and Hotaru's voices blending together in his mind until he could no longer tell who had said what. This was all he had left; he was not going to turn his back on it. They had both died for it. He had to believe his goal was still achievable.

He just needed to break it down into achievable steps. The Wall was problem number one. He turned his entire focus to solving that, going back over the few things Hel had managed to impart as she lay dying.

"You need to take this north. Present it to any of the towers along the Warcross Wall; it will grant you passage into Romanii."

He pulled the violet spell crystal shaped like a hound out from his pocket, studying it. It was a strange shape for a spell crystal, one very difficult to create. A key, maybe? She had clearly expected to be able to return through the Wall. It also didn't quite feel like a spell crystal somehow. Then again, he'd felt not quite right himself since that strange attack from the construct. His magic felt much better and hadn't even taken all that long to recover, but something still felt wrong. Actually, if he was being honest with himself, he'd been a little out of sorts since the trial. He'd attributed it to the drugs, but the feeling still lingered.

Another thing to add to the list.

He wrenched his thoughts back to the problem at hand. He had to somehow present the spell crystal to the Wall. What did that mean, exactly? Was there something he had to do to activate it, or was merely having it enough? *"It will grant you passage."* Was the "it" the spell crystal, or the tower? None of the magics visible in the aegis were violet or any other purple color, and even if Hel had been involved somehow in the casting of it, her death would have dispelled her influence. No magic of hers should be able to win him entry. Not quite sure what else to do, he held it up towards the Wall.

Nothing happened.

"Sorry. I was... rush."

After a few minutes of standing there, he lowered his arm, studying the crystal a little more carefully. He sent a small pulse of magic through it, curious to see if he could discern its exact purpose. The crystal flashed violet briefly, then returned to its original state, but now he could feel the presence of magic stored in it.

It was a storage crystal! Meant to hold extra power for a caster, they could be fairly tricky to make, and those with larger reservoirs even more so. He wondered how much this one could hold. However, while that was useful, he wasn't sure how it was supposed to gain him entry to the tower.

"...walk up and... Titus..."

Takeshi closed his eyes for a moment. He was so tired. He just wanted to lie down and sleep.

"WALL."

He jumped, head jerking up as he took a step back. He had almost drifted off standing up. He needed to find a place to rest, and soon. Food would help in the meantime; he forced fingers nearly numb with cold to open his pack and pull out some jerky. Absently, he checked that his katana was still in its place on his hip.

He chewed mechanically as he turned his attention back to the Wall. He approached the tower slowly as he considered the magics visible through the surface. Cautiously, he reached out to touch the stone. It was curiously warm.

Suddenly Takeshi froze, finding himself inside a large stone room. Had he somehow lost time again? Where was he? How had he gotten here?

"Safe, now."

Lines of magic in a warm blue spread across the walls, before fading back to the colorful mix he had just been looking at, and Takeshi realized that he had somehow gotten into the tower. Alarm shot through him. How had he managed that? Why couldn't he remember? Gods, what was happening to him?

"Safe! ... Titus brought..."

The walls flared blue again as he fought back panic. The situation was rapidly spiraling out of his control in a way that for any other mission would be a sign to abort. But what could he do now? What would aborting even look like? He had somehow gotten past an aegis and he had no idea how. Could he go back? Where would he even go? The nature of his mission was such that it was succeed or die.

"Ander!"

Some part of him distantly recognized that this was not unlike some of the symptoms Hotaru had suffered. Though this wasn't nearly as bad, thankfully; he could deal with this. He wrapped his arms tightly around himself as he squeezed his eyes shut, praying that he might share in the strength she had shown through even worse attacks. At least it didn't seem like a migraine was imminent.

"Breathe."

What was he going to do?

"It's not so bad, Takeshi. People always find a way forward."

He had to go forward at this point. There was no way back. Hel had mentioned finding someone named Ander who could help him. Takeshi was fairly certain she hadn't meant help him with... whatever this was, but it was the only thing he had to go on right now. Desperately, he tried to force himself to focus. He had managed step one... somehow. Step two was to find Ander. Ander was in Tarvishte, where Hel had said they should go. So slight revision – step two was to get to Tarvishte, and step three was to find Ander.

Small steps. He could do this.

He forced himself to take one deep breath, then another. When he felt more in control, he opened his eyes and checked that he still had his bag and katana. Both were present. Then he looked around. The inside of the tower was bare except for the lines of power, which were now flashing blue at an alarming rate, and a circle of glyphs in the center of the floor. He studied them intently for a moment, realizing they formed a gate pattern. He wondered where the gate led.

As he watched, the glyphs began to glow with the same warm blue light that the walls had been flashing a moment ago. A quick glance up revealed that the walls had returned to the multi-color mix of the exterior. He wondered why the colors kept changing. Shinobi often worked together to combine their spell weaves, but he had never seen anything like this before. Regardless, the glyphs in the floor were certainly being powered now. Where was the mage?

"The passage... safe."

He shook his head, wishing the voices would be silent. He needed to focus. He knelt down to get a better read of the glyphs to see if he could figure out where they were linked to, but the exhaustion was catching up to him and the symbols swam in front of his eyes. He hesitated; being forced to take one route like this made him uncomfortable, but there was literally nowhere else to go. At least he was mostly certain Hel had wanted him to come this way, and there didn't seem to be anything malevolent in the glyphs. He stepped into the pattern, which activated in a brilliant display of light.

As the brightness faded, Takeshi found himself standing on a slightly raised platform, sister-glyphs to the ones he had just left etched into the stone. Now he was in a small courtyard of brick and ivy, ornamental ironwork decorating the tops of the walls. There was a green-painted door under a small trellis against one side. It was the only way out.

Well, almost the only way out. He eyed the top of the nearest wall and scaled it quickly, dropping down on the other side onto a cobbled sidewalk, gaining a few curious glances from passersby. He looked around the wide, tree-lined street, taking in the charming brick buildings and copper pipes that made up the majority of the area. He had lost time, whether it was when he somehow passed through the aegis or at some other point; it was mid-morning now. He picked a direction and began walking, hoping to blend into the general population. Takeshi was pleased to see that a number of people walking around were armed; hopefully that meant his katana would not stick out as much here. He didn't feel up to keeping an illusion going for an indeterminate amount of time right now. There was also magic in the air. High above, he could see the tell-tale shimmer of power, though he couldn't discern its purpose. Overall, this place reminded him far more of home than the cities south of the Wall.

"Just like magic, I believe tech also needs to be bridged and balanced."

He paused for a moment, considering what to do. He hadn't expected to be teleported into the heart of a city. He wasn't even sure which city this was. He could guess based on the size of the gate pattern that it wasn't more than fifty miles from the Wall, and the presence of visible magic told him he wasn't in the Rose Empire anymore, but he needed more information than that.

So then, step two, part A: figure out current location. He just needed to keep focusing on one goal at a time.

Takeshi continued wandering. Unlike Charve and Bariza, this city was not laid out in a grid pattern. Mostly bare vegetation was everywhere – it probably looked beautiful in warmer weather – and the shops and houses followed no discernible pattern. He passed several statues, but most were covered with black or white fabric. Strange. He didn't look too closely; they reminded him of how Hel had appeared to him in the mirror. Luckily, he seemed to have arrived in a central area with many people out and about, Humans and Avari both. He was able to ask a pair of women lounging near a storefront where the nearest train station was. They helpfully pointed him in the right direction, and before too long he found himself staring up at a large structure made of stone and marble, heavily engraved with decorative motifs. Above the entrance, "Braila Train Station" was deeply etched into the marble.

Well, now he knew the name of the city, though not where it was. He strode through the large doors and glanced around, disappointed at the cool temperature of the building. He was pleased to see a large map crossed with brightly colored lines for the train routes against one wall. He headed in that direction, noting that there weren't very many people in the building. He would have thought a train station would have been busier.

"It... *affect you.*"

Tiredly, trying to push the memories aside and reminding himself yet again to focus, he studied the map, looking for Braila and Tarvishte. He found the city he was in fairly easily – it was close to the Wall, as he had suspected – but his heart sank when he found Tarvishte almost two thousand miles away. That was a significant distance. Did he even have the money to go that far? It would take weeks, maybe months if he had to go on foot. If he was at his best it wouldn't be a problem, but he wasn't sure he could afford the time that would take right now. Something was wrong, and he just knew he needed to get there as quickly as possible.

Perhaps he could go as far as his money could take him by train, and then finish the journey on foot. It wouldn't be ideal, but then nothing about this mission had been, and he didn't see why it would start now.

"The pressure and expectations we put on shinobi is dangerous. We rely on them for so much, and yet..."

"It's... mission."

He mentally shushed them both as he walked over to the ticket counter, manned by a young Avari teenager with bright-pink hair and pale-blue eyes. She looked incredibly bored, flipping the pages of a book lying on the counter with one hand, chin resting on the other.

"Excuse me, but how much would a ticket be from here to Tarvishte?" he asked, hoping against all hope it was a figure lower than what he had left.

The girl blinked at him, almost seeming surprised she was being addressed, before straightening up. "Oh, um, I can look that up for you," she said, grabbing at a sheet on her desk and scanning it quickly. "That would be one hundred and forty notes."

Takeshi abruptly realized he had no money. The currency here was different. Because of course it was; this was a different country. How had he completely failed to consider that? What was wrong with him?

"But none of the trains are running right now anyway," the girl continued apologetically. "Everything has been shut down since the attack in Tarvishte. I'm sorry."

"When it rains..."

It really was just going to get worse and worse, wasn't it?

"Hey, kid."

Takeshi glanced behind him at the interruption to see an older Human man frowning at him. He was tall, with very short salt-and-pepper hair, wearing a black vest over a white shirt. A silver chain for a pocket watch stood out sharply against the dark fabric, from which hung a violet crystal hound.

Takeshi stared at it. It was the same as the one Hel had given him.

"Drop that illusion before you kill yourself," the man continued, seeing that he had the shinobi's attention.

"What?" Takeshi asked, confused. He glanced back at the Avari girl, surprised to see her sketching a quick but respectful bow in the man's direction.

He didn't so much as glance her way. "The illusion. Drop it. Before I drop it for you." He gestured towards Takeshi's left hand.

He looked down, realizing belatedly that he was still feeding the illusion sewn into the glove. Had he walked the entire thirty miles through the Waste with it still active? He couldn't remember. He must have, though; he hadn't reactivated it when he reached Braila. He would remember that.

Wouldn't he?

Takeshi flinched as the persistent drain on his magic suddenly ceased, power snapping back weakly like a rubber band stretched for too long as his connection to the pattern was severed. Violet shards of a pattern Takeshi hadn't seen woven dissolved into the ether as the echo of the man's snap faded. The same violet of the spell crystal in his pocket, and of Hel's magic. How was the color the same? Not just close, but the exact shade?

"Focus!"

Well, his ghosts were trying to keep him on track now too. At least they were making themselves useful.

He looked again at the hound crystal. "Ander?" he tried, vaguely hopeful that if he had the same crystal, then maybe this was the person he was supposed to find.

The man's eyebrows rose to his hairline. "No," came the drawled response. "My name is Jak, but good try. Ander is..." – he trailed off for a moment, eyes flicking to the side – "...still in Tarvishte," he finished confidently.

Takeshi fought down a wave of disappointment. "I'm supposed to find Ander," he said slowly, though at least it seemed like he had found someone who knew Ander. A step in the right direction. "Where did you get your pendant?" he asked suddenly.

Jak eyed him with an unreadable expression. "Yup, I know, and the same place you got yours." He ignored the sharp intake of breath from the girl. "When was the last time you ate?"

Takeshi felt very off balance talking to this man. How did he even know Takeshi had a matching spell crystal? How many of these things had Hel made? "At the Wall?" he hazarded, fairly certain that was correct.

"Okay, great, but *when* was the last time you ate?" the man repeated carefully. "You know what, I think the answer is probably 'too long ago.' You're coming with me." He turned to the girl. "Thank you!" he stage-whispered in an over-exaggerated manner, causing her to smile shyly, even if she still seemed a bit confused. "Come on, kid. Let's get out of here."

"Excuse me?" Takeshi had lost control of the situation. "I need to get to–"

"Tarvishte, yes, but quick stop first," Jak interrupted him, grabbing his wrist.

Takeshi yanked away, refusing to be dragged anywhere without more of an explanation, but they were no longer at the train station. Instead, he and the man were now standing in a fairly large sitting room, modestly decorated in neutral colors. One wall had three floor-to-ceiling windows, allowing for a breathtaking view of the city below them. He looked around, confused. He hadn't even noticed any casting, but there clearly had been if he had been teleported here. "Where...?"

Jak glanced at a large mirror hanging nearby. "*You* can stop shrieking now. He's fine, I'm fine, everyone's in one piece. Relax." He turned his attention back towards Takeshi after that utterly bizarre outburst. "And you, sit down and eat," he all but ordered, indicating a table already covered in various platters on the other side of the room. "After you've eaten and slept, we are absolutely going to go to Ander, I promise. She's already told me everything."

Takeshi faltered. "She... Hel?" he tried to clarify.

"Me."

Jak grimaced. "Yeah, and we are going to have that conversation too, but food. Now." He gestured towards the table again. "For right this second, this," he held up the spell crystal, "is a marker – we call it a *crystallus canis*, a 'crystal hound.' It signals to other people that you have her protection, and that they should give you whatever help you require, as well as a bunch of other stuff we can get into later. So you have one, I have one, and I'm helping you. It's not that weird."

Privately, Takeshi disagreed with that. It *was* weird, even if he finally had an explanation as to why she had given him the crystal. It made sense that they were fairly unique because of the complexity of the shape. He was worried that he was the bearer of bad news, since Jak didn't seem to think she was dead. But the delicious smells wafting off the table were reminding him that not only had it been some time since he last ate, but he had also been casting non-stop for over a day. He was ravenous.

"Then... eat."

Jak sauntered past him and plucked a roll from a tray, taking a large bite as he just stared at Takeshi silently.

He gingerly stepped towards the table, feeling very off-kilter. Keeping his eyes on Jak, who seemed content to merely watch him and chew, he slowly took a seat and one of the rolls and began to eat.

"I hate these formal dinners. They can be so... stuffy, and awkward."

"Alrighty then," Jak declared after an uncomfortable amount of deafening silence. "You continue eating, and I will start explaining some things. Fun things. And not fun things."

Takeshi was almost certainly too tired for this, but he was also tired of not knowing. He nodded.

"So, from my understanding, you were trying to help Hel rescue herself from a military base in Charve, right?" He didn't wait for Takeshi to respond before continuing. "And then she went and got stabbed, causing her to explode out of existence, so you think you failed. Which is, by that metric, technically true. But – and here's a big 'but' – there's a lot of information you've been missing, since her ability to communicate with you was pretty hit or miss at best. The good news is, that body was a magical construct, and not actually *her*, so to speak."

Takeshi's eyes widened. "A construct? That perfectly mimicked an Avari form *and* channeled magic? How was she controlling it?" He realized that the cracks he had seen on her arm were likely the first sign of the construct breaking down.

"You are eating right now, not talking." Jak's voice was firm. "And I have no idea how it worked; that is not my area of expertise. So the good news is, she is still... well, 'alive' is sort of a weird term for it. She exists. Is definitely still around."

That was excellent news. Possibly the first really good news Takeshi had received since coming to this blasted continent. "But then why didn't she contact me? Tell me–" He cut himself off, suddenly having a sinking feeling.

:For what it's... understand.:

Takeshi wanted to bash his head against a wall. What in the names of all the gods was wrong with him? How had he not noticed?

:Jak... explain!:

At least she didn't seem angry with him.

"Yeah," Jak said with a wince. "She tried. But, to be fair to you, it does make sense why you thought you couldn't hear her."

"It does?" Takeshi asked, feeling utterly confused by all of this.

"And this is where it gets a little bit complicated." Jak paused, glancing again towards the mirror. Takeshi wasn't at the right angle, but he realized she was probably appearing to the other man in the mirror the way she had to him in Charve. "You see, it takes a very special sort of person to hear her at all, usually." He looked back at Takeshi, who vaguely remembered her saying something along those lines. "Because while Hel is a name she goes by, the more common one is Hades."

Takeshi blinked at him. "She was named after the Silent Goddess?" He could understand why she might choose to go by a different name. Who would do that to their child? And what did that have to do with his ability to hear her?

"No," Jak said after a moment, as the shadowy figure in black veils Takeshi remembered from Charve coalesced behind the other man, draping herself over his shoulders. "She *is* the goddess."

Takeshi felt himself freeze as he stared at her, his face going pale. Suddenly, a number of things made much more sense, such as her strange method of communication that seemed to work better in the temple, why all the statues in this place were dressed like her, Jak having the same color magic – he was probably channeling *her* power, not his own – and her complete lack of concern over her own death. A god couldn't die. And if anyone could create such an amazing construct, it would be a deity. He tried desperately to go back over their interactions to see if he had done anything that would be offensive to her.

He felt a growing sensation of dread as he realized there were a lot of things he would not have said had he known he was speaking to a god.

Gods – *she was a god.*

:It's okay... stand on ceremony...: She sounded reassuring, head tilting to the side.

Jak shook his head. "Yeah, don't do that to yourself. We yell at Her all the time. She's not really into the whole 'holier than thou' thing, even if She literally is. Kind of."

Faintly, Takeshi managed to ask, "Why me?" He couldn't think of a good reason he would be singled out by a god. In fact, he had been very content with his distant relationship with the divine. Gods only tended to meddle in the stories when things were about to go catastrophically bad in ways he preferred not to be a part of; he hadn't thought the political situation Ni Fon found itself in was something that they would care about at all.

"Okay, this is going to get more complicated. So, if we want to be really technical, everyone has the ability to hear any god. But they have to believe, truly *believe*, that they can hear that god. Any doubt at all renders them deaf to divine communication." Hades was nodding as Jak explained. "But sometimes there are certain people who sort of... align to that deity. For whatever reason, they're more receptive to that god. Can hear them, talk to them, even use their power to a greater or lesser degree."

"You are describing a... a saint, or a priest," Takeshi protested in baffled panic. "I am not a member of Hades' clergy. Or any clergy." That he absolutely would remember happening, he was certain. If nothing else, he was confident he had not joined a religious sect at any point in his life.

"Both those points can be true simultaneously?" Jak offered, though it sounded more like a question. "I think you may be thinking of it a bit backward, though. You don't hear the god because you're a priest; you're a priest because you can hear the god."

Takeshi slowly put the fork he was holding down as he tried to make this information make sense. How had this mission come to this sort of spectacular... was it even a failure, at this point? He didn't know. He was so, so very tired, and it was making it difficult to think. Everything was spinning around in his head, words almost devoid of meaning.

And he was still cold, which wasn't helping him concentrate either.

:...*still cold?*:

:Please don't right now,: he whispered, still trying to reconcile what she was. He felt her pull back.

She was a *god*.

"Hades says it's been over forty hours since you last properly slept, though you stretched it a bit with meditation. I think the best thing to do right now is get some sleep," Jak suggested firmly. "Gives you some time to rest and think all this over. We'll all still be here when you wake up, and then we can go to Tarvishte. There's more, a lot more really, but it can wait until then."

Sleep sounded wonderful. Had it really been over forty hours? That could explain why it was so difficult to concentrate. "Yes, I think sleep is a good idea," he agreed.

Jak nodded as the goddess's form dispersed into wisps of shadow. "This way."

The conversation kept playing itself over and over in his mind, an out-of-sync jumble of voices that made comprehension an impossibility as Jak showed Takeshi to a bedroom. Takeshi all but collapsed into the bed, desperately wishing for silence in his head.

He was asleep almost instantly.

Chapter Three

Ander had a dilemma.

The half-Avari strode briskly through the palace complex, heading back to the Temple of Night Rising after yet another meeting concerning the Abominations. Or whatever they were being called nowadays; Jamirh's "bionics" was catching on, even though Ander thought there was probably a better term. He was still working on it.

:I only suggest none of you overdo it because they'll *start to get upset. Three times in three hundred years is not overdoing it,:* Hades pointed out mildly, bringing him back to the problem at hand. Well, it wasn't a problem per se, but it was definitely adjacent to one.

:Jak acquired him earlier today?: he asked Her instead.

:Yes.: It was a good thing She was used to his side-stepping from topic to topic. *:Jak needs to rest a bit himself, and then he will gate them both here. He is very concerned, Ander. Takeshi is... not well.:*

:Have his symptoms progressed?: he queried, dodging around the furry bodies lazing about in front of the Temple. One would think they would be too warm in the direct sun, but he had never observed any behavior that would validate that idea.

There was a brief silence. *:It is difficult for me to tell. Reaching him is still extremely difficult, even though he can now hear me in some capacity again. But he has not felt very... coherent, maybe? Since the battle in Charve. He hadn't slept since then, either. He was also cold, even in the church apartments in Braila. It doesn't feel right to me.:* Her tone was frustrated.

Ander could understand why; Hades loved and cherished all those called to Her. And while bringing a priest into the fold had often been a challenge in the past, She was afraid She was going to lose this one before She even got the chance to try.

What he didn't understand was what was wrong with the potential priest. Hades' reports had been confusing and occasionally contradictory. He himself had been unable to reach Takeshi at all the one time he had tried. All he had heard was something like static, which was unusual and concerning on its own. *:Did you sense the Abomination again? Has he experienced any other migraines since Charve?:* He closed the door to his lab behind him and took a seat at his desk, reaching for his notes.

:No.: That was a good sign. *:It was so strange, Ander! It felt like it was* in *him, but then it felt like it was attacking him from far away. Shielding him did work, though it was clear he was still suffering aftereffects for some time.:*

:And you couldn't tell where the attack originated from?: He flipped back several pages to review what She had told him before.

:Not a precise location, no; I prioritized the shield. Whatever it was, it was killing him slowly.: He wasn't surprised; Hades always

prioritized saving life over everything else. And Ander would never question Her on whether something was deadly.

:Did Jak ask about his symptoms?:

:No. Jak made him eat, then partially explained the crystallus canis *and that I'm not dead, and got started on the fact that he is called to my service, but I'm not sure how much of that Takeshi actually absorbed.:*

Ander brought a hand up to his own crystal, hanging from his neck and tucked under his shirt. *:You are full of negatives, today,:* he pointed out wryly before marking down the information. Hopefully he would be able to ask the man himself when Jak brought them to the Temple tomorrow, but any information was better than none.

:Then you should ask me more questions I can say 'yes' to,: came the prim reply. *:Jak says he could only get that feeling of static from him as well.:*

Well, that was alarming, and it fully killed the possibility that distance had some part to play in Ander's failure to connect with Takeshi. *:And you didn't?:*

:No. It is more like I have to push through something thick and cloying. I have never experienced it before. Not that I remember, at least.: He got the impression that She was tilting Her head to the side. *:A new experience is a novel thing for me, in this day and age.:*

Ander did not roll his eyes. *:You've said that to me more than seventy times over the course of our acquaintance.:*

:Is that so? Strange. It feels very uncommon.: He sensed a hint of laughter in Her tone.

:There are always new things. It is the nature of the universe to move forward,: he thought at Her absently as he considered the oddity of the static. *:Even your kind will never truly encounter everything.:*

:Possibly. Possibly not.: Now She was definitely amused. *:I'll keep your theory in mind as the ages pass.:*

:Indeed, you should.: Static; white noise. The sound made when tuning to an unused frequency with a radio, or an interference of signals. Not something usually associated with the mind and telepathy. People with tinnitus might hear static or buzzing, but it should not affect their thoughts. From what Hades had told him, it didn't seem that Takeshi himself perceived the static, either – only those trying to reach him telepathically. Ander sketched a few radio waves crossing as he thought. The option that made the most sense was an interfering signal, even though that wasn't how telepathy worked. Two minds touching one did not interfere with each other; they were able to communicate with the target mind just fine independently of one another.

Static was something associated with tech, not magic. Tech and magic did not work together.

Would tech and magic interfering with each other cause static, or a static-like effect?

Ander noted the possibility down as Hades began to hum in the back of his mind, losing interest as Her priest's thoughts drifted towards tech. She had no interest in understanding it the way a fish had no interest in understanding the atmosphere.

:What does it matter? As cycles pass, such things come and go like the tides. Only magic persists.:

:If they come around time and again, perhaps a basic understanding might be helpful,: he countered. *:If such things as* that: – he indicated the remains of the Abomination on the nearby table – *:have existed before, or even something like them, then your previous knowledge would be extremely useful. And if they come to exist again in some far future, perhaps your attention now might save some other priest of yours a good number of headaches trying to figure it out.:*

Her form coalesced above the table, looking down at the cloth covering the dismantled corpse. She shrugged gracefully. *:Abomination too comes and goes. If it has moved on from demons to this, I think it more likely that when it comes around again it will have evolved further. Taken a different form, looking for new ways to succeed in rending reality apart.:*

:Evolution implies it grows from what was. Understanding the 'was' could be crucial to understanding the 'is.': It was an old argument between the two of them. In the end, he knew his cause was futile – She lacked the capability to understand tech. Even when She tried, more for his sake than Her own, the result was... less than successful.

:Perhaps. Does my understanding of demons help further your knowledge of this?: From anyone else, the question might have been a rebuke, but there was only honest curiosity in Her tone.

:Not as of now,: he admitted. *:I won't rule out a possible connection at this time. I need more data.:*

Her tone turned grim. *:You will likely have many chances moving forward to gather it. It will not stop until it is made to do so or it succeeds.:*

Ander hummed thoughtfully, spinning his chair around to face Her. *:And it has never succeeded, correct? Else we would not be here.:*

:It came very, very close exactly once. In a world with far more tech than what mortals utilize now, and even then, it took a different form,: She answered after a long silence. *:But that world is gone, now. The problems it suffered are not the same as our own.:*

Ander said nothing. Hades rarely spoke about the far past, choosing to situate Herself firmly in the present. Trying to prompt Her to say more would end in failure. He had always gotten the impression that whatever had happened, She and the other deities hadn't liked it. Instead, he just filed the crumbs of information She dropped away, hoping that one day they might form a picture of an era so long gone it only existed in the memories of the gods.

He turned his attention back to the table. He had finished his notes on the bionic Abomination that morning; he no longer had a use for the remains. He would have to look into getting them removed, or perhaps destroying them himself was the safer option. He did want to keep a sample of the metal for testing purposes, but the rest of the bionic should be disposed of.

He grimaced in disgust. Even he was now referring to it as a "bionic."

Her mental laugh was turned into a cough at his sharp glare. *:Does the name really matter that much? It will still be what it is no matter what you call it. And it's not like it's going to be offended if you all settle on a name it doesn't like.:*

:Proper nomenclature absolutely matters,: he argued. *:Why assign words any meaning at all if you are going to use them imprecisely?:*

:I think you might be taking that concept a little too far,: came the wry reply as She poked at the sheet. *:Communication is not an all-or-nothing concept.:*

:Please confirm it is dead. And that it is going to stay dead,: he requested, suddenly uncomfortable and alarmed with how closely She was studying the remains. He was certain all the systems had been dismantled, and no life had been present while he was dissecting it, but Her powers revolved around death and rebirth and also had a bad habit of going awry around tech. It didn't hurt to be safe. *:I don't need one of those things running around my lab.:*

Her head tilted in his direction. *:It is dead,:* She confirmed. *:I'm just looking at it. I do not wish to reanimate it.:* She looked back at it, curious. *:Considering how many pieces it is in right now, I would not reanimate it even if I could. That would be a cruel thing.:*

Ander took a deep breath as the panic subsided. He wondered if priests from other religions ever had to worry about their divine patrons potentially causing unmitigated chaos. He didn't think so, but who knew? Maybe priests of the Nyphoren occasionally had to be concerned with the possibility of the water twins capsizing random fishing boats for no discernible reason, or the Aradians had to talk the Faleri out of setting something important on fire simply because they wanted to.

Somehow, he had a feeling this was a Hades-specific problem. He could be wrong, but he had a feeling.

He hadn't even been around all that long. What must it be like for Jak?

He felt a wave of exhaustion wash over him, and he closed his eyes briefly as he felt Hades' attention snap to him. *:I'm fine,:* he said quickly, trying to stave off Her concern. *:It's just been an intense couple of days.:*

:Everyone seems tired right now,: She agreed quietly. *:Jak is tired from gating to Braila; Vlad is tired from dealing with the fallout of the attack. Takeshi is literally passed out right now because of, well, everything. You are tired from dealing with the attack and then dealing with the corpse. I've received prayers from many who are tired from the past few days of near lockdown.:* She paused for a moment, head turning to look towards the wall. *:Even Jamirh feels tired.:*

Ander had been nodding along, but that last one threw him. *:You are sensing Jamirh?:* Jamirh didn't worship Her.

:He's just outside. I think he's trying to decide if he wants to enter the Temple to... talk to me, maybe. Or you. There's quite a bit of confusion there.: She shrugged.

He blinked, wondering what that was about. *:Well, let me know if he figures it out.:*

There was a sense of amused exasperation. *:You know, the job of a priest in most religions is to help people 'figure it out' when it comes to communicating with the deity, from what I've observed.:*

:How mundane. I have better things to do with my time.: He waved a hand dismissively, turning back to the parts on the table. *:Such as deciding what to do with–:*

:He's coming into the Temple proper now,: She interrupted mildly, form dissipating into the ether.

Ander sighed, mentally debating whether to get involved or not. He could just stay out of the way in the lab and let Jamirh do whatever he had come here for. It wasn't even that he didn't necessarily want to talk to Jamirh; he just didn't want to *right now*, when there were so many other things to do. Though maybe he should check on him, since as Hades had pointed out they had all been through a very harrowing night not that long ago. That was what most people did, right?

:It is considered polite, if nothing else.:

There was a quiet knock on the door.

:Yes, it would be rude to ignore that,: She informed him, clearly amused.

He ignored Her, striding to the door and pulling it open. "Jamirh. Are you well?"

:Really just going all in there, huh?:

:It's efficient,: he defended himself. He'd never really seen the point of all the unnecessary words people added to the beginnings and ends of conversations.

Jamirh was looking at him a little oddly though, ears twitching slightly as his shoulders slumped. "Uh, hi. Yeah, I'm fine? I just had a question."

:The emotion you were looking for there was 'resignation.':

"How can I help you, then?" he asked, hopeful that perhaps they would be done quickly if that were the case. He had told Jamirh he could ask him questions at any time, but he felt that it was less imperative now that the kid had the Crystal Light Blade.

:I think it might actually be more *imperative now,:* Hades countered.

Ander would be the first to admit that his feelings about Jamirh and the Blade were complicated, though only to himself. Shouldn't Ander's part be over? He felt like he'd already put in more than enough effort to be able to wash his hands of the mess. He'd even left the palace grounds to meet the kid. Now that Jamirh had the Blade, the rest would follow in time, quite without any input from him.

"Well, maybe a couple of questions." Ander arched an eyebrow as Jamirh glanced past him into the lab. "Have you seen the news about the Charve Military Base? On the Empire's channels?"

That was unexpected. "No, I've been busy with other things. Why do you ask?"

:Maybe ask him to come in and sit down, rather than stand in the doorway?: the goddess suggested.

That felt unnecessary and Ander would do no such thing.

Jamirh's ears twitched again, and he reached up to fiddle with the key Ander had noticed he always wore, similar to how he wore his *crystallus.* "Well, Jeri and I were watching it a little while ago, and they were showing pictures of the damage and it got me wondering. That Human, who was trying to save Hel? Did he make it? The base looked... pretty destroyed."

Jeri was back from Pitesh? She must have run the entire way; the trains were shut down. He ignored the feeling of pride from Hades over the mention of the destruction She had likely caused, more interested that Jamirh was concerned for Takeshi. "He did, yes."

:Actually, I'm going to manifest and take this one,: Hades murmured.

:You are going to talk to him directly?: That was a surprise. She normally didn't do that.

:He's earned a little more help than most.: She began to pull from Ander's magic so that Jamirh would be able to see Her. *:It reminds me a bit of the olden days, when it was easier to reveal ourselves to petitioners and I spoke to many without having to feed off of a priest's presence.:*

For a deity, it really hadn't been that long. *:The olden days of a thousand years ago?:*

:Shush, you.: He felt Her manifest behind him, draping Her arms over his shoulders. Jamirh's eyes widened into silver saucers. *:It was a different time. More people believed. For all that the years are still dated as the 'Age of the Gods,' it really isn't anymore.:* "Hello, Jamirh."

"Hel," the Avari squeaked. "Hi."

She waved at him cheerfully before tilting Her head. "You are interested in Shuurai Takeshi? Why?"

"Wait, what?" Ander regarded Jamirh silently as the boy faltered in confusion. "Wasn't that the name of the banished Human from Ni Fon? The one who killed the duchess's daughter?"

"Yes?" Hades seemed to realize Jamirh had been missing the important information of which Human exactly had been aiding Her. "Oh, yes. Well, that situation is a little more complicated than we expected. But he was the Human helping me in Charve, yes."

Ah, yes. That reminded Ander of his dilemma.

Jamirh peered at her, eyes squinting. "How did you go from 'never hearing from him again' – which is what you told me in Ardwick – to 'destroying a military base together'?"

"These things happen, believe it or not." Now She sounded tired, hugging Ander a little tighter. "It wasn't under ideal circumstances, I'll give you that. Maybe when he comes here and has had time to recover he'll share the story with you."

"He's coming here?" Jamirh asked, ears twitching.

"Another of my order is escorting him, yes," Ander interjected. "They should be here tomorrow, though based on Hades' reports he may need to spend some time in the hospital."

Jamirh frowned. "It's just that out of everyone, he seemed to be the only person interested in helping you get free. And I get that no one else was concerned because you are actually a goddess, but... oh, I don't know. I just kind of feel bad for him, I guess." He ran a hand through his hair. "I didn't realize he was the guy that killed that girl in Ni Fon, though good for him if that's the case."

Ander cocked his head as he tried to work his way through that logic.

"Like I said, that situation is more complicated than what you have heard," Hades stated firmly. *:He doesn't really care for Humans as a general rule,:* She added silently to Ander, who gave a mental shrug in response – he himself didn't really care for most people in general. "It might be best if you withhold judgement on that for now. He was also unaware of my divinity, though for different reasons than you were."

Jamirh shot Her a look but said nothing.

Ander frowned. "Wait, I cared about the avatar. I put significant time and resources into its creation; having it be destroyed less than two years after completion was notably disappointing. Its recovery could not be justified as a high priority, however."

Hades gently patted his head while Jamirh stared. "That's... not really what I was talking about. But since you brought it up, are you going to make another one?"

"I intend to, yes. Some general modifications and improvements can be made to the original design and process, so hypothetically She will have another avatar in" – he did some quick math – "fourteen years or so."

"That's quite an improvement on time," She exclaimed, clearly pleased, while Jamirh looked... disappointed? His ears were drooping, at least.

"And it will be up to you to make it last longer," Ander warned Her. "It's not meant to hold up to the things you are used to doing as an incorporeal collective of magic. You have to treat it more gently, or it's going to break."

"I wasn't trying to get stabbed," She protested. "I was trying to bring it back with Takeshi. By the way, being stabbed hurts. Zero out of ten; would not recommend."

Ander was abruptly reminded of the scar running down his face. "It does, yes." He turned to Jamirh. "Advice to live by."

"Literally," Jamirh deadpanned.

Ander turned his head slightly to look at Her. "A 'new' experience?"

"Yes, actually," She replied with a sniff. "There's no need to poke fun, you know."

He turned back to Jamirh. "Anything else, kid?"

"Uh, no? No, I was just... the damage was really impressive," he blurted out.

"Thank you," came the cheerful reply, "but I can't claim all of it. Takeshi helped."

Silver eyes regarded Her quietly for a moment. "Well, I'm glad to hear he'll fit right in with this madhouse," he finally sighed. "I hope he's ready for it."

Ander could *feel* Hades' wince. "There might need to be an adjustment period," She admitted.

Jamirh just shook his head, looking unsurprised. "Let me know if he needs anyone to commiserate with," he snorted. "Thanks for the info. See you around!"

"Bye, Jamirh!" Hades chirped as She disappeared in a swirl of shadow. "Come back anytime!"

"Goodbye," Ander echoed as Jamirh waved and briskly trotted out of the Temple. He glanced around, then stepped into the hallway, closing the door to his lab behind him and heading into the sanctuary proper. *:That wasn't too much for you, I hope?:*

:Not at all. He does believe in me, which helps. And we were in the Temple, and you were right there. I could do it again, if it were necessary,: She reassured him.

Absently, Ander wondered why it was such a struggle for the gods to manifest in this day and age. Surely things weren't that different a thousand years ago? Was it really just that the number of people who truly believed in them was so diminished?

:Many people go through the motions. Comparatively few mean them.:

A problem for another time.

He faced the altar, considering his dilemma. He supposed the wise choice after everything he had learned in the past day or so was to just do it and see if he could fill in the pieces he was missing. But the last time he had attempted this, the results had been less than satisfactory. The spirit he had queried had refused to speak to him at all. The dead often resented being called on.

At least Jamirh was talking to him now. And was alive.

:I don't think you will have the same problem with this one,: Hades reassured him.

:She is not one of my dead.: He looked around. The Temple was as impeccably kept as usual. He did not need to be in the Temple to perform the ritual, but he thought this spirit might appreciate the location from what he understood of her. *:She may very well refuse to speak to me.:*

And one of the few things Hades would not do was speak for the dead. If their secrets were to be sought, it had to be directly – not even Her priests could use Her to cheat answers from those who had moved on.

Would this spirit be willing to answer questions concerning someone who was still living? And if she was, did she even have the information he sought?

If he didn't at least try, and Takeshi died before he was able to Choose, he would blame himself.

The ability to summon the dead was not magic; it was a gift. As easy as breathing. He closed his eyes and waited.

"High Priest, you wish to speak with me?"

She was floating in front of him, long hair so black it was almost blue pinned up with decorative combs, wearing court finery that moved with a breeze he could not feel. Her voice echoed in the complete stillness of the Temple.

"I do. Will you answer me?" he asked respectfully, bowing.

"Yes, I will," Kobayashi Hotaru answered him gravely. *"Ask."*

Rhode finished straightening his uniform as he prepared to leave the hospital room. One whole day lost to injury was more than enough; he needed to get on top of damage control immediately. Major Sherri Cole had been doing her best, but she lacked the experience necessary for dealing with these sorts of disasters. He also wasn't willing to just throw her at the mercy of the dukes and duchesses, who were sure to be breathing down his neck looking for answers soon.

He wanted to have answers for them. Hell, he wanted to have answers for himself. Why had the prism sphere failed? Why had no one noticed? Why had six Truth Seekers and two assets all failed to recapture the Avari mage? Who was the Silent One who had come to rescue her? Where had she gone?

The answer to that last one was probably north to Romanii, fleeing like a rabbit back to her warren. But there had been no sign of a woman with her description heading north. It was as if she had vanished into thin air, taking all his leads with her.

The powers that be weren't going to like that, either.

He took a moment to ensure that his vision was going to cooperate before striding confidently out into the hall where Cole and Lieutenant Berif were waiting for him. His vision was still blurring occasionally, though hopefully that would clear itself up in a day or two. "Anything more to report?" he asked his second-in-command.

"We've managed to get the city back under control again." Cole's professional tone was exactly what he needed to hear right now. "Civilians are under lockdown, and military personnel have been distributed to deal with the cleanup. The Truth Seekers are on high alert; four more arrived early this morning."

"And do they have any ideas as to what caused the mass... hallucination?" He wasn't sure what else to call it.

"Valen has suggested that it was very old magic of some sort. None of the Truth Seekers admit to being familiar with it."

Berif cleared his throat. "Sir?"

"Yes?" Rhode allowed.

He glanced around quickly. "I've heard eyewitness accounts from other military personnel who were near Truth Seekers at the same time the mage screamed. They said that to a one, the Truth Seekers all stopped what they were doing and turned in the direction of Charve."

That was... bizarre. Rhode turned to Cole. "Surely we have footage of that, then?"

The major shook her head, frowning at the other soldier. "None of the footage I've managed to pull shows it. We only have eyewitness accounts, no hard evidence."

The story seemed preposterous – if the Truth Seekers had noticed something that had affected all of them, why wouldn't they have reported it? "Could the footage have been doctored?"

"I managed to acquire eleven security tapes from various bases around the Empire. I've already run a tier one analysis; nothing showed up." Her eyes flicked to the lieutenant. "That is why I didn't want to bother you with this."

Rhode had worked with Cole for a long time, and he trusted her judgement. Still... "And the eyewitnesses?" he asked, just to be sure.

Berif raised his chin. "Friends of mine, people I trust. Something strange is going on, Colonel."

Something strange had been going on for the past four weeks. He glanced at Cole. "Use my credentials; see if a higher analysis reveals anything." It didn't hurt to be sure.

Cole snapped a salute. "Yes, sir!"

Speaking of the Truth Seekers, Madine had saved his life when the Avari had attacked. Perhaps she would have an insight she was willing to share.

There was so much to do, and so little time.

Chapter Four

Ander.:

He didn't look up from his notes at the sound of Jak's voice in his head, the echo indicating he was using Hades to reach Ander from far away. *:I'm here.:*

:We'll be gating in shortly.:

:Understood. What is his status?: He finished writing his sentence before sweeping out of his lab into the main sanctuary.

:Not great.: Jak paused. *:Really not great. He massively overtaxed himself yesterday on top of everything else, and he's paying for it now.:*

Ander shooed the three wargs that had been napping in the center of the sanctuary out of the Temple proper. *:How so?:*

Jak's tone was exasperated. *:On already low reserves, he'd been running an illusion spell for almost a whole day. It was a low-effort spell, but still. Not great. I'd let him sleep longer if I dared, but I think he needs to be in the hospital.:*

:I would think he'd know better than to run himself so low.: Ander frowned.

:I don't think he knew he was doing it,: Hades interjected. *:He's not thinking clearly.:*

Ander considered brewing a cup of sillna to help the man with the effects of magicore exhaustion while he waited, but dismissed the thought. They would be going to the hospital immediately anyway.

:I don't think he's thinking at all,: came Jak's disgruntled reply. Ander got the impression the older priest was unhappy with the whole situation. *:Kid has got Problems with a capital 'P,' let me tell you, and I don't think they're all his fault.:*

This was not news to Ander. He thought back to his conversation with the former Nifoni princess the day before. Hotaru had been far more cooperative than he could have hoped, but even her knowledge was limited. The dead only knew that which they had known in life. Still, the insights she had offered were... something, and the picture they painted was not a good one.

"My mother does not see people as people, she sees them as tools. She is the power behind Ni Fon. Everyone, including me and Takeshi, was to be used advantageously and then discarded when she saw no more use for us," Hotaru had told him. *"I did not like her plan to gather information on the continent, the little of it I heard, but in the end I was so very tired and did not have the strength to argue the way I should have. She offered me a way out that would be quick, and I took it."*

Because, it turned out, Hotaru had already been dying, and those involved had all known it.

Vlad had already suggested to him that there was something bizarre about the whole banishment situation, though his probes into it had failed to turn up anything of substance. It checked out just fine on the surface, but if you started to poke at it, things started to fall apart. No amount of "service to the throne" should have mitigated Takeshi's sentence when the crime was murder of the princess and attempted murder of the Empress. Kobayashi Rikona was not known for her overwhelming habit of granting mercy. So she had wanted Takeshi alive despite her daughter's death; the only question had been why.

The woman truly was willing to grasp at any straws possible to win Ni Fon's freedom from the Empire. Without any legitimate intel, she had decided to set up this whole scheme to get Takeshi onto the Empire's mainland – a scheme that hinged on the death of her oldest child and the banishment of that child's fiancé. It would never even pay off; there was no rebellion. Ander could not understand the way she thought. It was such a bad series of decisions it was frustrating to contemplate.

Unless they were still missing something?

Ander shook his head to clear it as violet light lit up the floor of the Temple, glyphs blooming into existence as Jak built the gate from Braila. Absently, he wondered what it must be like for Jak to have to rely on the Lady's power for everything, as he had no magic of his own. Ander found using Her magic to be taxing – mortals weren't really meant for divine power. Still, gates were Jak's specialty, and he was very good at shorter-range teleportation as well – if you needed fast travel, you asked Jak.

So, of course, Jak liked to disappear for long periods of time doing goddess-only-knew what. At least he had brought himself back to help Ander and Hades try to figure out this mess. Even the others, though far away and dealing with whatever problems suited their fancy, were keeping an eye on the situation in Tarvishte, according to the Lady. Ander found himself wondering if he could expect Siva to show herself any time in the near future; she liked to appear whenever there was a new priest. So did Mara.

A final flare of brilliant violet light, and Jak and Takeshi appeared before him. Jak had not been exaggerating, Ander noted as he hurried forward. Takeshi was leaning heavily on the older priest, and his eyes fluttered as though he were struggling to keep them open. He was horribly pale, from what Ander could see over the black cloth mask covering the bottom half of his face. Dark circles under his eyes looked almost bruised, and there was a thinness to him that suggested reserves gone so low often enough that the body started to eat itself for energy. He was moving slowly and stiffly. The late November temperatures were not cold enough to warrant that amount of shivering; Ander wouldn't be surprised to discover he was also running a fever.

"Do not misunderstand – I believe my mother does still see Takeshi as useful. She sent him here for a reason, and she does acknowledge his power and skill. But she will cut herself free of him the moment she believes he has nothing left to offer her. Takeshi does not think of it that way; shinobi are conditioned to be loyal to a fault," Hotaru had warned. At what point would Rikona abandon Takeshi? It seemed likely to Ander she already had. How had she even been hoping to connect with him? Hotaru hadn't known, but perhaps Takeshi did.

"I feel like you probably should have just gated directly to the hospital," Ander suggested to Jak as he moved to help support Takeshi.

"I'm not as familiar with the hospital," Jak muttered, "or I would have."

:Vlad–:

:Everything is ready here,: came the smooth reply at Ander's touch. *:Jak can use me as an anchor if you want to take a shortcut.:*

"Ander?"

He was taken aback by how desperate Takeshi's voice sounded. "Yes?"

"She told me to find you…" The Nifoni's voice trailed off, sounding relieved. "Step three done?"

Ander turned a questioning look on Jak, who shrugged awkwardly. "He's been a little fixated on that point."

:If focusing on that is what allowed him to drive himself here, I'll take it,: Hades informed them flatly.

"Fair." Ander decided to move on. "Vlad says you can use him as an anchor to teleport to the hospital room."

"Good times. Hold on," Jak warned.

Ander allowed himself a moment to be impressed with how Jak never seemed to need to materialize the array for a teleport as the world whited out around him. Ander himself always liked to visually check his teleport arrays to make absolutely sure they had no errors that could lead to unfortunate accidents, but Jak clearly had no such worries. Perhaps because he had been casting them for so long?

They rematerialized in a bright, airy room in Haven Hospital. Vlad was standing near the door, looking concerned, as Jak and Ander got Takeshi sitting on the bed. His eyes had closed, and he was listing slightly to one side.

"Takeshi? Can you hear me?" Ander asked as Jak stepped away.

Dark eyes fluttered open; though unfocused and exhausted they tracked to his general direction as Takeshi shivered. "Hmm?"

Ander reached out mentally, just to check, and was answered only with that strange static-like sound. What in the Lady's name was causing that?

:Nothing in my *name.:*

He ignored Her. "Can you tell me your full name?"

"Shuurai Takeshi." He was a little slow to respond, but he was responding, which was a good sign.

"Do you know where you are?"

Takeshi blinked at him, considering. "Tarvishte? He said he would bring me to Tarvishte to find you." His eyes flickered to Jak, who had remained nearby. "We gated here? From... Braila." He looked around. "We are in a hospital?"

"Good." He was at least partially aware of what was going on around him, even if he didn't seem to be. Ander took the syringe Vlad offered him. "I'm going to take a blood sample. When was the last time you ate?"

"Yesterday?" Takeshi asked, glancing at Jak again.

Jak nodded. "Got him to eat a meal when we arrived at the Braila apartments."

Ander nodded. It clearly wasn't enough, but it was something. "Can you tell me what hurts?"

"Everything. It's just... muscles and joints, sore from overuse on too little energy. Pushed too hard, reserves too low, but had to keep going. Find Tarvishte, find Ander. So tired now, and cold. Why is it so cold here?" He shivered violently again.

Ander frowned as he drew blood, movements practiced and efficient. He handed the syringe back to Vlad, preparing a scanning spell to see if he could determine why that was. Magicore exhaustion didn't cause that.

:Be careful casting into him,: Hades warned. *:I think there is something wrong with his magic. We were both hit by that blast of whatever from the Abomination, and it definitely disrupted me, but I think it did something to him, too. Every time he has used magic since, he has gotten worse. Neither gate affected him, but Titus' pull into the tower did.:*

That was interesting. He let the magic dissipate for the moment. *:How does Titus bring people into the tower? What makes it different from teleportation or gate magic?:* He had crossed through the towers once before, but it had been long ago, and he had been preoccupied with other things. He didn't remember thinking there had been anything strange about the experience from a movement standpoint, but there could have been.

:The tower mages generally find it easier to pull mages in by touching their core because the magic is easy for the Towers to sense. People with no or very little magic are harder for them to affect, so they do teleport them the more standard way – it just takes more effort,: She explained.

:I see.: He reconsidered the array he usually used and modified it to have a lighter touch, sending power as gently as he could through Takeshi's body. "How does this feel?"

"A little strange," Takeshi admitted. "Warm, though."

The results definitely *felt* like magicore exhaustion to Ander. He wasn't sure what would cause Takeshi to feel chilled, but everything else was textbook exhaustion, aside from the strange echo of static he was getting back. Thankfully, the scan didn't seem to be affecting Takeshi negatively. He sent another gentle pulse of healing magic through the muscles, hoping to help alleviate some of the pain.

Why static?

At a loss for the moment, he moved on. "Have you had any more migraines since last week?"

Takeshi looked confused for a moment. "You know about the migraines?" He almost immediately seemed to remember. "Right, *she* told you. You told her to tell me to take more painkillers. And drink more water. No, not since... not since Charve. I haven't had any migraines."

That was also good, but it left Ander a little stumped. He glanced over at Vlad, who was sipping at the blood Ander had drawn. The Vampire's nose scrunched up slightly. "There's a heavy metallic aftertaste; I'm getting elevated iron levels." He started digging around in a cabinet for the supplies to draw more blood. "It's not at critically dangerous levels yet, but we should draw some blood to try to reduce those numbers. Other than that, there are no foreign substances I can detect."

Takeshi blinked at Vlad a little vacantly. "Right. There are Vampires here." It sounded surprisingly matter-of-fact, given everything. "I'm not sure I know what that means."

"There will be plenty of time to explain that later," Ander assured him. "It doesn't affect you right now." Satisfied that he was stable and not in immediate danger of death, Ander decided the best thing for Takeshi right now was rest under observation. If they could deal with the exhaustion, they might be in a better place to determine what was or had been going on between Takeshi and Abomination. He wouldn't be attacked here at least.

:Certainly not.: Her voice was coolly determined. *:If it tries again, I* will *deal with it.:*

"And speaking of drinking things, drink this." Jak stepped forward with a mug of steaming liquid, the strong herbal scent of sillna filling the room.

"The sillna will help with the magicore exhaustion," Ander explained as Jak helped Takeshi wrap trembling fingers around the cup. "After that, it would be best if you slept." And Ander needed to set him up with an IV. He needed nutrients just as much as sleep. He looked back at Vlad, who had clearly anticipated this and had included the relevant supplies on the counter along with those to draw blood. He considered carefully what he knew, then added, "And it would also be best to refrain from any magic for the time being. Give yourself time to heal from the attack in Charve. You are safe now; you have time."

Takeshi stared at him dully for a moment. "Do I?" His eyes fluttered closed again.

Ander didn't know how to respond.

It was the next night when Ander was summoned by the news that Takeshi was awake. He gathered his notes and his theories and made his way back to the hospital, followed by the one major question haunting him.

Why static?

Takeshi was sitting up and speaking to one of the nurses when Ander came into the room. He was pleased to see that though the dark circles were still present under his eyes, the shinobi looked far more responsive and aware. He was holding another steaming cup of sillna.

"Good evening," Ander greeted him as the nurse nodded to him and left. "How are you feeling today?" He felt Hades turn Her attention towards the conversation.

"Better," came the quiet reply. "Still a little cold, but I'm thinking much more clearly for the first time in a while."

Ander eyed the mountain of blankets, under which were three heating crystals, and decided that was still a problem to be solved. "Are you in any pain? Any headaches?"

Takeshi shrugged. "I am still aching and sore, but considering how much magic I used, that's not surprising. I had a slight headache when I woke up, but this tea seems to be helping. Nothing like the migraines."

Ander checked his temperature and was surprised to find him free of fever. Why did he still feel chilled, then? He marked that down in his notes and decided to get straight to the point. "Do you know why you are here?"

:Be more specific.:

"Why Hades sent you to us," he clarified.

Takeshi looked away, quiet for a long moment. "I've been sent by the Empress of Ni Fon to make contact with the rebellion against the Rose Empire. The only real lead I found and was able to follow was on… the goddess's advice. But I couldn't really understand her very well, and I think I may have made a mistake."

Right. Best to get that out of the way quickly. "There is no rebellion that we know of against the government of the Rose Empire. No organized rebellion, anyway. We – the country of Romanii – are probably the closest to that idea, but we are not rebelling against them so much as just very interested in curbing their power."

Takeshi just looked tired. "I see," he murmured faintly. "Then why bring me here?"

"Hades first contacted you in Bariza, correct?" Takeshi nodded. "Can you tell me the circumstances surrounding that meeting?"

As Takeshi told him about crossing the sea with a band of pirates, exploring a new country, and that first migraine, a small part of Ander pointed out that Hotaru had also suffered debilitating migraines. *"They started when I was twelve,"* she had told him when he asked what she had suffered from. *"That was the beginning. Strangely, I think they were worse when I was younger, though even towards the end I would sometimes take several days to recover."*

He frowned and pushed that memory aside. "Have you ever heard of the term 'Abomination'?" he asked when Takeshi finished.

Takeshi shrugged. "The goddess used it a few times, but I have no idea what it means."

"It is a term we use for a type of sin against the natural order that causes reality to begin to warp and break down," Ander continued. "Traditionally, demons have been the classic expression of this in ages past. Not to get too far ahead of ourselves, but the bionic construct you fought in Charve is the current expression of Abomination."

"I see," Takeshi said slowly, clearly thinking that over. "Why bring this up now, then?"

"The reason the Lady found you was because you made a Prayer of Agony – understandable, given the severity of the migraine – but when She investigated, She found traces of Abomination on you, as though you had come into contact with one recently," Ander explained. "When you proved able to hear Her, She also realized you had the potential to become one of Her priests. That is why you are here. She correctly surmised that you were in danger, and since you fall under Her purview, She manufactured a way to bring you to us."

Takeshi stared at him. "Oh."

"She's worried about you," Ander clarified after a moment. He sensed Her whole-hearted agreement.

:He hasn't actually been talking to me since he found out,: She whispered to him as though Takeshi could somehow hear Her direct communication with Ander.

:I sincerely hope the lesson you take from this century is that pretending to not be a goddess to people who need to know that you are a goddess is a bad idea,: he replied waspishly. Glancing at the shinobi, he was surprised to see a very concerned look appearing on Takeshi's face. "What's wrong?"

"What *exactly* is Abomination?" he asked. "How does it affect a person?"

"We are not sure how exactly it has affected you; in theory it can manifest in a number of ways." Ander tried to be gentle. He didn't know how well he was succeeding. "We just know that you came into contact with it sometime while you were in Bariza, most likely. The migraines are part of it; we just don't know how or why. That's why you are here – so we can help." He figured it wouldn't hurt to reiterate that.

"Things haven't been right since the trial," Takeshi almost whispered. "Something is wrong."

Ander couldn't disagree with that. "The more you tell me, the better we can help."

"I don't remember six months of being in prison in Ni Fon," Takeshi admitted. "When the pirates told me, I almost didn't believe it. I thought it had been two months since Hotaru's death, not eight. I don't understand why this happened. I thought it was the drugs, but ever since Charve I've still been forgetting things and losing time – hours will have gone by without my notice."

"They drugged you for six months?" That was incredibly dangerous. Ander made another note. "Do you know what drugs they used?"

Takeshi shook his head.

"Well, the good news on that front is that Vlad did not find any drugs or substances lingering in your blood. They aren't affecting you now," Ander continued.

Takeshi looked at him, puzzled. "Is that a good thing? I think I've lost time on at least four occasions since Charve."

"Sometimes I would forget something I had just done, or occasionally the last few hours. It wasn't something that happened often, but it was scary when it did."

Ander paused, remembering Hotaru's words, then conceded, "It is likely that does have to do with the Abomination, but I can't definitely link that to what happened while you were in Ni Fon. You were attacked by a bionic in Charve, and Hades says the wave it attacked you with disrupted magic."

Takeshi nodded. "And knocked out every electrical system nearby as well. It felt... very strange, like my magic had been shattered into pieces and had to pull itself back together again."

The Abomination in Tarvishte had also interrupted their power grid, even though Romanii and the Empire used very different systems.

Static could be caused by an interrupted signal, his brain reminded him.

He shook his head. "How do you feel now?"

Takeshi looked thoughtful. "Okay? It seems to have recovered back to the way it was before the blast, which still feels... a little off. I can't really put my finger on why."

"Hades thinks things that affect your magic might be triggering the dissociation," Ander mused. "So holding the illusion spell for as long as you did would not have helped. The attack from the bionic may have even triggered it." The theory worked, but it was incomplete.

"And that's why you told me not to cast magic." Takeshi took a sip from his cup and came to the same conclusion Ander had. "But the migraines started long before I came into contact with it."

"Yes. According to Hades, the first migraine was on the third of November, and the second on the seventeenth. You didn't come into contact with the Abomination until the early hours of the twentieth." Ander wrote the dates down. How did it all fit together? He started another column, writing Hotaru's name above it and jotting down the symptoms she had mentioned. Migraine attacks and dissociation had been the most dramatic, but that hadn't been the whole story.

"Slowly, over the next sixteen years, it became more and more difficult to move without pain in my muscles and joints. I tired easily, and towards the end, even breathing became difficult."

Ander added these to Hotaru's column. Those he hadn't connected since he had thought they were being caused by the magicore exhaustion, but those symptoms were common to a large number of maladies. It was possible they were worse due to the overuse of Takeshi's magic, but their root cause was something else. "You and Hotaru share the same symptoms?" He made it a question.

Takeshi looked surprised. "To some degree, I suppose. She had attacks that were... similar to my migraines. But she had them ever since she was little. The doctors said it was genetic."

"No one could figure out what was wrong with me. I just got sick one day and never truly recovered. The doctors said it must have been something genetic, but I always had the feeling that there was something that had made me sick, caused the attacks. Something that

poisoned my body and turned it against me." Hotaru had been insistent on that.

Hades had said it first felt like it was inside of him before thinking it was attacking him. Because Her shield had worked, She had thought She'd made a mistake, but... what if She didn't? What if both observations were true?

Takeshi's symptoms matched Hotaru's on an accelerated timeline, though he hadn't yet reached the difficulty breathing stage. Hotaru thought there was something poisoning her, and Hades thought She had sensed the Abomination in Takeshi.

Static could be caused by an interrupted or interfering signal.

Vlad had said his blood had an aftertaste of iron. Elevated iron levels could also cause joint pain, fatigue, and weakness. Was something leaching iron into his system?

Hades had gone very still in the back of his mind as She saw the shape his thoughts were taking.

It wasn't just Takeshi's magic that had been affected by the Abomination's attack. But, if he was right, what was its purpose?

:I didn't follow the thing that attacked him in Charve, and I don't know its point of origin, but it came from the direction of Ni Fon.: Her voice was filled with quiet fury. *:He felt like something was being removed from his brain.:*

That didn't fit with Hotaru's situation if he was correct, but it made the most sense for Takeshi's. The dates of the migraines were exactly two weeks apart, starting exactly two weeks after Takeshi had been banished, as if they had happened on a schedule. "This is going to sound like a bit of a non sequitur, but how did your Empress say they were going to contact you once you were in the Rose Empire, exactly?"

Takeshi's face fell. "She didn't. I was told that it wasn't my concern and 'it would be dealt with.'" His voice was bitter.

Ander slowly put down his notes on the counter. Migraines were the first symptom; location was thus likely in or near the head. "I'm going to check for something. It might hurt, but I'll try to make it quick."

Takeshi nodded, placing his cup on a nearby table. Ander approached, carefully putting his hand on the back of Takeshi's head, and *searched*.

Takeshi cried out in shock and tried to jerk away, but Ander had been prepared for that and grabbed him. And yes – there, attached to his spine at the base of his skull, was a small, answering buzz of static.

Hades' presence abruptly vanished.

Ander withdrew and felt Takeshi go limp. He sent a wave of healing energy into Takeshi, carefully avoiding what he now knew was the trigger, trying to ease the pain he had caused.

:*Ander?*: Jak's voice was filled with alarm. :*What happened?*:

:*I found the source of the Abomination affecting Takeshi. I'll need to report to you and Vlad shortly.*: Hades only ever fully withdrew from Her priests like this when Her emotions became so intense they could overwhelm and harm them. Mortals weren't meant for divine rage. Even the fury She had felt when She sensed the Abomination attacking Takeshi hadn't reached this level. Somewhere in the void She was probably screaming.

He sensed agreement from Jak before he withdrew.

"Takeshi?" he prodded after several minutes had gone by.

"Here," came the weak reply. "What did you do?"

He settled the man back against the pillows, making sure he was properly covered with the blankets as he had started shivering again. At least he had likely found the cause of that, too. "I was searching for the source of the Abomination Hades sensed." It didn't feel right without Her there. Hopefully She would return to them soon.

Takeshi paled. "Oh." Then a look of dawning horror, but he asked the question anyway. "What does that have to do with Ni Fon contacting me for information?"

What was wrong with people these days? Tech *did not belong* in Humans, Avari, or any of the other races. First the bionics, and now this. "There is a microchip attached to your spine at the base of your skull. I think that's how Ni Fon has been getting its information from you – by accessing the chip through some sort of tech and taking it."

He watched Takeshi struggle to process that for several minutes, before his face crumpled and he buried it in his hands. "Get it out," he finally whispered. "Please, just... get it out."

Chapter Five

Jamirh sighed in disgust, ears drooping as he stared at the world outside the doors of the palace.

He was soaked in mere moments as he trudged across the palace grounds, rain pelting him as it fell. The weather fit his mood, if nothing else, since he was dreading training today – the first training session since Jeri had returned to Tarvishte. It had only been five days since their last session, but he had a feeling she wasn't going to like how he'd slacked off in her absence.

He was trying to avoid the large puddles when a huge furry form almost barreled into him, rushing across the courtyard. "Hey!" he snapped reflexively at the warg. "Watch where you're going!"

It stopped, turning to look back at him. He could see the luminous violet of its eyes through the downpour. Jamirh winced, looking at all that wet fur – while they liked playing in the rain, most wargs tended to stay indoors when it was pouring like this.

It trotted back towards him, eyes full of far too much intelligence for an animal. It abruptly sat, making a hopeful whine.

"I'm not petting you," Jamirh said flatly, hoping it would take "no" for an answer. If it was anything like the goddess it was sacred to, it probably wouldn't. Hell, this was one of the wargs that even had her colors of white and violet. "We are both way too wet."

It stood and circled around him, before giving him a careful nudge.

Jamirh stepped away. "No, I'm not petting you right now." He turned to head back towards the training grounds. He was going to be late.

The warg moved to block his path, then nudged at him again, pushing in the same direction it had before. It looked up at him hopefully.

"What do you want?" Jamirh muttered crossly. He just wanted to go inside out of the rain, and this oversized dog was preventing that from happening. He wished the wargs had names so he could scold this one more effectively, but as far as he could tell none of the "wild" wargs in the city did. He hoped they weren't waiting for Ander to name them; the half-Avari showed little interest in the creatures he supposedly oversaw.

It nudged at him again, this time with enough force to cause him to stumble, then darted in front of him and woofed hopefully, wagging its tail. It took a few steps away, then stopped and turned back to Jamirh, waiting.

Oh gods, it wanted him to follow it somewhere. Somewhere in the wrong direction. "Will this be quick?" he asked rhetorically, hoping he wasn't being roped into some sort of new game they were playing.

It nodded its head.

Jamirh's mouth went dry, and he made a mental note to ask Jeri again just how smart the wargs were. He hadn't thought they were at the "understands speech" level of intelligence. "Okay," he said slowly, beginning to head in that direction.

The warg made a pleased huff as it turned to lead him wherever it wanted to go.

It was only a few minutes later that Jamirh found himself standing by one of the side entrances to the hospital. Like the Temple of Night Rising, Haven Hospital was on palace grounds for reasons unclear to Jamirh. There was a small overhang above the doorway, granting some shelter from the weather, which Jamirh took instant advantage of.

The warg sat by the door, looking intently at Jamirh, then to the door, and then back again.

"You want me to let you in?" Jamirh asked. He guessed paws were particularly bad at opening this kind of handle, but then he immediately decided that wargs opening doors was probably the last thing society needed. "Why couldn't you just go to the front door, where probably anyone inside would have helped you?" The front of the hospital had many glass windows; the staff would have definitely seen the warg had it just gone around to the front.

Its eyes somehow got bigger and more liquid as it gazed at him hopefully, completely ignoring his question. Its tail gave one small wag.

He shook his head at it in exasperation before trying the handle of the door; it opened easily enough. He pushed it open to reveal a well-lit stairwell opening up into a hallway. There weren't any people immediately visible. The warg pushed past him into the building, shaking itself vigorously as soon as it was fully inside. Jamirh flinched in disgust as drops of water rained on him from the white fur. "Stop it! Is this really how you are going to thank me for... whatever this is?"

It looked back at him consideringly, then glanced up the stairs before looking back at him.

"Oh no, this is all you're getting out of me. Good luck with whatever you're doing," Jamirh exclaimed, shutting the door in its face before it could convince him to be its hands any longer. He was already dreading how late he was to training.

Briefly, he considered how bizarre Tarvishte was. The only real similarity it had with his previous home of Lyndiniam was that they were both cities. Everything else, from the architecture to the people to the religion and government, was almost unrecognizably different. Different holidays were celebrated. Vampires and magic and weapons were a part of everyday life. Humans and Avari lived side by side in harmony. Large dogs strutted about like they owned the place.

He darted back into the rain, determined to at least *try* to make it to Jeri on time.

He still couldn't seem to utilize his ability as a Master of Blades reliably. Not that he'd had a chance to work on it with Jeri yet, but he'd tried to figure out how to achieve the same feeling as before. No luck. It was like he was missing the switch to turn it on or something.

He knew he was going to have to fight the Abominations again. They had proven capable of getting into the capital of Romanii, somehow crossing the Warcross Wall, so Jamirh figured they were probably capable of getting anywhere. Since he appeared to be number one on their list of targets, that meant he was definitely going to have to fight them again. He wanted to be ready when that happened. He couldn't rely on having someone following him for every waking moment; that was actually a little pathetic. Just because he didn't want to be like Ebryn didn't mean he was some wilting flower in need of protection. He needed to take responsibility for his own defense.

It would just be a lot easier if he could do the super-special thing he was supposed to be able to do.

It would be a lot easier if anyone else had done anything while waiting for him, too. Surely it wasn't *all* expected to fall on his shoulders? A lot of people had died while they were waiting for him.

That wasn't fair at all. To anyone.

He skidded into the main courtyard of the training grounds a few minutes later, earning a few turned heads in his direction. Even in the rain there were people facing off against each other for friendly bouts – Jeri had once commented that the weather was not a guaranteed deterrent for a fight, so training happened in all kinds of weather. Jamirh counted himself lucky that his beginner status meant Jeri was using one of the private, covered training rooms for their own sessions. He'd start wet, but at least he wouldn't have to deal with rain in his face the whole time.

His lungs were burning by the time he slid into the room Jeri had reserved for them. "Sorry I'm late!" he managed to gasp out as he nearly collapsed on the floor.

Jeri raised one delicate white-blonde eyebrow. "Are you okay? Goddess, you're soaked."

"It's raining," he pointed out unnecessarily, panting. "And yeah, just got... a little distracted... on the way... and didn't want to be late."

She hummed, looking down at him with a faint frown. "Do you not have a raincoat? Or an umbrella?"

He shook his head wordlessly.

"We should add that to the list of stuff you need. I'll be right back." She disappeared into the hallway.

Jamirh watched her go as his breathing evened out, hand coming up to touch at the key hanging from around his neck.

He'd never owned a raincoat before. Or an umbrella.

Jeri returned a minute later, tossing a large towel at him. "Here, dry off with that. Did you run all the way from the palace?"

He shook his head as he wrung his ponytail out. "From the hospital."

Her eyes widened. "The hospital?"

"One of the wargs needed a hand," he explained. "It was very insistent I follow."

"Oh, okay." She looked relieved. "Yes, they can be pretty... wait, what did it need at the hospital?"

Jamirh shrugged. "I have no idea. Maybe it didn't feel well?"

Jeri was frowning. "They usually go to Ander for that, though I guess he has been at the hospital quite a bit the last few days."

He rubbed at his head with the towel, perking up. "Yeah, because of the Human, right?"

Jamirh hadn't been involved, but Shuurai's arrival had triggered a flurry of activity among many of the people Jamirh knew – apparently, the man was sick or injured due to something Abomination-related. Jamirh hadn't seen Ander or Vlad around since. He hoped they figured it out; somehow the Human had managed to survive against all odds after having been banished from his home province of Ni Fon, and he had even tried to help save Hel from an Empire military base in Charve. It didn't seem fair to Jamirh that Shuurai would make it so far only to die once he reached safety.

Still, life wasn't fair, he reflected. Not even here. If that were true, he would've never had to take up the Crystal Light Blade and the mantle of "Hero" based on who he had supposedly been a thousand years ago.

Though, he supposed that if Shuurai's appearance was good for one thing, it was that people were focused on him and not Jamirh. And someone really important had shown up with Shuurai, apparently. Probably the other priest Ander had mentioned. Jamirh didn't care enough to ask, pleased that he was allowed to fade into the background while everyone else focused on the new arrivals.

"Yes. He's in bad shape, but if anyone can help him, it's Ander." She paused, eyeing Jamirh critically. "The hospital is farther than the palace from here, but you still shouldn't have been that out of breath. We'll have to work on your stamina."

He sighed. One more thing to work on. Apparently all-out sprinting wasn't the same as dashing away from the law to a hiding place.

"And start working on stretches once you've mostly dried off," she added.

He groaned. Did the stretches even help, really? He couldn't tell. Still, he obediently tossed the towel against the wall and re-did his ponytail before starting the routine she'd taught him. He winced at the stiffness in his muscles.

She frowned at him, planting her hands on her hips as her lips thinned. "You didn't practice while I was gone, did you?"

"You were gone for, like, a day and a half," he tried to deflect. "It's been less than a week since we last–"

"Jamirh, consistency is everything!" Her eyes narrowed as she began to pace back and forth. "You're twenty-something–"

"Twenty-two."

"–which is late to begin weapons work!" She ignored his interruption. "Normally that doesn't matter so much, but we've already seen that either the Empire, Abomination, or both are willing to try to hunt you here, so we need to get you proficient as quickly as possible."

"I *know* that!" he protested, shuddering as he remembered the bionic bearing down on him. "I don't want to die, either." And besides, how long were Jeri and the other members of the Black Watch going to want to follow him around for?

Her eyes narrowed. "Then you need to keep up with the exercises I give you, not shirk them." Her expression turned thoughtful. "Actually, I have a few ideas of what we should add to them..."

Jamirh groaned again, dropping his head to his chest as his ears sank. He didn't want to die either from bionics *or* Jeri's training regime. "We could just continue on as we were," he tried.

"We didn't know they could get to you here, then," she disagreed with a shake of her head.

"Do we know how the bionic got past the Wall?" he asked, trying to change the topic.

"Unfortunately, no. The Waste is unguarded besides the Wall – that's been more than enough to prevent any unwanted interference for the past five hundred years – and none of the Towers noticed anything unusual. They'll do what they can to prevent a repeat performance, of course, but until we discover how the bionic managed the crossing we can't be sure it won't happen again." Her mouth pressed into a thin line. "We have to remain watchful. And make sure you can defend yourself."

Damn. That hadn't worked at all. "You were right about Ander, at least." He sank down into the next set of stretches. "He did defend me."

"Of course he did. He's not about to let you die after all he's done for that Blade." She glanced away, lips pursed. "There wasn't anything he could do for the... for your predecessor, but he was never just going to stand by and let you die."

"All he's done...? You mean stealing the Blade?" Boy, that had to be a story. Jamirh had never really cared about the circumstances of how the Blade had gone missing from the museum in Norik, but given recent events, he found himself curious. He'd heard a number of theories over the years, but the Blade had gone missing a long time ago, and none seemed to match up with it ending up here in the hands of Ander.

She shrugged. "I'm not privy to the details, but he wasn't..." She looked down uncertainly. "However it occurred, I think it cost him a lot to deliver it here. He doesn't talk about it. But when he first came... he shut himself in the Temple for a while. Didn't really talk to anyone. Mara and Vlad had to–" She cut herself off abruptly. "It doesn't matter. To make a long story short, Ander is an ally, even if he occasionally chooses to act as though he's not. I may not like how he interacts with people, but he is still one of the Lady's priests."

"Mara?" Jamirh prompted. Perhaps he could distract her that way.

"Another one of the Lady's priests," Jeri said absently. "You aren't doing that one correctly. Here, move your leg like this..."

Jamirh sighed as she corrected his placement. It was odd, though. While he also wasn't Ander's biggest fan, he had never really gotten the impression that Ander wasn't on their side, even when he was beating Jamirh into the dirt. That was just a more intense version of what Jeri did. He'd meant that Ander had been very effective at protecting Jamirh, not surprised that he'd done it at all. "You and Ander don't really seem to get along."

She blinked at him, then raised one shoulder. "Like I said, I don't like the way he interacts with people. He always seems to think he's better than the rest of us. And to be perfectly frank, he doesn't get along well with most people for many of the same reasons. He has rank purely based on his status as a priest, so people will show it differently, but... well, he's just not the kind of person who gets close to others. He probably talks to the Lady more than anyone else."

Jamirh had found Ander to be overly blunt and kind of bizarre, so that checked out. "Not even the other priests?" Though none of the others apparently lived here, so...

Jeri hesitated. "I couldn't say, really. They're a mixed bunch and aren't often in one place. All of the Lady's priests can be a little... odd, I suppose, though Ander is by far the most standoffish of them. And it's not that I don't *respect* Ander, per se – he's a brilliant surgeon and healer, after all, and amazing with shields – I just don't *like* him all that much."

Jamirh considered that. Jeri respected Ander's ability but didn't care for him as a person. He guessed that was fair. He wasn't a hundred percent sure where *he* stood on Ander as a person, though he didn't ever want to spar with him again, and he could attest to the priest's shields being excellent.

He sighed. Why was everything so complicated?

Aether would have known how to deal with Ander. Aether had always known how to get other people to work with him, often despite themselves.

"Hey, what's wrong? Does it bother you that much, that the two of us don't get along?"

He glanced up at Jeri's concerned face and realized his ears had been slowly sinking. "Oh, no, sorry. It just reminded me of someone else." He clenched his hand into a fist to prevent it from drifting to his key.

She blinked. "Oh. I'm sorry you had another person like that to deal with."

"No! It wasn't... wasn't like that." He looked away. "Don't worry about it." He shifted into another stretch.

"Okay, then," she said slowly, frowning at him. "If you say so."

Jamirh decided this was not a safe topic. "Can we start with daggers and then work our way up to a sword?" he asked, pathetically trying to delay the inevitable. Hell, it was even an inevitable he had asked for, though now that the moment was here he found himself wanting nothing more than to put it off a little longer.

She rolled her eyes. "No. We need to get you going on the longsword as fast as possible. We'll still spend some days with the daggers – there's no reason to let those skills go – but our priority should be the Blade, since it will do some of the work for you against Abomination."

Right. Since it was a special, Abomination-killing sword. Made for him. Or, well, made for an earlier version of him. Great. He sent a look of disgust towards the wall of wooden practice weapons.

Oh, come on. It can't possibly be that *bad, can it?*

Yes, yes it could be. But he had to do it anyway.

Three hours later had him feeling nothing but disgust for himself.

"Let's give it one last try, hm?" Jeri offered. "Then we'll call it for today."

Groaning, Jamirh set himself into the stance she had shown him. He pictured the movements he was supposed to make, even quickly running through the motions. Perfect. He reset.

Jeri swung her own wooden practice blade for a moment, giving him time to prepare, then lunged–

Jamirh swung his own weapon to meet hers, but he knew immediately it wasn't right. The blades met at an awkward angle, and Jamirh's momentum carried him to the floor, leaving him annoyed but thankful for Jeri's early lessons on falling.

Yes, he'd been successful in quickly picking up the forms Jeri was teaching him, but it didn't feel anything like when he had just... *reacted* fighting Ander or avoiding the bionic. According to Miravu, the Aradian ambassador assigned to Romanii, it should be as easy as breathing for him to copy what he saw other people do. And while he did seem to be learning quicker than most people, it didn't feel right.

It was leaving a sour taste in his mouth. Even Jeri seemed to be disappointed, though he was doing about as well as he had with the daggers. She'd pushed him harder than usual, maybe to make up for the missed days, or maybe to punish him for slacking. He didn't want to ask.

"Okay, that's enough for today. We aren't going to get much more done at this point," she said, though her smile looked forced. "You did really well, considering today was your first attempt!"

"There's got to be a better way to figure out this whole Master of Blades thing," he muttered, scrubbing at his face.

"The best thing you can do right now is just keep practicing," Jeri said gently, holding out a hand to pull him back to his feet. "We'll try again tomorrow, hm?"

Jamirh didn't even want to think about tomorrow. All he wanted was a hot shower, some food, and his bed. He almost whimpered, thinking about the downpour he still had to go through to reach the palace. Maybe it had let up while Jeri had been torturing him? Still, he wished he had a better grasp on how to use his inherent. "Ugh. Why can't I do it?"

"Hey," she said, resting a hand on his shoulder. "Don't be so down on yourself. We know you can, right? It was enough to keep you alive against the bionic, and that's the most important bit. With Ander's report we know quite a bit more about what they are capable of, and none of it is good, but you still managed! So let's try to focus on the positives for now?" Her voice rose hopefully. "We can get you there, I promise."

He closed his eyes, ears drooping. He could only hope.

Chapter Six

Takeshi lay on his side wrapped in a cocoon of blankets, looking at the city lights through the rain falling against the glass. Every joint and muscle ached. His left arm itched from where the needle giving him nutrients had been inserted. Even after sleeping for most of the past few days, he was so tired his eyes hurt. He still felt chilled despite the several heating crystals tucked at the foot of the bed. Knowing the cold was a side effect of what had been causing the migraines didn't make it easier to bear. He wasn't sure when the last time he had felt properly warm was. He had definitely been warm on the *Sea Spirit*; he remembered the heated blanket Ashi had given him. Had he been warm since then? He wasn't sure. He hadn't even recognized that as a sign that something was wrong; he'd just thought the weather had been abnormally cold.

But it turned out a lot of things he'd thought had been wrong.

So many questions, and so many lies. Everything he'd thought he'd been doing was predicated on lies covering up more lies. How far back did it go? Was anything this mission was based on true? It was almost a relief to come to that realization; things started to make sense once you acknowledged that none of it was ever supposed to.

Why did they have so little for him to go on regarding the rebellion? Because one didn't exist. Of course no one wanted him to know how they were going to be retrieving the information he gathered – the method was going to be slowly killing him.

He wanted the chip out. Part of him wanted to rip it out right now with his bare hands, tearing at flesh until he was free of the violation. Ander had told him that was a bad idea, that he just needed a little time to figure out how to do it safely.

Takeshi refused to believe that the Empress and those who had sent him hadn't known death was a possibility, if not an inevitability. Ni Fon, though a nation of magic, had adapted to scientific techniques and strategies wholeheartedly; nothing was done anymore without thorough testing and research. If Ander was somehow right and Hotaru had also been slowly deteriorating due to a chip placed in her, then they had absolutely known. Takeshi didn't understand why a chip would have been placed in Hotaru, but he wasn't naïve enough to believe it was outside the scope of possibility. He wondered how many people had been involved. Surely the doctors; otherwise they would have found the chip, wouldn't they? If they already knew about it, it cost them little to say they didn't know what was killing her. Had they even been real doctors, or scientists masquerading as doctors? Takeshi was ashamed to admit that he hadn't paid close enough attention to notice either way.

The Empress would have known. Takeshi knew how ruthless she could be, and though he hadn't thought she would go that far, he recognized that she was capable of it. He had just thought that was a line she wouldn't cross. He guessed he had his answer to how little she had valued her daughter's life. In that light, what was his own worth? Probably nothing.

And if he acknowledged that were true, did it mean the whole murder and banishment were actually a complicated coverup for *Hotaru's* death? Had that actually been the reason? Why, if everyone involved in her care already knew? What was the point? The worst part was that any evidence was long gone – and he had been unwittingly instrumental in getting rid of it.

What a complicated web of lies.

How had Ander known Hotaru's symptoms?

Takeshi had to be honest – a large part of him just didn't care anymore. He felt horribly betrayed, both for himself and on Hotaru's behalf. He had pushed so hard through so much in her name, only to find out she had been manipulated as well. It was literally only due to divine intervention he had made it this far. Without Hades' interference, he would probably be slowly dying in some hotel in Alenci, searching fruitlessly for something that didn't exist.

As it was, the room he was in here had been practically covered in protective patterns and glyphs. Ander was certain of his theory that Ni Fon attempted to access the chip in Takeshi's head every two weeks, especially after learning that the migraines had begun at the same time of day each time. But since Hades had interrupted the previous signal, no one was sure if they would try again sooner, and today marked one week since his last migraine. Everyone was on edge, uncertain if anything was going to happen. Additionally, no one was sure if Hades alone was capable of shielding Takeshi, so in her absence Jak and Ander had implemented every defensive spell they could think of. Both of the other men thought that if Takeshi was attacked again Hades would intervene, but no one wanted to take any chances. He was under orders to alert someone immediately at even the slightest sign of an oncoming migraine.

Hades was an entirely different problem to consider. He hadn't heard her since he had asked for silence, though Ander had explained none of them could hear her right now. Ander and Jak were both priests of hers, it turned out. Takeshi guessed it made sense that she had wanted him to go to them if she thought he should also be a priest. He didn't know what to think about that; he certainly didn't feel like something desirable right now, much less something a god would want. He wasn't even a particularly religious person. He was a warrior and an assassin, and while he did pray and make offerings to the gods he had never done so in Hades' name. As it was, he was phenomenally lucky she wasn't offended by how he had spoken to her before, no matter what Jak said. Plenty of myths and stories existed of those who had failed to take care when speaking to a deity and paid the price for it. Granted, he didn't think any of them featured Hades specifically, so maybe she was just... very casual, for a god? What a strange thought.

And yet, she had been the one consistent thing in this whole mess since Bariza and had attempted to be genuinely helpful. He couldn't be angry at her for the communication errors; those had been caused by the chip embedded in his spine and his own assumptions trying to fill in the gaps. When they had finally been able to communicate accurately, other things had taken precedence, and then she had... "been exploded," was how Jak put it? He was right that "died" was clearly not the correct term. Been removed from this plane of existence, perhaps?

In almost exactly the same way he had removed Hotaru from this plane of existence.

Gods, Hotaru. How could they have done that to her? Why? What purpose did it serve? Hotaru had been one of the loudest voices for finding a way to try to live with both magic and tech in harmony. Hotaru had been a mage, though a fairly weak one. It may have been that which allowed her to live so long with the chip, whereas a more powerful mage such as himself who used magic more often would have succumbed more quickly. It was horribly ironic that she had spent her life fighting for something that was slowly tearing her body apart.

She would have been so young when they implanted the chip. Why? The Empress must have known.

And so his thoughts had kept going round and round since he had woken up in this foreign hospital. At this rate, it wouldn't be surprising if he gave himself a stress headache. At least he could think again. Ander appeared to be correct that using magic was what triggered the strange memory loss, so as long as Takeshi did not use magic he was actually able to remain aware and cognizant. Which was what was allowing him to over-analyze and agonize over the situation.

He sighed heavily. As long as he didn't use magic. Magic was a part of who he was; he'd been weaving patterns for as long as he could remember. What if the chip permanently damaged his ability to weave? What would he be then? No home, no people, no mission, no magic. What was a shinobi without those things? Would he even technically *be* shinobi? In the end, how much of what made him "Takeshi" would the Empress claim?

He curled a little further into the blankets as he fought to focus on something else. This hospital was strange compared to back home. They had given him warm, soft clothing to wear, instead of scratchy cheap fabric, and had allowed him to keep his mask. The room and the bed were both larger than what he was used to, and he wasn't sharing the space. There wasn't even a second or third bed for more patients. The staff had all been far more friendly than the professional but brusque attitude he was accustomed to in hospital staff. Except for perhaps Ander, who had been somewhat sympathetic, but much closer to what he would expect. Though... Ander also didn't seem to technically be hospital staff, so did that count? He wasn't sure. It didn't really matter.

Nothing really mattered anymore.

What was he supposed to do with himself now? There was no point in continuing his mission. Ni Fon did not need information on a rebellion that didn't exist. He believed the Empress was certainly looking for ways to break free from the Rose Empire, but he didn't believe his mission was one of them. He had no idea what the information he was providing to them was being used for. Maybe they did think he was going to learn something they could use.

He didn't care. He wasn't going to help her anymore. He just needed to wait for Ander to figure out how to remove the chip without killing him in the process.

He briefly acknowledged the fact that he had *actually* been banished. They had told him it was pretend, that it was to throw the Rose Empire off his scent, and he had believed them. Just one more lie to add to the pile.

Part of him did understand the reason for the chip, of course. It didn't really matter what information he found. The Empress would collect it from him *in case* it could be useful, using him to the very last until the chip killed him. She was efficient that way.

He closed his eyes tiredly. He still needed rest to recover from draining his reserves so thoroughly. Ander had called it "magicore exhaustion"; Takeshi wasn't sure if the fact they had a specific term for it made the situation seem better or worse. It made it sound like he had a condition – a condition that required him to rest and eat to recover, but he'd barely managed to pick at what had been offered him earlier. He just hadn't felt like eating, even though he knew he should. A tray filled with nutrient-heavy snacks was within reach if he got hungry, but eating would require sitting up and partially leaving his nest of blankets, and he didn't feel like doing that right now.

A puff of air ghosted across his face along with the sound of a soft huff. Takeshi opened his eyes to see a black nose attached to a white muzzle inches away from his face, luminous violet eyes looking at him curiously over them. Startled, he tried to pull away as best he could, but it followed after him and licked his face happily, bringing with it the scent of damp dog. Annoyed, he abruptly sat up to try to get out of its reach before realizing that there was no way to achieve that – the thing was enormous. White fur covered a very wolf-like body that had to be at least three, three-and-a-half feet tall. He pushed its snout away and it sat next to his bed, wagging its large tail enthusiastically, clearly visible even in the dimly lit room.

"Where did you come from?" he asked it, wondering how such a creature could have gotten into the hospital. Its fur was just barely damp, as though it had been outside in the rain but had since mostly dried off. Maybe it belonged to someone here? Hopefully it did. Did people here have pets this big? It was practically a monster, though a very friendly one. Cheerful joy radiated off it, completely eliminating any fear or worry Takeshi might have felt at being confronted by such a large canine. There was no malice in those eyes. In fact, it was looking at him just like any of the palace dogs back home when they wished to be petted. He reached out a hand and began scratching behind one of its ears. It gave a thoroughly satisfied huff of enjoyment and leaned into the attention, eyes partially closing in bliss.

"Okay," he started slowly. "We need to figure out where you belong, I think."

It pulled back, eyes wide as it stared at him, then jumped up on the bed. Takeshi had a moment to be thankful for the size of the furniture in question before it lay down on his legs; it never would have fit on a hospital bed back home. As it was, it took up the vast majority of both the available and unavailable surface.

"This is not what I meant," he muttered, beginning to attempt to push it off before he realized the thing was practically radiating heat. It was so warm it was even penetrating the perpetual chill he had felt for the past several weeks. He wavered. "Very well then; maybe just for a little while."

It placed its head in his lap and looked up at him hopefully.

Sighing, he gave in and began to pet it again. "We do still need to determine where you belong," he informed it dryly. "Someone must be missing you right now. A creature as big as you disappearing must cause a stir, no?"

One triangular ear flicked in his direction, but it gave no other indication that it heard him, absorbed as it was in receiving scratches along its jaw.

"Do you have a name?" he asked it, eyeing its neck, but there was no collar or any other means to hold a tag. It scooted forward so it could press its nose into his chest, demanding more attention and conveniently spreading its warmth.

The heat must have encouraged Takeshi to doze off, because the next thing he knew he was blinking awake at the sound of a knock. The dog-creature was still there, curled up on the bottom half of the bed and his legs, keeping him warm. Its head had popped up and was looking towards the doorway. He spared a brief thought that his legs should be asleep with something that large lying on them before glancing towards the door.

Ander stood there, staring at the canine for a moment with an unreadable expression, before demanding, "What are you doing in here?"

It made a soft woofing sound, wagging its tail.

"It just sort of wandered in," Takeshi tried to explain as the half-Avari stepped fully into the room, turning the lights on to half-power. "I'm not sure how long ago; I think I dozed off for a bit. It's keeping me warm, actually." He raised a hand to its head, and it leaned in. "I assume it belongs to someone here? What is it? I've never seen a canine so big. It's a good thing it's so friendly."

"She's a warg. And she doesn't belong in here; get out! You know better." Ander gestured towards the door, one hand on his hip as though his disappointment would be enough to make it get up and move.

The creature didn't so much as twitch away from Takeshi, staring down the priest with a look that said, "make me."

"Go back to the Temple. You can't just wander through the hospital; go bother someone else." The priest was clearly exasperated. "Please?" he tried after it became clear the canine was not going to move, sounding as though it physically pained him to ask.

"Do they normally respond to verbal commands like that?" Takeshi asked curiously. The dogs back home could sometimes be trained to verbal commands, but they had to be fairly simple. Ander was talking to this one as though it could understand full sentences and context. "She, you said? She's a beautiful creature. Is she yours?"

Her mouth dropped open in the dog-equivalent of a grin, and her tail wagged even more enthusiastically.

Ander grimaced. "No, she's not mine. Most of the wargs don't really belong to anyone; they just sort of wander around the palace grounds and the city like overgrown cats with no sense of personal boundaries. However, they are not supposed to just wander into the hospital, and they know that. Wargs are extremely intelligent; do not let them trick you into thinking otherwise. This one knows exactly what she's doing, which..." He trailed off.

"Which?" Takeshi prompted when he failed to continue.

Ander sighed. "They do usually obey me, given my status as priest and their association with the Lady. If I can't coax this one out, and I'm fairly certain I've failed, it's very likely she has decided to adopt you."

Takeshi's hand stilled. "Pardon?"

The warg pushed her head under his hand, clearly disapproving of Takeshi no longer petting her.

Ander sighed. "Well, you said she was keeping you warm?"

Takeshi nodded slowly.

"It could be worse, then. This one here is two years old, if I remember correctly, and probably not quite at her full size. You might as well start thinking of a name." He started pulling various tea-related items out of one of the cabinets.

"I don't... what?" Takeshi was very confused. He was being adopted by a dog? Didn't that usually work the other way around? He looked at her, perplexed, only to have her lick his face again, tail thumping against the bed.

Ander watched as Takeshi tried to push her snout away. "Wargs are creatures sacred to the Lady. They are definitely not normal animals; for all that they live among us they have their own rules and understanding of how things should be. Occasionally, one decides to, well, 'adopt' really is the best word... one decides to adopt a member of the bipedal races. It's nearly impossible to convince it not to once it has made up its furry little mind. They usually do this if they feel like they are needed by the person in question." The white-haired man tilted his head to the side. "Most are also empathic. Are you picking up any emotions from her? She's emoting at you to the point where it feels like she's shouting. I'm almost getting words out of the emotions." He considered for a moment. "You can't actually emote so hard empathy changes to telepathy, but she's giving it a good attempt."

Takeshi looked back at the large creature, who tried once more to lick him in response. "No, no foreign emotions I recognize, anyway."

Ander nodded. "The chip probably interferes with that sort of communication too." The large head turned in his direction. Ander looked at her quietly for a moment before turning back to brewing the tea. "She doesn't like that you can't sense her, but she figures she has other ways to communicate. She doesn't seem to think you are very bright," he added with a snort.

Takeshi stared at her, affronted that a dog was judging his intelligence. "*What?*"

"They don't have a high opinion of bipeds in general," Ander assured him. "It's not just you. They think we over-complicate things and that their way is superior. That seems to be part of the 'they need us' narrative they tell themselves. This one, for example, doesn't understand why you might not want her help, since in her eyes you obviously need it." A small green pattern lit up under the mug, which began to steam.

"Didn't you just say she was two? I'm thirty-five," Takeshi protested. "What does she think she knows that I don't?"

Ander shrugged, bringing the mug over. "And I'm three hundred and forty-two. It doesn't stop them from thinking they know more than I do. They'd probably question the Lady Herself if they had the opportunity. Drink this."

Takeshi took the mug carefully. The warg backed off slightly to give him room, but continued to watch him closely. He stared back at her as he sipped. It was the same tea they had been giving him – sillna, they called it? It was the best thing he'd ever had for dealing with the effects of low magic reserves, even if it tasted bland.

Had Ander just said he was three hundred and forty-two? Surely he had misheard that. He looked to be around the same age as Takeshi. Maybe he had said forty-two? A young forty-two?

And he was a priest of the goddess of death, which meant... what, exactly?

He decided to leave that alone for now and go back to trying to wrap his mind around the fact that this creature was adopting him, completely without his agreement. "Do I get a say in whether or not I belong to her?"

Ander actually laughed, the sound dry. "You can try to negotiate, but I've never seen someone successfully dissuade a warg who had claimed them. No matter what you do, she'll follow you now. They are awfully patient; you'll give in long before she will."

She made an annoyed whine in Ander's direction.

"And she does not like the suggestion that she ever would give up," the priest added. "They are very possessive creatures."

"How am I supposed to care for a dog this large?" Takeshi asked, trying to point out the obvious. "I don't have the slightest idea what her needs are."

Ander was already shaking his head. "You are thinking about it the wrong way around. She is more than capable of taking care of herself, no matter where you go. Even if you leave Romanii, she will follow you and she will manage just fine. I honestly do not know if it is possible for you to outrun her. She might get annoyed at the fact you are hampering her ability to take care of you, but the wargs handle themselves."

She put her head down in his lap, looking up at him with big eyes.

"But... the food alone must be excessive for a creature of this size," Takeshi protested.

Ander shrugged. "I've never seen a warg starve. They can eat almost anything, and they are willing to get creative about it if food is scarce. I wouldn't worry about it; if she thinks she needs something from you she will let you know. They are extremely straightforward."

Takeshi wasn't sure he liked how easily Ander seemed to be accepting this new development on his behalf. "But..." he tried again before trailing off, not sure where to go with that.

This was just what his life was now, he reflected tiredly. A complete, absolute mess. He didn't have the energy to argue with a three-foot-tall dog about whether or not she owned him. Why was he even considering arguing with a dog? He shouldn't have to do that; he was the person. He was above arguing with an animal.

A large white snout carefully pushed the mug he was holding up towards his face. It did not take a genius to realize she wanted him to continue drinking it.

"Oh no," he muttered, very belatedly realizing what she had gotten him into.

"Yes," Ander agreed. "They are like that. Good luck."

Uncomfortable with how closely that mirrored his thoughts, Takeshi gave up and obediently took another swallow. They could revisit this after the chip had been removed from his head and he was feeling better.

She put her head back down, radiating smugness.

"How intelligent did you say they are?" he asked, frowning.

"Intelligent enough to make your life easy or difficult, depending on how you approach it. Most wargs are more intelligent than even above-average dogs or cats, but those who adopt people tend to be... more than that. Just treat her like another person, honestly. She'll understand you. And she'll make sure you understand her, for better or for worse." Ander took the empty cup from him and headed back to the counter with it. "All of that aside, how are you feeling? Any headaches, pain, or discomfort?"

"I'm still very tired, but it's not too bad. I was cold until this one decided to lie on me." He waved a hand in the warg's direction; she licked it. "No headaches, thankfully. That tea is amazing."

"It's meant to deal with the effects of magicore exhaustion, which you are still suffering from, on top of everything else." His mouth twisted into an expression of distaste. "Even if you weren't showing signs of something worse, you'd have had to be hospitalized for several days. Your body started eating itself."

Takeshi hadn't been aware enough to recognize how bad things had gotten, but he could recognize it now. He stayed silent, not sure how to respond while the warg snuggled somehow closer.

Ander cast a critical eye over the untouched tray of snacks on the small table by Takeshi's bed. "And this is not how you should be going about recovering from that." He turned to the warg. "If you are going to be a nuisance anyway, make sure he eats."

Her tail wagged in response like some sort of furry flag. Takeshi looked over her bulk again; how was she not crushing him?

The priest glanced at his watch. "Based on the timing of the previous events, I think if they were going to access the chip today they would have done so by now. Excellent. Perhaps it must be every two weeks; did you ever happen to observe any pattern to Hotaru's attacks?"

Right, Hotaru. Takeshi shook his head mutely, feeling a pang of grief for her along with a stab of hurt betrayal.

Ander hummed thoughtfully. "No matter. Well then, you have clearly indicated you want the chip removed. Let's talk about what that surgery will likely entail."

Takeshi sighed and resigned himself to going over a number of medical protocols for the next hour or so. He hadn't known the other man for very long at all, but he had observed that Ander was incredibly thorough when it came to such things. In truth, Takeshi didn't really care what it took, or what he had to go through. He ran a hand over the warg's soft head, trying to distract himself.

He just wanted the chip out.

"I'm a busy woman, Colonel. I don't come to Espon often, and when I do it is for pressing matters of great importance. Why are you disturbing me?"

Rhode hated Kobayashi Rikona. Of all the dukes and duchesses, she was the most difficult to work with. Rhode didn't believe she ever had the interests of the Empire at heart, only her own.

"I'll make it quick, then," he replied smoothly. Never show weakness in front of a shark. "One of your shinobi was involved in the Charve Base incident. Why was he there?"

"You've been misinformed, Colonel," she responded calmly. "All of my shinobi are accounted for back in Ni Fon, aside from the two who accompanied me here." An elegant gesture, and two shadows briefly made themselves visible to Rhode, masked faces giving nothing away before they faded back out of sight. It disturbed Rhode that even though he knew they were there he still couldn't find them. Blasted magic. "And these two came with me; neither they nor I were on the continent five days ago."

Cole stepped up next to him, handing him a tablet with the relevant data. "Perhaps you could explain this footage, then?" He turned it so she could see, then pressed play.

Kobayashi was silent, her expression giving nothing away as she watched the shinobi fight the asset, clearly protecting the Avari witch. The footage fizzed out when the asset utilized its EMP, which had unfortunately harmed base systems as much as the mages. Her dark eyes studied him carefully for a moment. "I wouldn't have thought you to be that careless with your research. That is no shinobi, and he is certainly not one of mine." She leaned back in her chair, lounging in it as if it were a throne. When she continued, her voice was cold. "Perhaps you missed the banishment that took place over a month ago?"

Rhode's mouth thinned in anger. "Do you really expect me to believe you sent your former future son-in-law into the ocean to die instead of doing it yourself, and then he just randomly pops up weeks later at a military base in the heart of the Empire while a prominent Romanii captive breaks free? That timing seems a little too coincidental; surely you must agree?"

She shrugged, the movement as poised and elegant as any other. "He *was* shinobi. They are capable of many things beyond you or me." Her eyes flicked to the Truth Seekers flanking Rhode and Cole. "Even beyond your blind dogs. If he survived the ocean, it was by his own efforts. I put forth none to help him, and by the law neither did any of my people. I wouldn't worry about him for too long though, Colonel. A banished Nifoni rarely survives for long on their own, even if they do make landfall." She turned her attention back to the stack of papers sitting on her desk. "Good day, Colonel."

For all his accusations and theories, Rhode didn't dare push her any further. He still had no proof. "Good day," he responded stiffly, turning and striding out of the duchess's office. Major Cole and the two Truth Seekers followed him out.

It was almost half an hour later, in the car on the way back to Charve, that one of the Truth Seekers coughed politely. "Sir."

Rhode, stewing in his anger over Kobayashi's lack of cooperation, was taken aback. "Yes?"

"She was surprised," the Truth Seeker said succinctly.

Rhode blinked, then turned to look more directly at the Seeker. They didn't usually offer this kind of information. "What?"

The blindfolded head tilted slightly. "When you showed her the footage of Shuurai at Charve. She hid it very well, but she was surprised to see him."

Rhode stared at him, wondering what that meant. Was she actually innocent in Shuurai's involvement? Rhode had a hard time swallowing that; Kobayashi was the queen of plots upon shadowy plots. He couldn't fathom something happening involving one of her own that she didn't know about, and he would sooner believe pigs could fly than that she had truly banished Shuurai. She had her hooks in this somehow; Rhode just had to find them.

What was going on?

Chapter Seven

It had been a long week for Ander, and it wasn't over yet.

He was the first one to arrive at Vlad's office, so he let himself in and settled down into one of the plush chairs to wait for the other two. He glanced around at the dark wood furnishings and gold-and-black decor, as familiar to him as his rooms back at the Temple, then closed his eyes. The place that Hades normally inhabited was still vacant, adding to his general state of being out of sorts. She had been with him so long that it was... unbalancing to be without Her.

"You okay, kid?"

Ander opened his eyes to shoot a silent glare Jak's way.

Jak grinned as he dropped into another armchair. "Sorry, I sometimes forget you prefer a more formal address. Let me try again. Are you okay, child?"

Ander rolled his eyes, but there was no changing Jak. He'd been alive far too long for that. At least he hadn't tried to ruffle Ander's hair this time. "I'm fine. Just a little tired, given everything."

The other priest nodded in agreement. "Fair. Hopefully She gets over Herself sooner rather than later and drags Herself back to the land of the living with the rest of us. These old bones don't work quite right without Her around."

"I'm amazed anything works right at your age," Ander mused. He wasn't quite sure how old Jak was exactly other than "ancient." Older than Vampires as a race, and Vlad said Jak had been old even then. Siva said Jak had been old when she had become a priest long before that. Six thousand years, or maybe eight? Older even than that, perhaps? How long ago had Hades found Her first priest? It seemed to Ander like Jak had always existed. None of the younger priests were brave enough to ask for actual numbers, and Hades just laughed if you asked Her.

"It is something of a miracle, yes," Jak agreed easily. "A miracle I am happy to continue performing, though it's always easier with Her." Brown eyes slid in Ander's direction. "Will you be okay for later?"

He nodded. "If I have to pull energy from my *crystallus* I will, but I don't believe that will be necessary. I won't be using magic for the greater part of the surgery itself anyway. I don't dare use it that close to the microchip; I don't know how they would interact. Probably badly, if the way it reacts to Takeshi casting is any indication."

"Yeah, try not to explode him. I don't think the Lady would be too happy with that."

Ander shot him another glare.

"Who are we not exploding?" As impeccably dressed as always, Vlad breezed in with an armful of papers, which he placed none too carefully on the solid wooden desk.

"Shuurai Takeshi," Jak informed him, making a song out of the syllables.

"Ah, yes. We are in fact trying very hard to keep him alive," Vlad agreed. He looked around the room as though trying to remember something before his gaze settled on Ander. "Are you all set for this evening?"

It was apparently the question of the hour. "Yes, everything has been prepared. I don't foresee any issues, and Kyra will be assisting. I expect it to take one to three hours, depending on how it is connected to him."

Jak grimaced. "I don't even want to think about that."

Vlad's attention refocused, and he headed towards the large hutch against one wall. He pulled three mugs out of it and began digging around in a drawer. "Luckily, you don't have to; Ander does. How sure are you of a successful outcome?" he asked, glancing over his shoulder at the half-Avari. "What if you cannot disconnect it?"

"I've been able to study it a little more in small doses now that I know what I'm looking for. It has been integrated very elegantly and neatly; the six months Takeshi does not remember were probably spent introducing the microchip to his system. Maybe they hoped that his magic wouldn't reject it if done that way. Regardless, it makes my job much easier – I'm removing a foreign body, not introducing one, and the tidiness of the work is also a boon. Once it has been removed I will also be able to use magic to assist in the healing. He would have had to recover the long way when they put it in."

"Thus six months," Vlad mused, grabbing milk from the cold box next to the hutch.

"Thus six months," Ander agreed.

"And... no one noticed the Nifoni princess go missing for half a year in her childhood?" Jak drawled.

Ander shook his head. "There are a couple of possibilities on that front. One is that Takeshi is a very strong mage, and thus more likely to experience fatal complications they would have wanted to avoid. Hotaru was weak magically; she would not have been in as much immediate danger from the procedure. Another possibility is that they thought a long recovery period could offset some of the complications Hotaru experienced. It had been sixteen years since they tried with her, and who knows how many times they may have tried between. The procedure likely evolved, leading to different protocols and strategies. We don't even really know what the original purpose was, or why they chose the princess to test it. Was it even a test, with her? Many questions are still outstanding."

"And how confident are you that the Kobayashi girl had a chip? Isn't that a bit of a reach, especially without a possible reason for it?" Jak questioned, leaning back in his chair and putting a booted foot on Vlad's desk.

"Just because we don't know the motivation doesn't mean there isn't one," Ander countered, eyeing Jak's foot. He missed having the Lady in his mind to help decipher other people's actions. "The symptoms Hotaru and Takeshi suffered line up very closely; though it is possible that is a coincidence, it is very unlikely. We know at least one faction in Ni Fon has been trying to force tech and magic to work together, though usually in far more innocuous ways than what we've seen with Takeshi. I imagine there have been… accidents we don't know about, just due to the volatile nature of the relationship between the two. Ni Fon prides itself on being innovative. I don't think it's a stretch to think that they might have gone too far in their search for success."

"Then you think there is some sort of conspiracy going on in Ni Fon? Because I don't know how the chip would have gone unnoticed for sixteen years unless everyone was in on it." Jak sounded annoyed, as though the situation were personally offending him.

"That's not implausible," Vlad pointed out as he finished heating the concoction in the cups. He wasn't commenting on Jak's foot on his desk, to Ander's displeasure. "Ni Fon is very capable of keeping its secrets, even from those within it."

"Takeshi is convinced Rikona was involved as well, so it would go all the way to the top," Ander added as he took one of the mugs from the Vampire. "Her reputation for ruthlessness probably discourages leaks."

Jak leaned back in his chair as he took a large swallow from his mug. "I just think it's interesting that there weren't even any rumors about this sort of thing being worked on."

"Well, there sort of were," Vlad said slowly as he added a small vial of blood to his beverage. "There were some rumors coming out of the Empire that turned out to be about the bionic Abominations, such as the one that attacked us here. The bionics are tech integrated with a living person as well, even though they seem to be going about it completely differently." He glanced at Ander, eyebrows raised.

The younger priest nodded. "I'll know more when I can study the microchip in a safe, non-Human setting, but the tech involved does seem to be different. The Nifoni chip shows finesse, the bionic was more brute force. The bionic was also made with a metal I have yet to identify; I'll be interested to see if it is present in the microchip as well."

Jak frowned. "Honestly, I'm more concerned right now about where they're coming from. The Empire must be making these... bionics... somewhere. Where? How? And who came up with this idea? Or, well, either idea. They're both bad ideas."

Ander eyed him thoughtfully. Was Jak actually going to get involved? That would be a first. He usually preferred to stay as far away from the action as possible, managing the younger priests from a distance. He often said that creating the religion had been more work than he preferred, though from what Ander had observed their religion was haphazardly constructed at best. Still, perhaps a potential priest coming under direct attack from such a threat was enough to convince Jak to intervene?

He took a sip from his mug, unsurprised but disappointed to taste hot chocolate. Vlad loved the stuff and collected different variants. This one had more of a spiced taste than usual. Ander didn't know why he hoped for coffee even though Vlad only ever had hot chocolate in his office.

Sometimes, Ander felt like he was the only adult in the room.

"There are currently several members of the Black Watch south of the Wall trying to determine the answers to those questions," Vlad informed them. "When the Abominations were demons, we just needed to kill the summoner. Now that it looks like the Abominations are being manufactured..." He trailed off for a moment. "This complicates things significantly. Even if we destroy the place they are currently being made, I'm not sure we can say for certain that the problem would be solved."

"If they are being manufactured, then multiple people likely have the knowledge of how to create them. There's nothing to say that they couldn't just start creating them again somewhere else," Ander agreed.

Jak was still frowning. "Multiple people with the knowledge? Not just one?"

Ander shrugged. "I suppose it is possible that there is one mastermind behind the whole operation as far as the bionics go, but the fact that Ni Fon is also dabbling in similar sciences leads me to think that multiple people are contributing to the issue. I'll be honest; I'm not really sure how we are going to fully deal with the situation. There may already be too many people involved for it to be contained."

:It must be. Such things cannot be allowed to fester.:

Ander's eyes widened as Hades' presence made itself known, settling into Her normal place in his soul. He immediately felt better than he had in days as She strengthened him. Jak made a pleased hum next to him.

Vlad eyed them both. "Has She returned?"

Jak nodded. "Thankfully, yes. So if you'll excuse me – what the *hell*, Lady?"

Ander snorted a bit at that. And Takeshi had been concerned about the way he had spoken to Her.

:I needed time,: She responded quietly. Ander could feel the sadness in Her words, but at least the anger appeared to have run its course. *:How long was I gone? How is Takeshi?:*

Time passed differently for the divine than for mortals, Ander mused, but he had actually been wondering if She was waiting for the chip to be removed. "Longer than we'd prefer, but it's only been two days."

"Which is two days too long – don't trivialize it for Her, Ander," Jak cut in.

:I am well enough, now,: She soothed mildly. *:There is no need to be upset. I will always return.:*

Jak pressed his lips into a thin line, but whatever he said to Her in response he kept between the two of them. Ander decided that Jak's problem was not his problem and moved on. "Takeshi is doing as well as he can be. Severely limiting the magic he is exposed to has allowed him to recover somewhat from the effect of the microchip, and significantly from the effects of the magicore exhaustion. I'll be removing the chip later today and that should allow him to make a more full recovery. We'll have to wait and see if there are any lasting side effects." He paused, double checking that was everything. "Oh – and a warg adopted him."

Vlad choked on his hot chocolate as Jak's eyebrows went straight to his hairline. "When was this?" he asked, distracted from his admonishment of Hades.

"Yesterday evening," Ander informed them. "I have no idea how she got into the hospital in the first place, but she won't be moved now. She's able to keep him warm so I'm less inclined to try to remove her by force. She also promised to stay in his room and not get up to mischief, and I'm hoping she'll make him eat more than he has been."

Hades made a sound of delight, clearly cheered by this development. *:I am sure she will not cause trouble for you if she is so focused on her new Human.:*

"Unfortunately, the wargs have your definition of 'trouble', so I'd take that with a grain of salt," Jak muttered.

Vlad finished coughing. The frequency with which this happened was a testament to the fact that he seemed to be having no trouble keeping up with the conversation even though he couldn't actually hear Hades' end of it. Then again, he did know his mother very well. "Though, those that make the choice to stay with a partner do tend to be better behaved..."

There was a moment of silence while everyone thought about the other two wargs who had chosen priests of Hades.

"...But maybe keep a close eye on her just in case," Vlad suggested with a wince. "Has he given her a name yet?"

Ander shook his head. "Not that I'm aware, but he still thinks he might not keep her. I tried to explain that that's not really how it works, but... well, he'll figure it out eventually. I'm sure getting the chip out should allow her to reach him with empathy, and then he can hash it out with her more directly."

"Because that always works out so well for the two-legged end of the argument," Jak snorted. "Did you ever consider that perhaps you made them *too* smart?"

:No?: She seemed perplexed as to why he would even ask.

Ander just sighed. "Could you just remind them that the hospital is supposed to be off limits?"

:She had to go in, though,: Hades protested in confusion. *:Her Human was in there.:*

"Right." Ander gave up. He'd just have to remind the wargs himself for the eighteen hundredth time and hope it stuck. He took another sip of the hot chocolate, feeling another pang of disappointment that it wasn't coffee.

Jak leaned over and patted Ander's arm. "Is it any surprise they behave the way they do with a patron deity like ours?"

:They are wonderful examples of life,: Hades sniffed.

"Anyways," Vlad interrupted with a sigh, "we were discussing the Abominations, and whether or not it has already gone too far to be stopped. What does my mother have to say on that front?"

:There is no such thing. The Abomination must be wiped out each time it appears, or the world will tip into a final ending.: Hades' mental voice was firm. *:This cannot and will not be tolerated.:*

Jak and Ander exchanged a glance. "There is no such thing in Her worldview," Jak translated. "Because that would mean everything will be destroyed. How long, exactly, has it been kicking around? Forty years, give or take?"

Ander hummed in agreement. "We are on the second Ebryn attempt; we lost a lot of time because of that."

"Jamirh," Vlad corrected mildly.

"I'm not calling – I'm just saying this is the second try," Ander said, exasperated. "Whatever you want to call him, or whatever he wants to be called, there was one previously that died somehow and because of that we are twenty years behind where we should be. We almost had to go to attempt three when the bionic attacked him here." And that had been one of the most stressful moments of his life, trying to get to Jamirh before the bionic killed him. He was very thankful Jamirh had managed to stay alive long enough for him to intervene.

Jak nodded, but his brows were creased in worry. "Forty years is a long time for it to take hold and spread. Did we ever figure out how the previous Ebryn died?"

"I tried," Ander admitted. "He wasn't willing to speak to me."

"Huh. I wonder why?" the older priest mused.

"I just attributed it to his personality at the time; the first Ebryn was remarkably standoffish and uncooperative, from what I understand." Ander looked to Vlad for confirmation, who was already nodding.

"Incredibly so. Ebryn was an individual with a singular focus – to avenge his sister. Everything else was secondary to that. Rage and grief warred within him, to the point that they began to consume him. Though," the Vampire king murmured thoughtfully, "I wouldn't put my money on him having been a people person before all of that, either."

Ander looked down into the warm chocolate in his cup, watching the liquid swirl as he shifted it. "However, my first hypothesis might prove to be false. We have now had a fair amount of time to get to know Jamirh, and he is very much unlike his first counterpart in temperament. I am left uncertain of why the other was unwilling to speak to me."

:Those who are reborn are different people, for all that they have the same soul,: Hades pointed out gently. *:They have lived different lives, and they come from different places. Their core values tend to be the same, the very center of what they are, but that can show itself in remarkably different ways, like white light filtering through a prism.:*

Ander appreciated the analogy; it was very much tailored to him.

"Hades says that it's not surprising that Jamirh has a different personality than Ebryn, and She has nothing to say about the middle one," Jak informed Vlad. Ander was glad; he hated having to repeat everything She said.

Vlad shrugged. "Then it remains a mystery for the moment. It's unfortunate, especially if what killed him was an Abomination of some sort, but it can't be helped."

Ander gave a very slight mental poke to Hades, but She did not respond. The secrets of the dead were their own.

"Hopefully we will have an answer soon as to where the bionics are being created," Vlad continued. "We will simply have to deal with everything one problem at a time. If we can stop them from making more bionics, even if only temporarily, that will be a step in the right direction. We can go from there."

Hades gave a pleased hum.

"Yeah, She likes that." Jak sighed. "So be it. Man, I'm too old for this. Forty years," he drew the words out slowly. "Honestly, the Blade is not the only way to get rid of them."

"It's not, but they also did not show themselves to us once in that entire time," Ander pointed out, ignoring the twinge in his stomach at the implication that the Blade was unnecessary. "We couldn't even tell Jamirh what form the Abomination had taken, and when we did discover what it was he actually had more information than we did."

"It's almost like it hid, knowing we would try to end it," Vlad mused.

:Indeed. It would have been ended with extreme prejudice,: Hades said coolly. *:I will use every tool available to me to do so.:*

Jak nodded. "Yeah, that checks out. It is kind of weird, though – is the Abomination as a concept that smart? To hide itself out of some sort of survival instinct?"

There was an uncomfortable silence.

"Maybe," Ander conceded. "But I think what may actually be happening here is just that it has been developed in secret, and those secrets have somehow been kept successfully up to this point."

:The Abomination does not choose its form, per se, and it does not think,: Hades said slowly. *:Abomination is brought into the world by people. It is the people who end up shaping it. It is not a sentient existence like I am, it is just a name given to a certain form of corruption that occurs over and over again.:*

Ander considered that as Jak explained it to Vlad. In some ways, that was a good thing. Hades tended to personify the concept of Abomination, but that was because She tended to personify everything, not because it actively moved against her. Abomination was more like a virus – something mindless that simply sought to replicate itself in a way that would destroy its host. On the other hand, that meant that it was always people who were responsible for letting that virus take root in the world over and over again. A sin repeated since the dawn of time, warping and destroying reality until stopped.

They were just unlucky that this time it had been kept secret for so long that it was going to be incredibly difficult to burn out.

"Then you plan to stay for a while?" Vlad was asking Jak. "It's nice to see you more than once every millennium or so. It wouldn't hurt for you to visit more."

Jak was silent for several long minutes as he thought it over. "Yeah," he said finally. "Yeah, I think I'll stick around for a bit. At least until we figure out Takeshi's situation."

Ander stared at the first high priest of Hades. He was going to stay?

While he was glad to have the additional help, he had to wonder – how bad did that make this situation?

A few hours later found Ander knocking on Takeshi's door. The Nifoni mage was reclining against his pillows, dark circles still present under his eyes and still much too thin. The white warg was lying on the bottom two-thirds of the bed, happily taking an offered piece of cheese from his fingers.

"That's for you to eat, not her," Ander said disapprovingly as he strode in. The warg's ears flattened in annoyance, and he got the distinct impression he was ruining her plan. Hades laughed in the back of his mind.

Takeshi looked pained. "I know, but she's been in here since yesterday, and I hadn't seen her eat anything. I don't want her to starve just because she won't leave me, so I've been trying to convince her to eat the cheese. She was only taking a piece after I had eaten one until a few hours ago when I was supposed to stop eating, so we are kind of sharing?"

Ander kept his expression neutral. Trying to *convince* her to eat the cheese? He glanced at the warg and her smug expression – and had to wonder who was convincing whom to eat.

Well, as long as Takeshi did so. "Have you come up with a name for her yet?" he asked mildly as he started taking ingredients out for the tea he needed. Kyra was busy setting up the surgery downstairs, and he wanted to get started as soon as possible.

"No?" The man just sounded confused. The warg's tail wagged; she didn't mind waiting for a name until he was feeling better.

Ander continued brewing tea. "Well then, how are you feeling today?"

"Not awful?" For some reason, that was a question. "I'm still very tired and sore, but it's much improved from before. I haven't had a headache since I've been here, either, and while I'm still a little cold, she's been keeping me warm." He stroked the top of the warg's head as she leaned into his chest. "I'm ready for it to come out," he finished quietly.

Ander put a tablespoon of honey in the now steaming tea – this one needed it to be palatable – and brought it over to the other man. "Soon. Drink this. Quicker will be better; you'll start to feel the effects in about ten minutes."

The shinobi peered at the cup and the pale-green liquid, then pulled down his mask and drank the whole thing in one fluid motion. "What," he coughed as the taste caught up with him, "in the names of all the gods was in that?"

Ander took the cup back from him to be washed. "That is dormis tea."

"That is *not* tea," Takeshi protested as he pulled his mask back up. "I do not know what that is, but it does not deserve to be called 'tea.'"

The priest shrugged. "Tea is determined by what it is made from, not how it tastes. This particular plant's leaves are excellent sedatives and, mixed with a few other things that I will admit don't help the taste, will put you and help keep you asleep for the next few hours. Which we all want, trust me."

Takeshi shuddered. "But the chip will be gone after, right?" There was a tired, almost bruised look in his eyes. The warg made a soft sound and placed her head on his shoulder, the closest thing to a hug she could manage.

Ander found himself wondering how Takeshi was convincing himself that she was going to leave him. Even he could recognize that she'd attached herself to the shinobi. "Yes, it will be out the next time you wake up," he promised. "I am very good at what I do; you'll be fine. You'll have time to rest and process everything after we remove the microchip, as well." He was speaking as much to the warg as to Takeshi, since she couldn't come with him into surgery. She would have to wait here.

Her tail wagged once. She understood, though she didn't want to be separated from her Human. She knew he needed more help than just what she could provide.

Hades too knew better than to interrupt him while he worked; while he was glad She was back they had very strict rules in place about when he was performing surgery. He felt Her settle in the back of his mind. She would be a silent presence throughout, but that was all.

"I don't know that I want to process anything," Takeshi muttered a little uncooperatively, bringing his hands up to pet the warg.

That was a Vlad problem, if it came to that. "One thing at a time," Ander agreed. "How are you feeling now?"

Takeshi blinked. "Fine, still? Not particularly different, I think."

Ander nodded, noting that he was moving a little slower than before. "What was your favorite part of Charve?" he asked, aiming for a conversational tone.

"Charve?" Takeshi looked confused, then thoughtful. "I'm not sure. Both the Temple of Faith and the big park I went to were very nice..."

The priest listened to him describe the two attractions, prompting him with the occasional question to continue. Takeshi managed for a few minutes before starting to blink rapidly, words beginning to slur together as the dormis began to take effect. The warg gently licked at his face over his mask as he finally succumbed to the drug, eyes fluttering shut as his breathing evened out.

Ander shooed her off the bed. "Go do something else for a bit. This will take a few hours, but he won't be awake until later."

She curled up unhappily on the floor under the window, resting her head on her paws.

He shook his head, sending a quick mental alert to Kyra that they were ready as he prepared to bring Takeshi down. The warg could mope if she wanted to. He had work to do.

Chapter Eight

T akeshi was resting comfortably, reclining among a slew of pillows and blankets, the warg lying across his legs. Overall, he felt much the same as he had before – sore, tired, and a little chilled – but the sensations were one step removed, as though there were a cushion of sorts between him and the discomfort. The drugs here were very nice, he decided. Except for that "tea" Ander had made him drink before the surgery; that had just been disgusting.

But he was free.

He had been told that the procedure had taken almost three hours. The chip had been attached to his nervous system with extremely fine filament. Ander had needed to be very careful removing it to avoid damaging the nerves, and so he had gone very slowly. But it had been a success and Takeshi was now free of foreign tech in his body.

He had woken up sometime after the surgery, groggy and disoriented, and stayed awake just long enough for them to determine that there didn't seem to be any damage. Once it had been decided that he was responding within acceptable parameters, he had been given more painkillers and allowed to slip back into sleep.

He had woken up again some time ago, feeling significantly better than the night before. It was hard to tell currently if that was due to the drugs or the lack of a chip in his spine, but he had been able to eat some breakfast before dozing for most of the morning. The warg was still contributing to keeping him warm, content to remain a near-permanent feature of his bed. He'd given up any pretense of trying to make her move, even if he still wasn't sure about keeping her. Or her staying; apparently it wasn't up to him?

He roused again for lunch, but he wasn't particularly hungry. Some of the ache was starting to return as the drugs began to wear off, and the back of his neck was just beginning to itch. He found himself just pushing the food around on his plate without really eating. He'd already slept so much, but he still felt exhausted. Ander had said that he would need time to recover from the surgery, but he felt like he had already spent an excessive amount of time sleeping since he had arrived in Tarvishte.

Though... what would he do, once he was no longer confined to the hospital? He wasn't sure. He supposed he needed to really think through everything that had happened since he had left Ni Fon and look at it through the proper perspective, not that he had a better idea of what that was. He just needed to take things one step at a time.

A large black nose at the end of a white muzzle gently pushed the tray towards him a bit. The warg clearly wanted him to eat.

"I'm sorry," he murmured quietly, dropping the fork in favor of scratching an ear, "I'm just not that hungry right now."

Big violet eyes stared at him, and he got the distinct impression that he should try to eat more anyway.

He managed a weak smile for her. "Maybe later." Hopefully he'd feel more like eating in a little while.

The furry head tilted to the side. Why should he wait? The food was here now, and it was always better when it was first delivered. And he needed food. He was too thin.

His hand paused as he untangled that. It wasn't words, but pictures, ideas and emotions. More than enough to understand what it was she meant and what she wanted from him. When he had been speaking to Hades, he had been able to "hear" words, but the meaning had been very difficult to decipher. This was almost the complete opposite of that. "So this is how you communicate," he said thoughtfully. It seemed that Ander had been correct; the chip had interfered with her ability to reach him.

It was strange. He'd lived with magic his whole life, but since coming to Espon he had been introduced to several forms of communication he had never even heard of before. What else could speak, if only he knew to listen?

The warg gave off a sensation of surprise, followed immediately by unbridled excitement. Her Human could finally understand her! Her tail began wagging violently as her mouth dropped open into the dog version of a grin.

Takeshi realized that he had absolutely lost that argument, feeling the emotions wrapped up in the idea of "her Human." He was never going to successfully convince her to leave him. She was intelligent, frighteningly so, but it wasn't quite the same kind of intelligence as the sentient races he was familiar with. It was different in some way he couldn't quite put his finger on.

Love, acceptance, and joy washed over him as she greeted him. She would have loved him anyway, but she was glad they would be able to communicate properly. The tall-white priest did not lie, but she'd still worried.

Hotaru would have loved this. If he hadn't still been under a very strict "no magic" order until they could determine if there were any lasting complications from the chip, he would have tried to get a feel for her magic, because he had no doubt she had it. "Hello to you, too," he returned her greeting. "You are not an animal at all, are you? Whatever you are, you are much more than that." Of that, he had no doubt, now that he had a better feel for her.

She was pleased someone recognized that. Her Human was actually very smart for a Human! She liked that. She was special, of course – she was meant for him, and he for her, and she was so very glad she had found him! He needed her very badly, but that was okay – she would not leave him now that they were together.

His lips twitched in amusement, but he wasn't sure he could disagree with that. She was very sure of herself. How could he deny her? "My problems are a little more than the both of us combined, I think, but I thank you for your support regardless."

The two-feet often had problems that they over-complicated, but together, she was sure they would find a way. She was good at solving problems. She had even gotten into the hospital when the other wargs had told her she couldn't.

Takeshi considered asking her how, exactly, she had managed that, but decided he was better off not knowing. "I see."

And the most immediate problem in her opinion was that he wasn't eating. He could fix that. By eating.

He sighed, halfheartedly picking the fork back up. "I'm really not hungry right now, just so you know."

Why? He needed food. She could actually *see* that he needed food.

He hid a wince at the reminder of how far he had pushed himself. "I am aware, but that doesn't mean that I'm hungry. Maybe in a little bit."

Even if she agreed that the leafy stuff wasn't that appetizing, supposedly it was good for the two-feet. And there was some meat in there; maybe he could just eat that?

Takeshi obediently speared a piece of chicken from the salad to placate her and took a bite, chewing slowly. The soreness in his limbs was definitely starting to make itself known again, and he closed his eyes tiredly. He brought a hand up to touch the bandage at the back of his neck but forcefully brought it back down before he could scratch it.

Was he in pain? Was that why he didn't want to eat? She glanced towards the door. She could go get one of the healer-people if that was the case. They would not ignore her.

He smiled, scratching her head. "I think you are supposed to stay in my room, since you aren't supposed to be in the hospital to begin with."

Her tail wagged twice. That was true, but she'd do it for him if he needed her to. What he needed was more important than the tall-white priest's commands.

Takeshi wasn't quite sure what to do with that level of loyalty, or what he'd done to inspire it. "I am fine," he assured her. "I would prefer to avoid activity that could get you thrown out, if at all possible. I'm fairly certain you are the only thing keeping me warm, even with the chip removed." Ander had told him some of the symptoms might take time to fade. Unfortunately, they were dealing with a completely new procedure involving unfamiliar tech, so there were still many, many unknowns. At least they had been able to remove the damn thing, so he no longer had to worry about migraines set off by them trying to access his brain.

The warg snuggled a little closer. She could keep him warm. But if he needed her to go fetch a two-feet, she could do that too. She was not afraid of the wrath of the tall-white priest.

Takeshi abandoned the food entirely, running a hand through her soft fur. If he was being honest with himself, he had already grown used to her presence and didn't want her to leave. She had been clearly supportive even when he could not hear her directly, and had forced her way into the situation without a single care for anyone else's opinion – including Takeshi's. Wargs choosing to adopt people seemed to be accepted behavior in this country; Takeshi seemed to be the only person questioning this development. Oh, plenty of people were surprised to see the warg, but that appeared to have more to do with the setting than anything else. Almost everyone had asked the warg what she was doing in the room upon seeing her, but no one seemed overly concerned or surprised once they heard the reason.

It was just hard to wrap his mind around the fact that a large dog had adopted him. What did that mean, exactly?

There was suddenly the most peculiar sensation, like someone coughing politely to gain his attention, but mentally. Takeshi blinked, his tired mind trying to figure out what that could be before realizing what was happening. He suppressed a sigh; he should have expected this would happen sooner or later. The question was, did he want to deal with this right now?

It was a little rude to keep a goddess waiting.

:Hello,: he greeted her, wondering how this was going to go.

:Hello?: Though her voice was still quiet, Takeshi heard it far better than before. Removing the chip had solved quite a number of problems. Go figure. *:How are you feeling? Any better?:*

:Much, thank you.: He paused, then added, *:I have you to thank for that. Thank you.:*

:Oh? Oh! Yes, you are welcome.: Relief poured from her tone. *:Ander told me the chip removal was a success. And I watched it as well as I could. Not that I understood any of it. Are you in any pain? Are you comfortable? Is there anything I can do? Or that I can get someone else to do? I think Ander is asleep right now, but I might be able to convince Jak to be a pair of hands.:*

Takeshi blinked at the word vomit. Was... was this what he had been missing? Had she really been so verbose in her prior communications with him? Or was she just feeling exceptionally talkative now? Then again, she hadn't held back on information when they had faced the bionic construct, so maybe this was more in character?

No wonder he'd had so much trouble understanding her. He'd been missing far more than he'd thought, if this was the case.

:Actually, he's still a little mad at me. So maybe he won't help. But if I tell him it's for you he might?: She was still going, he realized. *:But I might be able to manage something, even if he doesn't want to.:*

In Ni Fon, the goddess of death was known as "The Silent Goddess." This, Takeshi was coming to realize, was a lie. *:I am fine, as I was just telling this warg.:* He scratched between her ears, and she pulled herself up so that she could press her head into his chest.

There was a sense of amusement. *:Ah yes, Ander told me you had been adopted. Congratulations! She seems very sweet. I like her colors.:* A beat, and then, *:Oh, are you hearing me completely now?:*

:I seem to be. I'm not sure what I could possibly be missing if I'm not,: he observed dryly.

:Excellent! It is much easier for me to reach you as well.: She seemed pleased with this development, but there was a thread of anger under it as well. *:What a horrible thing to do to a living being. That will have to be dealt with at some point.:*

Takeshi raised an eyebrow. *:How do you plan on going about that?:*

:I'm not sure yet.: She sounded frustrated. *:But it will be figured out eventually. Such things always are.:*

He closed his eyes. If he was going to be speaking to the goddess of death, then there was one real question he wanted to ask. *:Was Hotaru dying because of a similar chip in her?:*

There was a long silence, but he didn't sense the goddess's presence go anywhere. She just seemed to be thinking. *:The dead only know what they knew in life,:* she finally murmured. *:And even if she did know more, I will not tell the secrets of the dead. Those are for them to share, or not, as they wish.:*

He frowned, puzzled. *:How else would the dead share their secrets, if not through you?:*

:My priests may ask of the dead what they will. It is one of the gifts I give them, the ability to do this. Of course, it is up to the dead to decide if they will answer: She sounded awfully matter-of-fact about such a bizarre thing.

:Speaking with the true dead is fantasy,: he protested. *:Ghosts and the undead might be one thing, but it is impossible to reach a soul that has returned to the ether.:* He had to believe Hotaru had not become one of the restless dead; he would never forgive himself if that was the case.

She didn't answer verbally, but he got the impression that she was gesturing wildly about herself.

:Right.: Goddess of death; it was *her* domain. Nothing was impossible for her within it. He silently chastised himself for such a stupid comment. He must have been much more tired than he thought.

Ander had been awfully knowledgeable about the symptoms Hotaru had suffered. If her priests could speak to the dead… *:Did Ander speak with Hotaru?:*

He felt her regard him thoughtfully. *:Yes. He thought she might have known something that he could use to help you. He wasn't wrong,* *in the end; it was what she told him that led him to find that invasive piece of tech.:*

Takeshi didn't know what to think about that. How strange, that she had managed to help him from beyond the veil, even though he was the one who had sent her there. And Ander had spoken with her. Swallowing hard, he asked, *:Is she okay?:*

The response was gentle. *:She is dead. As such, she is fine. The dead rest, Takeshi.:*

The warg must have noticed him freeze, because she was sniffing at his face. Was her Human okay? Did he need anything? He felt upset. What was wrong?

He tried to pet her reassuringly. "It's okay," he whispered.

She placed her head on his shoulder, her version of a hug. She didn't know what was wrong, but everyone liked hugs.

He wrapped his arms around her, burying his face in her fur and letting her solid presence steady him. He couldn't bring himself to ask the other question he had concerning Hotaru, so he pivoted slightly. *:What about ghosts, or other undead?:* he asked instead. *:The restless dead exist.:*

:My priests – and many others, honestly; if it were just up to my priests nothing would ever get done – prioritize helping them pass through the veil whenever they come across them. Hotaru is not restless dead, don't worry,: she reassured him.

:Your priests don't often help the dead pass on?: That didn't seem right.

:Oh no, they do; there just aren't a lot of them,: she informed him quickly. *:So they need a lot of help.:*

A faint memory poked at him from when he had first come here. Ander had taken a sample of his blood, and then someone... someone had drunk it. There were Vampires in Romanii, he remembered abruptly. There were just too many new things to keep track of here, and he was far from the top of his game. *:Are the Vampires restless dead?:*

:Vampires are their own category of special,: she snorted. *:Technically dead, yes, but also their own thing. They are created through divine magic, not a corruption or perversion like most of the other things you are probably comparing them to.:*

An image of the construct he had fought with the goddess flashed through his mind, and he idly wondered if that thing had been alive or dead. He wasn't sure which answer was preferable.

He had fought a battle with a goddess, he realized. That was something insane he could take with him to his grave.

He found himself yawning into the warg's fur, and he shifted a bit so he was using her as a pillow. She didn't seem to mind, even though the angle she was at must have been uncomfortable since he was reclining against the pillows.

:You are still not fully recovered, and I am possibly straining you. My apologies,: Hades said worriedly. *:You should rest more. Are you sure there is nothing I can do for you?:*

:Not that I can think of,: he replied. *:I think I'll probably nap a bit more.:* Honestly, he hadn't even felt well enough to meditate recently, which was usually a sign that he needed to sleep.

:I am only a thought away, if you need me. And she will be with you, too. You are not alone here, Takeshi,: she reminded him kindly as her presence retreated from his senses.

He sighed, shifting a bit more. He was starting to actually hurt again, not just feel sore, and the itch at the back of his neck was becoming harder and harder to ignore. He started running his hands down the warg's sides to give them something else to do.

It was only a few minutes later that one of the nurses came into his room with a cheerful greeting, a steaming mug of tea in one hand. She took one glance at the mostly untouched salad before launching into a speech about how Takeshi needed to eat to recover. She checked his bandages and his temperature while he drank the medicine before admonishing him to eat more and then leaving. He almost breathed a sigh of relief as he settled back into the bed, looking forward to the drugs kicking in. All of this interaction with other people felt more exhausting than it should.

The warg, who had been banished to the foot of the bed so the nurse could do her work, returned to lying across most of his body. How did he feel now? Any better?

"I'm just waiting for the tea to kick in, and then I will be much better," he informed her. He started scratching under her jaw as he considered. "I know Ander said I should think of a name, but do you have a name that you prefer?"

Her eyes were half-lidded in pleasure. No, she was not called anything. The two-feet gave names; wargs did not. She had been waiting for him to feel better. What did he have in mind?

He continued petting her silently as the pain began to recede. What should he call her? "I'm not sure I have anything in mind. Maybe something to do with your coloring? Shiroko?"

She wasn't sure she understood what that had to do with her fur.

He smiled. "'Shiro' means 'white' in Nifoni," he explained.

Oh! She was not opposed to a foreign name, but she wasn't sure she cared much for that one. Did he often speak the other language?

He shrugged. "In Ni Fon it is the primary language, but I'm not sure I'll have many people to speak it with here. Yuki, perhaps? That means 'snow.'"

Snow! She loved the snow, but she didn't like the way that one sounded. This was a fun game. Maybe they could play in the snow together when he was feeling better?

Takeshi snorted. "Maybe." Ander *had* mentioned she was young. Takeshi wondered how old a warg had to be before they were considered an adult. How long did they live, for that matter? Didn't large dogs have shorter lifespans? But then... was a warg *technically* a dog, or their own species? "Asami? That is a popular name for canines back home. It means 'morning beauty.'"

She did like the sound of that one, and its meaning, but she didn't want a common name. She was special! If she was to have a name, it should be a special name.

"Fair." He supposed naming a dog was a lot easier when they didn't have a say in what the name would be. Or maybe it was just as difficult; he'd never had a dog himself, though he had enjoyed interacting with the dogs that frequented the palace.

He was never going to go back there. Maybe it was for the best, though it hurt to consider that. There had been so many lies he had been practically drowning in them, and he hadn't even known. He had been too caught up in his grief and the mission that he had failed to recognize the many, many red flags. And when he had seen a flag, he had justified it to himself, because he had been too confident in his own importance. He'd never even considered that they might be trying to get rid of him.

Well, now he was well and truly gone, there was no denying that. After what he and Hotaru had gone through, he didn't think he could ever forgive the Empress her lies.

The warg pushed her head under his hand. Was he sure he was okay? He had gone somewhere else. She didn't like that. He should stay with her.

He resumed petting her. "You won't lie to me, will you?" he asked quietly.

Never! She could not lie even if she wanted to. Emotions were true, always. She could even tell if someone else was lying if she was close enough.

He considered that. Like with the goddess's telepathy, it did seem impossible to lie through this sort of communication. "Jitsu," he suggested after a moment. "Truth."

She wagged her tail enthusiastically. Yes, she liked that one. She would be Jitsu!

"Very well, then," he murmured. "Jitsu it is."

November 27, 2026 A.G.
Notes – Nifoni Microchip

Abomination is a sin against magic, which is a sin against life. This absolutely applies.

The microchip allowed them to somehow access Takeshi's memories through a connection to his nervous system at the base of the skull. Unfortunately, I do not have information on what the other end of the process is like – having taken the information, how do they review it? Does it go into another person with a chip in their head? I certainly hope not; the chip is a death sentence – it poisons the host's magic over time, causing the body to fail, since magic is life. My current hypothesis is that the process is faster in individuals with more magic, but even those without mage potential would be destroyed by it eventually.

*Note: What will happen when they try to access the chip without a host? Consider monitoring the chip.

→Dec. 1 @~ 8 PM – next access attempt?

***Make sure chip is in a contained environment.

Why the sudden interest in integrating tech with a living being? First the bionics, now this. It is clear that this is the form the Abomination has taken, but two different sub-forms simultaneously? Because the two are the same only on a conceptual level; they are executed very differently. The Nifoni chip doesn't even use the strange metal seen in the bionic constructs but is made of recognizable materials (silicon, aluminum, iron).

*Note: I have yet to come up with a better name than "bionic" for the cybernetic Abominations. It will have to do for now; it is unfortunately catching on.

Unlike the bionics, I don't believe these chips are being mass produced or widely used. The recovery time is too long for it to be done unnoticed outside of special circumstances. I do think the long recovery time is necessary; the filament needs a chance to bond with the nerves to be properly integrated. Perhaps this is where they went wrong with Kobayashi Hotaru.

I think the bionics might also be difficult to create, but since I believe they are being manufactured there is likely to be far more of them. The Nifoni chip has to be tailored more to the individual. Since the bionics discard so much of the organic tissue there may actually be a little more room for error (though to be honest, there can't be much) than with the chip. Both processes have a very high chance to kill the host, but I don't know how much those creating the bionics care about keeping the host functioning on a high level.

A thought – the bionics seem to require a host with mage potential. Does the Nifoni chip also require a mage host? I'm not actually sure how I would test that. My sample size of one (maybe two, if Hotaru also had a chip) is nowhere near enough to draw a conclusion.

Another thought – the bionics don't seem to have a will of their own anymore. This denial of will is at least part of the reason it is classified as Abomination, if not the whole reason. Takeshi's will did not seem to be affected, and Hotaru lasted sixteen years, but it is possible that there is a final stage neither of them reached that would strip a host of its will, leading to perhaps a similar state to the bionics.

Perhaps the two methods are not as different as originally hypothesized: two paths to reach the same outcome.

-Ander 11/27/26

Chapter Nine

Jamirh seriously regretted asking Jeri to teach him how to wield a sword.

"Let's try again," she said cheerfully as he picked himself up off the ground for the millionth time that day. He used the wooden length of his practice sword to help leverage himself up, wishing for nothing more than to just lie there and do nothing in protest. At this rate, he wasn't going to make it to another battle with the bionics – training was going to kill him.

"Can we take a quick break?" he panted, ears low. Already he was in far more pain than he usually was. Jeri seemed to have stopped pulling her blows, leaving Jamirh covered in bruises. Apparently her new philosophy was that getting whacked encouraged better form the next time.

Jamirh did not agree with this theory. He was collecting lots of colorful evidence of how it didn't work all over his body.

The blonde Vampire regarded him for a moment. "Sure. Drink some water!" she added, striding over to where she had left a few bottles against the wall and tossing one in his direction.

Jamirh leaned to the side so it sailed past him, ignoring her snort. Drinking water was a solid piece of advice though, and he trudged over to sink to the ground beside where it landed. He unscrewed the cap and drank deeply from it, peering up at the sky and its slight shimmer high above him. They were training outside today, to Jamirh's dismay. He wouldn't have thought he would be sweating in the late November weather, but here he was.

It was the fourth day of this. Yesterday they had taken a break of sorts, spending the day with daggers instead of the longsword; he'd appreciated the return to the earlier training regime. Even though Jeri had still pushed harder than she had before, it hadn't been nearly as bad as with the sword. She almost became a different person than the one he knew when they used the longer blade. Less patient, more brutal. She reminded him – gently, but it still stung – that he should just be picking it up from watching her, that they didn't have the time most people had, and that he shouldn't need it anyway.

Which, to be fair, was how being a Master of Blades was supposed to work, but Jamirh couldn't do it. He was gaining a library's worth of techniques in his head, but it was almost impossible for him to do any of them successfully. Sometimes he could defend for an attack or two, but that was all before he was sent sprawling. In some ways, it was worse than fighting Ander – at least Ander had stopped after a point.

Though, he had also managed to score a hit on Ander, something he had yet to manage with Jeri.

"Okay, you ready to try again?" she called out as he lowered the water bottle. She moved to the center of the yard without waiting for his reply.

Jamirh dragged himself back to his feet, wincing at the soreness of multiple bruises. They were only about halfway through their time; he had a lot more punishment to go through. Hell, that "break" hadn't even been five minutes. "No?" he tried. It hadn't worked before, but maybe this time?

She shook her head with a sigh. "Get ready anyway. Remember, we don't have unlimited time to figure this out, and sooner is better."

He sighed. Again with the time thing. He understood that, he really did, but he didn't see how this sort of misery was helping him learn anything except *maybe* theory. "I know," he said begrudgingly. He'd already tried to convince her to take things a little slower after Thursday's session, to no avail. Still, if time was so important, they sure had wasted a lot of it waiting for him. "Maybe just a thought, but..." He trailed off, losing the nerve to say it out loud.

"But what?"

He shook his head. "Never mind."

She eyed him for a moment, lowering her blade. "I know this is a lot," she said, starting in again on one of her many pep talks, "but just remember that you *can* do it! You've done it before; it's just a matter of doing it over and over until it clicks, you know?"

No, he did not know. He forced himself to hold the wooden practice sword up, setting himself into a defensive position. At least she gave him a chance to prepare for her onslaught, unlike Ander had, though the more they did this the more he considered asking the priest for help anyway. If he didn't want Jamirh dead, surely he would have something to say about this, right? Because this couldn't possibly be normal training. Hell, it didn't even line up with the training she'd been doing with him before.

A flurry of motion, and Jamirh found himself dropping his weapon, fingers stinging as he staggered back. "Ow," he hissed as he rubbed his hand.

"Jamirh! What have I said about dropping your weapon?" Jeri exclaimed, sounding concerned. "Never do that! Hold onto it like your life depends on it. Because it does."

She was trying to help him, he reminded himself as he fought not to glare at her. How could she be so good at teaching daggers but so bad at teaching the longsword? He shook his hand out and picked up the sword. He wished his inherent worked the way she seemed to think it did. Then maybe he could actually best her for once, the way he'd bested Ander. He allowed himself to fantasize about that for a moment before turning back to Jeri, who was waiting patiently for him to recover.

"Some inherents are more difficult than others to learn to control. We know you can do it – it kept you alive in the battle against the bionic, and I saw the spar with Ander – so I'm sure it's just a matter of time before you figure it out!" She smiled at him.

A small part of Jamirh wondered if he even had used his ability as a Master of Blades to avoid the bionic. *"If we move like this,"* the voice had suggested. What if it hadn't been Jamirh at all, but whatever echo of Ebryn remained that had been in control? Not that "in control" was a good way of putting it; he had hit a lot of walls because he *couldn't* control it. So what if it hadn't been him at all? He supposed his bout with Ander could be the only time he had successfully used his ability. Though... throwing the daggers at the Festival of Night had been easy. Why couldn't he just go back to that?

Instead, he was holding the hilt of a practice sword in stinging fingers, waiting to get knocked down again. "Am I actually making progress?" he asked, feeling defeated.

She looked a little taken aback. "Of course! Jamirh, you've known about your ability for less than a month, and you found out about it pretty late, if I'm being honest. Most people find out about their inherent abilities when they are very young, but then, your environment didn't really lend itself to that. It's harder when you're older." She shrugged. "However, it's not impossible. And you've already proven you can do it, so once again – it's just a matter of time until you get in the swing of things. Practice is the best thing to do, I promise."

He wondered if anything could change her mind as he tiredly raised the sword again. "Yeah, okay."

Three exchanges later, and Jamirh was feeling no more optimistic than before. He still had yet to even defend himself from her, never mind attack. What had he done differently when he had fought Ander? He wasn't sure.

Wait, maybe that was it. He hadn't exactly been leaving himself defenseless, but what if he focused entirely on defense? That wouldn't necessarily win him any bouts, but it would cut down on the amount of damage he was taking. He considered all the techniques he had seen Jeri use, but none of them had been defensive in nature. She had been on the attack since the first moment. Desperately, he sifted through his memories – had he ever seen anyone fight defensively with a sword?

No, but there was one Avari from back in Lyndiniam he had watched fight a few times who had done a few things that might work. He wondered if he had paid enough attention to be able to execute any of his moves, but then, what did he have to lose? He needed to try something different.

"Ready?" Jeri asked, and Jamirh nodded, hoping for the best and trying to think about how he had just reacted against Ander, combined with how the other Avari had defended himself from his opponent.

She rushed forward.

He set himself in place, bringing his left arm up, crossed behind the practice sword to brace it–

There was a sickening crack, and Jamirh felt his body go cold as he landed on the ground. Cold and numb, he couldn't feel much of anything else at all as he lay there. Something was definitely wrong, he decided, and he should just keep lying here for a bit until he could catch his breath. Had that last blow actually broken the practice sword? That was kind of crazy.

Jeri's face appeared above him, skin ashen. She was kneeling next to him. "Don't move, Jamirh," she commanded, voice wavering oddly, and he realized she wasn't kneeling next to him – she was kneeling on his left arm firmly enough that he couldn't move it.

"Your arm is broken. Ander is on his way. No, no – don't look at it." She turned his face away as he reflexively tried to look. "That will make it hurt more."

He felt weirdly frozen, which a part of him pointed out was probably bad, but he was fairly certain looking at an injury did not affect how it felt. He wondered morbidly how bad it was if she didn't want him to see. "Doesn't hurt yet," he managed to say.

She winced. "Let's hope the shock lasts until Ander can get here. Oh, Marcus!" She looked away from him as another Vampire in Watch blacks came into view.

The new Vampire knelt next to Jeri and put his hand on Jamirh's shoulder. "Got it," he said, voice mild, and Jamirh felt a strangely soothing sensation rush through his body except for his arm, which he could no longer feel at all. "Hello, Jamirh. My name is Marcus. How are you feeling?" His blue eyes were kind.

Jamirh would have shrugged, but something told him that would be a very bad idea. "I think," he said slowly, "this is a bad day."

"It does seem to be so," the Vampire agreed.

"I can't feel my arm," Jamirh informed him. Was that bad? It seemed bad.

Marcus nodded. "Yes, I'm doing that. You don't want to feel your arm right now, trust me."

"Oh." Everything felt kind of distant. Was the Vampire doing that, too? "How bad is it?"

"It could be worse, but also could be better," Marcus informed him. "Don't worry, we'll get you fixed up."

Jamirh thought he might have blacked out briefly, because when he blinked Ander was kneeling on the ground next to him and an older Human man was standing just in his line of sight. "Yes, hospital," Ander was saying. "Jak, do you mind another teleport?"

The other man shook his head. "Sure; what's one more taxi to the hospital? I didn't realize this was what I've been missing out on. How exciting. Who am I anchoring on, and who's coming?"

Marcus shifted so that he was holding Jamirh's arm still, and Jeri slipped free. "Myself, Marcus, and Jamirh; that should be the whole circus," Ander said. "Follow this to anchor–"

Jamirh didn't know what that meant, but he was starting to realize it was a little weird he wasn't panicking. It was almost like he were watching this happen to someone else.

Suddenly the training grounds around them whited out, and Jamirh found himself on the floor in a much smaller space painted in soft greens.

"On the bed first?" Marcus asked, and Ander nodded.

"Eh, I got it," the third man drawled, and Jamirh felt himself lift up off the floor, his arm still firmly held by Marcus. He floated over to the bed and gently descended onto it. "I'd have teleported him directly to it, but the way you were all sitting I'm pretty sure someone would have dropped to the floor, and we don't need any more injuries around here."

"We certainly do not," Ander agreed as he turned to another woman who was standing just in the doorway, a mug of something steaming in her hands. Ander took it from her, bringing it to Jamirh. "Drink this," he commanded, helping Jamirh sit up to recline against the headboard.

Jamirh chanced a look at his forearm and wished he hadn't. Arms were definitely not supposed to bend that way. He felt his stomach turn.

"Look at me, please." Ander's fingers under his chin turned his head back. Green eyes met silver, and Jamirh felt the nausea instantly clear. "Now drink." He held the mug to Jamirh's lips.

Jamirh drank obediently, even though the taste left something to be desired.

"You all set, Ander?" the mystery man asked.

"Yes, we should be fine now. Thank you, Jak. Marcus?" Ander glanced at the Vampire as he placed the mug on the counter.

The dark-haired man was looking intently at Jamirh's arm. "Both bones are completely fractured, but only in one place and nothing broke through the skin, amazingly. Some internal bleeding, but I'm dealing with that now. Should be simple enough to set." He looked up at Jamirh and smiled reassuringly. "See? It could be worse."

Surreal! That described this. "This feels very surreal," he informed them.

Marcus cocked his head to the side. "Have you ever broken a bone before?"

Jamirh shook his head. "No."

"It is, luckily, not the end of the world," Ander commented as he gathered various supplies from one of the cabinets. "And also not an uncommon injury, though I wouldn't expect training on a beginner level to have any of the sort of force required to break both bones like that. What happened?"

Jamirh was slowly starting to feel more like himself, even though physically he still felt pretty numb. He explained the series of events as best he could, ending with finding himself on the ground with Jeri kneeling on him.

Both of them were looking at him strangely. "Jamirh, I realize the practice sword is made of wood, but you do know the actual sword has edges, right?" Ander asked after a moment.

"Yeah?" What did that have to do with anything?

"Sharp edges?" Ander added, one eyebrow raising.

Jamirh looked at him quizzically, not sure what he was getting at.

"You usually don't want to come into contact with any blade, including your own. You run the risk of injuring yourself that way – and not necessarily a broken arm, like now, but you can cut yourself badly doing something like that with an actual edged weapon," Ander explained.

Oh.

Well, now Jamirh just felt stupid. Why had he thought that would work? It was so obvious that it was a bad idea.

Marcus must have seen the look on his face and took pity on him, changing the subject. "We are going to set the arm now, okay? It should only take a moment or so."

Jamirh looked away, glad he couldn't feel anything lower than his shoulder. Still, when Marcus stopped doing whatever it was he was doing, Jamirh bet his arm was going to hurt.

"All set," Marcus informed him cheerfully. "Ander?"

Jamirh looked down at his arm again and was relieved to see it was straight once more. He looked at Ander, who was studying him with a puzzled frown. "What?"

"I'm trying to decide if I should heal it," Ander murmured absently.

Jamirh stared at him while Marcus chuckled awkwardly. "Ander, that didn't come out right."

Ander blinked. "What? Oh." He looked away, as though his attention had been drawn away by something else, before clarifying. "Jamirh, we usually don't use magic to heal these sorts of things. Too much magic used to knit a bone back together can actually lead to the bone becoming weaker when fully healed, so it's better to let the body heal the break naturally on its own. However, I'm honestly not sure we can afford to keep you out of commission for the next three to four months." He regarded Jamirh's arm like it was personally offending him. "You need to be getting better at combat, not worse."

"We could take a middle route," Marcus suggested. "If it is imperative that he heals quickly, we could start it now, then bring him back in for mini healing sessions each week for the next month or so. It's a more labor-intensive strategy, and a little rougher on the rest of him, but the bone should heal with minimal weakening done that way."

Ander sighed. "That seems like the best option, I suppose."

"So too much magic can be bad for the body?" Jamirh asked with a frown.

"Too much magic interfering with the body's natural processes can be bad," Ander specified. "And even then, it's not that your arm wouldn't be healed – it would be – it would just be more prone to breaking in the future, which we also want to avoid. Healing is a complicated discipline," he added, seeing the look on Jamirh's face.

"So my options are – heal it completely, and risk breaking it again, probably at the worst possible moment; let it heal naturally, taking three months at best, and waste time that could be spent training to avoid this sort of thing; or kind of heal it slowly over the next month and hope for the best," Jamirh summarized.

Ander started to say something but paused, eyes flicking to the side again, before nodding. "Yes, those are your options."

Jamirh considered what to do. As much as he did not want to have to deal with a broken arm, with his luck it would break the next time he came face to face with a bionic and he would be totally screwed. "The middle one," he declared finally.

Ander nodded. "Of course. Marcus, if you could assist?"

The next hour or so was a strange experience for Jamirh as Ander and Marcus did something to his arm that he couldn't feel, then put it in a splint. His arm had started to ache dully by the time they were done – whatever Marcus had been doing and the medicine Ander had given him had both begun to wear off. At least the rest of him was feeling far more normal.

"All set, Ander?" Marcus asked as they finished cleaning up.

"Yes, thank you. You can go. Maybe have a word with Jeri, if you can." He brought a hand up to his face, covering the scar that ran vertically down it for a moment, looking tired. "Jamirh, you stay here." He started grabbing several other instruments and setting them out on the counter.

"I'll see what I can do. Goodbye, Jamirh; feel better!" The Vampire disappeared with a wave in a swirl of shadow.

Jamirh also felt tired, for all that he hadn't done much today. "Do I have to stay in the hospital?" he asked with a frown. He wanted to go back to his rooms and sleep.

Ander shook his head, grabbing a few sheets of paper and a pen. "No, not for a broken arm. But this reminded me that we have no medical records on you, and I thought now might be a good time to start that file. I understand you probably didn't visit a doctor very regularly back in Lyndiniam?"

Jamirh snorted. "I might have gone to a doctor when I was very little, but not since my parents died."

"Do you know if you have any allergies?"

"I've never had an allergic reaction to anything," Jamirh said with a shrug.

Ander noted that down. "And I suppose you don't know anything about your parents' medical history."

It wasn't really a question, so Jamirh didn't bother to answer it. How long was this going to take? He wanted to leave and go sulk quietly by himself for the next two days.

The priest glanced at him, then heaved a deep sigh. "This isn't anything bad, Jamirh. I didn't really expect you to have these sorts of answers, but I thought I'd ask just in case. Here; we'll just do one more thing and then I'll escort you back to the palace." He put the pen down and picked up what looked like a very big needle attached to a glass tube.

Jamirh's eyes widened. "What is *that*?"

Ander looked down at the thing in his hand, then back to Jamirh, clearly confused. "A syringe?"

"What is it for?" Jamirh asked, concerned.

"Oh." Once again, he seemed to have thrown Ander. "I'm just going to draw some blood."

"You're going to what?" Jamirh didn't know what that meant.

Ander looked a little lost, like he didn't understand Jamirh's confusion, but rallied. "This," he pointed to the needle, "goes into a vein in your arm, allowing me to collect a sample of your blood."

He was going to stab him with that needle? His stomach twisted uncomfortably. "Oh hell no," Jamirh snapped, totally fed up with today. "Do not come anywhere near me with that."

Ander's patience also seemed to be wearing thin. "Do not make this any more difficult than it has to be, which is not at all. It doesn't hurt and will be over quickly. Then you can go back to the palace." He put the needle down on a small side table by Jamirh and turned around to grab something else from the supplies he had laid out on the counter.

Jamirh wasn't interested in finding out what. He could get himself back to the palace. While Ander's back was turned, he silently slid off the bed and escaped into the hospital proper.

Rhode took a deep breath, eyes closed, before taking two pills from the bottle on his desk and swallowing them dry. The headache was trying to return, and he just didn't have time to deal with that.

He needed to get to the bottom of the events that had led to the destruction of the Charve base, and Madine would be here any second. He opened his eyes and waved off Cole's concerned look as she watered the plants on the windowsill. She was good with plants, he reflected. It was probably why any of them were still alive; he never remembered to water them.

He reined in his focus and picked up the tablet on his desk, swiping through to review the relevant report. Even though he had been there, it was still hard to understand what had happened exactly. Hopefully Madine could shine some light on the subject.

"You wished to see me?"

He managed not to jump in surprise at the sound of the Seeker's voice. They were sneaky when they wanted to be, though nothing like what the shinobi were rumored to be capable of. He wondered absently if Kobayashi was ever surprised by her guards. "Yes, I'm looking for any further information you could share regarding the Avari prisoner. Specifically, how she managed magic under your noses, and while in the prism sphere."

The blindfolded woman regarded him silently for a moment. "You have my report."

"I do. It has none of the answers I'm looking for." He felt the frustration enter his tone. "I saw her do magic, right before the array lit up in the walls of the sphere. The shadows moved. Are you telling me you really sensed nothing?"

"There was no change in the levels of magic that surrounded her," Madine informed him. "Therefore, she did no magic."

Rhode considered that. "Can you elaborate?"

"When a mage does magic, there is a push and a pull of power from inside of them as they cast. There was no push and no pull from the mage." She sounded as disinterested as always.

"No, what do you mean 'the levels of magic surrounding her'?" he clarified.

At least Madine didn't seem to mind his questions. "All living beings are fields of magic. The prism sphere prevents the utilization of magic, but it cannot extinguish it without killing the subject."

Rhode had never bothered to really think about how the Truth Seekers did what they did, but he was starting to wonder if he should have. "So you perceive this... field of magic, and know when a mage casts because this field is disturbed?"

Her head tilted ever so slightly. "If we are paying attention, yes. We were paying her a great deal of attention. She did not cast."

He frowned. "Then how do you explain what I saw? I saw you react to it." She had stiffened when the shapes formed and dispersed, he remembered.

"It will not make sense to you."

"Try me."

Several long minutes passed before she spoke again. "There was no push and pull from the mage, but it felt like her field *remembering* a push and pull. The only thing we are sure of is that she did not cast."

Rhode tried. He really did, but he could not figure out what that meant or how it explained anything. "And yet, she somehow managed to turn the whole prism sphere into an array without any of you noticing."

"It is a mystery," she agreed.

"Do you have any theories?" He was definitely grasping at straws now.

"Magic," she replied simply.

Rhode stopped himself from dropping his head to the desk. That would not help his almost-headache.

"No, you do not understand," Madine offered, somehow noticing his frustration. "A living being who uses magic would show the push and pull. But we think that magic itself might not."

He stared at her. "I'm not following."

"It is possible she was not an Avari using magic, but magic shaped like an Avari," she tried to clarify. "This is the current running theory."

"Is that what made you all react?" he mused, trying to wrap his mind around that concept. Magic, shaped like an Avari?

She didn't so much as twitch. "I do not follow."

"There have been rumors that all the Truth Seekers reacted to something that happened at the same time the mage screamed." Should he still be calling her a mage, if Madine's theory was true?

"I do not know of what you speak," she replied calmly. "Perhaps something was misinterpreted? We are often feared by the rank and file."

At the time, she had been attempting to teleport him to safety, so he supposed it could be true. Except that the Truth Seekers were all connected, one web of minds that allowed them to instantly communicate with each other. He would almost believe that they had been reacting to the danger Madine and Teuri had been in, but he'd seen their complete lack of reaction at the death of one of their own before.

Though, most people did fear the Truth Seekers, and Cole had found no recorded evidence. He trusted Cole's analysis of the situation.

"Perhaps," he allowed. "That was all. If you come up with any more theories, or maybe even conclusions, please bring it to my attention as soon as possible."

What had they captured, if it wasn't an Avari mage?

Madine inclined her head shallowly.

Cole cleared her throat, brushing a finger along one of the leaves of a plant. "Since she was a follower of Hades, perhaps a visit to the Temple of Faith? It's not that far from here; perhaps they have some information on that cult."

That... was not a bad idea.

The only problem there was that Rhode was unaware of *any* specific cult to Hades. Most people tended to avoid the death goddess's gaze whenever possible, so the only real marks of Hades as a goddess in the Empire were small shrines one could find on occasion, such as this one, and they were meant more to appease her into looking the other way than to worship her. Who would worship such a god? And where were they?

Maybe Cole was right.

Maybe the Temple held the answers he sought.

Chapter Ten

Takeshi was feeling much better after a few days of rest. Bored, but better. At least physically. Much of the ache had faded, and he was able to stay awake for longer than an hour or two. He still felt chilled but at least it no longer felt unnaturally cold, and blankets, heating crystals, and Jitsu all worked to combat it. The stitches on the back of his neck still itched and he was looking forward to them coming out in a day or two. That was also when Ander had suggested he might be able to leave the hospital.

And... what then?

It was clear to him that these people wanted him to stay here. He had conversed with Hades several more times since the chip had been removed, and even though she wasn't pushing, he could tell she wanted him to join her clergy. They hadn't actually talked about it, but he still wasn't sure what that meant, exactly. The two priests of hers he had met both appeared to serve completely different functions and were nothing alike. Ander was a healer and also managed Hades' temple in the city, and Jak... actually, he had no idea what Jak did. What was her clergy generally like? What about him made her want him? She hadn't just flat out told him "You're mine now," so he assumed he had a choice; what would happen if he said no?

What would happen if he said yes?

It did hurt, to let go of Ni Fon. For all that he had been horribly abused by the Empress and manipulated into burning every bridge he had, it was home. It was the place he understood the best, and he missed the scenery and the people. He missed the prevalence of magic and weaving. He missed speaking Nifoni. He had been chosen at a young age to become shinobi; it was what he knew and what he took pride in. That title, and the legacy and honor that came with it, meant nothing here.

"There is something wrong with this whole situation," Satomi had whispered to him on his last night in Ni Fon. She had been far more correct than he had been, he reflected. At least she had known there were things she was missing.

He supposed the root of the problem was that now that he had been severed from Ni Fon and his "mission," he was directionless and adrift. As shinobi, that wasn't a situation he had ever found himself in. Structure was something baked into Nifoni culture and he wasn't sure how to exist without it. Perhaps it was just a matter of learning the structure of this place, and then trying to fit within it?

Jitsu huffed at him from where she lay on his legs. Her Human was thinking too much again when he could be petting her.

He smiled at her. "I can both think and pet you, you know," he informed her, bringing a hand up to the great white head to do exactly that.

She leaned into the scratch, even as she denied that possibility. Why would he risk lowering the quality of his attention by thinking?

Takeshi chuckled. "I can't just not think."

Well, that was unfortunate. She believed he might be better off if he figured out how to not think for an hour or two at least. He kept getting sad when he thought too much. Why did he keep doing a thing that was making him sad?

"A fair critique, perhaps, but again – not something I can just stop doing." Not without falling unconscious, anyway, and he didn't think that was what she wanted. He considered her for a moment. Perhaps she had a different perspective, one he hadn't considered yet. "What do you think about–"

He cut off abruptly as a younger Avari with red hair in a short ponytail darted into his room and ducked around the corner, keeping his eyes on the doorway. His left arm was splinted, and he was holding it close to his body. His clothing looked fairly disheveled, as though he had been doing some sort of physical activity. Takeshi hadn't gotten this far in life without being able to recognize when someone was hiding.

Takeshi would have been more concerned, but Jitsu wasn't alarmed, perking up in excitement. Her tail began to wag. He trusted her judgement. "Can I help you?" he offered, keeping his voice pleasant.

"Nope, sorry. I'll be gone in a minute; just need to wait for those nurses to pass by." He glanced towards the bed, and Takeshi was struck by the strangest feeling that he had seen this Avari somewhere before. Silver eyes landed on Jitsu and the stranger frowned. "What are *you* still doing here?"

That was interesting. Many people commented on Jitsu's presence, but it was always "What are you doing here?" The addition of the "still" was new.

Jitsu dropped her mouth open in a grin. This was a very helpful two-foot! She liked him.

"I have been adopted," Takeshi explained gravely. "I don't think she's left since." He poked at his memory, trying to remember why this Avari looked familiar.

The Avari looked at Takeshi and blinked in surprise. He glanced towards the hallway again, then moved back further out of sight. "Hey, you're that Nifoni Human who got banished for killing the duchess's daughter and then broke Hel out of that military base!"

Takeshi was taken aback. Did many people know about these things? His banishment was understandable, having been plastered all over the news, but the incident in Charve? That was strange to contemplate, almost like... when he had read that newspaper article about himself, and...

"And you are the Avari who broke out of a prison in Lyndiniam," he said, mildly amused at the fact he had found him after all. Who could have guessed?

"Not gonna lie, I did very little of the actual breaking," the Avari muttered, ears flattening. "That was about ninety percent Hel's doing." He paused. "Maybe a hundred percent, actually; I mostly did a lot of running, followed by an unholy amount of walking."

Ah. "An unholy amount of walking?" he asked, smiling under his mask. Hades was literally divine, though he wasn't sure if this Avari knew that. No one said it was a secret, but he had mostly been interacting with her clergy and they were the ones who were most likely to know the truth about her.

"Yeah, which is... a little ironic, now that I think about it," he answered with a frown. Perhaps he did know, then. "Anyway, my name's Jamirh."

"Shuurai Takeshi," he introduced himself. "May I ask who or what you are hiding from?"

Jamirh's expression soured immediately. "Ander," he said with such venom that Takeshi almost flinched on the other man's behalf. "I just wanted to go back to the palace, but no – he has to stick *needles* in me. Needles! To take blood. What kind of psychopath does that?" His tone had taken on a thread of fear.

"It's a fairly common procedure." Takeshi was surprised at the vehemence in the other's voice. Ander might be standoffish, but "psychopath" was a little harsh in his opinion. He glanced at Jitsu, but she was just amused at the situation.

"For what possible reason?" Jamirh argued unhappily. "When I came here Jeri said they were not going to eat me."

Jitsu was seriously considering going over to him and letting him pet her. He was very afraid. He had not liked the big needle, even though in her opinion it wasn't that big.

Takeshi assumed Jeri was a Vampire. "I am not a healer myself, but to my understanding you can learn much about a person's health from their blood. When I first came here, they were able to find out that I had too much iron in my blood, which was contributing to making me sick. There are other things they can test for as well." He owed Ander; maybe he could make this situation a little easier for the priest.

Jamirh was frowning at him. "Really?" He didn't look convinced.

Takeshi nodded gravely.

"But I'm not sick," Jamirh pointed out.

"True," Takeshi conceded. "But you are injured, aren't you? And sometimes they just like to check to make sure everything is all right."

Jitsu nudged at Takeshi's shoulder. People were coming who were looking for the helpful-red two-foot.

Takeshi considered the room. "Hide over here, quickly" – he gestured to the far side of his bed from the door – "and don't make a sound."

The Avari darted into place at a respectable speed, folding himself into a small shape out of sight from the door with a wince, clearly favoring the damaged arm. Why didn't he have a sling for it?

Ander appeared at the door, knocking briefly and looking extremely stressed.

"Come in," Takeshi offered pleasantly, ignoring the slight flinch from Jamirh.

"Takeshi, we've lost a patient. Have you seen an Avari with red hair running around? Or has she noticed anything?" He indicated Jitsu.

The warg turned to look at Takeshi, clearly uncertain how they were going to proceed. He scratched her ears as he met Ander's eyes.

"It's just been the two of us here," he lied smoothly, even as he reached out mentally to the scarred man. *:Allow me to handle this.:*

Ander blinked at him in surprise, then closed his eyes and took a deep breath. "I see. Should he come by here, could you please let someone on staff know?" *:He broke his arm this morning, and he is missing a number of things such as pain medication and a sling in addition to fleeing from the blood test.:*

:I will promote him staying as still as possible,: Takeshi agreed. "Of course. Would you like to borrow Jitsu to track him?"

The warg licked at his face. She wasn't quite sure what was going on, but it had the feel of a game. She liked games.

"Hopefully that won't be necessary, but I'll keep it in mind," Ander said with a shake of his head. "Sorry to disturb you." *:I will be nearby.:* He swept out of the room.

Takeshi waited a few minutes, silently stroking Jitsu's head, before saying, "He's gone. Why don't you sit in that chair over there and rest your arm? It's out of sight from the hallway. I haven't had many visitors since coming here, Jitsu aside, and I'm a little bored."

Jitsu licked him again before nestling into his chest, clearly wanting more pets.

The Avari popped up beside him, glancing nervously at the door. "Thank you," he breathed, clearly relieved, as he settled down in the armchair Takeshi could only assume was for visitors. "Why did he call you 'Takeshi'?"

"It is my name," he reminded him, raising an eyebrow.

"Well, yeah, but isn't it your last name?" Jamirh asked, sounding puzzled.

"Our names are reversed in Ni Fon compared to here. 'Shuurai' is my family name; 'Takeshi' is my given name," he explained. "It is more common to address someone by their family name in Ni Fon. The opposite is true here."

"Oh." The Avari appeared to be thinking hard about that. "Then... which do you prefer to be called?"

"Takeshi is fine." Most of the people he'd met here were already calling him that.

"And you called the warg Jitsu?" Jamirh pointed at her.

Takeshi nodded. "Do you know her?"

Jamirh hesitated. "We, ah, met once, briefly. I didn't know she had a name. Or that she was a she, honestly."

Jitsu's amusement was palpable as her tail flipped back and forth. She had still managed to get him to do what she had wanted, though he hadn't been injured at that point. Maybe Takeshi could ask what happened?

Takeshi eyed them both, feeling like he might have an idea of how she had snuck her way into the hospital. "Jitsu tells me that when last you met, you were uninjured. She is wondering what has befallen you since then."

"Nothing good," Jamirh all but spat. He looked away. "It's a little complicated."

Takeshi settled back on his pillows. "I have nothing but time."

The Avari shifted uncomfortably. "I guess I have an inherent magical ability – have you ever heard of a Master of Blades?"

Takeshi shook his head.

"Well, it's supposed to mean that I can learn to fight with bladed weapons really fast. Like, all I have to do is see someone fight to be able to do the same stuff." He looked down at the splint unhappily.

"That sounds like an Aradian ability," Takeshi mused as he considered that. He was unaware of the particulars, but those who had it were known for quickly becoming masters of their craft and any craft they faced. "It is an impressive ability, though I can't say I know much about it. How does it work?"

"Hell if I know," came the bitter reply. "It's only ever worked for me once or twice, and it was by accident both times."

"When did you discover this ability?" Takeshi asked, curious.

"An Aradian told me about it a month or so ago," Jamirh admitted.

Takeshi frowned. "I see." An inherent discovered that late? No wonder he was struggling. Inherent abilities were magic and Jamirh had fled from the Empire, where they were told magic did not exist. The Avari looked around twenty years old; that was a long period of time to be denying a part of himself. Magic was belief. It was going to be difficult to repair that internal faith.

"It kind of works?" the Avari tried to explain. "I only need to see a technique once or twice to memorize it. It's the execution I can't seem to do correctly."

Takeshi could see how that would be frustrating.

"So the Vampires have been trying to help me figure it out. I've been doing... passably with daggers, and we decided to try adding in the longsword. And that has been a disaster." His eyes shifted back to his splint.

"How so?" Takeshi prompted.

"I don't feel like I'm learning anything at all!" came the explosive reply as Jamirh looked back up, eyes fierce. "She just attacks and attacks and attacks; she never explains *anything*. It's like she's hoping to beat the ability into working."

Takeshi recalled a situation where a technician had hit a computer to make it work. People rarely functioned the same way.

Jamirh was continuing. "I tried to explain that it's not working, but she just keeps telling me that if I just keep trying I'll get it. It's even worse than the fight I had against Ander, because at least I managed to hit him once. I can't even successfully dodge Jeri."

Takeshi assumed Jeri was the "she" Jamirh kept mentioning. "You succeeded in using it against Ander?" One success was a good start, but constant failure was a self-fulfilling prophecy.

Jamirh nodded, perking up. "Yeah, and that was amazing. We were using daggers, and he kept doing things I had no hope of countering, but this one move he did was really cool... and then I did it successfully against him and scored a hit."

Interesting. "How does this then result in a broken arm?"

The kid's face fell. "I was getting desperate against Jeri and I thought of something I saw an Avari do once in a hand-to-hand fight. It wasn't my best moment, honestly – I somehow forgot the practice swords stand in for bladed weapons – and I tried to brace the blade like this." He held up the splinted arm slowly, so that it crossed the other in front of his face. "And... well. I didn't realize she was coming at me with enough force to break bone. So here I am," he finished dejectedly.

Takeshi considered the situation as he ran his hands through Jitsu's soft fur. That was a sloppy mistake on the part of the instructor, even if the stance had been poorly thought out by the student. "Does your ability merely allow you to learn the forms, or also how to use them in a fight?" he asked finally.

Jamirh looked up at him, confused. "Isn't it the same thing?"

"Not really. You can execute the forms without an understanding of how or why to use them against an opponent," Takeshi informed him. "Does your ability give you this knowledge? Or should it?"

"I thought so," the Avari said slowly. "But to be honest, I don't understand much about how it works at all."

Takeshi wasn't sure Jamirh's idea had been as poorly thought out as it seemed on the surface, especially if the ability guided choice in combat. He would have to develop that theory a little more before he presented it. And if he was right, he had an idea that might help the Avari tap into his ability successfully, though neither of them would be in any shape to attempt that in the near future. His eyes slid to his own katana, leaning against the wall by the bed.

But in the meantime, he still had a promise to keep.

He changed the subject. "The way you are holding that arm makes me think that it is bothering you."

"Oh, yeah. A little." Jamirh frowned at the arm like it had betrayed him.

"Do you have any medicine to take for it?" he asked conversationally.

The Avari shook his head. "No. Ander gave me something before they set it, but it's definitely wearing off now."

Jitsu whined unhappily. Why were all the two-feet so stubborn?

The way Jamirh had talked about it made Takeshi think he had never come across the idea of getting blood drawn before. He supposed that on a conceptual level it could be quite scary if you lacked the context. He reached out mentally to Ander. *:Would you care to put on a bit of theater?:*

:What did you have in mind?: came the instant reply.

:It has been a while since you've checked my iron levels, hasn't it?: he asked cheerfully.

He got the sensation of a sigh. *:It's going to be very awkward doing this in such a way that I theoretically can't see him.:*

:I could cast an illusion?: Takeshi suggested slowly, a fluttery feeling making itself known in his stomach. He hadn't cast any magic over the past week, trying to allow his core to heal, but... *:It doesn't have to be very good; you already know he's here. And Jitsu can also help hide him, if I can suggest it to her without him knowing.:*

:She will hear you if you project at her this way,: Ander informed him. *:I'm not sure how I feel about you casting.:*

Takeshi considered his core. *:My magic feels better than it has in a long time. It will be a very simple illusion, very little power required. Like I said, it doesn't have to be good; it just needs to fool him. A good test for me, I think.:*

And it would be a test.

What would he do if the chip had permanently damaged his ability to weave? He couldn't even imagine a life without magic. He would rather the chip had killed him than that it should sever him from such an integral part of himself.

Ander sighed again. *:Very well.:*

:Jitsu?: Takeshi projected, and was rewarded with her turning to look at him, curious. *:We are going to play a game.:*

Her tail wagged happily as her ears perked up. She loved games!

"In theory," he started aloud, "I think Ander should have given you something to help manage the pain. That, and also a sling, so you don't have to keep holding it that way." *:Alert us when Ander approaches. We are going to "hide" Jamirh from him – don't worry, Ander knows he's here – and he can watch me get blood taken. When Ander shoos you off the bed, just go sit next to Jamirh in case he decides to do anything rash.:*

Oh, she could do that! She liked the helpful-red two-foot, and she was very good at comforting people. And if he tried to run, she could stop him and sit on him.

"Uh," Jamirh started, then winced. "I didn't stick around long enough to get to that point. On account of the stabbing that was going to happen."

"I see," Takeshi stated mildly as Jitsu twisted around to face the door, suddenly alert. Jamirh went pale. "Stay there," Takeshi commanded, putting some force behind his words. Jamirh blinked at him in surprise, but stayed. "I can hide you," he explained, raising a hand. He hesitated just a moment before squashing the doubt down as hard as he could, rallying his will, and demanding the pattern do as he bid.

Blue-white light formed a neat circle, glyphs perfectly balanced, and Jamirh and the pattern both disappeared from view.

Relief, in addition to the gentle pull of magic feeding the pattern.

"No one will be able to see you now." He closed his eyes briefly as the sensation washed over him. It felt the same as it always had. He still had his magic. The realization was almost dizzying.

There was a sound of surprise from the chair, and Takeshi could see the air ripple as Jamirh looked down at himself. He hadn't bothered to account for motion. "Wow," the Avari exclaimed. "This is amazing!"

Takeshi hid a smile, settling back against the pillows as he tried to relax. "Try not to move too much, and don't make a sound," he warned, moments before Ander knocked on the door.

"I'm sorry to disturb you again, Takeshi," the priest started, though Takeshi noted with some amusement that he didn't actually sound sorry. "Vlad would like me to check your iron levels. Hopefully they've stabilized since the surgery." *:Which is true, so at least this is not completely farcical.:*

:It is efficient,: Takeshi agreed as Ander pulled supplies out of a cabinet. "That would be nice. The soreness appears to have mostly faded."

"That's a good sign." The priest was putting the supplies on a little metal tray. *:We are going to do this all at once this time, though Goddess help me if you try to run away...:*

Takeshi hid a snort. *:I'm not going anywhere.:*

:I do have a backup plan in case this goes south, though it doesn't look like he'd get past Jitsu regardless. How did the casting feel? Any irregularities?: Ander was eyeing him critically. "Any headaches?"

"No, thankfully. If I never get another migraine again, it will be too soon. And while I still feel a little cold, it's not too bad." *:The* *weaving worked as expected, and felt... correct. Normal. Nothing hurt. I did feel a touch of lightheadedness, but I think that was due to relief.:* His magic was still his own. She hadn't taken that from him, at least.

He glanced at Jitsu and could see her fur was weirdly flattened in some places with some small ripples nearby. Jamirh was probably petting her. It was a good thing they weren't actually trying to hide him.

"Hm. I don't like that the temperature sensitivity hasn't gone away. We'll have to keep a close eye on that. But the rest of the symptoms subsiding is a good sign that there won't be any permanent damage." He cleaned Takeshi's arm with a damp wipe, and Takeshi felt the tingle of magic against his skin tightening around his upper arm. *:There is a wave of adrenaline leaving your system right now; the lightheadedness is likely from that. Relax. Do you need to drop the illusion?:*

:No, the illusion is barely pulling anything.: Takeshi didn't know how to explain how important that test had been to him, so he didn't try. He watched the other man's practiced movements. *:When you do this with him, it might not hurt to explain what you are doing before you do it,:* he suggested mildly. *:He has never even considered that this is something that is done. Jitsu said he is afraid.:*

Ander shot him a look that was just shy of annoyed as he positioned the needle. *:He is making it harder than it needs to be.:*

:He doesn't know how it needs to be,: Takeshi pointed out. He had known Jamirh for less than twenty minutes and he could tell that was the case. As much as he appreciated Ander's expertise, he hoped he wasn't called in to deal with children very often.

There was a snort in the back of his mind that had the distinct flavor of Hades to it. He sent her a wordless greeting as he watched the syringe fill with red liquid.

Jitsu sneezed. The helpful-red two-foot was petting her very aggressively. She did not think he was enjoying this.

:I suppose.: Ander withdrew the needle and pressed a small square of gauze to the puncture site. "Hold that there."

Takeshi obediently held it in place while Ander dealt with the syringe and other supplies, carefully labeling the vial. "Did you find your runaway?"

"No," came the short reply. Ander finished everything off by bandaging the small wound. "I'm sure he will turn up soon. He left some things behind," he added pointedly.

Takeshi almost winced; Ander's acting could be improved. "I see," he said instead. *:Hopefully I will be able to convince him to return shortly.:*

:Indeed.: "How do you feel?"

"Fine, thank you." He shifted against the pillows as Jitsu returned to the bed. He glanced at the chair, but Jamirh was still.

Ander nodded once. "Dinner should be up in an hour or so; please be sure to eat it." Without waiting for a reply he swept from the room, white coat flaring dramatically behind him.

"Well, no one can say he doesn't have a certain flair," Takeshi chuckled after a moment. He turned back to the chair and dismissed the illusion, revealing a rather pale Jamirh, fist clenched tight around something hanging from his neck. "See? I am fine."

The Avari swallowed hard. "Does it hurt?"

Takeshi shook his head. "It pinches a bit, but that's all. I have suffered through far worse at the hands of doctors." Though it probably wasn't fair to count the insertion of the microchip in the same category as bloodwork. "My arm is a little sore now, but in a few hours that will fade. You have certainly suffered worse during training."

Jamirh inspected the bandage morosely. "*Both* my arms are going to hurt."

"Only briefly, and one far less than the other. It's more uncomfortable than painful. Think of it as the price paid for your medication. Your arm must be starting to ache quite a bit at this point," he prodded gently.

"I guess," Jamirh muttered sullenly. He tucked whatever it was he had been holding under his shirt before Takeshi could get a good glimpse.

Takeshi was struck with sudden inspiration. *:Would you go with him?:* he asked Jitsu.

There was a pause while she considered that. She was not overly opposed to it since she liked the helpful-red two-foot and she did kind of owe him, but she did not want to leave her Human by himself.

:I will be fine for the twenty minutes or so you will be gone,: he pointed out dryly. *:And we might want to work on your nominatives.:*

She swatted him with her tail. There was nothing wrong with the way she referred to two-feet.

"Why don't you take Jitsu with you?" he offered. "You can focus on her while Ander does what he needs to. And it will seem like she caught you, so it doesn't look like you giving in to Ander, if that is a concern." They did seem to be mildly antagonistic to each other, but Jitsu's presence would help mitigate that, too. Hopefully.

Jamirh grimaced, but didn't deny it. "Are you sure?" he asked, expression fading back to worry.

She jumped down from the bed with a big stretch, then turned to look at her temporary charge. They should go quickly so she could be back quickly.

Takeshi nodded reassuringly. "I will be fine without her for a little while."

Jamirh took a step towards the door, then paused. "It really doesn't hurt?"

"It should not, no." He didn't think Ander would be that petty. He seemed to take pride in his work.

The Avari sighed, shoulders slumping. "Well, goodbye, then. It was nice meeting you."

"And you, as well," Takeshi said, smiling beneath his mask. "We will see each other again, I'm sure." He watched as Jitsu gently nudged Jamirh out the door, expressing to Takeshi that she would be back soon. He sent a quick thought to Ander. *:I'm sending him back to you with Jitsu.:*

:Excellent. You experienced no complications when you dropped the spell?:

:None. I am not even particularly tired.:

Ander seemed pleased to hear that. *:Good. Make sure you eat later; I don't want you accidentally setting yourself back.:* Takeshi felt him withdraw from the mental contact.

:I am impressed with how you handled that situation,: Hades murmured thoughtfully, finally choosing to speak up. *:They can both be… difficult, in their own ways.:*

Takeshi considered the bandage on his arm. *:Jamirh said you broke him out of the jail?:*

:Yes.:

He was surprised at the brevity of her answer. *:Is he also a… possible priest, then?:*

She was surprised. *:Oh, no. No, I broke him out for a different reason.:*

Why was she being cagey about it? *:So he is important to you in some other way. Otherwise, you would not have freed him and brought him here, and the Vampires would not be so desperate to see him trained that they are taking dangerous shortcuts.:* He allowed a hint of disapproval to enter his tone.

:I am certain you will find out eventually, but it should be from him, if you can manage it. He does not care for the situation he finds himself in, and someone not knowing is something of a novelty for him right now.: He felt her regard him carefully. *:He would want you to see him for himself.:*

Takeshi's brow furrowed. *:As opposed to what?:*

She remained silent.

He sighed. *:They are botching his training,:* he informed her bluntly.

:They are doing their best. It is imperative he learn quickly.:

:And now he will be unable to do anything with a weapon for some time,: he countered. *:That cannot possibly be anyone's goal.:*

He felt her agreement. *:Fair point. Do you have a better idea?:*

:Yes.:

Chapter Eleven

Takeshi did not have as much time to consider Jamirh's situation as he might have wished over the next few days. Ander submitted him to a battery of tests to determine if there were any lingering problems from the microchip, magically and physically. They left Takeshi feeling exhausted, even if he wasn't doing all that much other than experiencing the tests. He still wasn't perfectly well, plenty of sleep and good food notwithstanding. Still, Ander seemed optimistic that he was recovering as well as he could be, reminding Takeshi that he had also exhausted his core on top of the damage the chip had been doing.

He supposed that when looked at in that light, he was doing phenomenally. The only thing that didn't seem to want to go away was the persistent chill, and even that was nowhere near as bad as it had been those last few days after Charve. It was enough progress that Ander finally declared that he was well enough to be discharged from the hospital as long as he took it easy.

And so Takeshi found himself standing by his bed, staring at his very few possessions. The bag the pirates had given him, filled with food, a first aid kit, two changes of clothes, and his katana. The violet spell crystal shaped like a hound lay next to the bag.

He touched the hilt of the katana gently, running a finger along the cotton wrapping. Each shinobi was gifted their katana when they left the training barracks; this one was a special gift from when he had become Captain of the Imperial Guard. Hotaru herself had presented him with it. It was a symbol of loyalty, of *being* shinobi. He wanted nothing more than to hold it in his hands and let the familiar weight ease him into meditation.

But at the same time, the thought of doing that made him feel sick.

Did the Empress still deserve his loyalty?

Part of him screamed yes, that he was merely a tool for her to wield, that what she chose to do with him was to be accepted without hesitation, even if she chose to get rid of him. But it hadn't just been him she'd tossed aside, had it? And he didn't think he could forgive her for what she had done to Hotaru. To her own daughter.

And who was to say that it would end with them? What if there were others who were being... modified... against their will? The Empress was the kind of person who would chase something until she had it. What was the end goal of the chip? How many more lives would she ruin in pursuit of an unknown goal?

How many shinobi would let her?

Jitsu leaned into him, drawing him out of his spiraling thoughts. She looked at the items on the bed curiously. That was not a lot of things. Most two-feet had many more things. Did Takeshi need more things? She could try to find what he needed for him.

He absently ran a hand over her head, stroking the soft fur as he tried to push the thoughts away for now. It wasn't like he could return and do something about it, after all. He'd been banished. "I probably do need more things, but let's see where this is going before we start collecting them."

"Where what is going?"

Takeshi glanced back over his shoulder at Ander, who was just coming in. "Me, specifically. I am glad to be leaving – as nice as it is, this is still a hospital – but where will I be going?"

"Ah." Ander paused, looking uncertain. "You have a few options–"

"Which I am going to share with you!" Jak breezed in, looking for all the world like he owned the place and ignoring Ander's faintly put-out expression. He eyed Takeshi critically. "Well, you look miles better than before. Good for you."

"Thank you?" Takeshi offered, taken aback at the other man's sudden appearance.

Jitsu shook herself, moving forward to sniff at the new Human curiously. He smelled old. And like magic. And... ah, yes. This was another priest!

"Anyway, as I was saying, you do have options. All of them are equally valid, so don't feel like you have to pick one over any of the others." Jak was ignoring Jitsu, but he wasn't discouraging her, either. He held up a hand and began ticking off fingers as he counted. "Option one – you can stay at the Temple of Night Rising, where Ander lives and I technically live. Option two – you can stay at the palace. It's nearby and has excellent accommodations. Option three

– we can find you an apartment elsewhere in the city. That one will take a little more time than the other two, so maybe we should have asked you this earlier, but it is still very doable."

Takeshi raised an eyebrow. He wasn't sure what he had expected, but it wasn't that.

"Don't feel like you are making a binding decision, either," Ander added, shooting a glare at the other priest. "You can pick one now and switch to any of the others at a later date."

:We want you to be comfortable here, Takeshi,: the goddess piped in. *:Choose the one you think is best.:*

Takeshi was still getting used to Hades' tendency to join a conversation at any point. He hadn't even made a decision yet on that front, but he wondered if he would hear her for the rest of his life regardless. Still, the decision of where to stay was, for him, an easy one. He had lived most of his life in the palaces of Ni Fon, or at the very least on the grounds of those complexes. Hopefully the palace here would be the most familiar option. "I will stay at the palace, if that is acceptable?"

If they were disappointed he had not chosen the Temple, they didn't show it. "Alrighty then! I'm going to slip on ahead and make sure it's ready for you when you get there. Ander can show you the way. See you in a bit!" Jak disappeared in a shower of violet sparks Takeshi very much did not associate with teleportation without waiting for a reply.

Jitsu snorted as a spark landed on her nose before dissipating. She liked very-old priest!

Ander glanced at the warg before turning his attention back to Takeshi. "Very well, then. We might as well start making our way over if you are ready to go. I can give you a very rough tour on the way, but it's not far."

Takeshi nodded, reaching for his bag and katana. His hand paused over the hilt, thoughts straying back into their earlier direction, but then Ander turned to look at him impatiently and he found himself following, belongings in hand.

The weather looked surprisingly mild for early December, but he was glad for the warmer-than-average temperatures. He needed to look into getting more clothing soon, no matter what; the grand total of three outfits he had were not made for snow and cold weather. He was not looking forward to that.

The air outside the hospital was brisk, and Takeshi found himself glad they would not be outside for long. Ander pointed out the Temple as they passed, and Takeshi found himself surprised that the palace, Temple, and hospital were all part of the same complex. Didn't that make it difficult for citizens to seek medical help? Or was this hospital only meant for those on palace grounds?

He quickly revised that thought as he noticed just how many people were coming and going in the area. He was no stranger to the number of people needed to keep a state building functional, but there were too many out and about for that. He was forced to come to the conclusion that for some reason the palace was a public structure, not a private one.

Ander must have been watching him fall into confusion. "I didn't think it could possibly work when I first came here, either," he offered. "Yet somehow it does. Romanii's citizens are for the greater part responsible and understanding of their civic duty. They respect the palace for what it is, and so we have very few incidents on palace grounds."

Takeshi considered the grand entryway as they passed through into the building proper. The whole building was steeped in magic, with brighter sparks scattered about. "How is it defended?"

"The Black Watch guards the palace. They are not unlike shinobi in Ni Fon, or Truth Seekers in the Empire proper, except that they are exclusively Vampires. Wargs also tend to come and go as they please, and they will gleefully call out or deal with anything they think is wrong," Ander explained.

Jitsu's tail wagged proudly.

"Three hundred pounds of canine is a decent deterrent," Ander finished blandly.

So the bright sparks of magic were likely the members of the Black Watch, hidden, but watchful. Interesting. The palace itself also felt watchful, which was more agency than Takeshi felt comfortable attributing to a building. Perhaps his senses were still a little off from the chip. He resolved to take a nap as soon as he was settled.

And the wargs were also far more integrated into the defenses of this place than he had realized at first. He supposed that made sense – they were not actually dogs, no matter what everyone kept telling him – but it made him wonder how this balance came to be.

Takeshi had to admit that some part of him was fascinated by this place. This was a completely different harmony with magic than what he was used to. They did appear to have some form of tech –

a hard feeling to put into words, but Takeshi distinctly remembered the *wrongness* of the thing that had fought him.

Ander was nodding. "That is the feeling of Abomination. Most mages can sense it, though few know what it is in this day and age. Even non-mages can be affected by it."

:Few throughout history have ever been able to put a name to it, though the feeling is wrong enough to convince most to try to right it even without perfect understanding,: Hades interjected. *:Magic will always try to right the balance. Abomination will always try to upset it. These two forces have been in conflict since the beginning of time.:*

"Then is a final victory even possible?" Takeshi mused.

"I'll take a temporary victory over nothing," Ander muttered. "Against a primal force, that might be the best we can hope for."

They considered that in silence as they made their way through the palace, which to Takeshi appeared to have been built by someone who had no concept of spatial logic. Trying to learn his way around here would be difficult.

Jitsu nudged him playfully. He had her, and she was very good at getting herself to where she needed to be. He would not get lost with her around.

Well, that was another thing to be thankful for. He patted her head as they came upon Jak leaning against the wall, twirling a brass key with one hand.

"There you both are," he greeted them cheerfully. "The very nice lady who runs housekeeping nowadays assigned you this suite, Takeshi." He gestured to the closest door.

Takeshi frowned. A suite?

Jak unlocked the door and pushed it open, revealing what could in fact only be described as a poshly decorated suite of rooms. Takeshi glanced around, wondering what he was expected to do with all this space. As Captain of the Imperial Guard of Ni Fon he had had his own quarters, but those had consisted of one room roughly half the size of the sitting room he was standing in now and an attached bathroom. Most shinobi were quartered in barracks, and some part of him had expected something more like that. At most, he had considered he might be given something the size of his room in Ni Fon. This felt excessive.

Jitsu did not share his uncertainty, investigating curiously as she sniffed her way through the rooms. This was a good place for her and her Human.

"This is... a lot," he stated after a moment, when it became clear the two priests were waiting for him to say something. At least the cream, brown, and blue color scheme was pleasant to look at.

Ander raised an eyebrow sardonically. "Where did you think we were going to put you? The stables?"

"This is pretty standard for guest accommodations, believe it or not," Jak reassured him. "Living quarters are often even more than this."

More? What did these people do with more? These rooms were almost to the standard of the Imperial family.

"The Temple is sponsoring you while you are here," Jak continued. He handed Takeshi a small pouch. Takeshi opened it to see a pile of brassy coins, each stamped with a winged glaive. "You can give one of those anywhere you would normally pay for something.

It allows the business to bill the Temple for whatever you want to purchase. Feel free to pick up more clothes or food or whatever you want."

"If you run out, I will replenish them," Ander added. "We do realize you've come here with basically nothing, so don't feel like you have to be frugal." He considered Takeshi carefully for a moment. "If you are still chilled, I suggest you invest in sweaters and a good-quality coat. It is only going to get colder."

"Oh yeah, winters here are kind of miserable," Jak mused. "I forgot about that."

Ander ignored him. "If you need more bedding, Gerit in housekeeping is the person to ask." He pulled three red spell crystals out of one of his pockets. "And these heating crystals are yours as well. Between them and the warg, you should be fine, but if not please let me know as soon as possible."

Jitsu wandered back over to them, having already thoroughly explored the bedroom. She was good at keeping Takeshi warm. The tall-white priest did not need to worry.

"On a related note, I do still want to keep an eye on your recovery. I'd like to schedule your first checkup for two days from now on Friday morning, if that is acceptable," Ander continued while Jak apparently lost interest, looking around the room.

"I don't believe I have anything else scheduled for that time," Takeshi said agreeably.

Jak snorted.

"Right." Ander paused, then rallied. "Do you have any questions?"

Takeshi considered his surroundings. "None that I can think of at the moment." He didn't think "What do I do with all this space?" was a question that would go over well.

Ander nodded. "Jak and I are only a thought away, as is Hades, if anything comes up. You should be able to reach us from here, but even if you can't you will definitely be able to reach Her."

Takeshi felt the goddess's wordless assent.

"For what it's worth, you might want to carry the *crystallus canis*," Jak suggested, fingering his own where it hung by his vest. "It will signal to people that you are of the Temple."

Takeshi tilted his head to the side curiously. "Is that appropriate? I have made no decision on whether or not to join your order."

Jak shrugged. "It doesn't really matter. Even if you don't choose to become one of Her priests, the *crystallus* will not be revoked. It is yours, and it marks you as one of Her chosen. People may assume that you are a new priest, or that you are at least considering it, but it is a gift for you. You might as well use it."

Takeshi wasn't sure he felt comfortable doing that, even if Hades felt like she was nodding in agreement in the back of his mind. He glanced at Ander but didn't see one on his person. Takeshi wondered if he carried his out of sight, and if so, why.

"You are also welcome to eat with the court if you want," Jak continued. "You can also get meals delivered here if you let the servants know, or you can join us – we've been doing our own thing the past week or so." He indicated himself and Ander. "Just shoot us a thought so we know to have food for you. There are many options in the city itself if you want to eat out, too."

"Just keep in mind that just because you are no longer in the hospital does not mean you can neglect eating," Ander said sternly, shooting a glance at Jitsu. "You are not quite fully recovered from the magicore exhaustion, and so rest and nutrients are still your biggest priorities."

The warg sat next to Takeshi, leaning against him. Her head came up almost to his chest, making it easy to scratch her ears. "I understand," he agreed. As it was, he wasn't used to this level of physical exertion anymore. All they had done was walk from the hospital to the palace and then stand in the middle of a room, and he was beginning to feel exhausted.

"Very well then. We will be within reach if you need us," Ander reiterated.

"Yup! Let us know if you need anything," Jak agreed.

"Thank you. This is more than sufficient, though," Takeshi assured them, folding into a shallow bow of thanks.

He spent a little time looking around after they left. These rooms were ridiculously decadent in his opinion. Jitsu watched him do his own exploring from the couch, of which she took up the majority. He paused, frowning as he considered her.

"I'm sorry. I never asked you for your opinion on where we should stay," he realized. "Where were you living before?" Had he taken her away from something?

But Jitsu was almost immediately dismissive. Anywhere her Human was worked fine for her. Most of her kind lived somewhere on the palace grounds anyway. There was a lot of space in here, which was nice, but she was sure that the tall-white priest and very-old priest would not allow Takeshi to live in cramped quarters. She needed to fit too, after all, though she felt she could make anything work.

Takeshi hadn't considered that. She had somehow managed just fine with him in the hospital, but she was absurdly large for a canine. It made sense that she would be more comfortable in a large space, even if he wasn't. And she was probably correct that she had played a part in the size of the area granted him. If she was going to be staying with him from now on, he would have to be more careful to factor her into his calculations. He eyed her curiously. "When I am a little better, we should train together, you and I." He had no doubt she was able to fight, but he preferred that they would be able to fight together. The ways they could communicate opened up possibilities that he never could have considered before, and he was excited to find out what they could do as a team.

Jitsu was equally excited by that idea, tail wagging enthusiastically. Together, they would be a force to be reckoned with!

He smiled faintly as she pressed herself up against him, nearly knocking him over in her joy. "And perhaps you can also help me with your helpful-red two-foot?" It had been less than a week since the Avari had broken his arm, and Takeshi himself was still not up to any sort of physical exertion on that level, but he still wanted to solidify some of his ideas. If the Vampires were determined to have Jamirh be competent at swordsmanship, he needed to have a plan ready to go.

Jitsu was doubtful of that. The helpful-red two-foot could be nervous around her kind at even the slightest hint of aggression, and others had told her he did not react well to those kinds of suggestions. But, if Takeshi thought she could help, she would certainly try.

Takeshi raised an eyebrow. "He seemed fine around you at the hospital."

Yes, she had made sure to be as non-threatening as possible. And he had already met her. And he had been more afraid of the tall-white priest and his needles, which had been helpful.

Takeshi considered. "Do the wargs often talk about Jamirh amongst themselves?" he mused.

Jitsu was immediately affirmative. He gave very good scratches, and very rarely pushed them away. Word had spread quickly. And the tall-white priest had asked them to keep an eye on him, which they were more than happy to do in exchange for pets and scratches.

Takeshi hummed thoughtfully. In the end, it didn't really matter why Jamirh was important. He was sure he'd find out why eventually. The actual important thing was that the Avari was able to defend himself effectively, and Takeshi was certain he would be able to get him to that point. If the inherent worked the way he thought it might, it just required a slightly different angle to encourage success. And even if it didn't, he was confident he could do better than whatever the Vampires were managing.

Desperation could be a dangerous thing. He was intimately aware of that. His distance from whatever this situation was would be better for Jamirh because he would not be driven to make the dangerous shortcuts the others had been taking. He could allow himself to focus entirely on the problem in front of him, and not the theoretical future issue that was driving the Vampires.

One step at a time. He could make this work.

Chapter Twelve

Jamirh sat on one of the marble benches, listening to the music filling the courtyard. Master Bard Caelessa had decided to perform an impromptu concert in the palace gardens. About fifty people were scattered about, enjoying her skill and talent.

It was a strange experience, though a pleasant one. Even though there were no instruments, he could still hear the music behind Caelessa's lyrics, could feel the songs connect with him on a level he had never experienced before. Jeri had explained that Voice magic was capable of creating a connection of sorts between the Bard and the listener. It felt a little like he *lived* the song through Caelessa's words. He had heard concerts broadcast in the Empire before, had liked some of the songs and disliked others, but he wasn't sure how anyone could dislike this kind of music. Even if the concerts he was used to were far flashier, he found himself preferring Caelessa's subtle mastery.

It was also going a long way to distracting him from the dull ache in his arm. It had been almost a week since he had broken it, and he hadn't noticed much improvement, even if everyone said he was getting the best possible care. It made sense – he knew broken bones could take a long time to heal – but he found himself chafing at his limited ability to do anything. It felt like everything was a production now, requiring far more effort than before. He guessed he was lucky it was his left arm; he didn't even want to think how much more difficult life would be if it were his dominant arm out of commission. He might have just begged Ander to heal it fully at that point out of desperation, future weakness be damned. Trying to eat would be so much more difficult with only his left hand.

At least he was spared training for the foreseeable future.

Jeri had been extremely upset with herself, worlds tumbling over each other as she apologized over and over. Jamirh didn't believe she had meant to hurt him. No one here seemed to want to cause him harm – at least not directly. They were okay with him fighting Avari-tech nightmares in some theoretical future, and they seemed pretty desperate to get him to the point where that would not instantly result in harm, but Jamirh just wished they would be a little more careful about how they got there.

And what was training going to look like, after? Would Jeri continue to train him? Jamirh wasn't sure if he wanted to keep training with her. She'd always pushed him hard with the dagger training, but this had been something else entirely. Marcus had told him that training accidents weren't uncommon, but still. Jamirh found it hard to justify the brutality of hitting him hard enough to break his arm. Right now she was treating him like glass, but there was no way that was going to last. Still, who else was there? Another Vampire? Ander?

Jamirh couldn't see training with Ander going any differently.

What if it didn't matter, because the problem wasn't with Jeri's training methods, but with Jamirh himself? What kind of super-special swordsman got their arm broken in a training accident?

About the only good thing out of the whole situation was that he now had more time to consider his ability and how it worked. Maybe if he understood more about it and how it was used by others, he'd have better luck, because trying to rely on instinct was not working. He had prepared a list of questions for the Ambassador next time he saw her based on his conversation with Takeshi.

Takeshi. Shuurai Takeshi, because Ni Fon reversed the names for some reason. Jamirh had liked him. He had asked questions Jamirh hadn't even thought of, and had been understanding of Jamirh's situation. He had even gone so far as to lend Jamirh his warg for the whole needle-and-blood thing. He hadn't been able to actively pet Jitsu, since one arm was broken and the other one was getting a needle stuck in it, but she had pressed herself close to his back and rested her head on his shoulder. It had, surprisingly, helped him feel better about the whole process. Takeshi had been right – it didn't hurt nearly as much as Jamirh had feared, and it had been over pretty quickly. Jamirh just wasn't sure why anyone would come up with such a bizarre procedure. At least it was over now.

He found himself wondering what exactly had happened to Takeshi to land him in the hospital. He tried to remember what he had heard about him, but it wasn't much outside of that he had tried to save Hel from that military base. There had been some mention of a... "prayer of agony" at some point? And even though he seemed okay, his iron levels were high, whatever that meant, and apparently headaches were involved. Though he hadn't moved from the bed, Jamirh had still gotten an impression of strength and competence from the Human, almost like he hadn't gotten up because he didn't want to, not because he couldn't.

He'd been nice, and even though he had recognized Jamirh it seemed to be purely based on his breakout from jail, not because of Ebryn. That was refreshing. Did people in Ni Fon even know who Ebryn Stormlight was? It was far away, and Ebryn had lived a long time before Ni Fon had become part of the Empire. What had communication been like back then? Jamirh wasn't sure. He didn't remember anyone from Ni Fon featuring in any of the stories.

And... maybe that was actually another option. Maybe he should try to examine the stories of Ebryn that survived and see if he could pull out more details about how he had used the Master of Blades ability. The Vampires might be of more help there, since some of them had actually known Ebryn, or perhaps even Miravu. An Aradian named Sukra had traveled with the Hero, and Miravu had hinted she had left her own take on their shared adventure to her people. Perhaps that would shed some light on a solution he could actually use? Would Miravu share that information?

No matter what, he needed to do something. What they were trying now wasn't working.

He sighed as he listened to Caelessa's voice, singing something soft and sweet and full of longing. This was also an inherent ability if he remembered correctly. He wondered if she had ever struggled with it like him, or if it had always come easily. People kept telling him that some abilities took practice to master, but no one seemed sure what to do when it could only be used once in a blue moon. How did he start using it reliably, never mind mastering it?

A cold black nose sneezed in his face.

Jamirh flinched back, noticing for the first time the white warg standing in front of him. Her violet eyes peered at him curiously as she settled down on her haunches, clearly demanding his attention.

"Ah, sorry about that." A cheerful voice sounded from behind him. Jamirh turned to see Takeshi himself standing nearby. The dark fabric covering the bottom half of his face hid most of his expression, but the crinkling of his eyes suggested that he was smiling. He also did not sound sorry in the slightest. "She wanted to come over and say hello."

The warg's tail wagged twice, and she leaned a little closer to Jamirh.

He obediently started scratching under her chin. "They always do," he said with a sigh, ears twitching down. He took in the Human. He looked a lot better than he had in the hospital, though maybe that was due to the clothing. A long, slightly curved blade hung in a sheath on his hip.

Takeshi's eyes flicked to Caelessa. The Bard's voice cut out after a high note, and the crowd broke out into applause. "It seems that the concert is over," the Human mused as Caelessa bowed before striking up a conversation with several people nearby. Others began to disperse. "How is your arm?" he asked, turning back to Jamirh.

Jamirh shrugged awkwardly. "Not great, but I've been told it could be worse."

Takeshi chuckled. "Bone can be a tricky thing. How it heals can vary from person to person. Is Ander the one in charge of your healing?"

Jamirh nodded.

"Then I am sure your arm will be fine," the Human finished, radiating a confidence Jamirh found hard to share. It wasn't *his* arm that was broken, after all. Takeshi must have seen Jamirh's expression, because he continued, "Bones break all the time. It is not an uncommon injury. I am certain most of the healers here are familiar with the healing process."

Jamirh considered that, then shrugged again. "I guess. The place I used to live wasn't exactly the safest, and other Avari were injured in accidents all the time, but I always managed to avoid the worst of it. Figures my luck would run out here." Aether had also managed to remain mostly uninjured, at least until... well. Jamirh's fingers found his key.

Dark eyes regarded him thoughtfully as the Human hummed in agreement. "You are from Lyndiniam, aren't you?"

"Yeah, but the worst part of Lyndiniam. Blackfields. It's kind of a slum, I guess. Avari only. They'd knock it all down if they could, but I think it would cost too much, so instead it's just a crumbling mess," Jamirh explained.

One eyebrow rose. "And you have never broken a bone at all." It was a statement rather than a question.

"Yup!" Jamirh agreed. "It works out best if you avoid getting injured in the first place, since the options for healing aren't exactly the best." It would have put a major dent in his ability to steal things, too.

"I see," the man murmured.

"And I see you're out of the hospital," Jamirh exclaimed, trying to turn the conversation away from his shitty previous living conditions as he rubbed the key between his fingers. "Congratulations!"

"Thank you?" Takeshi sounded a little confused. "It is nice to not be in the hospital anymore." He paused as Jitsu tilted her head in his direction. "She also prefers our new lodging, as there is more space."

"She took up, like, a third of your hospital room, so I can believe that." Jamirh snorted as Jitsu licked his face playfully. "Where did you end up?"

Takeshi glanced back towards the palace. "In there," he said with a nod in that direction. "I had options, and I chose the one I thought would be most familiar, but it wasn't what I had pictured at all."

Jamirh shook his head. "I get that. Nothing around here makes sense to me, either. I don't so much have rooms as I have a decently-sized apartment."

"The space allotted to each suite does seem a bit excessive," Takeshi agreed. "The palace is... very strange," he added slowly. "Watchful."

"Don't even get me started on the palace," Jamirh muttered. "It is insane how that thing works."

Takeshi tilted his head, confused. "How it works?"

"Oh! Don't tell me they didn't tell you," Jamirh exclaimed. "The palace is magic. You have to know where you are going, or at least think you know, or you won't get there. I spent the first few days here getting horribly lost."

"The palace... interesting." The Human looked like he was thinking hard about that. "The theory makes sense, but it is a strange thing in practice. The building is not laid out very logically, I noticed, but that could be a side effect of that sort of magic rather than the true shape of the building. The effect of the translocation is so subtle I didn't even notice. Jitsu's presence has probably kept me from the same fate as you. I have been trusting that she knows where she is going."

The warg huffed in agreement.

"Yeah, I think it changes as it wants, too," Jamirh added, not sure he understood everything Takeshi had just said. "My room sort of grew a kitchen when Vlad asked it to, not that I know what to do with a kitchen."

"Cook things," Takeshi offered blithely.

"Why bother? Every meal is provided by the palace," Jamirh pointed out. "And I have no idea how to use any of that equipment anyway."

The Human hummed noncommittally.

"Have you cooked anything since you've been here?" Jamirh asked.

"No, but my rooms do not include a kitchen. I shall keep an eye out for one appearing, however." Takeshi sounded amused.

Jamirh eyed the sword at the man's hip again. Was he really the only person who didn't know how to wield a weapon in this entire country? That was a little pathetic. His ears drooped. Still, it didn't look like any of the swords he was familiar with. "What kind of sword is that?" he asked.

If Takeshi was bothered by the sudden change in subject, he didn't show it. Jamirh wondered if anything really bothered the man. He seemed unflappable. "This is a katana, a common weapon in Ni Fon, our equivalent to your longsword, I suppose," he offered. "This one was gifted to me when I became Captain of the Imperial Guard."

It looked kind of plain for that, in Jamirh's opinion. "Does it have a name?"

Takeshi shook his head. "In Ni Fon, a blade is only named if it has some sort of special qualities, or it is named for its maker. While my katana is an excellent blade, it is not particularly special, except to me."

Jamirh blinked. "Oh. I kind of thought most swords got named."

"Perhaps in this country, but not in mine," Takeshi said with a shrug. "Naming a normal blade is seen as... a bit tacky."

Jamirh's ears twitched up in amusement, wondering what Takeshi would make of "The Crystal Light Blade." Then again, it *did* have special properties. That he hoped to one day be able to use. He found himself wondering again... "Have you ever heard of Ebryn Stormlight?"

Takeshi's expression was blank, what he could see of it. "Who?"

Huh. Perhaps he didn't know. "Ebryn Stormlight. He's a famous hero in the Empire. And here, actually."

Takeshi shook his head after a moment. "It does not sound familiar, but then I am not well-versed in the legends of the Rose."

Jamirh blinked at that. "The Rose?"

"The Rose Empire, yes? Where you hail from?" Now everyone was confused.

"Oh. *Oh.* That's... a very old name. No one calls it that anymore. It's just 'the Empire,' now," Jamirh informed him.

"Is that so? It is common in Ni Fon to refer to it as the Rose, to separate it from the Empire of Ni Fon," Takeshi explained.

"But... Ni Fon is part of the Empire?" Jamirh was ninety-nine percent sure that was true.

"Not by choice," Takeshi muttered dryly. "And not forever. Ni Fon will free itself one day." His voice turned sad. "With the lengths the Empress is willing to go to, it is only a matter of time."

Jamirh was getting more confused. "The Empress?"

"Ah, yes. I suppose to you she would be the Duchess of Ni Fon, Duchess Kobayashi Rikona," Takeshi conceded. "But the Nifoni are taught to hail her as our Empress."

"And the Empire allows that?" Jamirh exclaimed, eyes wide, remembering the cold woman from the vid screen at the gas station so long ago. Her dress had looked like it cost a fortune.

Takeshi shrugged. "We do many things they don't particularly want us to, though we do refer to her as "Duchess" in official documentation and communication with the Rose. Their hold on us is weak, and will break eventually." His gaze was distant.

"Won't the Truth Seekers keep that from happening?" Jamirh asked, ears twitching interestedly.

The Human's eyes refocused on him, once again looking amused. "They can try, but Ni Fon's shinobi are their equal in magic. Their fear tactics will not work on us, and they are not inherently better than us."

Jamirh shook his head. "Truth Seekers don't use magic. They use tech. Really, really advanced tech."

"I can assure you, they use magic," Takeshi corrected him dryly. "I am not sure if they also use tech, but I observed a significant amount of magic in my short stay south of the Wall."

Jamirh stared at him. "But... but the Empire doesn't use magic. They don't even have magic."

Takeshi shook his head slowly. "That is most definitely a lie. From what I saw, I would say the Rose Empire suppresses knowledge of magic, which then suppresses the expression of magic in the general populace, and reserves the use of magic for its elite forces. Tech is merely a smokescreen. I imagine that if one does not believe magic exists, it is fairly easy to explain it away as 'advanced tech,' especially if that is what they expect."

Jamirh thought back to the few encounters with Truth Seekers he had experienced while fleeing to Romanii. They hadn't done anything he would call magical, but then, they hadn't had time to. He had gone out of his way in Lyndiniam to avoid them, so he had never seen them do anything there, either. Did they really use magic? Hel had mentioned that the Truth Seekers "scanned" when looking for something; had she meant with magic? Jamirh had assumed tech.

Which, he guessed, sort of proved Takeshi's point.

It occurred to Jamirh suddenly that he was likely to have to fight them, too. How the hell was he supposed to fight people with magic? He didn't think the Blade would do anything special to help against normal magic people. The more he thought about this situation, the worse it got. He felt his ears droop.

"It's not surprising you were fooled," Takeshi tried to reassure him, apparently misinterpreting why he was upset. "I'm not sure how the Rose started its campaign of 'there is no magic,' but you can't deny it's been successful. Collective disbelief on that level... I am actually more surprised there are people who are able to become Truth Seekers at all. How does one become a Truth Seeker, do you know?"

"I can't say I've ever really thought about it," Jamirh murmured, still caught up in the realization he would have to fight them too. "They are all Humans, so it's not like there was ever an opportunity to look into."

Takeshi hummed thoughtfully. "Interesting."

"Is it?"

Takeshi nodded. "On the whole, Avari tend more towards mage abilities. Yet only Humans are members of their elite mage unit?"

"Well," Jamirh started, trying to figure out if Takeshi really didn't know, "Avari aren't put in positions of power. I don't even think there are any Avari in the Guard, never mind the military."

"No, no, I saw that." Takeshi waved it off, continuing, "Where are the Avari with mage potential going? Statistically, there are likely to be more of them, even with the suppression policies in place."

Jamirh's stomach dropped as he was reminded of the bionic Abomination that had attacked him. His hand clenched around his key. "It's not uncommon for Avari to just go missing. And we think they are being turned into bionic constructs, like the one that killed Hel."

Takeshi was silent for several long moments. "That fits, unfortunately," he finally said. He sounded disturbed, and Jitsu pried herself away from Jamirh to go rub up against him. "How many of them exist, then?"

Jamirh shuddered. "That is something I try very hard not to think about."

"Jamirh, I'm back!"

They all turned to see Jeri approaching, holding two cups filled with a bright-red liquid. Since the accident, she'd been trying to make it up to him by waiting on him hand and foot – at least as much as Jamirh would let her. It made him uncomfortable. He didn't know how to tell her that what he really wanted was some space. He understood that she felt guilty, but it was really beginning to feel like she thought he was helpless.

The Vampire took in the addition of Takeshi and Jitsu curiously. "Hello," she greeted them.

"Hello," Takeshi responded.

"Jeri, this is Takeshi, the Human who tried to save Hel," Jamirh introduced him. "Takeshi, this is Jeri."

Takeshi raised an eyebrow. "*The* Jeri?"

"Yup," Jamirh answered blandly.

Jeri flushed, and her eyes found Jamirh's sling. Jitsu made a soft woof.

"And this is his warg, Jitsu," Jamirh added, rolling his eyes.

"It is nice to meet you." Takeshi inclined his head as Jitsu wagged her tail violently.

"Likewise," she answered, not meeting his eyes. She bit her lip, then handed one of the cups to Jamirh. "You'll like that; it's both fizzy and fruity."

Jamirh took the cup carefully in his good hand. "Thanks." He took a sip. "Oooh, this is good!"

Jeri smiled weakly as she looked around, taking in the few people still in the courtyard. "I see the concert is over," she commented. "What did you think of it?"

"Also very good," Jamirh stated, taking another sip. "Different from the concerts back in the Empire, but still good."

Takeshi hummed. "I saw pieces of a concert while I was in Charve – some sort of Avari fundraiser concert? It was much flashier than this, but I prefer the skilled use of Voice that the Bard showed. She is very talented."

Jeri nodded. "Caelessa is a master of her art. We are lucky she chooses to grace us with her Voice, and not another city. Does Ni Fon have bards?"

"We do have those who use Voice to perform, but our music can be... more eerie, I think one diplomat put it. And there is less repetition than in what I have heard since crossing the sea," Takeshi explained. "Our instruments are different, and our bards reflect that in their Voices."

"Eerie?" Jamirh asked. "That sounds interesting."

"Perhaps we have some recordings in the archives, but they would be very old," Jeri mused. "We have not had contact with your people for some time, I'm afraid."

Takeshi simply inclined his head again.

Jamirh found himself eyeing the sword on Takeshi's hip again, and felt the beginnings of a plan start to form. The Human had said the katana was like a longsword, after all. But he'd have to consider how best to approach it.

I think it's a great idea.

"Well," Jamirh said slowly, taking another sip of his beverage, "I think it's almost dinnertime. Who wants to eat?"

Rhode didn't actually have many leads, despite what Hel had told him about traces of her being "everywhere."

It was difficult to even know what that really meant. Rhode had run searches for Avari matching her description, but while there were a few in the Empire matching her colors, ages or genders did not match. They could find no trace of her existence before she had broken out of prison. Her name didn't come up in any of the databases either, though Rhode would put money on it being a fake name anyway.

He studied the small statue centered on the altar in the alcove. It was old, most of its features having been worn away over time, but it was definitely the form of a woman with long hair in a flowing dress holding a staff. It could be any woman, given the utter lack of detail. There wasn't even any color to the damn thing.

He had asked one of the priests who tended the Temple for any information, but she had claimed that Hades' shrine was maintained more out of tradition than anything else, and she hadn't known anything about what the goddess's religion might be like. There had never been a priest of Hades who served at this temple. She couldn't even think of a place that housed a priest of Hades.

He sighed, turning away. Perhaps the archives would have more information about Hades and her followers. Cole might be able to help him there; she was very good at ferreting out information.

"If I may, sir."

Rhode glanced at Madine. "What is it?"

The Truth Seeker's face was as expressionless as always. "The last known location of one of Hades' clergy was in the Nyphoren Islands, some two hundred years ago."

He turned to face her more fully. "What? How do you know that?"

"The Truth Seeker who met her died," Madine answered blandly. "However, he informed the rest of us before he was ended."

That was... interesting. Rhode hummed speculatively. "The Nyphoren Islands, hm?" It was two hundred years out of date, but perhaps something might still be there. The Truth Seeker had died; that meant the priest had probably survived. Perhaps that was where the cult was centered.

It was the best lead he had. He had to find out what the Avari was. She was the key to everything; he just knew it.

Chapter Thirteen

Ander was finishing up the list of supplies he was going to need when he heard the knock. "Just a moment," he called as the door swung open anyway. He sighed in mild annoyance as Jak strode in. "I said a moment."

"If I wait a moment, one will become two, which will become five, then ten, and next thing you know I've been out there all night waiting for you." Jak's voice was dry. "We are eating now. You can get back to... whatever *this* is after." He gestured to the multitude of papers in varying sizes and colors covering nearly every available surface. "Actually, what *is* this? You don't normally allow your office to become this much of a disaster. Not with paper, anyway."

"It's not a disaster. This is organization," Ander protested. "I needed to review and consolidate a selection of notes from some time ago into a more easily referenced format."

Jak eyed him, then looked around the room again. "Uh huh." A pause. "Where I'm from, we call this 'a disaster.' Let's go before I have to drag you out of that chair; I'm hungry."

Ander shot the older priest another annoyed glare as he purposefully wrote the last two ingredients on his list before primly putting the pen down. "It's only a disaster if you don't understand what you are looking at," he pointed out. "This is perfectly organized from my perspective."

"Let's split the difference, then. It's organized chaos," Jak snorted. "*Food*. Let's move it." He waved impatiently at the door.

Ander stifled a sigh as he smoothly stood from his chair. He swiftly returned the notes of his experiments with chemical compositions to one neat pile, aware Jak was not patient enough to let him file them properly, before stalking out of his lab. He waited for Jak to exit behind him before shutting the door and casting a quick locking spell, array integrating itself into the door.

Jak took the lead, heading to the stairs around the back of the sanctuary that led to the private apartments of the order. It was a little strange, Ander mused, to share the space with another person after all this time. Though rooms were assigned to each of Hades' priests for when they were in Tarvishte, he usually had the run of the whole building to himself. Jak's presence shook that, and most of his routines, up. Like now, when the older priest interrupted his work for dinner of all things. Honestly, the food could wait.

:It can, but sometimes you do have it wait a hair too long,: Hades pointed out mildly. *:For all that you've been on Takeshi's case about eating, you could stand to remember that you also need consistent meals.:*

:Our situations are completely different. I do not drive myself past the brink of magicore exhaustion; I occasionally skip a meal when my attention is better served on my research. You cannot compare the two,: Ander protested.

He felt Her amusement. *:"Occasionally"? Is that how we are defining multiple times a week now?:*

Ander rolled his eyes. *:I am not going to be lectured on how and when to eat by an incorporeal personality that has never had to.:*

:I did have to eat to some degree while inhabiting the avatar,: She corrected him. *:And I've watched people eat for millennia. And I talk to Vlad occasionally. Your eating habits are not what most people would describe as ideal.:*

He decided to ignore Her, glancing instead at the large aquarium in the sitting room as he passed. The fish looked fine, patiently awaiting their next feeding in a few hours. Content that particular experiment was going well, he followed Jak to the kitchen. Dinner had been delivered and set up on the small dining table, with two places set. "I see it's just us today. Again."

The older priest nodded. "Mhm. I'll make a more explicit invitation within the next few days. But it's not a bad thing that he's trying to find a place for himself in the palace, either. We have time."

Ander considered that. "I don't believe my situation was this complicated."

"Not even remotely. You got here and were basically like, 'Where do I set up?', according to Vlad," Jak chuckled.

That wasn't entirely accurate and Jak knew it, but Ander didn't like to think about it. He had eventually made the best of a bad situation. He found himself gazing back towards the fish tank.

"But then, you had already made your Choice. He hasn't."

Ander's Choice had been an easy one, he supposed. Literally the difference between life and death, and even though he had never seen

Alice again, at least he knew she and Fredrik had survived that night. *:We can save her,:* had been Hades' first words to him as he had tried desperately to stop the bleeding–

He shook his head to free himself from the memory. That time was long gone, and there was no point in dwelling on it anymore. He was the only person who still remained from that night. And Hades, he amended, feeling her fierce love and affection for him. And on that note... "Has he been talking to you any more, Lady?" he asked as he took his place at the table.

There was a thoughtful hum. *:He responds to me when I reach out, but he almost never initiates the contact himself. And he keeps me at arm's length,:* She added, having noticed the bent of Ander's question. *:He has not truly let me in, but few of you did so until the Choice had been made.:*

Jak snorted but didn't add anything.

Ander looked at him uncertainly. "This is typical, then?" Takeshi was the first new priest since Ander himself. He wasn't actually sure how the process worked from this end.

"There has been a grand total of eleven of us over thousands of years, coming from a variety of backgrounds and catastrophes. I'm not sure there is such a thing as 'typical,'" Jak said wryly as he started to eat.

:Yes, all of you have been very unique,: Hades agreed cheerfully. *:Keeps an incorporeal personality on her toes, you know?:*

Ander ignored Jak's raised eyebrow. "The warg at least seems like a good sign."

"He does seem to have taken to her very quickly," Jak agreed. "And he's stuck with her no matter what, so that's probably for the best."

"I think he'll stay, even if he doesn't Choose to serve Hades," Ander mused after considering the situation. "From my conversations with him, he seems to have found purpose in helping Jamirh figure out his inherent, of all things."

Hades was silent. Strange; he would have expected a comment of some sort.

Jak winced. "Ah, yes... Jamirh."

Ander glanced at him in surprise, waiting for him to elaborate.

"Is this... hm. Well. How are you doing?"

He blinked. "What?"

Jak shrugged. "I wasn't exactly around at the time, but I know what you went through to bring us that Blade."

Bringing them the Blade had been entirely incidental, and Ander was glad to be rid of it. "And?"

"Well, it's just... from everything that I've heard, Jamirh's very reluctant to be what he needs to be to survive this. He's supposed to literally be some sort of magical combat expert, but he broke his arm in a training accident, which is – let's admit it – not a good look. If he does actually have the inherent, then he has no control over it, which in a practical sense is nearly the same as not having it." Jak gestured in the air with his fork. "And to make matters worse, he's on an accelerated timeline, since he's late to the show. The Abomination has a forty-year lead. And the broken arm has stopped any progress he was making."

Ander waited for him to get to the point.

"I don't think many people would blame you if you were... ah... upset with Jamirh, I guess," Jak finished.

Oh. Oh no. Jak wanted to have... what, a heart to heart? Absolutely not. "It's up to him to figure his own shit out," he snapped, trying to keep the agitation out of his voice. "How I feel about him does not matter one way or the other."

"Well, no, it doesn't, but I'm asking for you, not Jamirh." Jak shrugged. "Mara told me–"

"Mara is not here right now," Ander said hurriedly. "And she doesn't need to be," he added as he felt Hades' attention begin to drift in that direction. This was exactly the sort of well-meaning nonsense he liked to avoid. He did not want to talk about himself. "I am fine."

Jak eyed him. "It would be okay if you weren't."

"But I am." Or he would be, as soon as Jak dropped the topic. His scar was beginning to itch. "Our current problems have just as much to do with a lack of information as they do with Jamirh's... situation. The previous Ebryn attempt apparently didn't work out. If we knew how, and why, we might be in a better position now, but we are not."

Jak pressed his lips together for a moment, but thankfully moved on. "And when you tried to speak with him, he just... refused? Did he seem angry?"

Ander shrugged. "He didn't seem angry, no. He seemed... distant. As though his attention were elsewhere, and I were a distraction, perhaps. A distraction he was content to ignore."

There was silence while they both considered that. "Anything you want to add to that?" Jak asked finally.

Hades said nothing.

Jak sighed. "Not much we can do about that now that Jamirh exists." He took a bite of his stuffed cabbage. "Hey, is the Vampire going to keep training him?"

"Jeri? I have no idea, but I would guess so. Why?"

"You were able to teach yourself magic. Maybe you... could..." He trailed off at the withering look Ander sent him.

"No." Yet another thing he wasn't going to entertain. "I taught myself learned magic. I do not have an inherent. They are completely different."

:'Completely' might be taking it a little far,: Hades mused.

"The point stands. What I did – which was read a book, by the way – won't work for whatever Jamirh's problem is." Why was Jak so invested in Ander's involvement in this? "It sounds like Takeshi is working on that anyway. I have other things to do."

"So you *are* upset with Jamirh," Jak declared.

"*No,* I am not. There just isn't a reason for me to be involved," Ander tried to explain, exasperated. "He has the Blade. What he needs now other people are better equipped to provide for him."

Jak raised an eyebrow. "Jeri broke his arm."

Ander refrained from throwing his hands in the air. "Because Jamirh tried something stupid, which isn't that uncommon with amateurs. Training accidents happen. He'll get over it."

"From what I understand, this isn't going to help him figure out his inherent, though," Jak argued.

"And I'm sure Takeshi has already considered that." Ander glared at his plate.

:Probably. There's not a lot Takeshi hasn't considered regarding Jamirh's ability from what I can tell. He's very thorough.:

That was more than enough for Ander. "See? He'll be in great hands. We know it can be very difficult to learn how to effectively utilize magic as an adult. This is well-documented."

"But you managed it."

"It's not the same thing," he repeated. Why must the conversation continue to move in circles? "My situation is not applicable to Jamirh's. Takeshi is – according to the Lady – already working on the problem. Perhaps the Nifoni are more familiar with overcoming this sort of situation?"

:The Nifoni are pro-magic, so that seems unlikely. But perhaps,: Hades conceded. *:Takeshi certainly seems to think about the hows and whys of Jamirh's inherent more than most.:*

"That's probably better than thinking about the Kobayashi girl." Brown eyes regarded Ander carefully. "Does he know you spoke with her?"

:I told him, yes,: Hades admitted. *:He asked. It was important to him to know that she had not become restless dead.:*

Excellent. "Did he show any interest in talking to her himself?"

There was a pause as Hades considered the question. *:Not explicitly, no,:* She finally responded. *:I think it might be something he is interested in, but he did not ask me directly. I just got the impression he still had something he wanted to ask her.:*

"We should offer that," Jak stated. "Whatever his Choice may be, that we can make happen, if it is that important to him."

Ander was surprised that was on the table, especially considering that the decision to speak was ultimately up to the dead. "And if she refuses to speak with him?"

:That is unlikely to be a concern,: came the firm response.

Jak nodded. "Great. We can work on that too, then." Ander felt a moment of dread at the look Jak gave him, but the older priest only asked, "In the meantime, have you made any progress on that chip?"

Ander shook his head, relieved and on stronger footing with this topic. "Since it shorted out, there is little to study. It is a useless collection of metal, filament, and circuits. My best guess is that being in a living being was at least part of what made it Abomination, if not entirely. It's just science now. Unusable and inoffensive tech. And unfortunately, there are few similarities between the microchip and the bionic, aside from the fact that they were both integrated with living beings."

Jak raised one eyebrow. "Did the Avari used to make the bionic count as a living being?"

"Yes," Ander said bluntly. "She was definitely not dead. Not until Vlad made her so."

The older priest shuddered. "It sounds so much worse with the pronoun; thank you for that."

Did it? The Avari had a gender; why did acknowledging that make it worse? Was there room for it to get worse? It was already utterly appalling.

:Agreed,: She whispered to him.

"Is there any information on where they are being… see, if you add the pronoun, 'manufactured' also sounds so much worse." Jak sounded incredibly disgruntled. "And so do all the other options. 'Made'? 'Created'? 'Doomed to eternal suffering'?"

"'Manufactured' is probably the most accurate," Ander stated mildly. Honestly, it was just a word. "And not that I've heard. Vlad is prioritizing finding out, however, so hopefully we will know something soon."

"If they aren't dead, we can't even try to use the Lady," Jak said with a sigh.

:Not that that would get you anywhere, since that would be information belonging to the dead,: Hades interjected dryly.

"But for a good reason," Jak wheedled.

A disapproving silence.

Jak tried to bend the rules often, Ander had noticed. It didn't ever seem to come to anything. Hades would not cross certain lines. Or perhaps it was that she could not. Certainly different rules applied to Her kind than to mortals.

As they finished eating and began to clean up, Jak asked, "What exactly are you doing down there with all that stuff, anyway?"

Ander, who had already been mentally reviewing the next few steps of his project, took a moment to process the question. "I am starting the process of creating a new avatar for the Lady."

He could feel Hades' pleasure at the idea as Jak cocked his head to the side. "Oh? I never got the chance to see the first one, though Hades bragged about it a lot." He paused. "There was a time when such things weren't necessary."

Ander finished packing the serving dishes to be returned to the palace. "The power of the gods wanes in the modern era. If science can be of assistance, then so be it. I am happy to oblige."

Jak seemed to be weighing his next words carefully. "But is now really the time for this?"

Ander shrugged, wary that Jak was going to try to pull Jamirh back into the conversation again. "Until more information becomes available, there is little else to do. I might as well get the process started, since it is likely to take over a decade to complete."

"*Wow*, that takes a while." His eyebrows rose.

"A lot can go wrong." And many things had the first time. Hopefully he had worked those kinks out. "Being very careful can help mitigate that. And there are some steps that require a fair amount of waiting."

Jak shook his head. "Still... the forty-year head start makes me nervous. I'm not sure you all appreciate how bad this could get very, very quickly."

"It's been worse." This, Ander was certain of. Hades had told him. The world was still here.

"I know," Jak said grimly, gaze distant. "I'd like to stop it before it gets to that point."

There wasn't much Ander could say to that.

"Have there been any other lingering symptoms?"

Ander eyed Takeshi, who was sitting on the bed in the examination room. It had been just over a week since he had released the shinobi from the hospital, and on the whole he was much improved.

"No. I feel fine, otherwise," Takeshi answered, shaking his head. "And it's not nearly as bad as it was. More like a chill, rather than a freeze."

Ander hummed, glancing at the warg sitting on the other side of the bed, but she seemed unbothered. He cast another scanning spell, paying especially close attention to where the microchip had been attached to the nervous system, but he could see no damage or anything that would cause the side effect to linger. Takeshi claimed his reserves were still on the low side, but that tracked correctly with the level of magicore exhaustion he had suffered. *:Lady?:* he asked, just to check.

:Not even an echo,: She confirmed. *:I have been paying* very *close attention. It is much easier to tell now that I can reach him clearly:*

So there was nothing left of the Abomination to continue to cause the issue either. That was both good and bad. Good, because he was free of an existential poison; bad, because...

"There is nothing that is causing it," Ander admitted. "It is possible your body tried somehow to adapt to the presence of the Abomination, and if it hasn't gone away by now..." He went to make the note in Takeshi's file.

"Then it is likely permanent," Takeshi finished, sounding strangely resigned to the fact. "It makes sense there would be some sort of lasting manifestation of such a thing, if it is inherently anathema of life itself."

"It is probably permanent, yes," Ander agreed. "It may yet fade with time, but if it has stayed fairly consistent this long after the removal of the microchip that seems unlikely."

"At least it's better than it was. And warmer clothing, Jitsu, and the heating crystals all do help to mitigate the effect." The warg shifted to rest her head next to Takeshi on the bed, looking up at him. He started to pet her. "It is not the end of the world."

There were worse ways to look at it, Ander supposed. "It is something to keep an eye on, though. If it does start to get worse again, let me know." He didn't think it would, but better safe than sorry.

Takeshi nodded his agreement.

"Then you are free to go. I don't think we need to schedule another appointment, though you know how to reach me if you need to." Ander finished the note he was writing and closed the file, pausing when he noticed Takeshi hadn't moved. "Was there anything else?"

The other man hesitated, then asked, "Do you have time to answer some questions?"

Ander blinked. "About?"

He could almost feel Hades' sigh of exasperation as Takeshi answered. "About Hades, and her priesthood."

Oh, of course. He didn't bother asking why Takeshi didn't ask Hades; Her answers were sometimes evasive or confusing in their own right. He briefly thought back to his conversation with Jak the night before and decided this was a good sign. "If you'd like, though we don't need to have this conversation here. You can follow me back to my office." He still needed a few more things from his notes in order to start the process of creating another avatar.

Takeshi nodded, standing to follow Ander out. Jitsu cleared the bed with one hop to join them.

"What did you wish to know?" Ander asked as they headed into the hallway, the warg's massive frame taking up much of the space.

"I have been unable to determine what it is, exactly, the priests of Hades are supposed to do," Takeshi admitted, sounding puzzled. "And I have yet to meet any others besides Jak and yourself, and you both appear to serve very different functions. If Jitsu is to be believed, you are the only priest usually in residence in the city?"

Ander felt his mouth twist in wry amusement. What did they do? "If you find out what our purpose is, you will have to let the rest of us know. I'm not sure even Hades has thought that much about Her own clergy." He got the impression of a shrug from the deity in question. "As a result, we more or less do whatever we wish. And yes, I am usually the only priest present in Tarvishte."

They walked in silence for several minutes as Takeshi digested that. When they reached the outside of the hospital, he asked, "How many of you are there, at present?"

"Eight, currently." The number was painfully small, especially considering how long they tended to live. "There have been eleven in total."

Takeshi squinted at him, as though he were trying to parse that. "Eight right now? And eleven... in recent years?"

"Oh, no. Eleven total. Since the beginning of time." It was hard to believe, Ander had to give him that. "It's a very exclusive club," he added, amused.

"Eleven," Takeshi repeated faintly. "This explains much."

Ander shrugged. "It is what it is. Very few are called to Her service, and She will not settle for anything less than a true vocation. And when She finds it, She doesn't tend to let it go easily."

:Well, there are so few of you to begin with.:

Takeshi glanced around as they entered the Temple. "If there are only eight of you, why do you all not stay here? There seems to be plenty of room."

"That is part of the 'doing whatever we wish' bit. The others simply choose to live elsewhere or travel. They stop in on occasion, but it is fairly rare. I imagine that if you Choose to join they will make more of an effort to do so over the next decade or so to meet you." Which meant his peace and quiet would be touch and go for a while, unfortunately. Would Mara or Siva make it back first?

"But Jak is here now? I gather that you are a healer, and some sort of scientist, but his function remains a complete mystery to me." He still sounded like he was trying to make sense of it.

"Jak usually makes it a point to swing by every century or so, and he doesn't tend to stay long. He likes to travel. I didn't actually meet him until I had been here for five years." Ander considered the question. How to best explain what Jak did? "Jak is the first of us. Perhaps there were others who were called before, but Jak is the first who answered. He and Hades worked together to create the religion. As a result, he generally manages the rest of us from a distance. And by 'manages,' I mean he travels around and checks in on us on occasion. I am unsure how he spends his time outside of that. You, stay out here." He aimed that at the warg, who sneezed dismissively.

They entered his office, sans Jitsu. Takeshi's mask hid most of his expression, but Ander could see his eyes dart over the room, taking in the papers pinned and taped to various surfaces. "So then, it seems to me that the priests of Hades deal with being priests of Hades by ignoring that status almost completely?"

"Well, there is the addition of hearing Her, and there are some general expectations. If you come across any of the restless dead, you would be expected to put them to rest, for example. But Hades knows any ritual or duty you might be required to perform and will let you know should you come across such a situation. Additional duties would be up to you. Since I reside here, I usually help manage any festivals in Her name, but that is by my own choice." He sat at his desk. "Actually, where you choose to live will also be up to you, though I would recommend staying nearby for the first few years just in case of any oddities."

Takeshi had moved so that he was in the position farthest from any paper. "Could you define 'oddities'?"

"Probably not, honestly," Ander said with a grimace. "Anything strange will probably be based on what you choose to do. You have only been here for a few weeks, most of which you spent in the hospital. No one expects you to know what that is yet, goddess or no goddess."

The shinobi shifted slightly. "You chose... medicine, and research? How long did it take you to decide?"

Ander blinked. "That was merely a continuation of what I was already doing in Elbe. I was good at medicine, good at science, and had already earned my degree. When I was forced to leave it behind, I simply tried to recreate the position I desired. With some added religious duties, since to me it seemed strange to have none." Especially given what She had done for him.

"You were forced to leave Elbe?" Takeshi asked. Ander could hear the frown in his voice.

Ander hesitated. "Most priests find the call to Hades in some sort of catastrophe. When the dust settles, few are welcome to return to the lives we had, no matter what good or bad we may have wrought."

And sometimes, it was the good that tipped the scales out of their favor. He had healed Alice *after* she had died. He had known even as he did it he would never be welcome there again, that his presence would make her and Fredrik targets. Magic wasn't supposed to exist, after all.

He would do it again if given the choice.

Takeshi hummed thoughtfully. "I see. My being unable to return home is thus more the rule than the exception."

"Give it a few hundred years if you wish to return. They will forget the face, if not the name. The one thing we have on our side is time," Ander advised. "You will outlive those who would bar your presence, and the memories of mortals are short."

The other man tilted his head to the side. "Did you ever return home?"

Ander shook his head. "There was no point." He could feel Hades' sorrow on his behalf, but he spoke true. Nothing had bound him to Elbe in centuries. He doubted he ever would return, but there was no need to share that. And seeing how twitchy Jamirh was made him think the Empire really had not become a better place to live in the intervening time.

"What a picture you paint," Takeshi said dryly. He glanced around the room again. "I'm not really sure if you are trying to sell me on this or not."

Ander shrugged. "*You* have to make the Choice. I can only offer you facts. Do we need more priests? Probably; we are a religious order so small it is practically pathetic. But that's not something that is going to change overnight no matter what you decide, and our faith is based on the tenet of choice. Trying to trick, coerce, or otherwise influence your decision would be sacrilege. Even if you do Choose to become a priest, She will not dictate what you should do with your life – all you are really agreeing to is letting Hades be part of it. Oh, She'll make suggestions," he added, seeing the look of disbelief on Takeshi's face despite the mask, "but in the end, what you choose to do is up to you."

:I'm not even entirely sure why I bother with the suggestions, when you all carry them out only like ten percent of the time,: the Goddess grumbled. *:One would think the advice of an ancient being such as myself would be treated with more respect.:*

:I'm sure that percentage is higher,: he disagreed, before considering how many times he did, in fact, ignore Her. *:Or maybe not. Have you tried giving better advice?:*

She sniffed at him in a huff.

Takeshi's eyes were unfocused, leading Ander to believe She was having a different conversation with him. He glanced over the notes on his desk, starting another to-do list while he waited.

"I see," Takeshi stated finally. Ander brought his attention back to him. "This explained some things and muddied others. I have... much to think about. Thank you for your time."

Ander inclined his head. "It is both simpler and more complicated than one might expect. Take your time; this is not a decision you need to rush."

Takeshi stepped carefully to the exit, where Jitsu was lying across the threshold like a furry half-door. She stood as Takeshi approached, backing up so he could pass her. He paused. "Thank you," he said sincerely, and then both he and the white warg were gone.

Ander realized belatedly he probably should have reinforced Jak's dinner invitation. *:What do you think?:* he asked Hades.

He got something like a shrug in response. *:It will be what it will be. He has made no hard decision yet, and isn't really leaning in any direction, either. He seems a little bemused by all the emphasis on choice.:* Which was, in turn, probably confusing Her.

Well, Ander had done what he could. It was up to Takeshi himself now.

Chapter Fourteen

J amirh realized Ebryn had lived a thousand years ago, but he wouldn't have thought information about that time would be so sparse in a nation ruled by people who didn't die.

To be fair, there were plenty of documents and even some people willing to talk about that period, but there was frustratingly little to find about the one person he was trying to research. Ebryn had not spent a lot of time in Romanii, it turned out – he had only been to Tarvishte twice, and even then only briefly. His life before the debacle with the evil wizard was practically unknown other than that he had been living somewhere in northern Agale. The quest itself had taken a little over a year. There were a number of stories about the things he'd done as he traveled around the globe collecting the crystal lights and forging the Blade, but Jamirh wasn't sure how much was fact and how much was fiction. Some of the stories even flat-out contradicted each other. There was absolutely nothing about what had become of him after killing the wizard and setting Queen Saran back on her throne.

Ebryn was beginning to seem like he had been a ghost even in life. None of the information Jamirh managed to hunt down came from his predecessor directly. Apparently he had been very focused on his task and not interested in talking about himself. Perhaps the only person he might have been close to was Sukra, the Aradian who had followed him for most of his journey.

Jamirh was starting to get annoyed. If Ebryn – and by extension, he himself – was supposed to be so important, what were these people doing? Ebryn was so important that no one knew anything? He kept trying to work that out, but it didn't make sense. It was like everyone was only pretending to care about the disaster, content to wait for Jamirh to solve it for them.

Which was why Jamirh found himself and Jeri sitting at a garden table across from Miravu, the Aradian ambassador to Romanii. He'd wanted to come by himself, but Jeri had insisted on accompanying him, and in the end he didn't have a good reason for her not to be there.

He just wished she'd give him some space.

The ambassador's violet hair was in a thick braid over her shoulder, and the dark pigmentation of the skin around her eyes made it look as though she wore a decorative mask. The blue and green colors of her eyes flickered like flames behind glass as she regarded him with interest.

"So then, you wish to learn what Avhad Sukra taught her House of Ebryn of Storms and Light," she stated pensively after Jamirh had explained the situation. "I will share this knowledge freely, but I am uncertain if it is what you are looking for."

"Honestly, any information is better than what we've managed to find so far," Jeri sighed. "I met them both, but I was very young at the time and that situation is not relevant to what Jamirh is looking for. Even the other Vampires who met him don't have any information concerning how he used his ability. No one even knew he had one until you told Jamirh; everyone just thought he was an exceptional swordsman."

Miravu hummed thoughtfully, the flames in her eyes banking to smoldering coals. "Where to begin, then? I suppose the story for us begins with Avhad Sukra long before she was Avhad of the House of Blood, when she was a young Hunter looking to make something of herself. Occasionally, a Hunter will feel that the call of their destiny lies beyond the sands of Dalmara, and seek their glory on the other continents before returning home a Warrior. Avhad Sukra was one such Hunter. She traveled to Espon, and after some time heard rumors of a sorcerer wishing to summon demons. Demon summoning is dark magic, forbidden magic, and it was in this the young Hunter found her calling. She would bring an end to this expression of the forbidden and return home victorious.

"She tracked the sorcerer inland across the continent, hoping to bring about his end before he was successful. The Hunter discovered she was too late when she came upon a young Avari fighting three demons on his own. Demons are... tricky to kill, yes? Very resilient, able to shake off the loss of limbs or other significant damage. Fire is the easiest way to destroy them, though other destructive magics can be effective as well. They are also competent fighters, and many have wings, making them extremely difficult for a non-mage to fight." Miravu paused. "The Hunter was surprised to find that the Avari was managing quite well against the three demons even though he lacked fire, hacking them to pieces until there was nothing left that could rise. She added her flames to his carnage, and so did the Hunter meet he who would become of Storms and Light."

Jamirh found himself wondering if it was just an Aradian thing to refer to everyone by titles instead of names, or if the fact that Ebryn and Sukra were heroes demanded that they have special titles.

Miravu was continuing. "The Hunter spoke with the Avari and discovered they hunted the same quarry. The sorcerer had taken the swordsman's sister and sacrificed her to achieve his dark purpose. He was thus committed to ending the sorcerer himself. The Hunter decided that two would have higher chances of success than one and joined her journey to the Avari's. It did not take her long to determine that the swordsman was a Master of Blades."

The Ambassador was regarding Jamirh carefully, flames flickering in her eyes. "As I have said before, the ability is most common among the Aradians, so we are the best at identifying it. The Hunter soon realized that the swordsman's skills grew exponentially when he saw her fight, and asked him about it. He did not seem to have any answers – he simply said he had always been a fair hand at picking up skills with a blade – and to her disappointment was completely uninterested in developing or exploring his ability any further. For the remainder of their time together, the Hunter would often try to convince the swordsman to branch out and utilize his gift to its fullest, but by her own account he just was not interested.

"And so you ask me how Ebryn of Storms and Light used his ability. The answer is tricky, because while he used it, he did not *utilize* it. According to Avhad Sukra, he probably used it unconsciously for the entirety of his life, learning how to wield the longsword faster and better than other students of the blade, but that was all. I'm not even sure he truly believed her when she told him he had an inherent ability, even though Masters of Blades are often able to pick up techniques at unbelievable speeds. He preferred to believe he was merely a good swordsman." Miravu brought her hands together in front of her as she finished.

Jamirh understood not wanting to be special. Miravu had already told him that Ebryn had not taken advantage of his ability, but still... "So he was likely using it before he knew about it?" he asked, just to clarify.

Miravu inclined her head gracefully. "It is thus with many inherent abilities."

"Usually, the parents are able to identify the signs when their children are very young," Jeri explained. "Many inherents tend to be more common among certain races or even geographical locations, so there is usually an understanding of which inherent it is. If the signs are missed, either because they are too subtle or because the parents or the community doesn't know what they are seeing, the inherent can go unnoticed, though that doesn't mean it goes unused."

"But then how does that work?" Jamirh asked, frustrated. He felt his ears sink. "How do you use an ability you don't know you have?"

Miravu shrugged. "We do many things without thinking of them. Rarely do you think of breathing, though you do so without being taught. You know how to sleep, and how to dream, without being taught. And the young are often known for speaking without thinking, as well," she added, an amused twist to her lips.

Jamirh ignored that last bit. "But then how do I start using an ability that I've never noticed before? If it is supposed to be innate, why am I not innately doing it?"

"But you can't say that, either," Jeri protested. "You've definitely used it – with the knives at the Festival of Night, and turning Ander's own attack back at him during training. And against the bionic, you said?"

He shrugged. "I don't know how else I could have survived. And I moved... fast. Much faster than I'd have thought possible."

And... there had been that other voice, as well.

Miravu was looking at him curiously. "It is extremely unlikely that the ability manifested itself for the first time a month or so ago. It is much more likely you have used it in some capacity before, even if you didn't realize it."

Jamirh shook his head glumly. "Even if that's true, it doesn't really help me. Using it without knowing I used it in the past doesn't explain how to use it on purpose in the future. And trying to figure it out through trial and error doesn't seem to be working, either." He looked down at his arm, still in a sling.

The Aradian's head tilted. "An unfortunate accident indeed. How does your arm fare?"

He shrugged again, glancing at Jeri, whose face had flushed at the reminder. "I'm told it's not as bad as it could be, but it feels like it's taking forever."

"Bone needs time to knit back together," Miravu chided gently. "This is not something you can rush."

"Well, it is," Jeri muttered with a sigh, "it's just not normally a good idea."

"I will amend – it is not something you *should* rush, no?" The Ambassador chuckled. "Vlad has told me the decision was made to heal it quickly, however."

Jamirh picked at a bit of fuzz on the sling, eyes narrowing at it in displeasure. "It seemed like the best option at the time. I think if I had to pick again I might choose 'heal me now,' consequences be damned. This has been a horrible experience. I hate that everything is, like, seventy percent more difficult now, and I can't wait to have full use of my arm again."

Jeri shot him a concerned look. "Will it be *fully* healed in two weeks? Or just enough to be free of the sling?"

He looked at her in horror at the thought he might have to wait longer. "I thought it was supposed to be fully healed at that point? Because they want me to be able to train as soon as possible?"

"Just checking," she said quickly. "I wasn't sure what Ander and Marcus had in mind. This is a very unusual method of dealing with a broken bone."

"Because it can weaken the arm," Jamirh concluded. "Yeah, they explained that too. But if I had to wait four months to start using my arm again, I think I'd go insane."

Miravu smiled. "Masters of Blades are not often injured, but they do fall to stir-craze easily when they are restricted in movement."

"Great." Jamirh heaved a huge sigh. "At least I'm doing one thing correctly."

Jamirh was a bit dispirited as he and Jeri wandered into the palace's main dining room for lunch. His conversation with Miravu had been enlightening in some ways, but it had left him without the most important answer – how to actually use his ability. Not even the promise of food was cheering him up. His ears felt like they were in a permanent wilt.

To some degree, he supposed it was good news. It looked like Ebryn had managed just fine without understanding his ability, so maybe there was hope in that sense for Jamirh. Then again, Ebryn had been able to swing a sword without causing massive harm to himself, and Jamirh couldn't say the same. Maybe having trained to use a sword for most of his life was the thing that Jamirh was missing. But if that was the case, where did that leave him? He couldn't go back in time and study swordsmanship. That ship had long since sailed.

He pushed his food around on his plate, not even hungry, ignoring the concerned looks Jeri kept shooting him.

"May we sit with you?"

Jamirh looked up and nearly flinched back as he realized how close a warg had gotten to his food, black nose sniffing interestedly. Belatedly he recognized Jitsu and Takeshi. "Hey," he said warningly, pulling his food away from her. "That's mine."

Jeri waved to an empty chair. "Be our guest," she answered Takeshi.

His eyes flicked to Jitsu. "I have food for you here; leave his alone." He sounded more amused than anything else.

Jamirh noticed Takeshi did seem to have a ridiculous amount of food on his plate. He considered the warg while still guarding his own. "How much does a dog this size eat, anyway?"

Takeshi shrugged as he slid into the chair. "I'm not entirely sure. If I ask, she tells me I shouldn't worry about it." He placed a few pieces of thinly cut roast beef on the table next to him. Jitsu eyed it hopefully, but did not eat it until Takeshi had pulled his mask down and taken a bite of a sandwich. He put more roast beef on the table. "For what it's worth, I don't think she will actually take anything off your plate without an invitation, but she will let you know if she finds anything interesting."

Jamirh glared at the warg, shifting over to put more space between her and his food. She didn't seem to notice, already looking at Takeshi for more of his.

"The wargs can take care of themselves," Jeri snorted. "Almost anyone will feed them if they ask, so I'm sure they get plenty of food."

Takeshi glanced at Jitsu, then back to Jamirh. "She says if you don't want your lunch, she will eat it for you."

Jamirh angrily took a bite of his sandwich. Emphasis on "his."

"Is everything all right?" Takeshi asked, a little hesitantly. "You were looking despondent when we came over. Is your arm healing well?"

Jamirh blinked, then shrugged. "I guess. I'm supposed to have another healing session later today, and then I'm supposed to be about halfway there. No, I was thinking about the Master of Blades thing again... I spoke with Miravu earlier, but it didn't really help."

Takeshi cocked his head to the side. "Did you ask whether you are supposed to know how to use the techniques you learn, or just memorize the forms?"

Jamirh stared at him blankly for a moment, then dropped his head down to the table in frustration. "Damn it, I forgot!" he all but wailed. "How could I forget!?"

Jeri's voice held a hint of alarm. "What did you forget?"

"Takeshi asked me a really good question in the hospital about my ability, and I didn't know the answer but I thought Miravu might, so I was going to ask her and I forgot!" His ears kept trying to twitch lower.

"Essentially, I was wondering if being a Master of Blades means he picks up when to use techniques as well as the techniques themselves," Takeshi explained. "He said he wasn't struggling with memorizing the individual movements, just using them in a simulated combat situation."

"That's quite a way of saying 'training,'" Jeri said, eyes flickering away. "But... that is a good question. We probably should be using the Ambassador for more information, honestly; she doesn't seem to mind." There was a thoughtful pause while Jamirh considered banging his head against the table. "From an outside perspective, I would say it is supposed to include the 'when' as well as the 'how', at least to some degree. Otherwise, I don't see how he could have effectively turned Ander's attack against him, or how he could have successfully dodged the bionic. Jamirh, it's not like she's gone or you will never speak to her again. She is quite literally on the other side of this room right now."

He raised his head and looked towards the main dais, where Miravu was in fact chatting with Vlad over lunch.

"I also think this is likely," Takeshi agreed. "Jamirh, you said you forgot the practice sword was a stand-in for a bladed weapon, and so you chose a technique that was unwise for the weapon type. But what if you didn't?"

Jamirh pulled his gaze away from the Ambassador and back to Takeshi. "What do you mean?"

"Your ability is untrained, and thus not at its full potential. At that moment, what you had in hand was essentially a stick. And the move you showed me works just fine with a sturdy, non-bladed weapon, at least when the difference in strength is not as severe as it was in your situation."

Jamirh's ears twitched upward slightly. "So it wasn't as dumb as I thought?" *Of course not. It could have been right.*

"I think your ability more or less read the weapon you had on hand, not the weapon it was standing in for, and so you were able to attempt that sort of cross guard – probably successfully, if your teacher had not come at you with full force." Takeshi fed Jitsu a few pieces of cheese. "I think your ability needs to be refined, but I don't think you aren't using it, either."

Jamirh started feeling the first stirrings of hope, before another realization made itself known. "But nothing I try *works*. Miravu says

I shouldn't have to think about it, but then how do I use it without thinking about it? Even if blocking that way did make sense, I still ended up with a broken arm. What's the point if it doesn't help me when I need it?"

Takeshi met his eyes. "Are you sure it hasn't?"

Jeri was looking between the two of them, a look of confusion beginning to give way to understanding.

"What do you mean?" Jamirh asked.

"You said you came from a rough part of Lyndiniam." He waited for Jamirh's confirming nod. "How common were broken limbs, or other severe injuries?"

Jamirh shrugged. "Pretty common, I guess?"

"And how many other people did you know who went twenty or more years without significant injury?"

He opened his mouth to respond, then paused, realizing he wasn't sure. Injuries were very common, to the point where they stopped being anything of note. Someone was almost always nursing some sort of injury. Had anyone else he'd known had his luck?

The realization hit him like a train. It hadn't been luck. *Who is that lucky?*

Jeri's eyes widened. "I *knew* it! I told you that you weren't supposed to be taking hits. What have I told you about dodging?"

"That I should be," he replied by rote, realizing that subconsciously, he had *always* been dodging. At least before the training had started here. Even the little hand-to-hand he knew he had learned mostly to get himself out of situations. "But then... what about the rest of it? Can it work offensively at all, then? Or do I have some specific brand of defensive-only super learning?" This was starting to make his head hurt.

"Unlikely at best."

Jamirh turned to see Ander stroll up to the table, hands tucked into the pockets of his coat. "The most likely theory is just that you've had more reason to dodge problems than confront them."

Takeshi winced. "That's not overly helpful, Ander."

"For real," Jeri muttered. "Also, hello. What have I said about greeting people in a normal manner?"

"No, seriously," Jamirh protested. "How does this work? I am so confused."

"Well–"

"The Rose Empire clearly suppresses knowledge of magic," Takeshi cut Ander off. "Since spell weaving requires study and knowledge in addition to ability and belief, it is possible to put policies in place and take steps that can end the practice over time. However, inherent abilities are much harder to stomp out since they can be used subconsciously. The knowledge of them may eventually be lost, but the abilities themselves occur regardless – magic will find a way. The flashier ones probably result in mysterious deaths or disappearances. For the rest... without the training required to bring out the full potential, the gift likely develops subconsciously in a way that is useful, but that can be explained away as 'being lucky,' or something else mundane. You were never exposed to bladed weapons, so your gift never got the chance to develop in that direction. Instead, you used it defensively to avoid being injured, a far subtler expression of what your ability does than waving a sword about. Belief is a requirement of all magics. *Subconscious* belief works perfectly fine, which is why the knowledge is irrelevant for inherent abilities; if you have always been good at dodging things, you trust in your ability to dodge, and your ability makes it so you begin to gain an uncanny ability to dodge. This feeds back into itself, and eventually it becomes – dare I say – a magical ability to dodge."

Everyone stared at Takeshi, silent.

"So then we know your ability works, and works well," Takeshi continued after a moment. "It is merely a matter of finding the correct angle of thought to get it to work in the desired direction – in this case, offensively, and preferably with a sword, if I've gathered the gist of your previous training correctly."

That was a lot to process. "So then... how do we do that?" Jamirh asked hesitantly, ears raising hopefully. If Takeshi was going to help him figure out how to use his inherent, then maybe he would be willing to teach him how to wield a sword too. He glanced around and was surprised to see Ander looking almost impressed at Takeshi. Jamirh had never seen anyone impress Ander.

"I have a few ideas," Takeshi said mildly. "None of which we should put into practice until your arm is better."

"Which is still at least two weeks away," Ander cut in, "though I'll have a better idea after today's healing session."

"You really came here to collect Jamirh?" Jeri asked, eyebrows rising.

There was an ever-so-slight pause. "Yes," the priest answered.

Jitsu sneezed.

"I promise I am capable of getting him to the hospital," Jeri said, looking stricken.

"Of course, but now you don't have to," he pointed out. "Take a break, or something."

Jamirh shook his head, turning back to Takeshi. He was already not looking forward to the next hour or so. "You'll help, then?" He liked the idea of the Human helping better than anything else he had put up with so far. Takeshi sounded like he knew what he was doing.

"Of course." He sounded almost surprised Jamirh was asking.

Ander's eyes narrowed at Takeshi thoughtfully before the scarred man turned back to Jamirh. He started to say something, then turned back to Takeshi. "Do you like the wargs?" he asked, completely out of nowhere.

Takeshi glanced down at Jitsu, who wagged her tail. He looked back at Ander. "Yes?"

Ander nodded. "Good." He switched his attention back to Jamirh. "Are you finished with lunch?"

Jamirh looked down at his mostly uneaten sandwich. "No?"

Jeri cringed. "At least let him finish eating."

There was a soft woof.

"Jitsu says eating is important," Takeshi translated, voice bland.

Ander rolled his eyes but gestured for Jamirh to continue eating. "Hurry up, then."

Jamirh took another bite of his sandwich. Now that he had started eating, he was actually hungry. Then he was struck by another thought. "Does Hel have any advice? About my ability?"

Takeshi raised an eyebrow, while Ander looked surprised at the question before shaking his head. "The concept of being unable to use magic of any kind is as foreign to Her as the concept of government to a bird."

"That... is a very strange analogy, though I guess it technically works," Jeri mused.

"In several ways, since she doesn't get the analogy either," Takeshi murmured as he sipped at his beverage. "*'Why does a bird have to know about government?'*"

Jamirh recalled that Takeshi could hear Hel too. That was what had prompted that first meeting between himself, Prim, Vlad, Jeri, and Ander – she had been excited that someone could hear her, though at the time Jamirh hadn't realized Hel was Hades or that Takeshi was the Human in question. He wished he could remember more of what they had talked about, but at the time he hadn't understood enough of the context for the information to stick. He remembered that it was rare for someone to hear Hel, but he didn't think anyone had said why, or what it meant. They had been very determined to have Takeshi come to Tarvishte because of it, he remembered, so hopefully it meant the other man would stick around for a while. He was beginning to think Takeshi was his only hope of figuring out how to be a Master of Blades.

"That's the point," Ander said with a sigh. He eyed Jamirh as he neared the end of his sandwich.

Jamirh took the last bite with some regret. He wasn't looking forward to this. The last time they had done this, his arm had been so sore that not even the painkillers seemed to reach deep enough to help. "All right, let's get this over with," he said unhappily as he stood up.

Takeshi smiled as he pulled up his mask. "It won't be that bad. And it will move you one step closer to being able to use your arm again."

"Exactly. Have fun," Jeri suggested with a weak smile. "I'll meet you afterwards in the hospital lobby."

Jitsu wagged her tail at him.

"Yeah, see you later," he said with a wave of his good arm as Ander swept towards the exit without a word, causing him to have to hurry to catch up. Takeshi wasn't wrong, and the sooner his arm healed the sooner they could try the Human's idea.

You could have asked me, some part of him whispered with quiet laughter. He shoved the thought down; he needed outside help for this.

Hopefully this time it would work.

Chapter Fifteen

Takeshi felt much improved from when he had first arrived in Tarvishte almost a month ago. The chill was the only thing that still persisted, and that was easily managed now that a three-hundred-pound magical dog-like creature had decided to attach herself to him. Even his magic reserves were mostly recovered from both the construct's strange attack and having been run so low for so long.

He'd been trying to fill his time by focusing on Jamirh's situation, since he felt that was something he was capable of helping with. However, there was only so much he could do with theory, even if the theory was sound, so he now had to wait for Jamirh's arm to heal before putting theory into practice. He didn't dare try anything before the arm was whole – any failure at all was only going to make the situation worse, so he needed Jamirh to have the best possible set of circumstances for when they began. He was certain he could trick the Avari into the proper mindset, but he had to be careful it wouldn't backfire.

Since he now had to wait for Jamirh to heal, that left him with only one major question to occupy his mind and time – that of Hades, and her clergy, and his future concerning them both.

What was he supposed to do?

It was strange. Those he talked to about it were all very adamant that it was his choice, and they seemed to be going out of their way to avoid accidentally influencing him one way or the other. Ander and Hades had both stressed that it was his decision to make, even though he was fairly certain they wanted him to say yes.

Strangely, even though he saw Jak a fair amount in passing, the oldest priest was very difficult to pin down for a conversation. Takeshi wondered if that had to do with the aversion the other man had towards doing anything even vaguely priest-like, which Ander had alluded to. Jak seemed interested in his well-being, but not in discussing the choice Takeshi was beginning to dread having to make.

He was trying very hard to think back, but he wasn't sure he'd ever really had a say in any choice of this magnitude before. A nominal say, perhaps, but he had always been able to tell when a specific choice was expected, with potentially dire consequences if a different answer was given. There was none of that here. Hades had even gone as far as to say that if he made a choice and didn't like it, he could *change his mind*. At any time. What then was the point of the choice?

And this freedom to do whatever he wanted was leaving him adrift. Everyone emphasized that he needed to make the best choice for himself, but what was that? How could he make a decision when he didn't know? The lack of consequence for the decision was almost making it more difficult to come to a definitive conclusion.

Life in Ni Fon had been so much simpler in this regard. Everything was regulated and ordered and the consequences of actions were clear. There was very little uncertainty.

Takeshi did not like uncertainty.

He was also cognizant enough to realize that he still hadn't really let go of his previous life, for all that he was trying desperately to distract himself from this fact. How could he? It was a part of him, even if it had rejected him. He would never not be shinobi, no matter what he became in the future. It was all he had ever known, and that wasn't something so easily left behind.

Hotaru's ghost also still lingered. There was so much here that reminded him of her, or of something she would have liked. Romanii had succeeded in the thing she had chased for her whole life: a union of tech and magic. It wasn't fair she had never been able to see it. And he still had so many regrets about her death, especially now that he could see the shape of the manipulation that led to it. If only he had paid closer attention... could he have saved her?

He sighed, giving up on meditation for the morning. His thoughts were not cooperating and he'd been doing this long enough to know when it was a lost cause. He pulled the hound-shaped spell crystal from his pocket, looking at it morosely. What should he do?

Jitsu lifted her head off her front paws and looked at him from where she lay sprawled across the couch. Were they not going to do the sitting-thing today?

He shook his head. "No. It's just not the day for it, I guess."

She wagged her tail once, hesitantly. She was glad, because the sitting-thing was boring, but it usually seemed to make her Human feel better. So maybe this wasn't good?

He smiled. "It is helpful, but not essential to my well-being. I will be fine." He paused, eyeing her. "What do you think about me potentially becoming a priest of Hades?"

She snorted. What was there to think about it? He would or he wouldn't, it made no difference to her. Most wargs served the Lady in some capacity, but whether or not Takeshi did was up to him.

Takeshi nearly twitched in frustration. How could no one have an opinion? Surely there was someone who had information that could guide him.

:Takeshi?: Hades' voice interrupted his thoughts.

He took a moment to breathe in deeply and hold it before letting it out slowly. He didn't want to snap at her. *:Yes?:*

:Siva would like to talk to you.:

He tried to remember if that sounded at all familiar, but came up with nothing. *:I'm sorry, who?:*

:Siva is my second high priest. It is she who usually helps new priests get settled. She is currently in Dalmara, however, and is finding it difficult to leave, so she thought she would speak to you through the mirrors,: she explained. *:A long-distance call, so to speak. She could speak to you through me, but she thought that was a little too impersonal.:*

He perked up. Another priest wished to speak to him. Perhaps this one would have clearer answers. *:Through the mirrors?:*

:Yes, yes. Find a mirror, any mirror, and I will link them, and you can speak with Siva,: Hades elaborated cheerfully.

"Why mirrors?" he wondered out loud as he stood, scanning the room. There was an unnecessary mirror above a sideboard; that would do. He strode over to it.

Looking back at him was a tanned Aradian woman with pinkish-orange hair and violet flames tinged with gold dancing in her eyes. The darkened skin around her eyes made it appear almost as though she were wearing a blindfold, one long strip across her face. She looked to be a little older than Takeshi – or perhaps quite a bit older, considering Aradians had three times the lifespan of Humans. Darkly painted lips smiled at him.

"There are many traditions involving the dead and mirrors," she explained. "Some say they have the power to trap spirits and prevent them from passing on. Others say that mirrors have a way of reflecting what is true, and so if you wish to see a ghost that doesn't want you to, a mirror will reveal the presence regardless. Still others say mirrors are a passageway to the land of the dead. So many beliefs linking death and mirrors link the Lady Herself and mirrors, regardless if they were true to begin with or not, and so here we are."

Takeshi regarded her thoughtfully. It was the sort of thing he would expect a priest of the Silent Goddess to know. Ander had been fairly noncommittal about things the priests were supposed to know and do, saying Hades would let Takeshi know if something came up, but surely there was basic information he should know. Most religions had texts their priests studied. How was he supposed to learn these things? The other priests were scattered to the four winds for the most part, so learning from them seemed unlikely. Surely the goddess herself had better things to do with her time than answer such questions. "Are any of them true now?"

"In those places where a particular belief is strongest it holds true. We, and the Lady Herself, usually utilize them to communicate, as you and I are now. I greet you, Shuurai Takeshi. I am Siva of the House of Shadows, second high priest of the goddess Hades." She bowed her head in greeting, and Takeshi noticed small white blossoms poorly woven into her hair.

"Well met," he responded formally, returning the bow.

Jitsu wandered over, standing so she could rest her paws on the sideboard, and peered at the mirror curiously. Her tail gave a cheerful wave. Another priest!

"I apologize for being unable to come see you in person, but I have duties that will keep me here for the near future. I would have simply waited for them to resolve and then traveled to Tarvishte, but the Lady tells me you are struggling, so I thought it best to have this conversation sooner rather than later." Her voice had a pleasant, smooth cadence to it. "It is I who usually help explain things to the newly initiated, or those considering it, as the case may be."

Takeshi perked up at that, placing a hand on Jitsu's head. Perhaps Siva could actually give him answers that could help. "Is this your function in the order, then?"

The Aradian nodded. "Among others. It is what I chose for myself after seeing Jak struggle miserably to explain basically anything." Her tone was surprisingly frank. "You wouldn't think it would be so, since he was the one who came up with the basic framework for our religion, but it appears he and Hades mostly winged it and hoped no one would question the results."

There was a feeling of mild embarrassment in the back of Takeshi's mind that he knew did not belong to him.

"They meant well, but they had no idea what they were doing. And so allow me to welcome you to perhaps the most haphazard religion on the planet," she continued dryly.

"Ander said as much," Takeshi said with a sigh. "I just... how does the religion function like that?"

The gold-tipped violet flames in her eyes jumped in amusement as she smiled. "The truth is that with eight members of clergy, it doesn't need to function efficiently. The other religions have thousands or hundreds of thousands of people to manage among their priests. The more people who belong to an organization, the more rules and structure help that organization to not devolve into utter chaos. With a mere eight people, we do not run that risk." She shrugged. "Then there is the added bonus of Hades herself, linking us and providing a common thread to hold us all together. The other gods do not tend to exist in such close proximity to the entirety of their clergy, often only choosing to speak directly to a few of their priests."

Unfortunately that did make sense, even if it wasn't satisfying. Fewer people required less oversight. And if the oversight itself was directly linked to each of the moving pieces, then why should it bother with excessive rules and formulas?

Siva must have been able to tell that he didn't care for that answer, because she laughed gently. "You prefer rules and structure, no?

Though I have not had much reason to go to that area of the world, I have always had the impression that Ni Fon is a fairly regimented society."

Jitsu snorted, then dropped to the floor and wandered back over to the couch. Her Human preferred "rules and structure" far more than was healthy, in her opinion. Maybe the fire-eyed priest could convince him otherwise.

He glanced at her in amusement before answering Siva. "Yes, that is true. There is a rule to govern nearly every aspect of life in Ni Fon." He paused, then admitted, "I no longer know what to do with myself here, where that seems to be a foreign concept."

"Have you considered that you may set your own rules?" she mused thoughtfully. "Or perhaps work with the Lady to create a framework within which you may function? Her own nature will never allow it to reach the levels you are probably used to, but it may make it more comfortable for you to adjust to life outside of Ni Fon."

There was a sense of concern from Hades, but Siva's eyes flashed warningly and it subsided.

Takeshi considered that. "I don't think it will carry the same weight if the rules are self-imposed," he said after a moment. "I don't even know if that is what I want. Can you understand? My path has always been decided for me. How do I choose when I have never had to?" he finished, hating how lost he sounded.

She regarded him silently for several long minutes. "You are looking for someone to choose for you, but that cannot happen. This *is* a rule – the Choice must be your own."

Well, at least some rules did exist.

"This was the first precept laid down by Jak when he agreed to become the Lady's first priest – all living beings have the right to choose," she continued softly. "You have time, Takeshi. You do not need to make your decision now, or even soon. But... you said you spoke to Ander about being a priest?"

He nodded. "I asked what priests of Hades do. I was trying to figure out what would be required of me. The answer was frustrating. 'Anything or nothing.' But what would that mean for me?"

"Ander is very young by our standards, but he usually makes it a point to know what he is talking about. And he is not incorrect with that assessment." A white flower fell from her hair and she brushed it away. "However, he is unlikely to elaborate beyond the stated question. Perhaps this will help. Has anyone told you what you would gain by agreeing to become a priest?"

Takeshi blinked in surprise. "I thought Hades... what do you mean?"

"Being able to hear Hades is what makes you able to become a priest," Siva explained carefully. "And it is at its core what makes you a priest. But there are additional benefits for those of us who say yes besides being able to hear Her."

"Immortality?" he hazarded, uncertain where this was going. "Ander said that time would be on my side."

She nodded. "That is one gift, yes. Perhaps the most well-known one, but there are others. Access to Her power is another, and the ability to soulforge weapons and armor far beyond what mortal smiths could ever hope to make. She can teach you magics only known by those who have chosen to serve the cycle of life and death. There are things only we can do to send the restless dead on to peaceful rest." There was a slight pause. "And we may speak with the dead."

"Yes, Hades told me Ander had spoken with Hotaru... oh," he trailed off quietly, contemplating that. For some reason, he hadn't realized that he would be able to speak with her himself.

"None of us may tell you what to do," Siva said quietly, voice grave, "and I do not think one of the dead would either. What happens to the living no longer concerns them. But the Lady has told me about your princess, and I think you might find what you are looking for if you spoke with her."

He stared at her, frozen. He... he couldn't speak with Hotaru. "I killed her," he whispered, horrified at the thought.

"Yes," Siva agreed. "We are all of us broken, Takeshi. Hades fits into the cracks of our souls and holds us together. This is the final gift She gives us. But I think you might be able to find at least some measure of peace if you speak with your princess. It is not magic to speak with the dead, just a gift, and one the Lady will grant you at least this once even if you do not choose to follow Her in the end."

:Yes.:

"If you wish to speak to her, then do so. She will come to you." Siva looked over her shoulder suddenly, then turned back to Takeshi and bowed. "I must go. I pray you find what you are looking for. Be well, Takeshi. And remember – the dead only speak if they wish it." Her form faded from the mirror.

Takeshi reached out blindly for the one being who might be able to explain that. *:What?:*

:All you need do is wish,: Hades murmured softly.

He dropped to his knees. How?

A large, furry head pressed itself into his chest. He wrapped his arms around her, burying his face in her fur. This was too much.

Jitsu moved so that she was partially wrapped around her Human. Were they going to talk to Takeshi's princess? She would like to see her. Was she nice? Why was Takeshi sad?

Takeshi laughed weakly. "She'd probably like you too," he mumbled into her fur, miserably reflecting again how many things about this place Hotaru would have loved. He wished she'd had the chance to see them.

"Oh, she is lovely, Takeshi. And so large! Where did you find her?"

Takeshi went very, very still, scarcely even daring to breathe. He knew that voice speaking Nifoni, even if it echoed a bit strangely. He didn't want to look up. This could not be happening; he had killed her; what if she still looked that way, what if she–

Jitsu did not share his reservations, attempting to squirm around so that Takeshi could continue hugging her and she could see. She did not understand why Takeshi was so concerned. This two-foot looked very nice. And she was clearly admiring Jitsu, which was obviously correct. Jitsu could tell, even if she didn't understand the words. And the nice princess two-foot was on the floor with them, so Takeshi didn't even have to get up or let go of Jitsu if he didn't want to.

"Really, Takeshi? Not even an offer of tea? How rude."

The haughty tone startled Takeshi into looking up. Hotaru had never stood on such propriety with him even when she should have.

Hotaru was in fact sitting near Jitsu on the floor. She didn't look anything like the last time Takeshi had seen her – eyes glassy, blood everywhere, a katana, his katana, speared through her, he had killed her why didn't she–

:Focus.:

Hades' calm voice in his mind gave him something to anchor himself to, and he forced himself to actually look at the spirit on the floor with him. She didn't look angry with him even though she had every right to be. Instead, her eyes were glinting with mischief as she smiled at him, clearly pleased her ruse had worked. She looked... surprisingly well, for being dead.

With some confusion he registered her clothing. Instead of the elegant kimono he was expecting, she was wearing gray slacks and a lavender sweater. Her long hair was braided and pinned into a bun on the side of her head. While the style suited her, he was finding it hard to reconcile the image in front of him with the one he associated with her. At least there was less blood in this one.

She had always wanted to wear pants.

Hotaru tilted her head slightly, following his gaze and glancing down at herself. *"I am no longer bound by Mother's rules,"* she pointed out mildly. *"I can now wear what I wish."*

It was surreal to hear her speak, to see her sitting on the floor in foreign clothing as though it were normal. Takeshi didn't know what to do. Did she even know the truth behind her death? Hades had warned him the dead only knew what they had known in life.

:There is a certain understanding that comes with being dead,: Hades clarified softly. *:But they do not magically learn everything they didn't know before that point.:*

"I'm glad to see you again, Takeshi," Hotaru continued. *"You look well. I was worried after the priest summoned me, though he ended up asking more questions about me than you."*

So no, Hotaru didn't know. Should he tell her? It would make no difference to her at this point; perhaps it was kinder not to speak of it. Or would she somehow find out about it at some other point? How did the dead learn things? She clearly remembered speaking with Ander. Could they learn from others among the dead? Would it be better for her to learn from him?

"Takeshi!" He snapped back to attention at the sharp tone; she had moved closer to him, her expression a mix of exasperation and worry. *"Have you truly not even a single word for me?"*

"Do you hate me?"

It just slipped out, the question he had been wondering for some time now. Certainly she had every right to.

She sat back slowly, expression blank as she stared at him. *"Do I hate you?"* The question was repeated slowly, each syllable enunciated. There were several minutes of silence as they stared at each other. Finally, she asked, *"Is this because you killed me?"*

He managed a very small nod.

Hotaru took a deep breath, closing her eyes briefly. *"Takeshi,"* she said, sounding like she was picking her words very carefully, *"I asked you to kill me."*

He gave another small nod.

"It would be cruel to hate you for carrying out my request, wouldn't it?" she offered after another moment of silence. *"Please tell me you haven't been fixating on this."*

Takeshi wasn't sure how to respond to that, so he said nothing.

Hotaru sighed. *"Of course you have. What am I supposed to do with you, Takeshi?"*

He looked down at Jitsu's white fur. Everything about this was wrong; Hotaru didn't understand. How could she? "Everything was a lie," he finally admitted quietly.

"Of course it was. My mother was involved." Hotaru tilted her head in interest, studying him for a long moment. *"Tell me."*

So he did. He told her everything that had happened since her death and his banishment. The pirates, Bariza, Charve, and the tragedy of failure that had occurred there. The Wall, Braila, and Tarvishte. Finding out about Hades and her priests. Finding out about the microchip, and the truth of Hotaru's death and the Empress's betrayal. Jitsu. The choice he was going to have to make.

It was in essence the mission report he was never going to get to give back home.

Hotaru let him speak, listening quietly. When he finally came to a stop, she remained silent for some time, gazing off into the distance with a thoughtful expression on her face. He waited, wondering if she finally understood now why she should hate him.

"This explains quite a bit, unfortunately," she murmured. Her gaze refocused on Takeshi. *"I am going to make this explicitly clear. Are you listening to me?"* She waited for Takeshi's nod before contin-

uing. *"Takeshi, under no circumstances are you to attempt to avenge me."*

He started in surprise. "What?"

"I feel like I shouldn't have to say it, but I'm going to anyway. Do. Not. Avenge. Me." Her voice was fierce.

Takeshi wasn't sure how they had gotten here. "I don't–"

"I know you, Takeshi. You might be drowning in guilt now, but eventually you'll realize it is really my mother to blame, and then you'll start getting ideas. I'm telling you right now: no. Let it be. You have a chance to be free; don't let her ruin that for you. She has ruined enough."

He stared at her, head spinning. "But–"

"No," she repeated again. *"I mean it. Do not seek revenge on my behalf. I am dead. It is done."* She paused again, considering. *"You and I might have done great things for Ni Fon, but the way forward to that future is closed. For better or for worse, Ni Fon will now go in another direction. At least ours was not some great romance, lost now to the ages. Do you still accept my authority as princess of our Empire?"*

He nodded, feeling lost. He had never doubted her.

"Then I set you free, Takeshi, of any remaining responsibilities and ties to Ni Fon or to myself. You no longer owe anything to the life you lived before. You are free to find your own way, whatever that may be. Don't waste time grieving for me, or what could have been." Her eyes were kind. *"I know you are lost and uncertain, but if I may make a suggestion – if the Silent Goddess is willing, perhaps a trial period as one of Hers? It may give you the stability you need to make a more*

permanent decision. It will be different than what you were used to back home, but that may not be a bad thing."

There was so much to digest in that statement that he latched onto the easiest point. "She's not very silent."

There was a sense of wry agreement from Hades towards both of their statements.

"Religion is like that sometimes, I've discovered." Hotaru laughed gently. *"Wrong, but important to people nonetheless. In this, you have a chance to find out what is true. She cannot lie."* She paused, looking down at herself as though she were not sure what she was seeing. *"It's strange... being here wears on me. This is no longer where I belong."* She looked back at Takeshi. *"I feel that I should go."*

Takeshi swallowed hard, sorrow rising in his chest, but he understood that she could not stay. "This is farewell, then."

She shrugged. *"For a time, perhaps. I will always be here. Though I find myself becoming less interested in the world I left behind as time passes, I will remember you. I hope one day you can find your own voice, Takeshi. Don't let my mother strip it from you."* She rested one translucent hand on Jitsu's head, and the warg looked up at her solemnly. Hotaru smiled at her, then looked back to Takeshi. As she spoke, she began to fade out. *"May we meet again in a world less gray than this."*

"Goodbye, Hotaru. For what it's worth... I'm sorry. For everything," he whispered.

"Don't be. Go with my love, Takeshi, and much luck to you." She smiled at him once more, and then she was gone.

Jitsu huffed. She wished she could have understood what the nice princess two-foot was saying, and now she was gone. She twisted to look at Takeshi – was her Human okay? He still seemed sad. She hadn't been able to understand him, either.

Takeshi scratched one of her ears. "I'm... I'll be fine," he reassured her softly. Tiredly, he closed his eyes and took several deep, measured breaths. She snuggled closer as he took a moment to try to center himself. It hurt, and it would likely hurt for a while yet. He needed time.

And a distraction wouldn't hurt.

:All right, then,: he offered, reaching out to where he could feel Hades hovering nearby. *:How do we manage a trial?:*

Rhode wondered how much longer he could afford to stay here before he was recalled to the mainland. He had a feeling his superiors already thought he'd been here too long, wasting time on dead ends that would amount to nothing.

But Hel was the key, he was sure of it.

If only they could find one of the priests of the death goddess's cult, he could get some answers.

Who was she? What was she? How and why was she involved with Ebryn? How had she destroyed the prism sphere? Where was she now?

Well, that last one was probably a stretch, but he could always try.

Nevertheless, he, Cole, and Madine had been traveling around the Nyphoren Islands for nearly two weeks now, looking for any remnants of the cult of Hades. Madine assured him they had been here at some point, but he needed them to *still* be here. Unfortunately, every lead they pursued turned out to be a dead end. Not even the few Truth Seekers stationed at the base could offer any help – they despised being on the island and tended to rotate out quickly. He wasn't sure why they didn't like it, but Madine wasn't showing any discomfort, so he pushed it aside as irrelevant. He had other mysteries to solve.

Today's disappointment had been a possible shrine location high up on one of the forested slopes of Crescent Island's volcano. There had been an abandoned shrine there, but the mark looked more like an eroded sigil of the Espera than of Hades, and this further setback led to a downcast mood as they trudged back to civilization. Only Cole showed any signs of pleasure, interested as she was in the foliage around them, but she appeared to be trying to rein it in for Rhode's sake.

Suddenly Madine froze.

"I hear you've been looking for me?"

Rhode's head jerked up at the darkly amused voice, and behind him, Cole drew her gun. Madine did nothing, but that meant nothing for a Seeker.

Sitting in a tree was a woman dressed in black with blue-and-silver accents. Her skirt was very short on one side and long on the other, paired with a cropped halter top, barely visible under the long black cloak draped around her. Long dark-blue hair escaped from her hood, and aqua-colored eyes glittered from within its shadow. A violet crystal shaped like some sort of dog hung from her belt.

She also wasn't wearing shoes, black stockinged feet tapping against the trunk of the tree.

His eyes lingered on her feet for a moment out of confusion before meeting hers. "Are you a priest of Hades?"

She grinned. "I am, Colonel Rhode."

That gave him pause. "You know who I am?"

"We would all know you should we see you." Her tone was still amused, and her eyes shifted, aqua bleeding into violet.

He suppressed a shudder. "Then you have me at a disadvantage," he prompted, gesturing for Cole to stand down. He wanted to talk to this woman, not shoot her.

Her head tilted slightly. "I am the Witch of the High Tide, seventh high priest of Hades."

Mentally, he added "Witch of the High Tide" to his list of things to research. "I have questions regarding one of Hades' adherents, an Avari with white hair named Hel. Do you know her?"

"I do."

He glanced back at Madine, but the Seeker was as unreadable as ever. "She was recently in our custody, and we have some questions as to the nature of her magic. What is her type of inherent?" It was the conclusion that made the most sense.

"She was a sacrifice, to prevent you from finding what you sought. Even now, she fulfills her purpose."

He didn't care for the glee in her voice; it was putting him on edge. "Where is she now?"

The woman's grin grew wider, and she said nothing.

"She is Wanted," Madine stated. "She will be found, one way or the other."

Cole's gaze snapped sharply to the Seeker.

"Truth Seeker," the woman giggled, drawing out the word "truth" tauntingly. "You already know wh–"

Her form suddenly dissolved into water before his eyes, splashing down out of the tree. Stunned, Rhode tried to process what had just happened.

"Well, that was rude." The woman's voice echoed around them, petulant. Rhode spun, trying to pinpoint where it was coming from. "And here I thought we were just having a chat."

Angrily, he turned on Madine, but she was frowning and shaking her head, looking almost concerned for the first time since he'd met her. "It wasn't me."

"It wasn't," the woman agreed, singsong.

He looked at Cole, who shrugged.

Another giggle echoed through the forest. "Well, I think that'll be all for me. It was nice getting to meet you once, I guess. And oh – Hel says hi! She doesn't think it'll be too long now before you see each other again, for what it's worth. Good luck! Do you hear the hounds baying yet?"

Only silence answered his roar of frustration.

Chapter Sixteen

What, exactly, is a "trial period"?: Ander asked, utterly confused.

Hades laughed weakly. *:It's so he can test the waters, so to speak. He's not one hundred percent sure about committing himself to something he doesn't understand, and I don't particularly blame him for that, so he's going to feel it out before he makes a more permanent decision.:*

That cleared up nothing. *:That's just called "being a priest,":* he pointed out. *:Being one of your priests is a living choice; any one of us could decide to quit at any point. And I don't think any of us have a perfect understanding of what it means to be yours. Are we all in a perpetual trial period?:*

:I think the situation's a little different,: Jak offered wryly. *:If nothing else, it's making the situation easier for Takeshi to digest.:*

:He seems to be struggling with the concept that the Choice need not be permanent,: Hades added. *:Siva agrees this may help.:*

Ander didn't understand that. The difference, if Jak wanted to call it that, was purely semantic. They had all made the Choice to be hers, but that could be revoked at any time. Jak's own precept made it so.

He supposed it didn't matter what they wanted to call it. For all intents and purposes, Takeshi was a priest of Hades, at least for now. Which was why plans had been made for him to join them for the Longest Night; Ander had assumed it was Takeshi's official debut as one of Her priests. A trial period? Honestly.

:And he still hasn't truly let me in. He doesn't understand yet, the way the rest of you do,: Hades tried to explain.

So he was a new priest. That wasn't exactly a surprise. Ander added one last tablespoon of flakes to his aquarium, eyeing the fish as they fed. They all looked healthy and content, though he was going to have to prune some of the coral soon.

Jak peered at the aquarium. "How many fish are in here, anyways? I assume none of them are the original fish Mara gave you. Although... how long do eels live again? Have you been breeding these things, or does she just keep supplying you?" He tapped on the glass.

"Don't do that." Ander tried to keep the snap out of his voice with only partial success as the fish scattered. "You're bothering them."

Jak leveled an even look at him. "They're fish. They're fine."

"They will be if you leave them alone." Ander made a mental note to clean the glass later, tacked on to the end of his long list of things to do. At least he wouldn't have to worry about Solstice after tonight. Ostensibly, Jak was helping with the preparations, though Ander wasn't quite sure what specifically he was doing except strewing garlands and lights throughout the apartments. Ander had already needed to remove random strings of lights twice from the aquarium. Lady only knew what Jak was doing to the aquarium while he wasn't around. At least the fish didn't seem traumatized.

Hades snorted in the back of his mind.

"You let *Her* sit on it, but I can't even touch it? That's not fair," Jak complained, but he did take a step back.

Ander glanced at the see-through form of the Lady perched on top of the aquarium. "She's not real, so it doesn't particularly matter."

"Wow," Jak snorted as Hades shot Ander an offended look he could feel through Her veils. "Harsh."

Ander didn't bother clarifying. They had both understood what he meant, even if they chose to react as though they hadn't. He continued recording the water temperature and salinity in his logbook.

There was a knock on the door to the apartments.

Ander glanced over his shoulder as Jak strode over to answer it. That would be Takeshi, who had decided to meet them here before heading to the crown vigil. Ander thought it was inefficient, since Takeshi was already staying in the palace, but Jak and Hades thought it was "supportive" to all show up together. He slid the logbook into its place by the tank as the older priest opened the door.

Jitsu pushed her way in first with such confidence Ander thought it might have been she who knocked, because Takeshi stood by the door looking so uncomfortable even Ander could tell he wasn't sure if he wanted to be here.

Ander shot Jitsu a warning look as she eyed the aquarium with interest, before turning his attention back to the door. He checked over Takeshi with a practiced eye; the man didn't seem to be moving stiffly or slowly. He was dressed all in black, cutting quite a striking figure, though his clothing was a little heavier than the weather called for. Unfortunate that the temperature sensitivity persisted. He wasn't showing any signs of exhaustion or malnourishment, and overall he seemed to have recovered as well as could be hoped for. His katana was present on his hip, and Ander noticed he was wearing his *crystallus* next to it – a good sign, in his opinion.

"Takeshi… and Jitsu. Come on in," Jak drawled wryly with a pointed glance at the warg, who sat herself in the middle of the parlor as though she belonged there.

It was hard to tell due to the face mask, but Ander thought Takeshi might have winced as he followed his warg into the main room. He scanned the area, taking in the large, off-white sofas and armchairs scattered about the generously sized space, with their decorative lavender and gray pillows slightly chewed by little warg teeth. His gaze flicked from the marble-and-glass coffee table covered in Yafen's books to the gray stone fireplace, currently lit by Jak to stave off the December chill, to the yellow candles Siva had brought from Dalmara on the mantle next to one of Daiyu's butterfly-shaped incense burners. Dark eyes took in the upholstered window seats in the bay windows before lingering on Ander's aquarium, finally coming to rest on Jak. "I'm sorry to intrude," the shinobi began, "but this is the right time, is it not?"

:He wasn't sure about coming up,: Hades informed them quietly. *:Both Jitsu and I had to assert multiple times that it was fine.:*

Jak waved a hand, dismissing Takeshi's concern as Jitsu snorted. "You're not intruding, Takeshi – you have just as much right to be here as either of us. We have a few minutes before we should go, though. How're you settling in?" He motioned towards the couches. *:You, too,:* he added mentally to Ander just as he was considering returning to his lab for a quick check on how his compounds were developing.

Ander fought back a sigh and obediently sat in one of the armchairs while Takeshi moved towards one of the couches. Jak took a moment to move Mara's crocheted throw in shades of blue that had been thrown haphazardly across the other couch before sitting. Jitsu maneuvered herself so she was lying on the cream-colored rug at Takeshi's feet, sniffing at the dark wooden foot of the couch, which also showed teeth marks from one of the twins' wargs. The Lady remained where She was on his aquarium, kicking Her feet back and forth placidly.

Takeshi tilted his head slightly. "About that – should I expect to move in here?"

Ander wondered why his presence was necessary. It wasn't that he disliked Takeshi – on the contrary, he thought the man was extremely intelligent and competent, especially with the way he appeared to be handling the Jamirh situation – he just didn't see why this conversation required him. Why did everything seem to require him, recently?

Jak was shaking his head. "I've already assigned you rooms here, since that is something that we all get, but there is nothing that says this is where you have to stay. You may have noticed that the rest of our special club is missing in action at the moment, and to be honest their absence is far more common than their presence, so you should feel free to stay where you like. Ander can show you which rooms are yours later if you want," he added, causing Ander to stifle a twitch of annoyance.

"I see. Thank you," Takeshi responded, glancing at Ander. "In that case, I think we will stay in the palace, at least for now." He rested a hand on Jitsu's head.

:See? He's still uncertain,: Hades whispered to him. *:Treating this early period as a trial should help with that somewhat.:*

:If you say so,: Ander responded with a silent sigh.

"What should I expect from today's ceremony, then?" the shinobi continued.

Calling it a ceremony was a little much, in Ander's opinion; he wondered if Takeshi would be disappointed by it.

"You took a nap earlier, right?" Jak asked, waiting for Takeshi's nod before continuing. "Falling asleep during the vigil is considered bad form, unless you're a kid. There really isn't much to do during it, other than sitting there in prayer for literal hours. The crown vigil is boring."

Ander once again marveled at the head of his order. That was quite a view. "It's not supposed to be fun," he pointed out. "It's a vigil, not a party."

"But at least people tell stories in the smaller gatherings. We aren't even going to do that. We are going to sit silently until dawn," Jak complained.

"Yes, silently listening to the Lady sing," Ander countered.

"But that's just us! No one else is going to hear that," the older priest pointed out.

Takeshi coughed politely. "Is there anything I will have to say, or any formal prayers I should know?"

Ander saw Jak wince, but honestly, it was his fault none of these things existed. "There are no formal prayers to the Lady, at least not like there are in other religions. Prayers are kept between you and Her and are usually silent. You won't be required to say anything specific."

:Praying is speaking to a deity and believing they can hear you. That is all that is required,: Hades explained as dark eyes flickered to the shade over the aquarium. *:The rest of it is just dressing to stroke the god's ego–:*

"Which you certainly don't need," Jak interjected wryly.

:–or the petitioner hoping to curry extra favor.: Hades ignored Jak's interruption. *:You will be expected to light your candle, but I can walk you through it as we go, and it really is just lighting a candle.:*

"I also had a snack before coming here, as the Lady suggested," Takeshi informed them. "Other than that, there didn't seem to be anything else to do?"

"Oh yeah, dinner is... sparse," Jak muttered.

Ander was beginning to wonder who exactly started this tradition considering Jak's apparent aversion to it. "It's meant to remind us that the earth has little to give at this point in the year, of hardship and scarcity. There will be coffee and tea available to drink throughout the night, however."

"Is Vlad going to send over hot chocolate, too?" Jak asked, perking up.

"Yes." Everyone was an overgrown child. Ander had to remember that.

Hades hummed thoughtfully in Ander's mind. *:Takeshi liked that you explained why the dinner is the way it is, even if the explanation was short. I think it might not go amiss to explain more of these sorts of things.:*

:Feel free,: he advised, voice dry. *:You are in a great position to do so.:*

:And deny you the pleasure?:

Jak sighed. "We should head over if we don't want to miss out on our berries and twigs for dinner."

Ander rolled his eyes. How dramatic.

As they made their way down to the main sanctuary, Takeshi cleared his throat. "Aside from attending her holidays, what, exactly, should I be *doing*?" There was a hint of something in his voice Ander couldn't quite identify. Frustration, perhaps. "What duties am I expected to perform? Hades has been uninformative in this regard."

"Ah," Jak said, then paused. "There aren't really 'duties' in quite the sense you mean, I think?"

Which perfectly explained Jak's habit of doing as little as possible, save for the Solstice lights now hanging around the apartments and the little evergreen tree made of spell crystal in one corner. Ander, however, did have ideas in this regard. He gestured towards the furry bodies dozing in the sanctuary as he strode over to the altar to light the brazier for later that night. "How would you feel about taking over care of the wargs?"

Takeshi blinked at him as Jitsu's head came up, tail giving a slight wag. "The wargs? What does that entail?"

Hades snorted in Ander's mind. *:I see what you're doing.:*

Kade and Fen were more than willing to take over warg-watching duties when they were around, but that was rare. More often they were only able to give Ander advice on how to wrangle the oversized pigeons if he needed it. But like the twins, Takeshi had a warg – that made him a dog person, right? Ander was not, and he was fairly certain the wargs knew it. Surely Takeshi would be a better fit for working with the creatures. Jitsu seemed better behaved than many of her brethren, hospital break-in aside, and though Ander had spent too much time around wargs to attribute that to Takeshi's influence, maybe that was a good sign that the wargs would be more willing to obey the shinobi.

"It isn't anything terribly complicated. The palace delivers food for them once a week; you would oversee distributing it to any wargs that want it. They also don't have hands, so if they need anything that requires fingers they will come to you to sort it out. You would mediate any arguments that might arise." Ander paused, remembering how inane some of those arguments were. Better someone else deal with those. "We haven't had plowable snow yet this year, but the wargs are one of the main methods of clearing the roads, so you would be in charge of coordinating that as well." He double-checked that the box of solstice candles was in place by the door.

"I see," Takeshi murmured slowly, glancing down at Jitsu, who met his gaze, tail wagging. "Well, she certainly likes the idea."

Good luck to him, then. "Between Jitsu and Hades, you should have more than enough information to perform adequately, though if you need another opinion or have a question, I am usually available," Ander added as they left the Temple proper.

Hmm. Why had he offered that? He hadn't meant to; the whole idea was to wash his hands of the creatures, not continue to be involved. He could feel Hades regarding him curiously, and he decided it would be better to move on than to examine that further. "Besides that, I think it might be most efficient to focus on Jamirh and his training, something you have already expressed interest in and appear to show an aptitude for. His arm should be completely healed by the end of the week, so he will be able to resume practice."

Takeshi raised an eyebrow, glancing between Ander and Jak. "Training Jamirh counts as a religious duty?" he asked mildly.

Ander belatedly remembered that Takeshi did not know the whole situation as Jak cringed. "Not so much a duty as something... helpful? But it is something to fill your time with."

:Jamirh's situation is complex,: Hades cut in, apparently taking pity on them before the conversation got too out of hand. *:There is a vested interest in him, but he would not wish you to learn it from us.:* Her voice was firm.

:And yet Takeshi is involved. We can't keep him in the dark forever,: Ander warned Her privately. Someone as intelligent as Takeshi was likely to figure it out eventually, but in Ander's opinion there was no reason to play this game at all. Takeshi was a priest now. Upholding the natural order against Abomination was part of the job, and it

struck Ander as the sort of goal-based directive Takeshi was looking for. Keeping it from him for Jamirh's sake was unnecessary.

:There is time yet. Rushing will only muddy the waters further.:

What did that mean?

They walked in silence for a minute before Ander was struck by a thought. Siva had mentioned that Takeshi would want direction, but what if he could make do with the trappings of priesthood? It would be something for him to do, if nothing else. "There are things people associate with us that you could work on, as well," he suggested.

He ignored Jak's quizzical look as Takeshi hummed curiously. "Oh?"

Ander gestured to the katana. "Though wearing weapons openly is commonly practiced and no one will stop you, we generally don't need to. Our weapons are soulforged and so may be accessed at any time." A thought and a pull, and a glaive materialized in a shower of green threads, held across his open palms. "Soulforging is a technique unique to Vampires and the Lady's priests; armor can also be soulforged, though most start with a weapon."

:Yes, I can help with that as well, if you'd like,: the Lady offered. *:A weapon is easier than armor, which has many parts, but your weapon can take any form you would like and can even change forms.:*

Ander shifted the glaive into a pair of daggers to demonstrate. "Soulforged weapons are much stronger than both magical and mundane weapons and cannot be taken from you. They are a part of you, an expression of your will."

Takeshi did not look as interested in this as Ander had predicted, but still inclined his head. "Siva mentioned it, though I did not know what it meant. What would happen if someone were to take it?"

Ander shrugged. "Whatever you would want to happen. Dematerializing it is probably the simplest option, but you could increase its weight or change its form if you wanted to. There is a bit of an uncomfortable sensation if it is in another's hands. Your soul is meant to be yours, after all."

"On that note, a warning about using Hades' power in general," Jak cut in as they entered the palace. "You have access to it, of course, but mortals are not built with the idea that they can handle the power of a god. Too much of Her power will strain your body past its limits and cause problems."

"You can use it to supplement your own magic, but mortal bodies can only handle so much magic before magicore exhaustion, burnout, or even death becomes a risk," Ander clarified. "Using Her power on any large scale can actually cause you to become exhausted faster than if you only used your own resources."

Jak nodded. "Having said that, there are times when the risk is worth it. What I'm trying to say is just... be aware that it is a risk, and judge accordingly."

Takeshi nodded solemnly. "Thank you for the warning." He looked around briefly at the hall as they ascended the main staircase. Few people were out and about; most were settling into their homes for the Longest Night. "Are there titles or honorifics that I should know about?"

Jak's eyebrows drew together in confusion, though at the question itself or the change in topic Ander was unsure. "Uh... we are all high priests?"

Ander sighed. "No, not like what you are probably thinking. We don't use titles among each other. There aren't enough of us to make that seem anything other than ridiculous and pretentious. Civilians usually address us simply as 'High Priest,' or sometimes 'Lord'; we don't generally push for anything specific like 'Father' or 'Your Eminence.' Most people who know us simply use our names."

Takeshi was eyeing Jak. "That seems to fit with the rest of it. I just do not wish to accidentally cause offense."

Jak shrugged. "We're a pretty casual lot. Even if you did manage to somehow offend one of us, if it's due to a misunderstanding or lack of information no one's going to be upset."

"Perhaps, but I would prefer to avoid any issues rather than run blindly into them," Takeshi stated firmly. "If there are so few rules, there is no reason I cannot learn them effectively."

"Hades will warn you away from saying or doing anything disastrous," Jak reassured him. "That's one of the really good things about being one of Her priests."

There was a slight pause, then Takeshi offered, "But should she have to? Should not the responsibility for our behavior be on us?"

"She won't stop you, She'll just point out that it could be problematic," Ander clarified. "Feel free to ignore any and all advice from the divine being. Be your own person."

:Hey!:

Ander ignored Her. "She is not and never has been mortal. She doesn't think like we do, not really, and She has Her own view of how the world works. It doesn't always line up with ours. Divinity does not equal perfection, and it does not equal all-knowing. And while She can't lie, Her perception of things is not always one hundred percent accurate."

"So feel free to tell Her to shove it," Jak concluded, voice amused. He also appeared to be ignoring Her offended silence. "She won't hold it against you."

Takeshi looked... tired? Resigned? Ander wasn't sure. "I see."

He'd learn, Ander decided. It was hard to have someone living in your head for an extended period of time and remain oblivious to their flaws. That alone was probably the reason the other deities weren't as close with their priests as Hades was with Hers. They didn't want their priests to realize that they could be fallible. The Lady didn't seem to care if Her priests realized this. Or She had the self-esteem to continue thinking She was perfect regardless of what Her priests thought; Ander wasn't sure which.

There were roughly thirty people in the dining hall, all high-ranking courtiers and their families. A few people were still filtering in and finding their places at the tables, which had been set up in a "u" formation.

Ander steered them towards the middle table, where Vlad was chatting with Miravu and Prim. Jitsu happily bumped noses with Prim's warg Thorn as they settled under the table.

The Vampire king smiled at their approach. "Welcome! Happy Solstice."

"Are we all ready to stay up far too late?" Jak asked. "Oh, wait – this is normal for some of you. You'll have to forgive this ancient Human if I doze off at any point."

Ander very purposely did not roll his eyes as they sat down. "Happy Solstice." He paused. "Takeshi, you have met Vlad before, right?"

Takeshi hesitated. "Ah... you look familiar?"

Vlad smiled. "I was present when you arrived, but we were not formally introduced at that point. I am Vlad, the ruler of Romanii. With me are Miravu, the ambassador from Dalmara, and Primrose, the Captain of the Black Watch."

"I am Takeshi. I am... a new priest of Hades," Takeshi responded.

"Well met." Miravu returned Takeshi's shallow bow. "This is not the first time I have participated in the Vigil for the Lost, but to have three of the death goddess's priests present is quite the novelty, no?"

Prim chuckled. "Usually trying to keep any number of them in one place is like herding cats, but occasionally the stars align."

"So we like to travel. Sue us," Jak said with a shrug.

As Prim and Jak began discussing the merits and faults of a small religion's members frequently wandering about, Miravu turned to Takeshi. "Congratulations on finding your vocation."

Takeshi inclined his head silently, masked visage giving away nothing as Ander mused that it tended to be the vocation finding them.

"Do you plan on staying in the capital, as Ander does, or will you travel like the others?" she continued. "I will admit I am unfamiliar with the protocols for those called to the death goddess's service."

Dark eyes glanced Ander's way before returning to the curious ambassador. "Nothing has been decided yet, but I believe I will be staying here for the time being."

"It is different for each of us," Ander tried to reinforce. "There is no one way, but we all find our niche eventually."

Miravu nodded. "At home, an acolyte must serve as such for several years before standing on their own as a Hemjer of the Faleri. Yet the Lady Siva once told me that such a thing is unnecessary for the death goddess' order, so tightly are you bound to her."

Takeshi shrugged. "I don't know; a presentation or something could go a long way."

Ander snorted at that as the first course was served. He could do at least a little about that. "Fir bark soup," he interjected, indicating the small bowl that had been placed in front of each of them. "Meant to remind us that life can be nourished even from unlikely sources."

Miravu's eyes widened. "Oh! Are you to explain the meal?"

Ander met Takeshi's eyes as he accepted the challenge. "I'm teaching this year."

The shinobi tilted his head as he pulled his mask down. His lips twitched into a smile.

Chapter Seventeen

Jamirh couldn't help it – he was excited, if also a little nervous. The cast had come off two days ago and Ander had finally cleared him for training again. He was glad he didn't have to deal with it anymore; any longer and he would have been climbing the walls. He needed to move, and even though the cast had only been on his arm he had felt horribly restricted. Now that it was gone, he was free again. Good riddance.

It was even enough to make him look forward to trying again with the longsword. Jamirh didn't know what to expect this time, but Takeshi seemed to be very confident of success. If nothing else, Jamirh was sure the experience would be different from training with Jeri. It certainly couldn't get any worse.

Well, actually, maybe it could, but he had to hope it wouldn't.

Still, Jeri had insisted on being present as an observer to prevent any more "accidents." Jamirh knew she felt bad about breaking his arm, but the hovering was getting on his nerves. He found himself wondering if she thought he was completely helpless. And *she* was the one who'd broken his arm in the first place.

On the other hand...

It was strange to have someone so invested in his well-being after being on his own for so long. In Blackfields, you learned quickly that the only person you could really count on was yourself. Some part of Jamirh wondered how long it would be before Jeri left too. People didn't stick around; everyone left eventually. He looked down at his key, feeling a pang of sadness. Aether had also—

"Jamirh?"

His head snapped up, startled out of his thoughts. Jeri was waiting for him on the stairs. He dropped his key back down to his chest and bounced down the steps, Crystal Light Blade in hand.

Jeri eyed the Blade curiously before shooting him a questioning look.

He pretended he didn't see the way green eyes lingered briefly on his key and shrugged, ears twitching. "Takeshi said to bring a real sword if I had one. I don't know why, but... this is what I've got."

She studied him for another moment. "The sheath is nice. I don't remember seeing it before?"

"Vlad had it made for me after I took the Blade." Jamirh glanced down at the black leather. It was a little more ornate than he would have chosen, but at least the subtle silver detailing wasn't too flashy. Unfortunately it did nothing to hide the ridiculously ornate hilt.

"I wonder what happened to the original," Jeri mused as they started towards the training grounds. "Maybe Ander forgot it and it's still in that museum in Agale."

Jamirh was noticing that he – or rather, the Blade – was getting a lot of interested looks as they passed through the palace. It was beginning to make him uncomfortable. "Maybe? Vlad didn't say."

"I know you hate all things Ebryn," she started carefully, "but did you ever go? For a school trip, or something similar?"

He shook his head. "I never left Lyndiniam, not before I met Hel."

Jeri hummed, looking lost in thought for a moment before her head snapped in his direction. "And how is your arm? Any pain or discomfort? Ander said–"

"My arm is fine," Jamirh interrupted with a sigh, his mood beginning to sour. He really just wished she would drop it. "I already said I'll stop what I'm doing and let Ander know if something feels off."

"That's good! It's just that–"

"My arm is fine," he snapped, ears flattening.

Jeri looked away and didn't say anything in response, though he could tell she wanted to.

Takeshi was leaning against the wall near the arched entrance to the training grounds, Jitsu a white shadow beside him. He raised one hand in a casual wave as they approached.

"Hey," Jamirh greeted him, returning the wave with one of his own. "I brought the thing." He held up the Crystal Light Blade.

"Good." Takeshi turned to Jeri, nodding at her. "Good morning. Will you be staying for the duration?"

"Yes." The tone of Jeri's voice did not allow for any argument as she led them to what Jamirh hoped would be one of the private rooms. He didn't think he could handle training in public right now.

If Takeshi took any offense to that, he didn't show it. "You've been teaching Jamirh to wield daggers, have you not? You should be able to utilize this technique to improve his learning there as well, though hopefully after today it won't be necessary."

She glanced back over her shoulder at Jamirh with a small frown before returning her attention to Takeshi. "And what exactly is this technique? How are you going to help him... ah... 'find the correct angle of thought,' as you put it?"

Jamirh was wondering that too. If believing he could do it was necessary, but he kept failing whenever he tried, how was Takeshi going to convince him otherwise? It felt like some sort of paradox he just couldn't comprehend. It gave him a headache whenever he tried to wrap his brain around it.

Takeshi hummed. "You'll see."

Jamirh could tell by the twist of her lips that Jeri didn't like that answer, but she didn't push.

"Why did you want me to bring this, anyway?" Jamirh asked, indicating the Blade as they entered one of the large practice rooms.

Takeshi held out his hand for it, and Jamirh willingly passed it over. The Human studied it closely, taking in the fancy, wing-like cross-guard with its embedded violet gem and the pale-blue crystal of the blade itself. "Magic swords," the man said after a moment. "It's almost as though they have to let everyone know they are magic." He shook his head, handing it back to Jamirh. "Hades says its special properties are only effective against Abomination. That's... a very specific quirk."

Jamirh fought back a sigh. "Yeah, you could say that."

Takeshi stared at it, looking displeased. "How did you come by such a thing? It is a very powerful, if focused, artifact."

Jeri went still as Jamirh averted his eyes. "It was given to me. An... ancestor had it, originally."

"I see." A pause. "And so you are to wield it." It wasn't a question.

"Yup."

"I sincerely hope your inherent works as advertised, if we are to get you capable of fighting those things any time in the near future." Takeshi had clearly connected at least some of the dots on his own. "I have fought them. It was not an easy battle, and I have been training for most of my life."

Now Jamirh did sigh, ears drooping. "I have to try. One of them made it to Tarvishte and attacked me. All I was able to do was fling myself around and avoid getting hit until Ander came to save me." He was unable to keep the bitterness out of his voice.

One eyebrow raised. "It attacked you, specifically?"

"And others," Jamirh was quick to add. "Several Vampires died. I don't know what it would have done after, if it had succeeded in killing me." He shuddered at the memory of the thing's twisted body and blank face.

Takeshi glanced at Jeri, but she said nothing. There was a long pause as his gaze unfocused, staring off into space. Finally, he shook his head. "You used your inherent to keep yourself alive, at least. Surely you can see that?"

Jamirh shrugged. "Yeah, it makes sense, I guess. Especially considering how you described the way it probably developed."

"You could not have managed the same with normal, untrained reflexes. The Abominations are too fast for that," Takeshi explained.

"We are calling this iteration of Abomination bionics," Jeri advised helpfully.

"So we must then work on the more offensive aspect. Very well." The Human sighed, glancing at Jitsu, who had settled herself against one of the walls. "You said you were able to pick up on some of the techniques Jeri showed you, yes?"

Jamirh blinked, relieved but surprised Takeshi hadn't pressed for more information. "Yeah, I can picture them in my head just fine. And when I'm practicing with daggers, I can usually replicate it on my own, just not against an actual person."

The shinobi gestured, taking a step back. "Show me one or two."

Jamirh started to head towards the rack of wooden weapons to get the practice longsword.

"No," Takeshi interrupted, voice mild. "With the sword in your hand."

"Excuse me?!" Jeri exclaimed, spinning to stare at Takeshi in horror. "He can't practice with that. He'll hurt himself!"

Well, that stung. "It wasn't me who broke my arm."

Silence. Jeri flushed and swallowed hard, looking like she was groping for something to say.

"And he will not hurt himself now, either," Takeshi interjected calmly after a moment. "His ability requires the proper weapon in hand for now. He may well learn to wield a wooden blade as though it were steel, or crystal in this case, but right now he cannot. His inherent treats it as what it is, not what it is pretending to be. So we will use live weapons."

Jamirh's eyes snapped to the curved sword at Takeshi's hip, and his stomach twisted uneasily despite his earlier words.

"In Ni Fon, shinobi make the switch to steel very early in their training. You have some knowledge of forms, so I will treat you the same way." The evenness of Takeshi's voice cut through Jamirh's growing panic. "You will be perfectly fine, Jamirh. Neither I nor your ability will allow you to come to harm."

"What if I hurt you?" Jamirh blurted out.

"You will not harm me, either," came the confident reply. "I do know what I am doing, and I am very good at it. No one is going to be injured today."

"Your people train with actual weapons?" Jeri asked, shock coloring her voice. "How do any of you survive to adulthood? Accidents—"

"Those who teach know what they are doing," Takeshi repeated. "Accidents are few and far between in Ni Fon. I understand that an accident has already occurred with Jamirh, but it was caused by poor instruction and a failure on the instructor's part to pay proper attention to the student." His tone sharpened ever so slightly. "Such a thing will not happen with me."

Jeri flushed again, then her gaze darkened. "You have no idea what—"

Takeshi cut her off, voice firm. "He has a sword meant to fight a corruption of the world itself, and he has already been attacked by an incarnation of it. The goddess tells me he 'must' learn to fight, and with that context, I cannot disagree. He will come to no harm here with me, but he has already faced one *in the palace itself*. If even that place is not safe... you and I cannot be with him every moment of every day. Stand down, and let him learn to defend himself."

Jeri gaped at Takeshi, clearly taken aback. Jamirh gaped with her, uncertain how to respond to that.

The shinobi caught Jamirh's eye before he looked back at Jeri. "In fact, why don't we ask him?"

Jamirh blinked as he was suddenly the target of two very intense gazes.

"Ask him if he wants to train with live weapons?" Jamirh could hear the scorn in Jeri's voice. "He's a novice; decisions about training shouldn't be made by–"

"I'll do it."

The words slipped out without his permission, but Jamirh knew they were true.

Jeri took a step towards him. "Jamirh, I really don't think this is a good idea. You've already been injured once..."

"And I need to get better so it doesn't happen again, no matter who I'm fighting," he said, straightening up and trying to look more confident than he felt. His hand found his key.

Damn straight.

"I *need* to do this," he continued, meeting Jeri's eyes evenly. "Because I really, really don't want to die when one of those things finds me again."

He saw Takeshi raise an eyebrow out of the corner of his eye.

Jeri did not agree. He could see it in the thin line of her mouth and the storm in her eyes. But it was she who looked away first, turning to Takeshi. "If there is an accident…" Her voice trailed off but the threat was clear.

Even now, she refused to back down. Jamirh felt the sharp sting of disappointment.

"There won't be. And you could always leave, if watching him do this makes you uncomfortable." He turned back to Jamirh, ignoring the darkening of Jeri's expression. "A string of three or four attacks, please," he said calmly, as though there had been no interruption.

At least the Human's confidence was somewhat reassuring. Jamirh glanced at Jeri, but she had schooled her expression into something unreadable, green eyes glued to Jamirh. He looked back down at the pale-blue blade in his hands before tentatively placing himself in an attack stance, left foot forward. He thought back to the attacks Jeri had performed. "Anything? Are you looking for something specific?"

"No, any will do."

Okay then. He picked an attack string he remembered Jeri using several times, picturing it clearly. Slowly, making sure he was doing it right, he moved through the forms, stopping when he got to the end.

Takeshi was watching him closely. "Again."

Ah, this was more like how Jeri trained him with daggers. He ran through the forms a second time, feeling a little more confident.

"Again. Faster, if you can."

Jamirh repeated the movements, picking up speed as he went.

"Again." Takeshi began to walk in a slow circle around him, giving him plenty of room to maneuver.

Jamirh ran through it. The Crystal Light Blade was a little heavier than the wooden sword and he was out of practice; he wondered how long he was going to be able to keep this up.

"Again."

Over and over, Takeshi ran Jamirh through the same drill, sounding bored. Jamirh lost count of how many times he repeated the same motions as Takeshi circled him like a shark, sharp eyes watching his every movement. Jamirh found himself moving faster and faster the more he repeated himself, his focus closing in on the blade and the forms as it grew harder to make himself complete the actions. He wiped sweat from his face and kept going, even though he wasn't sure what this was accomplishing. He had always been able to do the motions by himself.

Just as his muscles began to scream at him, Takeshi said, "Now add three more attacks to the end of the string."

Jamirh stared at him blankly for a moment, processing words that were not "again." Takeshi wanted him to *lengthen* the string? He wanted to take a break, already exhausted. How long had they been at this? He looked at Jeri, but she was sitting near Jitsu, scratching the warg's ears and watching silently.

He couldn't help but feel like she was judging him.

"Well?" Takeshi prompted. "Surely you were able to pick up more than just those four strikes."

Jamirh refused to back down now, especially with Jeri watching. At least he wasn't being thrown to the ground every few minutes, though this felt like more work in some ways. Doing the same motion over and over meant he was using the same muscles over and over. They were tired. He forced himself to run through the drill anyway, adding the requested three strikes to the end of it.

"Good. Again."

Jamirh felt his ears twitch in frustration. He wasn't sure how long he could keep going. He had to give all his attention to the motion to complete it. No, not the motion; he'd done it so many times at this point he was sure he'd be dreaming about it tonight. He just had to focus on moving through the soreness, not how to move. It was just him, the blade, and a voice saying–

"Again."

Jamirh stepped forward into the first strike.

Takeshi *moved*, his sword meeting Jamirh's in a shriek of steel against crystal. Jamirh felt everything sharpen, come more clearly into focus as his body moved through the same attack string he had been repeating for what felt like hours. Takeshi met him swing for swing, dancing back as Jamirh pressed forward, muscle memory carrying him through motions he couldn't have stopped even if he'd wanted to. He flashed through the movements, but as the attack string ended he found himself on the defensive – Takeshi didn't stop.

There was no room for thought, anything outside of himself and his opponent and the dance of blades as Jamirh met Takeshi's advance, countering simply by *knowing* on a level beyond conscious thought how the Human was moving. And then there was an opening, *there,* and Jamirh went for it, even as Takeshi countered with a violent push that sent them spinning away from each other.

"Hold!"

Jamirh froze at Takeshi's order, breathing heavily as his muscles screamed and his mind was finally able to catch up to what he had just done. Takeshi remained where he was, regarding Jamirh silently. He didn't look even a little bit winded, to Jamirh's chagrin. He didn't look surprised, either.

But Jamirh had done it. And not just an accidental exchange like with Ander; this had been a continuous understanding of a sort Jamirh lacked words for. How many exchanges past seven? He replayed it in his mind, picture perfect… ten, eleven… fourteen exchanges! He'd met Takeshi's blade fourteen times past what he had practiced, and it was like his body had just known what to do!

He looked towards Jeri, eyes wide, and saw a stunned look on her face.

Jitsu looked like she was about to take a nap, completely unaware of the miracle that had just happened.

He looked back to Takeshi, who was still waiting patiently, probably for Jamirh to get his act together. "I did it," he whispered. *Yeah, you did!*

Takeshi nodded. "Yes, I think we can count that as a success."

The muscles in Jamirh's legs finally gave out and he dropped to the ground. It didn't matter. "I did it!" he repeated, looking back to Jeri. His ears twitched upward with happiness. "I really did it!"

She shook her head as if in disbelief. "You did!" Then she perked up. "You really did! You *can* do it!"

Jamirh felt a pang that cut through his joy. Hadn't she believed he could already? He felt his ears sink.

Takeshi sank gracefully down into a kneeling position to join them on the floor. "So now we know for sure – you are a Master of Blades, and all that that entails. If you were not, you would have performed poorly past the practiced strikes, yet you met me nearly as an equal."

At least Takeshi's words were reassuring. "How did you... how did you make it work?" Jamirh asked, breathless.

The shinobi hummed. "I waited until you had done it so many times you didn't need to think about it anymore, then when I stepped in, I defended in such a way that the logical move for you to make was the attack string you had already practiced. You answered me without thinking, and then when I switched to offense, you were already in the correct state of mind, and so – success."

"The 'correct angle of thought,'" Jeri murmured.

"Exactly so," Takeshi agreed. "You told me once that you used an attack against Ander that he had used against you earlier. It seemed likely to me that he had attacked you in such a way that his previous attack was a natural counter. So, I manufactured a similar scenario, then pushed it further. And now, since you have succeeded, and know for certain that you have, it will be easier to replicate, to find that same mindset."

Jamirh thought about it and decided Takeshi was right. There was something about the way everything had clarified, the way he had been able to take everything in and simply react, that seemed to sit just within his reach. He could reach that again if he tried, he was sure of it. *Of course, it's always been there, you've always used it.*

Right, he had always been able to do that... like when that beam fell down in the structure he and Aether had been sheltering in and he'd pulled them both out of the way before he'd even really noticed it falling, or the time he had nearly been run over by someone driving a car way too fast but had managed to roll out of the way...

Yes. He could reach that mindset again, now that he understood what it was. It was thinking and not-thinking simultaneously. It was reacting. It was learning and reacting faster.

He found himself thinking back over the exchange with Takeshi, analyzing it. Takeshi did not fight the same way Jeri did, but there were similarities. His sword was different – it had only one edge – but many of the movements had been familiar. Was that just because he was trying to make Jamirh's attack string make sense, or was that actually his style?

"So, then," Takeshi continued, "another minute to rest, and we try again."

Jamirh took stock of his legs. "I'm not sure I can stand."

Jeri winced. "It has been some time since you last performed intense activity like this. How is your arm, by the way?"

"It feels fine." And just like that, his annoyance was back. "Tired and sore, like the rest of me, but it doesn't hurt or anything."

"Repetitive motion can do that." There was no hint of apology in Takeshi's voice even though it was entirely his fault. "We should practice a little more, to help solidify the knowledge, though I think Ander might do me physical harm if I undo any of his work."

Jitsu huffed, sounding as amused as a canine could.

"Regardless, this is a good start," Takeshi continued. "We've proven that you can do it, and that is the most important thing. Remember, belief is key. But there is still work to be done – if you want to be able to fight the bionics, then you need to be much, much better than you are now. You still need to observe and learn far more skills, and you need to be faster."

Jamirh's ears sank a little at the reminder, and he found himself glancing at Jeri. "It is possible though, right?"

"Yes, but it will take time. Far less time than it would take someone who is not a Master of Blades, but time nonetheless. It is hard to estimate how much your inherent can cut out. Even among Masters of Blades, it is likely an individual variable." Takeshi looked thoughtful, dark eyes falling on Jamirh's sword. "Who is this ancestor who cursed you with such a burden? Did they share your talent?"

Jamirh stared at the pale-blue surface, seeing the red of his hair reflected in it. "Yeah, kinda."

Takeshi's eyebrows rose. "'Kinda'?"

"He was also a Master of Blades, but he only ever used a longsword," Jamirh explained. "I guess it annoyed the Aradian he traveled with."

Takeshi shrugged. "Some people only do one thing, but they do that one thing masterfully. Though if Masters of Blades primarily come from Aradians, I can see why they might feel some ownership over it. But inherents can be tricky things, nearly impossible to predict. I assume if your ancestor had an Abomination-fighting sword, he fought Abominations?"

Jamirh sighed. "He saved Agale from them, yeah. Some wizard was summoning demons or something and he stopped it. And he wasn't really my ancestor, I guess," he added, deciding to go all in. "Supposedly I'm his reincarnation. And because he made a deal with Hades, who created the Blade for him, I have to fight Abominations too."

There was a long silence, after which Takeshi stated, "I see."

"It's complicated," Jamirh finished lamely.

"If by 'it's complicated,' you mean 'a series of bad decisions,' then yes, I agree," Takeshi stated mildly. Jamirh wondered if he was getting more of the story from Hel. "And should you choose not to fight, they will find you and kill you anyway," he concluded.

"Pretty much," Jamirh agreed.

"So you see why we have been trying to teach him," Jeri insisted. "Why he must learn how to defend himself."

"Yes, I do appear to be seeing the whole picture now." There was nothing about his tone that really gave away what he thought about it. They might as well have been discussing the weather. "It's kind of a mess." Okay, that was a little more direct.

I mean, he's not wrong.

"The guy before me got killed too," Jamirh added, "so we know that they do want me dead. Actually, wait a minute; it makes sense the Abomination would want me dead, but why would the Empire be involved? Like, I know they are making the bionics, but what do they gain from my death? How do they even know about the reincarnation thing?"

Jeri looked uncertain. "What we know, we know from the Lady," she said slowly, glancing at Takeshi. "It was She who told us about you in the first place."

Takeshi frowned, looking as though he were listening to something else. "She says there is a prophecy made by a Truth Seeker concerning Ebryn, but she cannot say what the prophecy is about more specifically. The dead keep their secrets."

"That's not fair," Jamirh exclaimed. "Not if it's about me."

"I don't think that's negotiable," Takeshi warned. "She is very protective of the dead, which is fair to her domain. Besides, if she can tell me that much, that means someone else knows something about it. I can try to get more information from my end. And we do need information, let's be clear on that." His voice was firm. "The more we know, the more we can prepare."

"But what are we preparing for?" Jamirh asked, feeling thoroughly disheartened. Shouldn't everyone already have been preparing?

"...We might need more information on that, as well," Takeshi admitted after a beat of silence. "I'm getting a kind of vague 'to fight the Abomination,' but not what that means, precisely. I'll talk to Ander."

Jeri shrugged. "What will be, will be. She is probably vague because not even She knows what exactly we are in for, just the generalities. She does the best She can to help us."

"I think she extrapolates based on echoes of what has already happened," Takeshi mused thoughtfully. "Which does give us a starting point, but I think we can do better. In the meantime, the best thing to do is to continue learning to utilize your inherent to its fullest, Jamirh. That does appear to be one of the important aspects, regardless of the why or how of it."

"This thing, too." Jamirh lifted the Blade a bit.

"Luckily, it is not the sort of magic sword you need to do something to activate – it will do what it is supposed to merely by being in the presence of Abomination," Jeri offered. "All you need to do is have it."

"So it is good that we are training with it," Takeshi concluded. The shinobi rolled to his feet swiftly and with a grace Jamirh found himself envying. He was definitely not getting up that easily. "Come, let us have another few attempts at it before we call it a day."

Groaning, Jamirh forced his aching body to stumble into a standing position. Stopping had been a bad idea. Still, at least he knew what he had to do now. He pulled the Crystal Light Blade up, settling into a stance.

It is a good thing, yes. We will need it, but even that alone will not be enough.

January 4, 2027 A.G.

Notes: Addendum – Bionic Abomination

Another capability the bionics have is a proficiency in tunneling. It's not something I would have guessed based on how spindly they appear, but the structure of the artificial muscles and actuators do indicate a capacity to exact more force per area unit than an Avari or Human can (see notes from Nov 20). The four arms also give them an advantage in moving material. At least we know how they bypassed the Warcross Wall.

The tunnel found in the Waste near the Tower of Morden was six feet in diameter and twenty miles long, reaching a depth of thirty feet underground. I believe the tunnel was made at such a length in an attempt to avoid the sight of the Wall. The Empire may not understand how it works completely, but they certainly know enough to realize that the Wall is watched somehow. So the bionic began digging while still a ways out in the Waste, and emerged once far past the Wall.

*In my opinion, this was a risk, as they couldn't have known for sure the Waste extends the same way on our side of the Wall. Inference, or did they somehow gain this knowledge?

*Question: Did the bionic itself make this determination, or those in charge of it?

→ It is still uncertain how much capacity for thought each individual bionic has. The one that attacked Jamirh clearly had some problem-solving ability, considering that it was able to avoid detection for over seven hundred miles, and they must be able to function in a combat scenario, but how far does that go? Is it all programming, or does something of the original host intelligence still remain? If that is true, it implies that each bionic has a different level of intelligence based on the original Avari's. Interesting.

> → The lack of will does not necessarily preclude the lack of intelligence.

*Note: I would have benefitted greatly from being able to study a living bionic. Uncertain how to do so even should I come across another, considering the murderous intent.

> → Do they actually have intent? See above.

An intense search along the length of the Waste has not revealed any more tunnels, thankfully. The breach has already been sealed; they won't be able to enter that way again.

The Watch has put forth new security measures in an attempt to prevent any more of the bionics tunneling into Romanii, and they are on high alert for any others that may have come through with or after the original one, since it existed unnoticed for almost two months. Hopefully that will be enough.

-Ander 1/4/27

Supplemental: Takeshi has mentioned the Truth Seekers several times in relation to Jamirh and the Abomination scenario as a whole. They've been mostly ignored up to now, since as mages they are considered the most easily understood part of the Empire's military, but he brought up a good point: How do they fit in this picture? As mages, they must be able to sense the corrosion Abomination begets. How are they coexisting with this knowledge?

Chapter Eighteen

Ander looked on as Jamirh sent his opponent sprawling in the dust of the training grounds. "At least he's finally making progress."

Red eyes scanned the gathering below them as Vlad leaned on the balcony. "Takeshi has proven himself indispensable in this regard, though I must say I am also impressed with the effort Jamirh himself is putting forth. Miravu tells me he is improving at a rate impressive even for Masters of Blades."

Ander snorted. "What is there to it? Fight, and learn to fight better. It is not much different from standard learning; he simply does not need to practice as much to internalize what he learns."

"That might be oversimplifying it," Vlad murmured dryly. "Still, it is promising that Takeshi has opened up his training to other opponents."

"Of course. The more varied styles he faces, the more he can absorb," Ander pointed out. "It's almost unfortunate we couldn't capture the bionic and have him fight it in a controlled setting. That would probably be the most efficient use of his time, as he would be learning to fight the Abomination directly."

The Vampire coughed. "I'm not sure trying to contain a bionic would be what's best for anyone else. Or Jamirh himself, for that matter."

:That does seem like it would have some logistical issues,: Hades added. *:Also, Abomination is to be destroyed. I don't like the idea of purposely keeping it around, no matter the reason.:*

Ander sighed. No one had any respect for science.

"Besides, we have plenty of capable fighters in Tarvishte for him to learn from," Vlad continued. His eyes slid towards Ander as his mouth quirked up into a smile. "Have you considered giving it another go?"

"No," the priest responded shortly.

"Oh? You are content with only having taught him the one trick?"

"Physical combat is not my specialty," Ander stated. "He will learn best from others."

Vlad shot him an amused look. "What happened to 'the more varied styles he faces, the more he can absorb'?"

"There are plenty of varied styles down there for him to deal with," Ander dismissed with a wave. "He hardly requires mine."

A pause. "It's not because of the Blade, is it?"

Ander stared at the blue crystal flashing in the sun, veins of elemental power quiet without Abomination nearby. The more he saw of it, the more he was reminded of Alice and how he had come to possess the Blade in the first place – something he usually tried to avoid thinking about.

There was a reason he never visited its room in the museum.

At least it was being used for its intended purpose now. Or would be soon.

"It's just a sword," he said dismissively after a moment. "Better that than the daggers."

Vlad frowned. "That's not really how you feel."

Sometimes Ander hated empaths. "Does it matter? As long as Jamirh is able to do what he needs to, my 'feelings' shouldn't come into play at all."

"To the situation? No. But they should to you."

Ander fought back a sigh. First Jak, and now Vlad. Though he wouldn't put it past Jak to have brought it up to Vlad. He would really prefer to just move past it. "Everyone is unnecessarily interested in 'how Ander feels' about the whole mess recently."

"Because you are important too." The Vampire turned to face him fully. "People care about you."

Hades hummed in the back of his mind, swamping him with Her love.

"Perhaps their energy could be spent caring about more important things," he suggested with a pointed look at the bout below, not liking the feelings that declaration dredged up.

Vlad chuckled softly. "Like saving the world? Sure, that's important, but the people who live in it are important too. If we lose sight of them, then what is the point? Just because you aren't the one wielding the Blade doesn't mean that you don't matter. And besides, I think Jeri is worrying for Jamirh enough for the rest of us."

Ander glanced at the dark shadow brooding in the corner of the practice yard by Takeshi. "She will have to get used to him being in danger eventually. It might as well be here, where the situation is under control."

Vlad shrugged. "I think the better thing would be for her to get used to working with him in such a scenario. As it stands, I'm not sure she wouldn't try to take on more than she should, even though he will clearly be capable of holding his own."

"It would be foolish for her to think that he will be less capable than she is," Ander pointed out. "His inherent literally makes him a 'Master of Blades.' He will outclass her eventually if he's able to survive long enough."

That earned him a disappointed look from Vlad. "That was uncalled for. I know this whole situation is important to you; you don't need to pretend otherwise."

Ander looked away, eyes catching again on the Crystal Light Blade. He did not want to remember what he'd risked and lost for that artifact. Now that the time to use it was here...

The worst thing was he wasn't even sure what he had been expecting. But he was sure Jamirh wasn't it. He was just so... *passive.*

:The Blade is special, but it is also simply a tool. In many ways, Jamirh is the more important part of the equation. Ebryn existed before the Blade did, after all.: Hades' tone was gentle. *:There is more to people than the things that come with them.:*

:Says the being that bound him to Her,: he shot back, not in the mood to be talked down to.

:Yes, I did. And I used the Blade to do it. But the person came first. I could create the Blade; I couldn't create the person who would wield it.:

He knew that, logically. It was even something he'd managed to mostly convince himself of. But Jak had a point – Jamirh had not made a great first impression. Or second. Or third.

Though the kid was doing better now, Ander supposed as he watched the red-haired Avari dance around his opponent. Maybe there was hope for them yet. It wasn't like he wanted Jamirh to die; he just wasn't sure he had what it would take to stay alive. Being able to use his inherent effectively wasn't going to be enough on its own.

:He has a survivor's mindset. He will be fine.:

Ander almost startled at the mindtouch that wasn't Hades. He glanced down at the training yard to see Takeshi looking up at him.

:You are looking at him like he is a very confounding puzzle,: came the amused explanation. *:Jeri often watches him with the same expression.:*

Everyone seemed amused with Ander today, much to his disgust. He didn't care for the comparison to Jeri either. *:Jeri coddles him; I will do no such thing.:*

:He is very, very young compared to Jeri,: Takeshi pointed out as he returned his gaze to the bout. *:I would almost expect more Vampires to latch on to their mortal charges in such a way. Like having a pet – you know you will outlive it, but you still care for it and try to give it the best life it can possibly have.:*

The comparison completely derailed Ander's former train of thought. *:What? No, Vampires don't see mortals as pets.:* He glanced sideways at Vlad, who was watching the fight with interest. *:Half the council is made up of mortals; it's a symbiotic relationship–:*

:Peace.: He still sounded amused. *:I merely jest. You look so grim up there.:*

:There is much to be grim about, if we are being realistic,: Ander admitted, suddenly feeling very tired.

:That is why we need to know more,: Takeshi answered simply. *:Forewarned is forearmed, knowledge is power, and all that. We do not have all the necessary pieces yet to know which big steps we should take. Instead, we should focus on the small steps that are achievable. Jamirh's inherent has allowed him to progress to a level that would normally take several years in just under a month. He does well. This is a victory.:*

Ander frowned. *:And yet that is likely not enough. You fought them; you know what he's up against.:*

:He survived against one before; I trust that he will be capable of at least that again. The rest will come in time. Have there been any more sightings of the bionics in Romanii?:

Ander cleared his throat. "Have there been any more signs of bionics?"

Red eyes slid his way. "No, nor have there been any more power outages, thankfully. I'm still unwilling to declare that we are definitely free of them, and the Watch is still on high alert, but there's been nothing."

:None,: Ander repeated for Takeshi's sake.

:Then for now, we stay watchful and give him the tools he needs to defend himself,: the shinobi asserted. *:We do need to find out what that prophecy is so we can guard against it. We do need to find out where the bionics are being created. We do need to figure out what is*

actually happening at the upper levels of the Empire. We do need to figure out how the previous Ebryn died. We may need to figure out how the first Ebryn died; no one seems to know that, either. But until we are able to know these things, we should focus on Jamirh.:

It made sense. It was good to know Takeshi's priorities were straight at least.

Vlad was glancing back and forth between Ander and the field. "Are you speaking with Takeshi?"

Ander nodded curtly.

Vlad smiled. "How is he? Has he been well?"

Ander sighed. He hated being a go-between, and Vlad was very capable of reaching out himself. *:Vlad wishes to know if you are well.:*

:I am, thank you. It is kind of him to ask.: Takeshi stepped forward as Jamirh's opponent retreated from the field, easily falling into a stance.

"He says he is fine," Ander relayed.

"I am glad." The Vampire returned his attention to the new bout happening below. "I must say, for all that Takeshi lives in the palace I rarely see either him or Jitsu. Has he been settling in well?"

Ander fought back a twitch. "He keeps asking questions I don't have answers to. Mostly concerning Jamirh and Ebryn and some prophecy Hades will only allude to. He's really thrown himself into the whole mess over the past month since Jamirh told him. Have you tried looking for him in the museum? I'm sure he'll soon become an expert regarding anything ever even remotely connected with the Hero."

Vlad inclined his head. "So he is settling in well. That's good to hear."

"How am I supposed to know some random prophecy some Truth Seeker made who knows how long ago?" Ander continued. "Truth Seekers had only just become public knowledge by the time I left Elbe. Takeshi knows more about them than I do. Why am I the one fielding questions about them? And there are people here who actually met Ebryn; I can't answer any of those questions either."

"He's fitting right in, I see." Vlad nodded authoritatively. "Excellent."

"And Jak keeps disappearing, so he's no help. Where he's disappearing to, I've no idea, but he keeps leaving me to deal with whatever esoteric questions Takeshi has come up with." It might have been disrespectful, but part of Ander found himself wondering why Jak was even still here. Was it because Takeshi was still technically in that "trial period"? He was going to have to come to some sort of conclusion eventually; Jak's presence likely made little difference. Especially since he appeared to be dodging Takeshi. "Why would I have answers Hades doesn't?"

And the thing was, he *understood*. Ander also liked to know the answers to questions. He liked to know the context of any given problem. But they didn't have either the answers or the context, and Takeshi constantly reminding Ander of this was creating anxiety.

"Maybe he just feels more comfortable asking you," Vlad suggested. "Not everyone is immediately at ease with having a deity in their head. That's the whole point of the trial period, isn't it?"

Ander hid a grimace. Everyone was buying into this farce.

"And besides, while my mother does know a lot, She doesn't know everything. I wouldn't ask Her every question I've ever had." Vlad paused for a moment. "Definitely not. And besides, it's a little flattering, isn't it?"

Ander considered that. "But I am the wrong person to ask these questions."

"But he thinks you might be the right one. Is that truly so bad?"

They watched Jamirh exchange a series of blows against a member of the Black Watch, ending in a draw. "They are going easy on him," Ander observed, changing the topic.

"I believe they are doing whatever Takeshi tells them to do. And no few of them have been intimidated by Jeri, unless I miss my guess." Vlad's tone was dry.

Ander purposefully did not look at Jeri, instead studying the clash of blades happening in the center of the courtyard. He frowned. Why did it feel like there was something he was missing? "It isn't too impressive until you realize he's been at it for less than a month."

Vlad hummed as he studied the bout. "I find it to be impressive even without that knowledge. Were this a young knight, I would consider him to be full of promise. He has just fought six bouts and made no major mistakes. Just because he has not yet reached mastery does not make it less remarkable."

"If you say so," Ander murmured doubtfully, poking at the half-formed feeling but not getting any closer to what it might be. "Did you ever see Ebryn fight?"

But Vlad shook his head. "No, I did not. He never had reason to draw his sword in Tarvishte, and he wasn't the sort to engage in a friendly bout with any, save perhaps Sukra. He was an individual of singular focus. I can see a bit of that in Jamirh when he fights, but they aren't very similar otherwise from what I've observed. There is less sorrow in Jamirh, and for that I am glad."

Ander considered the Blade. Whatever it was that was bothering him, it did have to do with the artifact. But what? "He still lost his whole family."

Vlad shrugged. "Perhaps, but the circumstances were different. Ebryn was very attached to his sister, and when she was taken... do we even know if Jamirh had a sister?"

The priest shrugged. "Not that he's mentioned to me; Jeri might know, though."

Hades was predictably but unhelpfully silent. Ander got the impression Her attention was elsewhere.

"Jamirh has been on his own for a long time, regardless," Vlad continued. "It's left its own scars across his psyche. Different from Ebryn's, but present nonetheless."

"Life leaves scars on everyone. There's no escaping that," Ander observed, thinking briefly of Alice and Fredrik.... and Ida. He rubbed at the scar on his face, pushing away the memories.

"You're glaring at it." Vlad sounded amused.

"Something about it is bothering me. *No*, not what you're thinking of," he hastened to correct the erroneous conclusion Vlad had obviously come to as the Vampire's eyebrows rose. "Something... I don't know." The words tasted bitter. He hated feeling this way.

"What do you mean?"

"We are missing something," Ander murmured, frowning. "But what that could be…"

"Missing something about the Blade?" Vlad blinked and looked down at the bout. "It is a magical artifact created by a god, and Ebryn only had it for… was it about a year or so? It's very possible there are things about it we don't know."

Magic. Right, the Blade was magic. Because of course it was. Why did that matter? "I didn't realize he had it for such a short time."

"Like Jamirh, he didn't really care for it; he just needed it to avenge his sister." The Vampire returned his gaze to the match below. "Why did my mother choose Ebryn, anyway? Was it truly just for the convenience, the grasping of an opportunity?"

"I think it has to do with him, specifically. But…" He thought back to Her earlier words. "I have no idea what. It surely can't be just because he is a Master of Blades. And usually when She makes deals they are beneficial for all parties involved."

:Ander, Mara needs to speak with you,: Hades suddenly interrupted.

Ander paused. Mara *needed* to speak with him? Out of all his fellow clergy, Mara was the one who most often reached out just to chat. He had always thought that, as the seventh high priest, she considered it her duty to check up on him and make sure he was doing well. But it hadn't been that long since they had last spoken, and he could feel an undercurrent of building anticipation in Hades' voice. *:I will hear her.:*

:Hey, Ander!: Mara's voice was cheerful as always. *:How's life been going for you? The new guy settling in okay?:*

Ander resigned himself to having to answer the same question three times in one day. *:I am well. Takeshi seems to be managing fine now that he's training Jamirh to use his inherent.:*

He could feel Mara's grin. *:Oh good! I really should make the time to head back home so I can meet him. He sounds cool!:*

:How is the Emerald Shore? Still ignoring as many laws as you can?: he asked dryly. Mara had the least respect for authority out of just about anyone he knew.

:Hmm. Well, you see, that's actually part of the reason I wanted to contact you. I'm actually in the Nyphoren Islands right now. Got a tip someone was looking for one of the Lady's priests, you know? Like, really, really looking. Thought I should check it out, since I was the closest, and I rarely get the chance to be mysterious.:

Ander frowned, and not just because "Mara" and "mysterious" didn't go together. *:Please tell me you didn't get in some sort of trouble.:*

:Oh, no! No, I'm fine. Used an illusion to meet with him. Which did turn out to be a good call, since a dryad popped it. But Hades would let you know if something bad happened: She chuckled weakly. *:But I did find something else, and you're the one I know who's most likely to be able to tell Vlad.:*

:Oh?: he prompted after a moment of silence.

:Well, as soon as I got here – I'm on Crescent Island, by the way – things didn't feel quite right. It's kind of hard to explain? Like dirty, almost, or on edge. Wrong. Not quite broken. Oily? But not the air, or the cities, or the towns, or the people, the–:

Ander twitched. *:Mara.:*

:Right, right!: She tried to get herself back on track. *:So I did a little investigating, but carefully, 'cause Hades said to be careful because what I was sensing was Abomination–:*

He was going to strangle her. *:Mara. What. Did. You. Find?:*

:I found the place the bionic Abomination things are being made!: The words came out in a rush. *:I think. Maybe. Probably. Actually, Hades says definitely, based on the concentration of awfulness here. I thought you should know.:*

Ander's eyes went wide.

:It is the most likely conclusion, yes,: Hades confirmed. *:There is an upsetting amount of Abomination here.:* Then, in such a way as only he could hear Her, She added, *:Mara really wanted to be the one to tell you. She's quite proud of herself.:*

"Vlad!" Ander snapped, whirling to look at the monarch. "Mara says she has found the factory creating the bionics!"

Vlad stared at him. "What? Where? Hold a moment; I'm contacting Prim." His eyes unfocused.

:How precise can you get?: Ander asked quickly. *:Did you find the actual building? Or are you just sure it's on the island somewhere?:* Crescent was one of the largest islands that made up the Nyphoren, but at least that would significantly narrow down the search.

:I'd call it more of a complex, but yeah, this seems to be it.: She sent him an image of an industrial complex, surrounded by barbed-wire fencing and watch towers, followed by the coordinates. *:I didn't try to get in.:*

:Do not attempt to breach the perimeter,: he ordered, mentally reaching out to Jak and Takeshi simultaneously. *:Mara found it!:*

He received a start of surprise from Jak, and less than a minute later Takeshi was vaulting over the balcony railing to join them. He and Vlad nodded at each other in greeting.

"It's in the Nyphoren Islands, on Crescent. She found the complex," he explained.

Vlad's lips pressed into a thin line. "That could be problematic."

Takeshi tilted his head. "Oh?"

Ander hid a wince. In his excitement, he'd almost forgotten. "For some reason, crossing large bodies of water is... difficult for Vampires."

"It makes us feel sick, weak, unbalanced," Vlad added. "To get to the Nyphoren... that is a significant amount of water to cross. Then they'd have to make the return trip. There are ways to mitigate it, but they are a bit unwieldy, let's say."

Takeshi hummed. "Well, then we cross that bridge when we get to it. In the meantime, we should gather more information. What sort of defenses does the compound have? How it is being supplied? Is it integrated with a nearby settlement, or is it separated, either by distance or other means?"

Vlad cracked a smile. "Prim says she likes the way you think. Ander, can Mara answer these questions?"

:Yeah, I can get you that info!: Mara had apparently been concentrating to follow the conversation through Ander's thoughts, or Hades was relaying it to her. *:The new guy seems on top of his stuff. I can't wait to meet him. Like, really meet him; I could talk to him, I guess, but it's not the same thing. Give me a few days to see what I can*

find out; I have a feeling he's not going to be satisfied with my usual level of effort.: She laughed.

:Be careful,: Ander warned.

:I always am, but thanks for worrying about me! Cheers!: And she was gone.

They had different definitions for "being careful," but Mara could look after herself. For all that she acted younger than Ander, she was almost twice his age, and a powerful water mage in her own right with a goddess watching over her shoulder. She would be fine.

"She's going to investigate what she can, and she'll get back to us in a few days," Ander reported. "She has something else she wants to do there, but she doesn't think it will interfere." Now if only he could figure out what was bothering him about the Blade...

Vlad nodded. "Excellent. Then we wait."

"What a mess."

In Rhode's opinion, Duchess Cecile Leblanc of Gallia had certainly summed the situation up nicely. It was definitely a mess, physically and bureaucratically. They still didn't have the full damage estimates out of the Charve base, and it had been almost two months since the incident. He looked around at the assembled dukes and duchesses of the Empire, the true powers behind the throne. The Emperor wasn't even present at this meeting, more concerned with whatever social event had most recently grabbed his attention.

"So then, what do we do about Ebryn? Are we sure he has truly reincarnated again, or are we wasting resources on a red herring?" Tyra Strom, Duchess of the Emerald Shore, asked calmly.

"I don't particularly care. I want him dead," Stefan Belian, Duke of Agale, snarled. "He dared to touch my daughter."

The Duchess of Ni Fon leveled a cool look at the red-haired man. "We all know it's far more likely she dared to touch him," Kobayashi ruthlessly corrected.

"How *dare–*"

"Should we not be more concerned with the prophecy?" Duke Johen Cade cut in. His province of Nyphoren hosted the asset production facility, and Rhode was certain he was concerned that it might become a target if Ebryn was in fact alive again. The previous site had been targeted last time, after all. And though Rhode had not been involved in that incident, it had been far worse than the most recent one in many ways.

Duke Latif Hisham of Cartago-Mir shrugged, running a hand over his bald head. "Should we trust a prophecy made by a Truth Seeker in the first place? Has it not already led us to take actions we would not have otherwise taken?"

Rhode's eyes darted to the three Truth Seekers who were standing watch at various places in the room, but none of them reacted to the slight. Still, Rhode wished that they would stop insulting the Seekers to their faces. There was no need to breed any more resentment than he was sure there already was, even if they didn't show it. The Seekers were strange and arcane, a hive mind beyond Rhode's understanding, but he didn't believe they were as emotionless as most people assumed. One day, someone was going to push too far, and… well, Rhode wasn't sure what would result, but it probably wouldn't be good. For anyone.

"Is that not the point of a prophecy? To inform one's actions?" Duchess Mila Holzer of Elbe was by far the youngest of those present. "We must defend the Empire at all costs, should we not?"

"Even if he is not Ebryn reborn, what is the life of one Avari to be sure?" Leblanc said lazily. "We might as well kill him just in case."

"I think the Avari witch we held prisoner might be the key to that," Rhode suggested slowly. "The readings we got off her were very strange, almost like she was not actually Avari. I think that is why the prism sphere failed to hold her." He didn't dare present the evidence as having come from the Seekers. He appreciated their usefulness in ways this forum would not.

"Stop looking for reasons your little experiment failed," Belian snapped. "She got away and blew up half of the base with her, and Rikona's little mistake fled with her. Too bad. Focus on something useful for once."

Kobayashi glanced at Belian disdainfully. "Following custom is not the same as making a mistake, not that you'd have any experience in that regard. And besides, I have reason to believe he is dead by now."

Strom raised one dark eyebrow as she brushed back her long, wavy black hair. "Would you care to share why you believe that?"

"The Nifoni have our ways," Kobayashi said simply.

Rhode tuned them out as the conversation started to devolve into an argument. He would not get any support from them in his investigation into the Avari – Hel, she had called herself. They were too busy trying to save themselves from ruin, afraid of a red-headed Avari prophesied to bring an end to the Empire.

"Colonel."

He glanced to the side to see General Nashaat frowning at him. "Sir?"

"I want you to stop pursuing the Avari."

Rhode stared at him.

Nashaat ignored the dukes as they continued to bicker, running a hand over his bald head. "You've been to multiple provinces in the past month but have yet to come up with any leads. The Avari is a dead end."

Rhode took a deep breath. "She was able to overcome and destroy the prism sphere. That should be impossible–"

"We've only tested it against Truth Seekers before," the general cut him off. "Maybe she was just stronger than them, or maybe the fact they're all linked makes it affect them disproportionately. Who knows. Even if you did find her, I doubt your questions would be answered. The potential gain is far outweighed by the definite cost. I won't have you continue to waste resources on this."

"But if we could find out what she was–"

The general's eyes darkened. "What she was? She was a powerful Avari witch. You are overthinking it, Colonel. I've seen the reports on the prism sphere. You overestimate its usefulness. Move on. Try to figure out what actually went wrong with the sphere, or maybe try to improve it. But stop chasing ghosts. It's not your department." He turned away, ending the "discussion."

Rhode stewed in silence as the argument between the dukes ramped up. He knew Hel hadn't just been a "powerful Avari witch." There was something there, something worth discovering. Why couldn't anyone else see it? The general was wrong; if he found her he was sure his questions would be answered.

He'd just have to be more careful with how he went about it.

Perhaps Cole or Madine would have some ideas.

Chapter Nineteen

Ander finished building the array to Mara's specifications, putting in just enough power to keep it visible, and waited for her seal of approval. Illusions were her specialty and she had put serious effort into ensuring that this one would be correct. A mistake now could end up snowballing if their plans were formed based on faulty intel.

As she checked his work, he glanced around the table. It was getting a little crowded, he reflected wryly. Vlad and Prim were speaking to Frir and Elena quietly as they waited for Ander to finish. Jeri tapped her fingers on the table impatiently. Jamirh fiddled with his cup of water, eyeing the tray of little cakes that had been pushed to one side to make room for the array. Jak reclined back in his chair, staring up at the ghostly form of Hades hovering above, likely in conversation with Her. Takeshi was studying the bright-green lines of Ander's magic taking up most of the table. Thorn and Jitsu were out of sight; he hoped they were under the table and not causing warg-ish trouble somewhere.

Though at least that would be Takeshi's problem if they were.

:All set, Ander!: Mara chirped. *:Let's get this party started!:*

Ander focused on the lines, swirls, and glyphs of the array and allowed his magic to flow freely. It lit up in a blaze of green light that drew everyone's attention. Slowly, like water filling a cup, the shape of the military complex on Crescent Island began to rise from the table. It was detailed around the edges but faded into ill-defined blobs towards the center. Mara had been unable to find a safe way in.

"And this is to scale?" Takeshi asked as the illusion took form.

"Yes," Ander said shortly, unwilling to take his attention from the array until it had settled into its final shape. He could feel Mara's will superseding his as the lead in this particular spell. He was the physical component, providing the magic and his presence; she was the mental component, providing the shape and the guidance. It was uncomfortable. He hated this kind of "shared" casting, but they didn't have any other options. Mara knew what the complex looked like, but she was in the Nyphoren Islands. Ander was in Tarvishte, but he lacked knowledge of the complex.

The shape of the illusion filled in and the buildings settled into clearer focus as the drain on Ander's magic decreased significantly. Now all he had to do was maintain it. "Don't touch," he warned as Elena leaned in to get a better look. "Mara's illusions are excellent, but it doesn't take much to break them."

"Because she uses water as a base instead of light," Takeshi guessed. "It's incredible work. The detail is impressive."

:Aw, tell him I say thanks!: came Mara's pleased response.

"But isn't it your illusion?" Jamirh asked, eyebrows furrowed as he studied one of the revealed buildings. "Since you cast it?"

Jak shook his head. "Nah, Mara designed and guided it. Ander is just the... battery, for lack of a better term, since she's not here to do it herself."

Jamirh's mouth silently formed an "o" shape.

Ander shoved aside his annoyance at the "battery" comment as Mara sent a wry mental apology, acknowledging his effort on her behalf. "She says thank you," he passed on to Takeshi.

"Takeshi, you and the Lady were most recently on an Empire military base. Does anything about the layout look familiar? Any similarities to the base in Charve?" Vlad asked.

Takeshi was prowling around the illusion, gaze intent. "It is hard to say. Does Mara know the purpose of any of these buildings?"

:Some of them, yes. These over here are dormitories of some sort, and I think this building has food.: Ander passed along the information as she considered the illusion through his eyes. *:This small one is maybe an office? Do bases have offices? Paperwork's got to be done somewhere. There are a few larger buildings towards the center; I'm guessing that's where the actual production is taking place, though I don't have any real proof of that. Just makes sense to me.:*

"How much movement on and off the base has she observed?" Frir asked. "Are there multiple checkpoints?"

:There is an occasional truck from Star Light City, but they use the harbor most of the time. There's a lot of boats. The bay is pretty well-guarded, but I'm not completely sure about checkpoints. There's at least one for the trucks on the road leading to the facility, and then another at the entry gate itself,: she explained.

"Could one of these larger buildings be used for... uh... holding the Avari?" Jamirh wondered.

"The Avar– oh." Prim's face fell as she realized what Jamirh meant.

She wasn't alone; a number of faces around the table looked stricken. Takeshi was surprisingly not one of them. "That is likely, yes."

Frir frowned. "We are sure the Avari are alive when they are modified? Or are we looking at a morgue?"

Ander opened his mouth to answer, but Jamirh beat him to it. "Yeah, they're alive. Kept in small spaces, though."

Jeri tilted her head in confusion. "Small spaces? Why would you say that?"

Jamirh started to respond, then stopped, looking perplexed. He tried again. "I'm... not sure. It was just a thought I had." His hand drifted to that key he always wore.

"As much as I hate to say it, whatever is cheapest is likely the method of containment they use," Elena said with a grimace. She fiddled with a strand of bright-red hair, the saturation signaling that she was young for a Vampire. But she was good at logistics. "From what I understand of the bionics, they probably don't need the Avari in particularly good condition to be successful. Do we know if they keep the same parts from Avari to Avari? Or is each bionic uniquely formed?"

Takeshi hummed, looking up at Hades' form briefly. "The Lady has seen four. She says that the forms are similar, but not exactly the same. In all cases, the mechanical portion was greater than the organic."

Jeri winced. "So it's even less likely that their condition matters."

Vlad sighed heavily. "Unfortunately that seems to be the case. It is not surprising, considering what they become."

"There must be a baseline level of condition necessary, we just don't know what that is, or what it is in regard to," Ander pointed out. "A dead body doesn't work, but is that the bare minimum? Is it necessary for the organic component to be an Avari, or could it be a magically inclined Human? The head seems to be necessary, but why, when the victim appears to be functioning using programming rather than thinking?"

:I'm glad I haven't met one of these things yet.: Mara sounded perturbed. *:The way you describe them is disturbing. Do you think they can drown?:*

:Possibly, based on the surviving organic anatomy still requiring oxygen, but they have surprised us before.: "I could theorize more if I knew more about the process and what qualities they require, but I don't," he concluded.

Elena looked like she was going to be sick. "That's horrible."

Jak sighed. "Thank you for that analysis, Ander, but maybe we should be focusing on the base itself?"

"Knowing how the bionics are being constructed could cast more light on how this facility functions, so the information is not ir-relevant," Takeshi countered. "However, I do still have questions concerning the base. What is the surrounding terrain? You said it was situated on a bay?"

:Yup! Big bay area. Very nice. The base is quite a ways from Star Light City – maybe twenty-five miles north? And it's surrounded by forest, but they've cleared out a fair amount of space around the perimeter. I think there's about a hundred feet of barren ground between the fence and the tree line. That's why I couldn't get too close, you know? Well: – her voice became smug – *:not from the forest, anyway. I was able to enter the bay itself, but I didn't dare leave the water. There are Truth Seekers in there, too. At least three of them.:*

Ander saw Jak twitch as he relayed the information. Mara was almost certainly going to hear from him later about taking unnecessary risks. It did explain the very detailed shape of the dock area, though.

:The bay is pretty large, but also really protected. It opens towards the other islands, not the ocean. There's also a bunch of patrol boats prowling around the area.:

Takeshi frowned. "How was she able to get so close via the bay?"

"Mara is a Mer," Jak informed him with a sigh.

"A Mer?" Jamirh asked. A cake was missing from the nearby plate; had Jamirh taken it? Ander hadn't noticed anyone eating.

"A type of inherent magic," Vlad explained. "Mer are able to breathe underwater."

Jamirh blinked. "Like the Veren can? Are the Veren all... Mer?"

Jeri shook her head. "No, the Veren have gills. A Mer's ability to breathe underwater comes from their magic."

"Oh." Jamirh shrank back a little, looking embarrassed. "Got it."

"Actually, speaking of the Veren...?" Prim trailed off, looking at Ander expectantly.

:The Veren are not involved,: Mara confirmed. *:They've cut them-selves off from the surface for the most part, content with the couple of islands that are "theirs." And none of those are near the base. The Veren just want to be left alone.:*

Jeri leaned forward, resting her head on her hands. "And as deep-sea-dwelling fish people, they can achieve that, even with the Empire living directly over their heads."

"It must be nice to just ignore whatever you want to," Frir commented idly.

"In the end this matter will affect them too if the Abomination is not stopped," Vlad pointed out. "We could arrange a way to send word to make them aware of the situation."

"I'm not sure what kind of reception we could hope to get," Prim admitted. "The Veren have always been isolationist. Well, since the Empire took the islands, anyway."

Elena frowned. "Romanii never really managed strong ties with the Veren. They don't like to leave the Nyphoren Islands, and very few people cross the Wall. Those who do are usually Vampires, and... well..." She shrugged. "You won't find me getting in a boat over that amount of water any time soon."

Frir winced in sympathy, while Jeri leaned over to speak softly to Jamirh, who looked thoroughly confused. Takeshi's gaze settled on Hades briefly before returning to the illusion.

Another little cake was missing. Curious. It wasn't the wargs, was it?

:I could try to talk to them,: Mara offered. *:If you and Jak – and maybe Takeshi – think it would be okay. I don't want to leave Crescent if you think I should stay.:*

:We can discuss that later.: It was probably their best bet for any sort of successful contact, but Mara was likely more useful as eyes on the complex.

Prim cleared her throat. "For now, I think we should return to the problem of this." She gestured towards the illusion.

Takeshi nodded. "Indeed. So then, the base is well-guarded. What is our goal?"

"Destroy it, probably," Frir suggested.

"But," Elena exclaimed, eyes widening, "would that be enough? It goes back to Takeshi's point about knowing how the bionics are made – destroying the complex might not end production. How many people know the process? Could they just move production elsewhere?"

Jak's voice was grim. "Anyone who knows how to create the bionics has to die."

Silence.

"This is not up for debate," the first high priest of Hades continued. "Abomination cannot be allowed to continue. It must be stomped out."

"That could lead to many, many people dying. Maybe even people who don't understand what they are doing." Prim sounded upset.

"Yeah, well, a lot of people have already died." Ander was surprised by the venom in Jamirh's voice. "They've been dying in droves for the past forty years or whatever while you all have been doing nothing."

Jeri's eyes went wide. "Jamirh–!"

"No," he snapped at her. "What did you all expect to happen while you hid behind your big magic wall? Did you think the Empire was going to wait too? Because they didn't, I can tell you that much. There have been rumors of bionic super-soldiers in Lyndiniam for years. How many do you think they've made? Because she's right." He thrust his chin at Elena. "Forty years of production? You've got a way bigger problem than I think you realize. How many of them do you think there are now? Because I'm going to guess there's a lot. The Empire is good at making things and hating Avari, and the bionics are made of Avari."

He stared around the table, silver eyes flashing angrily. "I've been trying my best for weeks to learn how to use magic I never even knew I had because, for some reason, now is when we have to rush. Has it occurred to anyone that if someone had done anything earlier it might not be this bad now? Yeah, so the previous guy died. All of you were still here in your... immortal glory. Did you really have to wait for me?" He shook his head, raising his arms and dropping them in frustration. "What good is the magic if you don't use it?"

Hades abruptly manifested above the table, black gown and long white hair billowing in a non-existent breeze. The air thickened as Her power saturated it in warning. Ander's eyes snapped to Jak, whose mouth was pressed in a thin line.

"No one in this room besides myself knew forty years ago of the presence of the Abomination." Her voice was calm even as Her presence pressed down on them, revealing Her displeasure. "Forty years ago I wasn't even completely sure it had returned. Echoes and echoes... some signs were there, but nothing concrete. I recalled Ebryn to life out of an overabundance of caution more than anything else. I was not certain I was correct until shortly before his death."

"Then you should've done something then!" Jamirh exclaimed. "Why didn't you?"

"Because I could not." She sounded unbothered by this fact. "There are... laws, I suppose you could call them, that govern what gods can and cannot do, and when. I know it seems as though we act without thought whenever we wish to, but if that were the case, mortals... mortals would not have free will. I'm not sure there would even be mortals. I'm not sure this planet would still exist."

That was... an interesting thought.

"Doesn't the Abomination lead to the imminent destruction of the world anyway?" Jamirh wasn't having it, completely uncowed by the Lady's show of power.

:He might be one of the bravest people I've ever seen,: Mara whispered to Ander.

He didn't respond, trying to make it fit with his previous picture of Jamirh. Where had this come from? What had Takeshi been teaching him?

:No,: Hades whispered, even quieter than Mara had been. *:I tried to tell you. This has always been in him. He just needed to find it.:*

Had it? This was the first time Ander was seeing it.

"It can. It has come very close to victory in the past. The closer it gets, the more I can intervene," Hades explained to Jamirh. "Understand that, even now, it is far from the point where I can directly influence events. After the death of your predecessor, Ander began construction of a vessel through which I could circumvent this restriction. I am certain that should some of my siblings find out about it, they would be... displeased, to say the least, even though I limited myself to what a mortal would be capable of."

"Fine," Jamirh snapped. "Then what about twenty years ago? People definitely knew then. Even if you couldn't do anything directly, you seem capable of using people to do what you can't. Why bother waiting for me?"

"Because we have had this conversation in the time before. In accordance with the deal we struck, I have held to exactly what was asked of me." Her voice was cool.

Ander was surprised at Her candor, considering how She had danced around the topic before. He saw Vlad bring a hand up to cover his eyes. Frir and Elena both flinched. Jeri looked horrified.

Jamirh went pale, then red. Without another word, he turned and stormed out of the room. Jeri glanced at Vlad but didn't wait for his nod before hurrying after her charge. Hades disappeared too, though She no longer felt angry to Ander.

There was an awkward silence.

Frir opened his mouth, but Elena shot him a warning glare. "Whatever you are about to say, don't."

He shut it.

Takeshi's expression was hard to read, hidden as it was by the ever-present mask. "Not all of his points are without merit." He returned his attention to the illusion. "Action could have been taken sooner, and it does not need to rely on Jamirh's presence. I hope no one was waiting for Jamirh to master his inherent before dealing with this. Or was the plan to wait for him to volunteer?"

"Certainly not," Vlad asserted, anger tinting his voice. "While he remains in this country, Jamirh may do as he wishes. Not even my mother can override that." Red eyes glanced warningly at Jak. Words were going to be had between mother and son, Ander predicted.

Jak shrugged. "No one is taking away anyone's choice. And time is now of the essence – he was right about that, too. Forty years is too long to let this fester."

Ander was reviewing Hades' words. She had all but confirmed that the previous Ebryn's death was connected to the Abomination, if not directly caused by it. Not surprising, but good to know nonetheless. Unfortunately it did lead to more questions. Was it an accident, or was he hunted?

Or had he been hunting it?

"Then we strike," Takeshi was saying. "I will go and–"

He was cut off by numerous voices speaking at once. Ander hid a wince; a new priest going into such danger was not going to go over well, no matter how capable he had proven himself to be.

:I always forget how lively things are back home,: Mara commented as everyone tried to talk over everyone else. *:Maybe I should come back for a few years, soak in the excitement. Oh, maybe I could add to it!:*

:That won't be necessary, but do as you wish,: Ander sighed. He met Takeshi's eyes. The other man wasn't even trying to be heard over the cacophony. The shinobi shook his head very slightly. Ander could almost feel his disappointment with the whole situation.

Ander could sympathize.

:Do you still need this?: he asked, nodding towards the illusion.

:Oh, I like that idea,: Mara laughed, seeing Ander's intention, even if she couldn't hear his communication with Takeshi.

Takeshi shook his head again. *:No, I've learned all I can from it. Mara herself would be a better source for now, but I will have to go myself to get the full picture.:*

Ander hesitated. *:You are committed to that course of action?:*

:It is what makes the most sense, if Vampires cannot cross the ocean. If the Lady stands against Abomination, then why should her priests shrink from being involved in fighting it? I have always been a weapon in the hands of others; she should wield me as such. It does not offend me to do that which I was trained to.: His voice was matter-of-fact. *:If you are so concerned, you should come with me.:*

He blinked. *:What?:*

Takeshi's head tilted to the side. *:A good healer is always welcome on missions on the off chance something goes wrong. We could meet up with Mara when we arrive. Three strong mages with the power of the goddess of death and destruction behind them versus a military base with an unknown number of combatants of varying ability – I'll take those odds.:*

Ander's gut reaction was to say no. He hadn't left Tarvishte since he'd left Elbe. He had barely left the palace grounds, never mind the city. He didn't like to.

He didn't want to.

He'd decided that world didn't need him long ago, preferring to remain in the stability of the palace grounds. Everything he needed was here. His fish, the Temple, the hospital, his responsibilities. Let the other priests travel. After that last night in Elbe... anything else he might have wanted was far beyond his reach.

:That was three hundred years ago,: the Lady murmured gently. *:Tarvishte might not have changed much, but the mortal countries have.:*

Yes, they had. And the mortals who had lived then were long gone, too.

Jamirh... wasn't wrong when he said Romanii hid behind its magic wall. Frir had accused the Veren of being isolationist. In the end, were the Romanii any better? At least the Veren were honest about their level of involvement.

He'd be going west. It wasn't like he'd be going back to Elbe. And he was a much stronger mage than he'd been when he left.

He had shields now.

He could feel Hades watching in the back of his mind. She wouldn't push him to leave, he knew, nor would She hold it against him if he chose to stay. Her priests were given the right to choose the causes they championed. He wondered if She was as concerned for Takeshi as the rest of the table seemed to be, or if She had faith in the abilities of Her chosen.

:One can both be concerned and have faith that the outcome will be favorable,: She pointed out. *:Takeshi has proven that this sort of thing is well within his skillset.:*

:The last time I ended up involved in a situation involving the Blade, the outcome was... not what I had hoped for,: he admitted quietly.

He could feel Her regarding him. *:This is very different. The two situations are not equivalent. And you have me, now.:*

He did. And... Takeshi was very capable. So was Mara. They would be doing the invading, not getting invaded.

Ander forced himself to look at it logically. More capable people raised the chances of success. Between Mara, Takeshi, and Ander, they had a fairly well-balanced team.

:Takeshi thinks the three of us should take down the factory,: he informed the water witch.

She didn't even hesitate. *:Wow, three priests coming together to do a thing? And I get to meet him? Count me in!:* She paused, then asked softly, *:What about you?:*

He hesitated. He still didn't *want* to, but... maybe it was time. And Takeshi was correct about the presence of a doctor being useful. *:I think... I think I'm going to be joining you.:*

He felt a flash of surprise, but all she asked was, *:Are you sure?:*

:No,: he admitted wryly. Mara, of course, remembered when he'd first arrived at the Temple. *:But I think I should.:*

:Only if you're sure. Don't let new guy pressure you!:

:He's not.: He nodded at Takeshi. *:Both Mara and I agree.:*

:I will back this,: Hades declared. *:They will not dispute my will. Well, not much,:* She added after a moment of reflection.

:Then it is decided.: The shinobi looked back at the Vampires and Jak, who were all still talking over each other at Takeshi. *:Time to inform everyone else.:*

Ander took that as his cue and violently shattered the illusion, sending water everywhere and mercifully stopping the argument. The water wasn't real and was already returning to the ether Mara had pulled it from, but it was real enough for that moment. Mara giggled.

"Ander, what the hell!" Jak sputtered, wiping water from his face.

"A decision has been made," Takeshi stated calmly. "Ander and I will go to Crescent Island and meet up with Mara, and the three of us will deal with the facility. Hades has agreed to this plan," he added as everyone tried to speak again, holding up his hand to stop them. "This is no longer a debate; we are committed to this path."

"It is what makes the most sense," Ander added, deciding to back Takeshi up and purposefully ignoring the concerned expressions on Vlad's and Jak's faces and the shocked ones on everyone else's. Annoyingly, he knew it had more to do with him now and less to do with Takeshi. "Vampires will struggle to make the crossing. We will not."

"Wait, you–" Frir cut himself off as Elena whacked him.

"And how will you cross?" Prim asked, frowning. At least she wasn't making a big deal out of it. "We cannot help you with that. It is... difficult to get to the Nyphoren from Romanii."

"You could always go through the Empire? How risky would that be?" Elena looked thoughtful, but her eyes kept darting in his direction. Goddess, it was going to be all over the palace when this meeting was over, wasn't it?

Takeshi shook his head. "I might actually have a method of making the crossing, but I would have to return to Bariza. It wouldn't be impossible; I can disguise myself, and no one is looking for Ander. The risk would actually be quite minimal."

"The pirates," Ander realized, thinking back to Takeshi's story and ignoring the way Vlad's eyes were glued to him. "You want to utilize them."

Takeshi nodded. "They have already offered to take me to the Nyphoren Islands; they thought it would be better for me to go there than Gallia. I just need to get into contact with them again, and the best way I know to do that is in Bariza." He paused. "In retrospect, even discounting the chip, going to the Nyphoren probably would not have been the wiser choice if there is a strong military presence there."

Jak shrugged. "There's about fifty islands that make up the Nyphoren and some are better managed than others. And you could probably melt into whatever society you chose regardless."

"True, but I prefer not to have to be looking over my shoulder for the rest of my life." Takeshi shrugged.

Vlad raised an eyebrow. "So you've decided to go on an incredibly dangerous mission there?"

"Missions are not life," Takeshi countered. "Going there on a mission is different from living there. The mission will, one way or the other, end."

Jak grimaced. "Let's hope it ends successfully."

Ander couldn't help but agree.

Chapter Twenty

Takeshi woke up to a wet nose pushing at his face. Not quite willing to get up yet, he turned his face away and bundled himself more deeply in his blankets. Jitsu did not need him to get out, so whatever it was she wanted, it could wait.

He heard her huff in annoyance. She flopped down on top of him, still seeking his face. He hid under the blankets; it wasn't time to get up. She couldn't make him, not even by gently pawing at his shoulder. The bed was warm and comfortable and he wasn't willing to give that up yet.

A very sad whine originated from above him, along with the feeling of utter grief that her person was not joining her on This Great Day.

Takeshi sighed, snaking an arm out of the blankets so he could pet her. "Why is today great?" he murmured, still not onboard with getting up.

He felt Jitsu's tail beat against the bed as she perked up. It was wonderful! It was snowing! And not just little snow – fun snow!

Takeshi peeked out from under his blankets at the large window. It *was* snowing, big flat flakes falling lazily from a gray, cloudy sky, just barely light enough to be considered dawn. "So it is," he agreed, curling back under the blankets.

Jitsu pawed at him again. They needed to get up! They were in charge of plowing! Well, not totally in charge, but in charge of the wargs who wanted to plow.

Takeshi squeezed his eyes shut for a moment, then hauled himself into a sitting position as Jitsu jumped off the bed. He stared at the snow bleakly. She was right. He did, technically speaking, have a job he had agreed to. Even though he hadn't quite realized it would mean going out into the snow early in the morning. His sensitivity to the cold was going to make this much more unpleasant than it had to be.

He dressed quickly, adding a few extra layers as Jitsu sat at attention next to the window, nose pressed against the glass. He envied the warg her fur, which was certain to keep her warm. Maybe he should look into a fur coat? At least for when it snowed? He made sure to wrap his blue scarf snugly around his neck, overlapping it with his mask.

He was dismayed to find how much snow had piled up already as he left the palace. Jitsu leapt into it without any reservation, joining a number of other wargs who were also playing in the courtyard. Takeshi eyed the two feet of snow, then the distance between the door to the palace and the Temple where the equipment was kept. Not interested in having cold, wet feet and legs for the day, he was pleased to notice a deep shadow by the door of the Temple. He stepped back into the shadow of the palace, weaving the two shadows together into the pattern of a shadowstep, and stepped through the palace shadow into the Temple shadow. *:I'm over here,:* he sent to Jitsu. *:Come and help?:*

The warg immediately abandoned her playmates and bounded over to him, white fur blending in with the snow around her. He scratched her ear in thanks with one hand as he opened the Temple door, grateful for the surge of warm air. He followed Jitsu through the Temple. The door to Ander's office was closed, but there was light visible beneath it. Takeshi wondered how long the other priest had been up as he passed through the sanctuary to the courtyard, where wargs had already begun to gather.

He spent the morning hitching and directing wargs, thankfully not by himself. A group of four servants arrived shortly after him who were already familiar with the process and were happy to explain how it all worked. By the time they were done, Takeshi was exhausted. The wargs all seemed to share an overabundance of energy, and while they were excited to help, their excitement sometimes got in the way of them helping. They didn't always agree on what routes were most efficient, and some didn't care about efficiency at all, more interested in the experience of being in the snow. Luckily, Jitsu appeared to have their respect and was willing to enforce Takeshi's orders. He wondered how Ander had done it without a warg second-in-command and could understand why the man had been quick to pass this duty on.

Still, it hadn't been awful. The wargs had been having fun, and they wanted the two-feet to have fun as well. Nothing about their behavior was malicious and there had been some cute moments. It just wasn't the sort of thing he imagined Ander enjoying.

As he and Jitsu entered the sanctuary of the Temple, the man in question was standing at the door to his office. The half-Avari eyed Jitsu with disgust as she shook herself to get rid of the snow clinging to her fur, sending it flying every which way. "How was it?" he asked Takeshi, gesturing towards the stairway to the upper apartments.

"Cold, and hard work, but surprisingly entertaining. The wargs enjoy the process far more than I thought they would." He and Jitsu followed as the other priest led the way. "We won't be in Tarvishte for much longer; I assume we will have to make arrangements in case it snows while we are gone? Who will take care of the wargs?" He removed his wet shoes and set them by the door to dry.

"Jak is staying here so that we can still communicate with Vlad and Prim if we need to. We are going to hand everything off to him, and then pray that anything gets done in our absence. How long do you think this will take?" Ander indicated that Takeshi should sit while he headed into the kitchen, throwing a glance at the large fish tank opposite the fireplace. "Also, what sort of beverage do you prefer?"

"Tea, thank you." Takeshi considered the other question. "It is hard to tell. I'm guessing four or five days to get to Bariza. I'm not sure how long it will take to make contact with the *Sea Spirit*; I'll put a high estimate of two weeks. If they agree, another week to sail to the Nyphoren. Say another two weeks to investigate the situation, plan, and then execute that plan. Finally, the return trip. So a month and a half on average, with the possibility for it to take more or less time as the variables fall into place."

Ander grimaced. "How much more or less time?"

Takeshi shrugged. "The range could stretch anywhere from three weeks to six months. It's hard to say." He settled on a couch, Jitsu curling next to him to share her warmth. He stroked her head in thanks.

"We might be able to pare that down," Ander said thoughtfully. "Jak might be able to gate us to the Wall, or at least to one of the cities along it. Gating to the Nyphoren Islands themselves is too far, I believe, though that would solve a number of problems. You are correct about the number of variables though. How sure are you that you can get in contact with the pirates? And if you do, will they be willing to ferry you to the Nyphoren?" He set a kettle to boil on the stove.

"I know someone who can contact them, so that part should be straightforward. I'm just not sure how she does so," he admitted. "And they were displeased to see me leave. I was given something of an open invitation to return, so I don't foresee any trouble on that front, either." He watched Ander busy himself with gathering various supplies around the kitchen. It looked like there was coffee in addition to tea.

"Are you still cold? Feel free to use the blanket on the couch if you need to; it would probably make Mara's century," the priest commented as he looked over at Takeshi snuggled with Jitsu.

Takeshi twisted to look at the crocheted blanket behind him. The yarn was thick and soft, and multiple shades of blue created a wave-like pattern. "Why would it affect Mara so?"

"Because she made it. And she likes to know people use it." Ander's voice was dry. "But it is warm, if you need it."

Jitsu wagged her tail. Takeshi should use it. He needed all of the warm things.

He sighed, but he had already resigned himself to being told what to do by a large dog for the rest of his life. He pulled the blanket off the back of the couch, laying it across his lap. It was warm, and helped to ease some of the chill clinging to his bones.

Jitsu put her head down on her paws. She was always right about these things.

Takeshi frowned. "What about Jitsu?"

"What about her?" Ander asked, pulling the kettle off the stove.

"What will she do while I'm gone?"

Ander barked a laugh while Jitsu gave him an affronted look. "You think she's staying here?"

Jitsu huffed. What a stupid thought.

"Well, you can't come with us. We are going to need to travel through Gallia, and a three-and-a-half-foot-tall wolf is going to draw attention." Takeshi petted her apologetically, but he didn't see how that could work.

Jitsu flicked an ear dismissively. If she didn't want to be seen, the two-feet would not see her. She would not allow Takeshi to go so far without her.

"Wargs take care of themselves and make their own decisions, as I'm sure you experienced today," Ander stated. "You won't be able to leave her here. She will follow you no matter what you say."

Takeshi regarded her curiously. "What do you mean, that people won't see you? Can you turn invisible?"

Jitsu snorted. She meant what she said. A person did not have to be invisible to not be seen. Takeshi should know that.

He acknowledged her point. "Yes, I'm just wondering how a warg manages it. You can't hide in plain sight like I can."

Ander shrugged. "They don't need to. You will likely never meet a creature who can stay out of sight the way a warg can. It's not invisibility, but I wouldn't be surprised if it is a magic of their own. There are two other priests who have wargs, and they travel together without issue. Somehow." He had two cups steeping now, one with a normal tea ball and one with a coffee filter on top.

The warg nosed at him reassuringly. She would not give them away. She was good at hiding.

"I see." He stroked her soft fur. He did not want to be parted from Jitsu, but he wasn't sure this was the sort of trip she should come on.

:There is nothing to worry about. Ander is correct; the wargs have their own ways of staying undetected. You might as well consider her part of the mission.:

Takeshi almost jumped at Hades' mindtouch. She had been a silent presence since the altercation at the meeting yesterday. However, her faith in Jitsu's abilities was reassuring. He already knew that the wargs weren't simply intelligent animals, though what they were in actuality was a mystery.

"Have you given any more thought to soulforging?" Ander asked, changing the subject abruptly.

"Not particularly." He was familiar with using mundane weaponry, and besides, he was attached to his katana. He had no desire to use magic weaponry, though he couldn't deny the practicality of always having a weapon on hand. "How hard is it to learn?"

The other priest shrugged. "It differs from person to person. It sounds as though there will be a fair amount of downtime while we are gone; it would be a good project to work on."

Takeshi considered that. "And it is something associated with Hades, you said?"

"Yes." Ander nodded. "Her priests and Her children all have the ability."

"Her children... the Vampires?" he checked.

Ander nodded again.

Well, new skills could always be useful. Even though he preferred his own weapons, it wasn't difficult to come up with situations where being able to materialize one out of nothing was the better solution. And... he supposed that this was some way to quantify being one of Hades' priests. Something that he could do, that he could point to and say that it was because he belonged to the goddess. That felt right to him, somehow – grounding in a way he was realizing he needed. He had dismissed this ability far too easily when Ander had brought it up the first time. "Very well, then. You are right about the projected downtime; having something specific to work on is not a bad idea. What is the base array for the technique? I should begin internalizing it now."

The scarred man tilted his head slightly. "There is no array. It is not that kind of magic."

Takeshi blinked at him. "No array? At all?" He was familiar with non-visible patterns for spells, but the pattern still *existed* in the mind of the caster. Perhaps because the magic was from a divine source, it didn't need it? That would make it an even better goal to succeed at than he had thought. He found himself growing more interested.

"It is closer to an inherent than learned magic," Ander explained as he brought over the steaming cup of tea. "The first step is manifesting one's soul into a crystal."

Takeshi wrapped his hands around the tea cup, taking a moment to absorb the heat through the porcelain before asking, "What?"

He could practically see Ander asking Hades why he was the one explaining this. Too bad; he was the one who was here and he'd brought it up. "You must first locate your soul, then manifest it into a crystal. At that point, you can 'forge' it into weapons and armor."

"Locate my soul," Takeshi repeated slowly. "Of course."

Soft laughter filtered through his mind. *:I will help with that part, but it is not dissimilar to finding your magic core. Meditation usually helps, and you are well-practiced with that.:*

"She can help with most of it," Ander muttered, taking a sip from his own cup.

Sometimes Ander confused him. Had he not just offered to help with it himself while they were on the mission? Takeshi had noticed a number of such little contradictions in the other priest's words over the past couple of months.

He pulled his mask down and took a sip of the tea. It was a black tea, served at the perfect temperature and enhanced with just a hint of sugar. He nearly sighed with pleasure. "The tea is excellent, thank you. It is brewed perfectly."

Ander inclined his head. "Thank you. I enjoy many types of science. Brewing is one of them."

Privately, Takeshi thought of making tea as more of an art than a science, but to each their own.

"How have you been settling into your duties?" Ander asked, switching topics yet again. "Not just this morning, but in general."

Takeshi hummed. "Well, I think. I have been enjoying dealing with the wargs. They appear to be a force of... violent positivity." Jitsu's tail wagged. "I am more comfortable with Hades' constant presence as well."

Now both of the females in the room were pleased with him.

Green eyes studied him. "Have you made a decision yet?"

"No, something is still... I don't know," he admitted. "I'm not even entirely sure what I'm waiting for. It seems that the logical decision is to say yes, but something still feels out of place, or missing perhaps." Hades had not set a deadline on the trial period, but maybe she should have. Though perhaps this soulforging ability would fill that missing piece.

"I am not the right person to help with that," Ander stated frankly. "I chose... almost instantly. I can't even comprehend a different decision. But my situation was also very different." He paused. "Perhaps you will find what you are searching for while we are on the mission? It seems more like the sort of thing you would gravitate to."

Takeshi could only hope he was right, because right now he was in some sort of limbo. Eventually, he was going to have to make a decision. He couldn't make Hades – or the other priests – wait forever.

Takeshi was a bit miffed. Jamirh hadn't shown up for training.

He could understand the Avari being upset after yesterday's argument with Hades, but one had nothing to do with the other. He still had to learn how to defend himself. It didn't matter what Hades said or Ebryn had done. Yes, Jamirh had made good progress, but that didn't mean he could just stop learning. Learning how to fight was a lifelong process; not even the masters were ever "done." Jamirh needed to be here putting effort in.

The whole situation was a mess, though. Takeshi understood that. From what he could tell, there were both good and bad points being held on both sides, all intertwined with each other until it was impossible to tease them apart. It was likely there was no "correct" solution at this point.

What was then the "best" solution? Takeshi wasn't sure.

He was impressed with how Jamirh had initially stood his ground against the goddess. From a quick glance around, it seemed it hadn't been expected by the majority of the table. Hades had appeared the least surprised, but then again, supposedly she had already had the conversation with Ebryn and thus knew what to expect. It was interesting that Jamirh – who despised Ebryn and hated to be reminded of him – still occasionally acted in the same way, even though the few people Takeshi had talked to who knew both had claimed that they were like night and day.

Takeshi wondered if Ebryn had also sulked when things hadn't gone his way.

Instead of training Jamirh, Takeshi had spent the time training with Jitsu. If she was going to come with him, he wanted to be sure he knew her strengths and weaknesses and that they could work together in a fight. It had gone astronomically well. Fighting as one came almost as easily as breathing, each of them reacting to the other naturally and fluidly. Hades had commented that their bond was deep and strong, as they had barely been outside of each other's presence since Jitsu had found his hospital room, which helped them work together.

Jitsu was ridiculously proud, all but strutting as they left the training grounds, tail waving like a banner. Takeshi was watching her antics with amusement when he noticed a certain red-haired figure hovering nearby.

"Jamirh," he greeted him with some surprise. He glanced up at the position of the sun. "You are late for training today. Surely you didn't think we would cancel because of the snowfall?"

The Avari winced. "Ah, no, not really." He looked around as though noticing the snow piles for the first time. "Didn't even really notice the snow. I'm sorry; I lost track of time."

It was hours after they were supposed to have met. Takeshi didn't need Hades to tell him that was a lie, but he let it go. "I see. Please make an effort to be on time tomorrow; I need to make sure you have a routine while I'm gone."

Jamirh frowned, ears twitching. "While you're gone?" he asked.

Takeshi began walking back to the palace. He didn't want to be outside in the cold for any longer than he had to be. "Yes. Ander and I will be leaving in a few days to deal with the bionic factory."

Jamirh's ears swept down sharply. "What? Why?" he asked, following after Takeshi.

The shinobi glanced back at him. "Because it needs to be dealt with."

"But why you?" He sounded upset. "Haven't w... you already been screwed over enough by all this?"

Takeshi noted the aborted "we." "That doesn't really play into the decision. It must be destroyed, and I have a skillset that lends itself to that end. If I am to decide to be a priest of Hades, then I should act like one. If she stands against Abomination, so should I. It is my responsibility to destroy it when I come across it."

"But you won't be just 'coming across it,' you'll be seeking it out," Jamirh argued. "Why go through all that effort? If everyone is so sure it will come after me, then why not wait for it here?"

"As you rightfully pointed out yesterday, that will lead to more deaths, which is unacceptable. I have been trained to do these sorts of missions, Jamirh," he tried to explain. "I am perhaps one of the best options we have for dealing with it."

Jamirh raised an eyebrow doubtfully. "You've trained to destroy a world-ending phenomenon that a god has problems with?"

Takeshi shot him a wry glance. "The scale might be different, but the action that needs to be taken is still something I am familiar with."

They walked in silence for a few minutes. Jamirh looked like he was thinking it through hard, expression pinched and ears drooping. Finally, the Avari asked hesitantly, "Do you think I should be going?"

He immediately pushed down his instinctive "no." Jamirh's ability wasn't really what this was about. "Do you want to fight them?" he asked instead.

"I have to fight them anyway, don't I? That's why you've been teaching me," came the bitter reply.

Takeshi hummed. "There is a difference between preparing for a possible eventuality and seeking out an opponent." He forced himself to analyze Jamirh's ability objectively. "Should you come across them, the first few moments would be telling. *If* your ability can analyze a bionic's movements quickly enough, you could theoretically come out of the encounter the victor. I think you've grown enough into your inherent where that is a possibility. Not one I would feel comfortable betting on, but not unimaginable. The more important question is if you want to fight – because that can make all the difference."

"Does what I want really matter, if I have the Blade?" The question was quiet, a hint of defeat entering Jamirh's voice.

"We cannot assess our worth by magic items," Takeshi said confidently. "Ignore the sword. I do not have a magic sword, and it does not stop me. If you did not have it, would you fight?" He could feel Hades' attention in the back of his mind.

"Do *you* want to fight those things?" Jamirh grimaced, looking sick. "I can't imagine anyone wanting to face... one of those."

Takeshi fought down a sigh. "That's not really what 'wanting' means in this context." He paused, trying to put it into words. "You are correct – in a vacuum, I would not choose to endanger myself thusly. But they do not exist in a vacuum. The Abomination's existence causes harm to the living beings affected by them, many of whom I imagine cannot defend themselves from such a thing. But I can. And I can do more than defend – I can hunt, and I can destroy. So yes, I do 'want' to fight them, because I feel it is my responsibility to do so. Because by my actions, the harm they can cause is minimized, and people will be saved without even needing to be in danger. Is that not worth the cost of battle?"

They had arrived at the door to his rooms. He turned to face Jamirh fully. "But it is okay to not feel that way. Not everyone is meant to fight, and there is no shame in that. And even if Ebryn felt that way, that doesn't mean you should be beholden to the same feelings." He hoped Hades understood this too. "Do I think you should be coming on this mission? No – your combat ability is not yet at a level where you should be facing opponents who are trying to kill you. But I think this is a question you need to ask yourself. Not 'do I want to fight,' or 'do I have to fight,' or even 'do other people think I should fight,' but 'do I feel a personal responsibility to fight.' In the end, it must come from you. When you can answer that question truthfully, you will know if this path is right.

"You may always need to be able to defend yourself. That is dependent on the choices of others. But to take offensive action against those who would harm others – that is a choice *you* make. Do not make it lightly," Takeshi warned before slipping into his room with Jitsu, leaving Jamirh in the hall to think over his words.

Chapter Twenty-One

J amirh found himself back in his rooms, staring aimlessly out the window at the city below.

He had a lot to think about.

Takeshi's words kept running over and over through his mind until they blurred together and lost all meaning. Want, responsibility, choice. It kept coming back to the same concepts. He thought he had already made his decision to fight, but Takeshi had thrown everything into a different perspective. And it was true – Jamirh hadn't really been committed, had he? He'd just been doing what other people wanted him to do because he could.

If he were being honest with himself, Jamirh could admit that he had never had any sort of responsibility before. He'd always looked out for himself first and foremost. Sure, he'd help other people out if he could, but he'd never been *responsible* for them. Jamirh had spent his whole life chasing whatever he wanted. Not that he had often gotten it, but that was the goal. There was no point in doing anything else; life in Lyndiniam just didn't allow for it. He'd wished things would change, sure, but he'd always known nothing would. Trying to change things was pointless.

But if he could change things, would he? If his actions could actually make things better for others, would he put in the effort?

Is this really a debate?

He didn't know.

His instinct was to say "no," to do what he'd always done and look out for himself, but... that didn't feel right somehow.

He banged his head against the window in frustration.

I guess it is.

And that wasn't even touching the current fiasco. What was he going to do about that? Yeah, he had been training for a month now, but even he knew that wasn't enough to do what they wanted him to do. And they all seemed to be waiting for him before they did anything. Why did it fall to him? He hadn't even known anything about this before three months ago. What did they honestly expect him to do about it?

It was frustrating. Takeshi talked about personal responsibility, but where was theirs?

He felt bad about that thought immediately. Takeshi had been involved for even less time than Jamirh; none of this was his fault. But what about everyone else?

Why was Jamirh so important?

Yeah, let's just... focus on you for right now.

He had a sword that only he could use against the Abomination, but... Takeshi said the Blade shouldn't matter. His past life had fought the demons, but he didn't really care about that, either. He didn't want to fight the bionics – but no, Takeshi said that was the wrong idea too. His inherent made him uniquely suited to fighting in a way very few others were. Did he feel like it was his responsibility to fight the bionics?

For what it's worth, I felt it was mine. Not really sure about the other guy. But the Nifoni is right; maybe don't let that sway you.

...Wait, what?

Jamirh blinked, trying to figure out where that thought had come from. It hadn't felt quite right, somehow. In fact, it sort of reminded him of when he had been trying to escape the bionic...

Yes, that was me, too. We can't keep doing the whole "die and be reborn" thing; nothing is going to get done. As you've seen.

Jamirh felt a chill travel down his spine. He froze. Hesitantly, he offered a weak "Hello?"

Hello! Cheers for when your internal struggle becomes so great you start listening to the voices in your head. I've been trying to get through for a while now, but this is a lot harder than I thought it would be.

If nothing else, the voice sounded cheerful. Otherwise it sounded exactly like Jamirh, which was making it difficult to tell apart from Jamirh's own thoughts. "You've been what?" He dreaded the answer.

Trying to help, mostly. You seem way more lost than I was, for all that you found Romanii.

Jamirh didn't want to ask the logical question. He really, really didn't. But he had to stop dodging these things if he wanted to understand what was going on. "Who are you?"

There was a pause, during which Jamirh felt like he was being judged. *You anywhere near a mirror? I think I can do something with those.*

Jamirh glanced around. There was a large, rectangular mirror over one of the thin wall tables. That would probably work. He approached it cautiously, uncertain what was supposed to happen. He found himself staring at his reflection in confusion. What was he waiting for?

Hold on, I'm trying to work this out... I've never done this before.

"Done what?" Jamirh asked, perplexed.

Been a reincarnated fraction of a soul and tried to– ah, there we go.

Jamirh's reflection shifted slightly. It was still him, but at the same time it wasn't. The Jamirh in the mirror shared his ruby-colored hair and silver eyes, but he looked younger and was wearing his hair in a short braid over his right shoulder. The reflection's ears twitched happily.

Got it! That was somehow both harder and easier than I thought it would be. Nice. I think there's another way too, but this'll do for now.

Jamirh stared at him. This was... not really what he had been expecting. "Uh... hi?" he tried again.

So you see! I am you. Ebryn. He smiled, still not speaking so much as thinking.

"You are Ebryn?" Jamirh asked, completely confused. This was nothing like the Hero he had heard stories about.

The reflection shrugged. *We are all Ebryn, aren't we? But no, not the one you're thinking of. He's... cranky, most of the time. Doesn't speak much, though it was his idea for me to help you against the bionic thing. No, I'm your more immediate predecessor.*

Jamirh's eyes widened in shock. "Oh, *that* Ebryn!" He'd never really given the one that had died twenty-ish years ago much thought.

He hadn't even asked about him, come to think of it. Vlad had said he'd died mysteriously and hadn't talked to Ander. That was about the whole of his knowledge.

The Ebryn was nodding enthusiastically. *Yup, that one! Actually, maybe you have the right idea about the whole name thing... if we are all Ebryn, it could get confusing. You've already chosen Jamirh, so... I'll be Ryn!*

"Ryn," Jamirh repeated slowly. He could deal with this; at least it wasn't the Hero himself. And Ryn seemed friendly enough. "Yeah, okay." He nodded, then squinted at the reflection as he tried to process everything. "What's happening right now?"

Ryn's shoulders shook with silent laughter. *You are having a debate with yourself over whether or not it is your responsibility to fight the bionics. An echo of who you used to be is chiming in to help.*

Right, the bionics. What even was his life right now? This was insane, all of it. He'd been living a normal life three months ago. Had it been hard? Yes. Had it been miserable? Absolutely. But he had understood it. Now... now everything was weird in ways that were difficult to fully comprehend.

He blamed the blonde girl from the casino, Belian's daughter. Everything had been going just fine until she had stuck her nose where it didn't belong. And now here he was – in a country ruled by Vampires talking to his previous life about killing bionic super-soldiers that were actually corruptions of the world itself which the goddess of death seemed to have a vendetta against. It was giving him a headache to think about.

But what are you going to do about it, is the question?

Jamirh spun away from the mirror in frustration. He was going in circles. He caught sight of the Crystal Light Blade leaning against the couch and strangled down his desire to kick it.

It's not the Blade's fault. Ryn sounded amused. *From what I've managed to pick up, they don't even need it, technically. Like, if you don't fight and the Blade isn't used, that doesn't mean the world is doomed. I think we are just one piece of many involved in this battle.*

"But Hades–"

Of course She *wants you involved; She probably wants as many pieces in play as possible, but I don't think She'd create a plan that hinged on just one part. I actually think Her insistence on us might be more of a... return on investment sort of deal.*

Jamirh frowned, glancing back at Ryn. "What do you mean?"

Do we really know what it cost Her to make the Blade? If She went out of Her way and expended great effort to make it for our illustrious predecessor, then I could see why She would want the Blade used.

"But then why not make it usable by anyone? Why tie it to a singular individual?"

Ryn looked thoughtful. *I think he asked for that when he specified a soulforged weapon, but honestly, who knows? I never studied magic and I have no idea how it works.*

Jamirh looked at him curiously. "Did you know about being a Master of Blades?"

Didn't know that was what it was called, but I knew I was a wizard with bladed weapons. The pride in his thoughts was obvious. *I didn't have the special sword, though. Not that I think it would have mattered.*

He raised an eyebrow curiously. "Oh?"

But Ryn shook his head. *Later. We are trying to figure out what you* should do. *Let's ignore both the Blade and Ebryn's oath for a minute. And me, I don't really matter either here. If you were approached by someone and told that there was one specific – but also dangerous – problem that you were uniquely suited to help with, would you?*

Jamirh thought about that. It seemed pretty straightforward when put that way. "Yeah, probably. But with questions."

Ryn nodded. *So the real problem here is that you feel like you're being forced to help, even though you probably would have said yes if they had just come forward like normal people and asked nicely.*

Jamirh heaved a sigh. "I don't think it's that simple. There's all the magic stuff involved that I don't understand either. And it's really annoying that everyone appears to have just been waiting around for me."

Fair. But we can't do anything about what other people choose to do. As for the magic... well, we don't really need *to understand it, do we?* Ryn's head cocked curiously. *Like, whether or not we understand it, we know how to deal with it.*

"I guess." He studied his not-reflection in the mirror. "How did you die?" he asked softly.

Ryn's smile was sad. *By doing what they are going to do.*

Jamirh furrowed his eyebrows in confusion. "What do you mean?"

I attacked the plant where they were manufacturing the bionics. Myself and three of my friends – we were going to destroy it. It was in Gallia back then, not the Nyphoren, so it was easier to get to. But, yeah, no – it didn't work out.

"What went wrong?" Jamirh asked, feeling a chill travel down his spine.

A lot of things, honestly, Ryn admitted. *We were not prepared for what we found there.*

"Takeshi knows what he's doing. They'll be fine," Jamirh whispered.

We can't know that for sure, but a shinobi is far more likely to be successful than we were, yeah. So that's good. He eyed Jamirh carefully. *We could help, you know. I know things about the base.*

Jamirh's ears twitched. "How? Didn't you say it was in a different location?"

Ryn looked away. *Well, yes, but... I, uh... I might have made a deal. When I died.*

Jamirh stared at him. "With who?" he asked, even though he already knew the answer.

With Hades. At least he had the grace to sound sheepish.

Jamirh wanted to scream. "Why?!"

It was convenient? The answer was apologetic. *And I thought it would probably help us out when we had another go at it?*

"You have got to be kidding me." How did this keep happening? "What was this deal about?"

I wanted a way to... keep track, so to speak, of the factory. I can't really tell you the layout, but I know the layout. Does that make sense?

"No." Jamirh's voice was flat.

It's like I understand where everything on the base is, but I have no idea how to put it into words. I can kind of sense where people and things are, all the time. I just don't know how to share that information.

"Great. What did you promise in exchange for this near-useless knowledge?" Had he been an idiot in every incarnation?

I'm not actually sure, come to think of it. The whole thing is a little hazy. Ryn looked uncertain. *I was dying. That's mostly what I remember. That, and really wanting to make sure my death meant something, because I knew we'd failed.*

Jamirh started to snap, but stopped as Ryn's words caught up to him.

He'd wanted his death to mean something.

It struck Jamirh as horribly sad. Ryn looked to have been younger than Jamirh was now, but he'd already been trying to accomplish something. And he and his friends had died knowing they'd lost.

And what was Jamirh doing with his life? Sure, just surviving had been hard in Lyndiniam, but he wasn't there anymore. Maybe he should be trying for a little more now that he had the space for it. He'd picked up the Blade. He could fight, and he could fight well. He even enjoyed it, now that he knew what he was doing. Everything felt... more, while he was fighting. He felt alive. If he could use those skills to save other people...

...then shouldn't he?

Wasn't that what Takeshi had been talking about? That Jamirh should feel a responsibility to defend others?

He had never wanted that sort of responsibility, or any responsibility at all. But... this was something he was good at, something that aligned itself with a skillset he had and even kind of liked. And it wasn't like anyone else had stepped up until recently. Sure, Takeshi and Ander were going to the Nyphoren to try to stop the bionic production, but was that enough? What if it was too little, too late? What if they died when Jamirh's presence could have prevented it? Could he live with himself if that happened? They were excellent, but they weren't Masters of Blades. What if that could make all the difference? Or... maybe he was still thinking about it wrong. What if it was the combination of skills and abilities that mattered? Ryn had suggested that Hades wanted a number of pieces in play, but what if it wasn't about the number, but the type?

"One of the bionics killed you, didn't it?" he asked quietly as he tried to put the pieces together.

Ryn tilted his hand side to side. *Technically it was one that did it, but there were quite a few more involved in the process.*

"I'm sorry," he murmured.

Ryn's lips twitched into a smile. *What for? I made my own decisions. And besides, I managed to take a good number of them with me. Maybe it even set them back a bit. I like to think I might have bought you some time.*

"Then Takeshi is right, and I'm not ready to face them," Jamirh reasoned, uncertain if he was disappointed about that fact or not.

One red eyebrow raised. *Why do you say that?*

"Because – well, you were better than I am now, weren't you? And you still died." Even if he was going to fight, Jamirh didn't want to commit suicide because he had gone in over his head.

Eh, sort of. Familiar silver eyes considered him. *I'd been using a sword for a few years at that point, and I was really good, but you actually have something I didn't.*

Jamirh blinked in confusion. "I do? What?"

Me! Ryn grinned. *I can allow you to sort of piggyback off my experiences with the bionics, like we did when you were attacked by one a while back. You won't be starting from scratch against them the way I was. So even though you haven't been studying swordsmanship for very long, I think you have a better chance against the bionics than the Nifoni thinks you do.* He glanced at the Crystal Light Blade. *I guess you have that, too.*

Jamirh followed his gaze. "Oh yeah, you didn't have the Blade. Ander had already brought it here."

Yup. That should help you out a bunch, at least in theory. So I think you actually could go head to head with the bionics now. Maybe not a whole bunch at once, but you are way better prepared than you were when that first one attacked you. And even then we managed to survive! I think we've got this.

Ryn's confidence was reassuring. After all, he was the one who had fought the bionics before. Jamirh picked up the Blade, studying it. Takeshi and Ander were going to do the thing that had killed Ryn. Takeshi was his friend, and for all that he didn't like Ander he didn't want him to *die.* He knew they were both very powerful and competent, but... if he had information, and Ryn said he could go toe to toe with the bionics...

He looked back at the mirror and the strange reflection within. "How would we use your knowledge of the base, do you think?"

"I thought I was clear that you *shouldn't* come on this mission?"

Jamirh shifted his weight in his chair at Takeshi's puzzled exclamation. "Yeah, yeah, I got that."

One dark eyebrow raised as the shinobi leaned back against the sofa, clearly waiting for more.

Ander was not as patient. "At your current level, what do you hope to accomplish?"

Jamirh had broached the topic of joining them after his next training session with Takeshi. The shinobi had stared at him for a long moment, then brought him to the Temple, where they had met up with Ander in a comfortable sitting room above the Temple proper. Apparently, Ander "should be involved in this conversation," according to Takeshi. Jamirh wasn't sure he agreed with that, but since he was trying to convince Takeshi to come around to his idea, he didn't argue it.

Even though it meant dealing with Ander.

"It's not really about my... level," he began. He and Ryn hadn't practiced this pitch, but he was beginning to think they should have as sharp green eyes pinned him in place. "It's about what we bring to the table."

Now Ander was also regarding him quizzically with one eyebrow raised. Even Jitsu flicked an ear in his direction from where she lay next to Takeshi on the couch. "'We'?" the priest repeated archly.

Jamirh took a deep breath. "Yeah, Ryn and I. Did… did I ever tell you about the voice I heard, when I was trying to escape the bionic?"

"My voice?" Ander sounded perplexed.

Jamirh shook his head. "No, not you. There was another voice, helping me dodge the bionic. I did mention it to Hel afterwards. We thought it might have been Ebryn? Even though that didn't really make sense. Because he wasn't, like, helpful, generally. And the voice was. But I wasn't even really sure it was real, because it just sounded like me." He was getting nervous. This explanation sounded dumb even to him. "And it turns out we were kind of right, but not really. Because it was Ebryn, only not that Ebryn. It was the middle Ebryn."

"Stop for a moment," Takeshi interrupted. "Breathe. Then let's try that again."

"No, I think I followed that," Ander said slowly. "You are saying that the Ebryn who died twenty-three years ago helped you stay alive when the Abomination was trying to kill you."

Dark shadows coalesced into Hel's form so she was sitting on the large fish tank nearby, peering at him curiously.

Jamirh glanced at her before nodding enthusiastically at Ander. "Yeah, that's it. We decided to call him 'Ryn' to avoid confusing him with Ebryn."

"Because those are so different," Ander muttered.

Jamirh ignored him. "And Ryn has information about the base in the Nyphoren."

Now he had everyone's attention.

Hel hummed thoughtfully. "I wasn't sure he would be able to speak to you that way. Interesting."

Jamirh turned to her, confused. "Why not? You said it was possible for previous incarnations to talk to a new one."

Hel said nothing.

Ander's lips thinned. "He didn't talk to me when I summoned him after his death. I don't suppose there's a reason for that?"

Hel sent Ander an exasperated look as Jamirh shrugged, pushing down his annoyance at Hel's refusal to explain anything. He was still upset about the whole situation she had basically set up. "He didn't mention it, no."

I don't even remember the priest summoning me, to be honest.

"He says he doesn't remember you summoning him," Jamirh passed along.

Ander's expression darkened. "Doesn't remember–"

"Ander." Hel's voice was firm. "Let it be."

"So you are speaking to him now?" Takeshi asked as Ander shot a sharp look at Hel.

Jamirh considered that. "Kinda? It can be hard to tell when it's him and when it's not, and he said it can be difficult to make himself heard over my own thoughts. I'm trying to pay more attention, but it's weird."

"What information does he have about the base that requires you to be present at the location? Because I assume if you did not have to be there you would just give us the information now." Takeshi leaned forward in his seat, eyes intent.

Leave it to Takeshi to figure out the complicated bit. Jamirh glanced at Hel, but her expression was unreadable. "He can sort of sense where everything is on the base. Stuff, people... but when he shares it with me it just feels like one confused blob of activity far off in that direction." He waved a hand. "I can't distinguish anything. Our best guess is I probably have to be there to make heads or tails of it."

He could hear the frown in Takeshi's voice. "But this... Ryn can?"

He shrugged. "Yeah, but we can't figure out how to pass that info to you. I can't even really get it. We tried to map it, but... either his concept of space is warped, or the building doesn't make any sort of logical sense. What we ended up with didn't resemble anything like a building." He pulled a crumpled piece of paper from his pocket. He smoothed it out as best he could and put it on the coffee table. "See?"

Both Ander and Takeshi studied the strange, headache-inducing collection of intersecting lines overlaid with Jamirh's scribbled notes. "Is it possible it works the same way the palace does?" Takeshi offered hesitantly after a moment.

"Unlikely," Ander responded, though there was a hint of doubt in his voice. "I don't think you could create the bionics in a magic building without some sort of implosion happening due to the concentration of Abomination. Also, the palace is the result of thousands of years of magic evolving in a singular place. I don't think the factory Mara showed us could have that sort of buildup." He was gaining confidence as he talked it through. "However, if the Empire has managed to create something with a similar effect, the only safe way to navigate it would be with someone who could intrinsically understand the layout." Green eyes slid towards Jamirh.

"I do not like that idea," Takeshi said flatly. "I stand by what I said before, Jamirh – you are not ready for this sort of mission."

"He'd be with us," Ander mused, expression calculating. "And they won't find him as defenseless as they did the first time."

"Ryn actually thinks I'd do okay," Jamirh tried to explain. "He says I can kind of piggyback off of his experiences, so I'm not actually starting at zero against the bionics."

"And how did Ryn die?" Even though the mask hid his expression, Takeshi's voice was pointed.

Jamirh hid a wince. That was a low blow. He started to respond, but was cut off by Ander. "Actually, how did he die? That was something we were trying to find out." The priest's brow was furrowed.

He felt his ears sink a bit. "He says he and a group of friends tried to destroy the bionic plant when it was in Gallia. It... didn't go well. But!" He had to sell this. "That's why it's a good thing I can share his experiences, so I can avoid his mistakes. And if I can use what he knows" – he paused, having to force the words out – "maybe I can find a way to access Ebryn's knowledge too. That would give me effectively years of experience as a Master of Blades."

Takeshi looked unhappy. "I still don't like this. It's not the same as actual, practiced experience."

There was a long pause, during which everyone in the room except for Jitsu and Jamirh looked like their attention was elsewhere. The warg huffed at him reassuringly. He shot her a grateful look.

Finally, Takeshi shook his head. "I still don't like this," he repeated.

Ander shrugged. "I don't particularly care for any of it. But Mara cannot confirm whether the building is magic or not, and if there's a possibility we might need him..."

"I see what you are saying. I just don't think this is the right solution," Takeshi argued. "We might be risking too much."

"Isn't it my say, whether or not I am risked?" Jamirh cut in. He tried not to see the slow grin forming on Hel's face. It was her victory, after all. He reorganized his thoughts. "If I'm willing to risk it, then isn't that on me?"

"That's... not how missions work," Takeshi said, shaking his head slowly.

"And yet, it is how our religion works," Ander muttered. He looked up at Hel, but she dissolved into shadow without another word. He sighed. "How bad could it be?"

Takeshi's look said that he thought it could be very bad. "I just want it on record: This is a bad idea."

Ander shrugged, eyeing Jamirh thoughtfully. "Noted."

Success, then. He was going to the Nyphoren to help destroy the bionic plant. His stomach made an uneasy flop – deciding to do something and realizing you were actually going to do it were different things, apparently. There was just one last thing to do.

How was he going to explain this to Jeri?

Rhode slammed yet another useless book down on his desk. Since meeting the priest of Hades, they had learned nothing. Nothing! No references to the Witch of the High Tide, no idea what sort of inherent Hel had that allowed her to break free from the prism sphere, no word on Hel's whereabouts.

What was she?

"We did learn one thing of worth," Madine offered. "The priest was not like Hel. She was a normal, if powerful, mage. Not magic in the shape of one."

"She sort of implied Hel was created, didn't she?" Cole mused as she finished watering the plants on his desk. She took off her glasses to wipe the lenses. "Her 'purpose' was to be a sacrifice. Most people don't talk about other people that way. And it fits with what the Truth Seekers observed about magic in the shape of an Avari."

It felt like a stretch to Rhode, but he was willing to grasp at basically anything at this point. "Still no theories as to what caused the priest to flee?"

Madine shook her head. "She wasn't really there, from what I can tell. She was nearby – I could sense echoes of her – but the thing we were talking to was an illusion. Something disrupted it."

The more Rhode dealt with it, the more he found himself hating magic. At least tech had rules to it and was easily understandable. Magic was a chaotic mess that allowed people to do whatever they pleased. "For just a moment, while we were talking to her, I thought I saw her eyes flash violet, like Hel's did."

Cole frowned, stroking a leaf of the smallest plant. "I didn't notice that." She looked hesitantly at Madine.

There was a pause. "I hope neither of you are expecting me to weigh in on that." Madine's voice held a hint of disapproval.

Rhode coughed, eyeing her blindfold. Sure, they didn't see the way normal people could, but he thought they still were able to see in other ways. Maybe it was like a dog's vision, and they couldn't see color? Or maybe they just perceived things in a completely different way that he would never be able to comprehend because "magic."

Magic. Hel was magic.

But what did that *mean*?

"Excuse me, my presence is requested elsewhere," Madine declared. "I will return shortly." She swept out of the room.

Cole watched her go. She turned back to Rhode as the door swung shut. "Colonel?"

"Mhm?" He started rifling through the notes on the desk. Something had to be here; they must have just missed it.

"What do you think about the Truth Seekers?"

He glanced up at her, surprised. "What do you mean?"

She looked back towards the door. "You seem to tolerate them better than most of the other commanders."

He shrugged. "They are tools. Useful ones. While magic remains in the world, we need some method of counteracting it, and the Truth Seekers are our best bet until other options, like the prism sphere and the assets, are able to be moved into full-scale production."

She bit her lip. "So you think they will be replaced?"

"That seems to be the plan." He scanned another page. "They'll probably just be phased out over time. It's not like they live very long."

A pause. "Certainly Madine has been more useful to us than either of those options, though."

He shrugged again. "It's not my call to make. But since you've asked me, if there's anything we can take away from this whole mess, it's that magic is trouble. Anything that involves magic becomes exponentially more complicated. The Seekers are not exempt from that. Can you truly say you understand how *they* work? I'll admit they could be treated a bit better in general, but I think they were only ever meant to be a stopgap measure until magic could be dealt with in other ways."

"I see." Cole finished fidgeting with the plants and picked up her tablet. "Even though it was a Seeker prophecy that alerted the Empire to the threat Ebryn represents?"

"Prophecy." He snorted. "That 'when the Storm's Light reveals gods walking among mortals, the Empire will fall.' Who knows what that really means. Ebryn Stormlight died a long time ago. If it amuses the dukes and duchesses to kill red-haired Avari to avoid such a non-specific danger, let them. Help me review these notes, we may have missed something."

Hel was the greater danger to the Empire – a threat that not even the Truth Seekers could contain. If there were others like her...

He was going to find her.

Chapter Twenty-Two

Privately, Ander agreed with Takeshi when he said, "You must be joking."

Jeri had just arrived at the Temple carrying a wooden coffin over one shoulder. She met Takeshi's gaze evenly. "Don't worry; this will not affect the plan."

Jamirh stared at it. "Why...?"

The Vampire didn't blink. "I will need it to cross the ocean."

Hades had declared to Ander and Takeshi that Jeri was to be allowed to join them not long after the decision had been made to include Jamirh. The order came out of nowhere; Jeri hadn't even asked either priest about it beforehand. The Lady had not been forthcoming about the reasoning behind Her decision and She would not be dissuaded from it. Jeri was coming, and that was that.

"Besides, I thought it might serve an extra purpose," Jeri continued. "I know we were planning on using illusions to hide them, but I could store the weapons in here instead. They will be safe; no one will challenge the coffin."

The shinobi raised an eyebrow. "How can you be sure of that? This feels like introducing a large problem to solve a small one."

But Jeri shook her head, lips twitching into a smile. "It is not. Most Vampires are good at misdirection and suggestion. I am very good at it. Believe me – the coffin, and whatever is in it, will not be a problem."

Takeshi glanced at Ander, who shrugged. "She is not incorrect about her own abilities, and Jeri has been south of the Wall multiple times before. I see no reason not to trust what she says." Compared to the rest of them, Jeri was practically an expert at traveling south of the Wall, which... might explain her presence, actually. Lady knew Ander himself was far from an authority on the subject. Besides, the planned disguises now revolved around Jeri's presence. Even if the coffin were a problem...

Well. He supposed it didn't matter.

:It does not.:

Suppressing the desire to roll his eyes at Hades' amused interjection, Ander guessed from the look on his face that Takeshi had received a similar proclamation.

Jak, who had been waiting more or less patiently for everyone to arrive, cleared his throat. "We all good to go?"

Ander looked around as he hoisted his pack over his shoulder. Takeshi was still eyeing Jeri's coffin warily, but otherwise he was also ready. Jamirh shifted from one foot to the other, looking uneasy. A new pack sat at his feet. Jitsu was pressed close to her Human. And Jeri was standing unapologetically in the center of it all, coffin on her shoulder.

"Great," Jak said, taking the silence as an affirmative. "First of all, this is yours, Jamirh." The priest pulled a small purple pendant on a delicate silver chain out from his breast pocket. "Wear it."

Jamirh eyed it curiously, but obediently pulled it over his head. His hair turned bright orange.

"Perfect; keep that out of sight under your shirt," Jak ordered.

"What is it?" Jamirh asked.

"It has changed your hair color," Takeshi noted. "Is it a spell crystal? I can't sense any magic on it."

"Not from there you won't," Jak agreed as Jamirh pulled his ponytail over his shoulder to examine the color. "It's not a true illusion, more like... a yellow-colored filter, so to speak. Extremely subtle. You'd have to be on top of him to sense the spell."

Ander hummed in interest. Though he had no magic of his own, Jak was able to make use of Hades' magic in interesting ways. "The shape is also non-standard – at a quick glance, it won't be recognizable for what it is," Ander drawled. "Smart."

Jamirh frowned. "Why orange?"

"The less an illusion changes, the more effective it is," Takeshi explained. "Applying yellow over the top of your existing hair color takes very little magic. And an Avari with orange hair is believable."

"And also not what the Empire is looking for," Jak added. "Alrighty then, now that that's out of the way, everyone stand over here. Pretend there is a circle on the floor you are standing in, about this big." He indicated a large space, maybe nine feet in diameter.

Takeshi's eyes narrowed. "You are not going to draw it?"

"Nope! Never have, never will." Jak made shooing motions with his hands. "Into the imaginary circle. Please."

:I thought your people didn't usually draw arrays,: Ander mused.

Takeshi's eyes flicked in his direction. *:For our most used spells, carefully internalized, there is no need. To teleport four people and one dog twenty-five hundred miles? We would absolutely draw that gate pattern, and multiple shinobi would be part of the weave.:*

Ander hid a snort. *:Jak likes to live on the edge.:*

:It's not Jak's living that concerns me.:

:Fair,: he conceded as they all moved into the indicated space. *:But for what it is worth, Jak has never made a mistake with a gate.:*

:And I would prefer not to be involved in the first,: Takeshi responded primly, laying a hand on Jitsu's back.

Ander decided to drop it. The Lady could deal with it if She chose to. Instead, he locked eyes with Jak. "Don't forget about my fish."

Jak waved his concern away. "Eh, they'll be fine. I got it."

Ander twitched.

:Don't worry; I won't let him accidentally kill your fish,: Hades soothed. *:They will be fine while you are away. You can allow yourself to focus on the task at hand.:*

He allowed himself to be mollified somewhat as the ground lit up with violet glyphs under their feet. He took one last look at the Temple that had been his home for the last three hundred years.

"All right folks, here we go! Good luck storming the castle," Jak declared.

Before Ander could correct him, the world lit up with white light all around–

-and they were standing in the Tower of Jayne, gray brick walls pulsing softly with orange veins of magic. They grew brighter for a moment as Jayne herself sent a warm greeting towards them.

Ander sighed. Whatever went on in Jak's head was beyond him.

"Hello, Jayne." Jeri was returning the greeting to their temporary host. "It has been a while."

A feeling of cheerful agreement.

Takeshi looked around. "Orange instead of blue. The towers reflect the color of the... inhabitant's magic?"

"Yes," Ander confirmed. "You came through Titus previously, whose magic is blue."

"And Morden's was... dark gray, or maybe black," Jamirh added. "I remember thinking it was a weird color for a light."

Jayne felt amused.

"Any sign of Abomination?" Ander asked.

A sharp negative. The aegis might not extend down below the surface, but the Towers now knew to keep watch.

Well, that was probably the best they could hope for on that front. "Then we should be going," Ander concluded.

Jeri nodded in agreement. "Can you give us a bit of a boost? We have a long way to go."

Cheerful agreement, followed by a feeling of farewell. The walls flared with orange light, and when it faded, the group found themselves deep in the Waste. The Wall was visible to the north, the coast just barely to the west.

"That is convenient," Takeshi mused as they found their bearings.

"They can't reach all the way through the Waste without a permanent gate, and some can reach farther than others, but the Towers help out when they can," Jeri explained. "It is certainly better than having to walk the entire thirty miles."

Jamirh shuddered. "Yeah, not going to lie, was not really looking forward to this part."

Ander considered, firmly pushing away the thought that he was now far, *far* from Tarvishte. "It seems Jayne managed to cut our time here in half." He glanced at the horizon, still pink even after the sun had set and darkening quickly. "But we still have a significant amount of traveling in front of us."

Jamirh sighed.

Jeri shifted the weight of the coffin on her shoulder. "Indeed, and I would like to be out of the Waste sooner rather than later."

Jitsu huffed in agreement.

Takeshi nodded, eyeing the coffin with an unreadable expression. "Let's go."

They made good time. The moon was just beginning to wane and provided plenty of light to see by as true night set in. The February air was cold, but thankfully there wasn't any snow to contend with.

They traveled in silence, each lost in their own thoughts as they crossed through the barren wasteland.

Ander studied the Waste with a critical eye. He didn't remember much from his own flight across it centuries ago, and was forced to consider that may have been due to the fact there wasn't much to pay attention to. The ground was unnaturally flat and bare, thin gray dust occasionally being kicked up by their steps. There was no life to speak of – no trees, no brush, no grass or weeds, not even any insects that Ander could observe. Just miles of unnaturally dead land that refused to support even the hardiest of creatures. The Wall's magic was a faint buzz all around them, keeping everything just the way it was, and – as a side effect – disrupting any attempts to observe the Waste by the Empire's tech. They were still safe for the time being.

He remembered thinking all those years ago that he just had to keep moving forward. There was a certain amount of irony that he was using the same refrain now, but this time he was going in the other direction.

Finally, just before midnight, the Waste gave way to forest. Ander glanced at the abrupt line where the Waste ended and the forest began as they passed over it. How did the Empire explain such an unnatural occurrence? He couldn't remember. Though he also didn't think he had ever cared about the Waste one way or the other while he had been living in Elbe, for all that he hadn't lived terribly far from it. He couldn't remember anyone really caring too much about the Waste, save for the warnings not to go near it. So maybe that was how it worked. The Empire allowed fear and apathy to prevent having to supply any explanation at all.

Interesting.

They continued traveling south-east through the forest until just before dawn. They rested during the day, keeping a watch for any agents of the Empire or Abomination, but only forest critters came anywhere near them. At dusk they continued traveling south-east, and the pattern repeated.

"Why doesn't the Empire keep better watch over the border?" Jamirh asked as they trudged through the undergrowth. "This feels... too easy, you know? It's not like it's not marked by a giant wall or anything."

Jeri hummed. "The Wall – and by extension, the Waste – is a gigantic magical artifact. The Empire's tech is unreliable at best in that environment," she explained. "And it would take significant manpower to post a physical watch along the whole length of the Wall, so they generally only keep watch in the border towns."

"Which is why we are skipping past Vigeba to Muriz," Takeshi continued, "and will catch a bus there to Alenci."

The female Vampire nodded. "Yes. Muriz is far enough from the Wall that they aren't looking for people from Romanii there."

Jamirh snorted. "Ah, just the regular paranoid, then."

It earned him a few smiles.

They continued on in silence for a few minutes before Jamirh spoke again. "But doesn't it still feel too easy?"

"If given the choice, would you prefer to walk a hundred miles, or take some form of motorized transportation?" Takeshi asked dryly.

The Avari blinked. "Well, transportation, obviously, but there's nothing stopping us from walking."

"Most people in the Empire would make the same choice," Jeri pointed out. "Since things like buses and trains exist and are available to use, most people in the Empire – the military included to a lesser degree – won't even consider walking an option. Before you came north with Hades, would you have considered walking out of Lyndiniam to find a new life elsewhere?"

Jamirh opened his mouth to answer but then slowly shut it again, looking thoughtful.

"People are slaves to their assumptions," Ander added, thinking back to his earlier musings about the Wall. "Unless challenged, people tend to assume their assumptions are true."

"Jitsu says that is correct," Takeshi cut in, voice wry.

Ander hadn't seen the warg in hours, but that didn't mean anything. He ignored the interruption, glancing sidelong at Jamirh. "Certainly, as a thief, you utilized this premise?"

"Yeah, true," Jamirh agreed easily. "Guess I never really thought about it working on such a large scale before, though."

Hades' laugh was amused in Ander's head. *:If only any of you knew.:*

:Oh?: Ander prompted, curious.

But She refused to explain further, and the group settled back into silence as they pressed on.

Three days after leaving the Wall, they strode into the bus station in Muriz like they owned the place.

Ander made sure to follow just behind and a little to the left of Jeri, who oozed wealth and privilege as she stalked her way towards the buses. The few people in the station scurried out of her way. Takeshi, who had stopped by earlier to purchase their tickets, was to

Ander's right, and Jamirh trailed behind them all as he maneuvered the cart carrying Jeri's coffin.

They were the perfect picture of a rich Human woman, her father, his attendant, and an Avari servant, even if their luggage was a little macabre.

Jeri didn't pause, heading straight to the bus for Alenci. She turned and stood impatiently while Jamirh guided the coffin to be loaded in the storage compartment under the bus. The attendant loading the bags hesitated, glancing between the coffin and Jamirh and Jeri, before stammering, "Uh... I don't think that something of this size–"

Jeri's eyes narrowed, something cold and red glimmering deep inside. "The coffin comes with us. I'm sure that won't be a problem." Her tone was coaxing despite the aloof expression.

The attendant caved instantly. "Ah, no, no it won't be. Sorry for the delay." He began immediately loading the coffin into the compartment.

And that was Vampiric suggestion in action – a sort of weak hypnosis. Ander rarely saw it used – it was considered extremely impolite outside of specific circumstances. Vampires had once used it to put their prey at ease and convince them to make decisions they otherwise would not. It wasn't foolproof and couldn't be used to make someone do something that went entirely against their nature, but it had kept Vampires fed in the times before Vlad managed to form Romanii. Ander supposed it was quite an advantage for the Black Watch agents south of the Wall. It was easily broken by pain, but that wasn't a problem for how Jeri was using it.

Jeri kept her eyes on the coffin until it was safely aboard, then turned, snapping her fingers impatiently in Jamirh's direction. She adjusted her wide-brimmed hat and glided onto the bus, Jamirh trailing after her. "Come along, Father," her voice drifted back.

Ander hid a snort as he followed after her. She was more than three times his age, but his white hair made him look older than her as long as no one looked too hard. Luckily, his ears were short enough that a pair of earmuffs appropriate to the winter weather covered them.

Jeri slid into a seat near the front of the bus. As Jamirh went to pass her, she placed a hand on his arm, tilting her head at the seat next to her.

Ander frowned; that wasn't the plan.

Jamirh's lips thinned and he gave a subtle shake of his head.

Jeri tugged.

Jamirh's expression darkened and he yanked his arm away, stomping back several rows before choosing a seat.

Ander tried not to sigh as he took the spot next to Jeri. According to what both Jamirh *and* Jeri had told them, Avari servants did not sit with their masters. They sat near enough to be useful if needed. Why would Jeri want Jamirh to sit next to her? It would completely break the illusion they were going for of a wealthy Human noble.

Takeshi passed by to sit in the row right behind them. Ander looked away; the other priest's current appearance unsettled him. Takeshi's illusion was just close enough to his regular face that Ander's mind kept thinking the resemblance was uncanny. The fact that Takeshi wasn't wearing a mask added to the strangeness. He

found himself much preferring Takeshi's normal looks to this...
almost-Takeshi countenance.

Only a few other passengers were on board, glancing in Jeri's direction while trying to look like they weren't. That was good; Ander
wasn't interested in being crowded any more than was absolutely
necessary.

The bus started moving only a few minutes after they found their
seats. Perfect timing.

:Jitsu?: he asked Takeshi.

:I think she might also be in the baggage compartment,: the shinobi
replied after a moment. *:I am not entirely sure how she managed that,
but she still feels close by. And I do not think she is on top of the bus.:* A
slight pause. *:I hope she is not on top of the bus.:*

Ander raised an eyebrow as he leaned back in his seat and closed
his eyes. *:Unlikely. She probably wants to show off how stealthy she
can be, so she won't do something... odd like that.:* Then again, wargs
did sometimes have their own definitions for certain words, so who
knew.

Still, she probably wasn't on top of the bus.

It took a little over an hour and a half to reach Alenci due to
traffic as they got closer to the city. Ander watched the city pass by,
reflecting on how absolutely nothing felt familiar. That was good,
and not unexpected. After all, they were thousands of miles from
Elbe, and it had been three hundred years. Unlike Romanii, where
time seemed to pass slowly under the watch of their immortal king,
the Empire had moved forward rapidly, embracing their evolving

tech to the point where even if they had been in Elbe Ander wasn't sure he would recognize anything.

How ideal.

They disembarked without any fanfare. Jamirh collected another cart and stood in the baggage line to pick up the coffin while the others waited nearby. Ander looked, but he didn't see even a single tuft of white fur – however Jitsu was hiding herself, it was effective.

Coffin collected, they headed into the station proper. Alenci Station was the central hub for transportation in the city. Takeshi broke off from the group to purchase tickets to Bariza; a lady of Jeri's standing would never wait in a line.

Jeri and Ander both sat on a bench while Jamirh hovered nearby. Ander looked around; this was a very busy station. Humans and Avari were everywhere. The press of people was making Ander uncomfortable, and he found himself glad that their disguise made most people unwilling to come too close for fear of offending Jeri. She herself seemed oblivious to it all, adjusting her hat so it slanted fashionably across her face and studying her nails.

That was when Ander saw the Truth Seeker.

He was walking in their direction and came to a stop by the wall about twenty feet from where they were sitting. People were giving him a wide berth as they passed, causing a bubble of space to form around him. He stood there, looking out at the commuters as they did their best to pretend they didn't see him. Jamirh appeared to have noticed him too and was shifting so that Ander was between them.

Ah yes, the Hero reborn in action.

Still, Ander could appreciate that this was neither the time nor the place for any sort of confrontation, and Jeri's ability to suggest wasn't likely to work on such a person.

The Truth Seeker didn't seem to be taking any more interest in them than any of the other passengers in the area and wasn't actively searching for anything, so Ander concluded this was a routine appearance. He decided to take the opportunity to study the mage. Truth Seekers had been a fairly new addition to the Empire when he had left it all those years ago, and he had never seen one in person. The uniform was sharp, dark grays with red-and-blue trim. A pistol hung at one hip; he wondered if the accompanying sword was merely for show or if it was functional.

The blindfold was what interested him. Why a blindfold? Were the Seekers really blind? The Seeker wasn't looking in his direction, so he could only see half of it, but...

Ander narrowed his eyes and tilted his head slightly to get a better look. Were those glyphs on the blindfold? What were–

:Ander!:

The half-Avari nearly jumped from Takeshi's angry exclamation. *:What?:*

:Don't stare at him! No one does that; you are going to draw attention to yourself!: the shinobi snapped.

Ander nearly sniffed in annoyance. *:I was studying the glyphs. The blindfolds are–:*

:Non-circular patterns, I know.: Takeshi did not seem impressed by Ander's deduction. *:I noticed it while I was in Charve. The glyphs are distorted, probably to try to hide them. They don't look like glyphs*

if you look quickly, which is what they have trained the population to do. I'm not sure why; citizens of the Empire wouldn't recognize glyphs anyway.:

:How strange.: Ander considered this development. Even three hundred years ago the glyphs wouldn't have been recognized.

:Is it? They are mages,: Takeshi pointed out, appearing out of the crowd, tickets in hand. "Our timing is very good; the train leaves in twenty minutes."

"Excellent," Jeri declared airily. "We will wait here where it is more comfortable, if that is all right with you, Father?" Green eyes glittered in amusement.

"If that is what you would prefer," he responded dutifully, ignoring Jamirh's subtle wince. *:It's strange that it works at all,:* he continued to Takeshi. *:A non-circular array? Modified glyphs, sure; mages have been tweaking those for years to greater or lesser success, but the array–:*

:Is now really the time for this conversation?: The Lady's voice was exasperated.

:It's interesting,: he protested.

:Be interested later.:

He suppressed a sigh but did not return to studying the Seeker, no matter how much he wanted to. Still, he turned his mind towards trying to figure out how the array on the blindfold worked. It tied in the back; did the glyphs continue onto the tails? He wasn't sure. Would it make a difference? Inconclusive. What was the array meant to accomplish?

Jeri laid a hand on his arm, drawing his attention. "Time to go, Father," she murmured. "We don't want to miss our train and keep Mother waiting."

Hades snorted in the back of his mind.

The group gathered themselves and began to make their way towards the terminal. The Truth Seeker glanced their way briefly but gave no other reaction. They were out of his line of sight – if he even saw – a few minutes after.

Conversation was non-existent as they checked the coffin and boarded the train. Ander looked around, but still didn't see any sign of Jitsu. He wasn't sure if the increased size and activity of the station made it easier or harder for her to hide, but he figured she was doing fine. Takeshi would know if she got into trouble.

Their tickets led them to a pair of private compartments, which Ander fully intended to sleep in. They had been awake for almost twenty hours at this point, and the trip to Bariza was almost six-and-a-half hours long.

He followed Jeri into the first compartment, shutting the door and dropping his pack on the seat next to him as she drew the blinds shut on the large window.

She glanced at the closed door with a slight frown and Ander found himself wondering if she was going to protest Jamirh's absence. She looked away after a moment though, removing her hat and nearly collapsing onto the seat opposite his. "Well, that was close," she sighed.

"The Seeker? He didn't seem to be looking for anything in particular," Ander noted.

"No, but we try to avoid the Seekers altogether if we can. They are all linked; if it comes to a confrontation with one, all of them will know about it, and any hope of stealth is over." She fanned herself with her hat. "Okay, that was still far more sun than I prefer. I think I'm going to sleep for a bit."

"I also intend to rest," Ander admitted, studying her. Everyone needed to be at their best. "Blood would help, would it not?"

She blinked at him. "It would. Are you offering?"

Wordlessly, he pushed up his left sleeve, presenting his wrist. It wasn't the ideal or most common method to feed a Vampire, but it was a method.

Jeri looked at him with an unreadable expression, then slid from the bench to kneel next to him. "Thank you for this gift," she murmured formally, wrapping her hands around his arm. She placed her mouth over his vein in something like a kiss, and he felt the anesthetic in her saliva numb the area. There was a sharp pain as her fangs punctured his skin, then abrupt relief as the anesthetic entered his bloodstream, numbing his entire lower arm. He closed his eyes to wait for her to finish.

She only took a few mouthfuls before withdrawing, carefully licking the small puncture wounds to stop the bleeding, not letting even a single drop escape. She waited a minute to make sure the bleeding had stopped, then retreated back to her seat. "That feels so much better," she whispered, green eyes tinting red, the sign of a Vampire who had just fed from a live source.

"You're welcome," he responded, resting his arm on his lap. It would be half an hour or so before he regained feeling, though at least a Vampire's saliva cleansed the wound and aided healing. The marks would be gone in a day or two. "All that potential for healing, and early Vampires wasted it on killing," he muttered disapprovingly.

Jeri shrugged. "That was well before our time."

"True," he agreed, settling into a more comfortable position. "But still a waste." He closed his eyes. The first leg of their mission was almost over, and it had gone exceptionally well. Perhaps it was a sign that they were destined for success.

He considered the potential glyphs he had seen on the Truth Seeker's blindfold and let the possibilities lull him to sleep, almost able to pretend he was back in Tarvishte.

Chapter Twenty-Three

Takeshi pulled his scarf a little tighter against the chill in the air as he made his way back to the Dancin' Whale. It wasn't nearly as cold as what they had left behind in Tarvishte, but the temperature was still lower than Takeshi preferred, and the clouds were threatening to drop near-freezing rain on the city. At least he was better provisioned now than he had been on his first visit. He adjusted his hold on the stuffed paper bag he was carrying and increased his pace.

Freja smiled warmly at him as he pushed the door to the bed and breakfast open. "Welcome back, Mr. Tanaka. Looks like you beat the weather."

They had arrived in Bariza five days ago and Takeshi had wasted no time in leading the group to the Dancin' Whale. Freja had been surprised but pleased to see "Tanaka Yuki" again, even if he came with a mixed group of Humans and Avari. He supposed it helped that they were more than willing to pay for the accommodation and good food. More importantly, Freja did have a way of contacting the

Sea Spirit and had been happy to pass along a message. Now it was just a matter of waiting.

"Luckily, yes." He did not want to be outside when the weather broke. "Any word yet?"

She shook her head, ears twitching. "Not yet. Could be a few more days. Don't worry, though – they're comin'."

He inclined his head in thanks and glanced at the common room as he moved towards the stairs. No one was present, which wasn't a surprise, really. Jeri had retreated into her room and not come out since they arrived. Ander was preoccupied with something, choosing to remain in his room as well, though he at least would come down for breakfast. Jamirh kept sneaking out of the Dancin' Whale entirely against everyone else's advice. Takeshi wasn't sure why or how he was managing it, but it proved to him that Jamirh probably had been a fairly successful thief. He had an aptitude for stealth that some shinobi would envy.

Speaking of stealth...

Takeshi scanned the keycard to his room, slipping inside and shutting the door quickly behind him. The sound of a furry tail thwacking the bed greeted him from where Jitsu lay, having made herself quite at home on the furniture.

Big violet eyes regarded him hopefully. Had her Human brought back anything tasty?

He placed the bag on the desk and reached over to scratch behind one of her ears. "A few shrimp." Jitsu loved them. "I hope you stayed out of trouble while I was gone."

She put her head on her paws, wide eyes blinking innocently at him. She was deserving of the shrimp! She had not interacted with or terrorized anyone!

That was oddly specific, but since she couldn't lie Takeshi let it pass. He was glad to have her with him again, though how she had gotten into this room without being seen was beyond him. He assumed she had some way to come and go but had yet to see her utilize it. He pulled the shrimp out from the bag and tossed them one by one into Jitsu's waiting mouth as she practically inhaled them.

She licked her chops when he ran out and lovingly pressed her head up against his chest. She had the absolute best Human!

He petted her for a few minutes before reluctantly breaking away. "I'll be right back; I just need to deliver these," he told her, taking several microwave dinners out of the bag. He paused, then turned back. "Stay," he reminded her.

Jitsu wagged her tail at him cheerfully. She would await his return.

Takeshi slid back into the hallway, skipping Ander's room to knock quietly at Jeri's. A few moments of silence, then a very tired Vampire opened the door. "This was the best I could do," he offered as she took the meals from him.

She shook her head. "It's fine. These will do for now, though I will have to hunt soon."

He tilted his head. "How much blood do you need?"

"A comfortable amount for a fledged Vampire is about a pint a week. I usually manage just fine with a combination of hunting and stealing when south of the Wall." She shrugged one shoulder. "But I also only risk myself under normal circumstances."

"Have you considered asking Jamirh to steal blood from a hospital for you?" Takeshi asked dryly. "It might give him something productive to put his energy towards."

She cringed. "I would rather not put him at risk. I would also rather he not put himself at risk by going out as often as he does. What is he even doing out there?"

Takeshi blinked; he thought it was rather obvious. And while he didn't necessarily approve of the risk or the concept in general – he himself usually tried to avoid stealing, and it wasn't as if they lacked resources for this venture – it was a useful skill for someone with Jamirh's background to have and was something they might be able to utilize at some point. "Getting food," he replied blandly.

Jeri shook her head. "Is that all he ever thinks about?" Her voice was fond, though her face still betrayed her worry. "Well, thank you for this, Takeshi. I am going to continue hiding. No word yet from your friends?"

"Not yet. Freja believes this is normal, however," he reassured her.

Ander's voice drifted towards them: "You did say this part could take a while." Takeshi looked over his shoulder to see the half-Avari leaning in the open doorway to his room. "Your estimate was a possible two weeks. We are not quite halfway through that."

"So we could be waiting for a while longer." Jeri sighed. "All right then. I'm going to try to tolerate one of these." She raised the boxes in her hands.

"Hades said those were good," Takeshi offered weakly, though even he doubted that.

"She thinks everything is good," Ander pointed out.

:Because everything is good!:

"Everything is not good," Takeshi countered.

"Yes, I'm going to leave that conversation to you. Though that is something She and Jamirh have in common," Jeri murmured, quietly shutting her door.

"Well, if she can't stand them she can always pawn them off on Jamirh," Ander mused. "He'll probably eat them."

Takeshi shrugged. "'Good' is not a requirement for food."

Hades seemed interested by that idea. *:Then what is?:*

"The only requirement that matters is that it is edible." He made sure to pitch his tone so that it sounded like the obvious answer.

Ander stared at him for a moment. "I can't believe I'm the one who has to say this, but let's aim a little higher than that."

:Jak would be proud.:

"Shush, you." Now the other priest sounded annoyed. "Dare I even bother asking what the plan for dinner is?"

Takeshi hid an amused grin. "Would you believe it if I said–"

Ander shut the door in his face.

:Honestly, the dinners are not *that bad,:* Hades muttered.

"I guess we'll find out," he chuckled, heading back towards his room. His smile morphed to a frown, though. Seeing Ander had reminded Takeshi of his own failure to successfully soulforge. He wasn't even close, barely able to summon his soul crystal for a moment before having to release it. The feeling was painfully uncomfortable as everything in him screamed that what he was doing was wrong.

It figured that the one thing that priests of Hades were supposed to do, he couldn't. It didn't exactly bode well for the future.

:You've just started trying,: Hades soothed. *:Give it more time. As one of mine, it is something you are able to do, but the ability must still be learned. And sometimes it just clicks when you need it! Like shoving a baby bird out of a nest. I wouldn't worry about it yet.:*

Takeshi shook his head, pausing by his door. *:By what measure, exactly, am I a priest of yours?:* Nothing he had done so far was priest-specific. Even this didn't really qualify, since the Vampires could do it too, but at least it was something specific to the goddess.

:You are mine. That is all there is to it.:

Takeshi didn't usually struggle so much with magic. This didn't sit well with him.

"Mr. Tanaka?"

He veered towards the top of the stairs. "Yes?" he asked, seeing Freja at the bottom.

"I thought I heard you and your friends talkin' up there," she said with a grin. "I have good news – the *Sea Spirit* just docked."

"Li'l wizard! We missed ye!" The booming voice of Caron, captain of the *Sea Spirit*, greeted the shinobi as he swung himself on board.

"It hasn't been that long – only three months," Don pointed out from a deck above. The dark-skinned youth shot a lopsided grin in Takeshi's direction. "Welcome back, though."

"*Only* three months?!" came a shriek from just inside the mess. One of the twins popped her blonde head out from the door. "Did ye hear that, Salisha? Don says it's 'only' been three months since we were deprived o' our wizard's adorable presence!"

"What a travesty! T' think it be 'only' three months, Desha!" The other twin dramatically leaned outside as though in a swoon.

Somehow, Takeshi had forgotten this.

He had also kind of missed it.

"Y'all be a bit twisted," Marjori called down from the door to the bridge. "Honestly, he was only with us fer, like, a week."

"Yeah, two weeks o' intense bonding–"

"Nice to see you again, Shuurai," Benjen interrupted the sisters before they could spiral into more dramatics. "You look well."

"Far better than 'well'!" came Ashi's cheerful cry as she surfaced from down below. "He looks like he's actually sleepin' and eatin' regularly!"

"Ya do look less dead," Marjori observed.

"Thank you," he deadpanned. A little ironic, since the goddess of death was following him everywhere now, but that was neither here nor there. "It means a lot to me that you've noticed."

:I mean, they kind of have a point here,: Hades pointed out. *:You were not exactly in a great spot when you left them.:*

He ignored her, turning to Caron with a shallow bow. "Thank you for coming on such short notice."

"We be glad t' hear from ye, wizard!"

The captain was cut off by one of the twins. "Does this mean ye be done with yer super-secret mission thing?" she asked excitedly.

"And ye be joining us finally?" her sister added.

Takeshi winced. "The mission has pivoted slightly." He took a deep breath. "I – *we* – need your help."

Caron's bushy eyebrows rose. "Oh? Sounds like quite a tale, eh? All o' ye, int' the mess! Git!" He began shooing his crew back into the boat.

"You found the rebellion, then?" Benjen asked as everyone settled around the table.

"Ah, in a way?" Takeshi shrugged, deciding that an abridged version of events would do for now. "I think 'insurrection' might be the better term, since it is based in a different country. I took your advice and headed for the Warcross Wall. Along the way I made contact with... an agent of Romanii. She helped me cross the Wall."

Shocked exclamations came from the crew.

"I have learned that the Rose Empire is creating horrific bionic abominations by combining Avari with some sort of tech. Here–" He spun a pattern for an illusion, trying to show them what the Abominations looked like, though without any sort of preparation the image wouldn't be perfect.

:Here.:

He felt Hades help shape the weave and the image solidified in the middle of the table, leading to horrified gasps.

"What the hell...?" Don whispered.

"'Abomination' is certainly the right term for it," Ashi agreed, sounding sick.

"Yes. This cannot be allowed to continue," Takeshi explained. "And we have discovered that the location of the factory where they are being produced is in the Nyphoren Islands."

Caron eyed him knowingly. "And ye need a way t' get there," he guessed. "A non-Empire way."

Takeshi nodded.

Marjori's ears swept down. "Please tell me ya weren't sent t' deal with this mess all by yaself?"

"Again," Don muttered.

"No," Takeshi reassured them. "I need passage for myself, three other people, and a large dog."

Benjen's eyes widened. "A large dog?"

"She is an incredibly well-behaved dog?" Takeshi tried. "I have been told that I won't be able to stop her from coming with me."

"That don't sound like 'well-trained' t' me," Marjori snorted.

Takeshi acknowledged the point. "She's hard to explain."

"So four people and a dog to destroy a factory somewhere in the Nyphoren Islands?" Benjen hummed.

"Technically five people; we are meeting another mage on Crescent Island, which is where the factory is. Three of us are mages, one is a Vampire, and the remaining one is..." He trailed off. Jamirh didn't like people knowing. "...a skilled swordsman," he finished instead. That was close enough.

"A Vampire?" One of the twins laughed.

"Ye do find yerself with interesting people, don't ye?" the other giggled.

"And *more* wizards!"

"And a dog! Is it cute?"

"Any o' the people ye with be cute?"

"Let's stay on topic," Benjen interrupted. He turned to Caron. "Would be a tight fit."

The big man nodded. "'Twould, but not impossible."

"We can pay as well," Takeshi added.

"Pay is good," Marjori hummed. "But we ain't there yet."

Caron eyed Takeshi. "There be more t' the story."

"There is," he agreed. "A lot has happened since I left. But I promise that those are the relevant highlights."

Caron nodded again. "So mote it be, then. How soon can y'all be ready?"

Takeshi blinked as he processed that.

Marjori was less stunned. "Cap'n? That's it, ya just gonna do it?"

"Oooooh yes." The twins grinned.

Caron smiled at his navigator. "Now Marjori, the li'l wizard needs us! And he's right – those things need t' be destroyed." He waved a hand towards Takeshi's Abomination. "Nothing 'bout that be acceptable. And besides – there be a definite possibility for loot, if we be willing t' risk a bit with the military."

"And the military should be a concern," Benjen pointed out. He turned back to Takeshi. "When we suggested the Nyphoren Islands as an alternative to Gallia, Crescent Island was not where we were thinking. There is significant military presence on and around that island, though I suppose now we know why."

Takeshi frowned. "We don't wish you to risk yourselves any more than you are willing to. If it is easier to deliver us to a different island, I'm sure we will be able to manage–"

"NONSENSE!" Caron roared. "The *Sea Spirit* be more'n a match for those soulless ships the Empire tries t' pass off as top o' the line. We'll get ye t' where ye need t' go, wizard, and yer companions. Be here at first light, and we sail for the Twins' Islands!"

Takeshi cleared his throat. "Would it be possible to show up a little *before* first light?"

"Ye do look a lot better, Shuurai," Ashi proclaimed as she came up beside Takeshi. He was leaning on the railing, watching the sea speed by. "Whatever ye found out there, it did ye good."

They had cast off early, as soon as Takeshi had managed to shepherd Ander, Jeri, and Jamirh to the ship. Jitsu had melted out of the pre-dawn shadows as they boarded and almost immediately disappeared; how something that big and white managed to go unnoticed Takeshi still had no idea. Jeri had looked positively green as soon as she had stepped off the dock, and she had retreated to her cabin and coffin immediately. Takeshi wasn't sure, but he thought she might be planning to stay there until they reached Crescent Island. Ander had been muttering something about glyphs and balance and rectangles, and he had similarly removed himself to his cabin.

Jamirh, intensely curious about how the ship worked, was invited to the bridge to watch while they set sail, leaving Takeshi to his own devices while the crew handled their duties.

Takeshi hummed. "Found some things, and lost others."

Ashi smiled. "That's livin' for ye."

Jitsu's head popped out of the mess, and upon spotting Takeshi she loped over to join him. He rested a hand on her head as Ashi stared.

"I thought ye said ye had a dog?" the doctor asked, sounding uncertain.

"Her name is Jitsu. She is very friendly," he reassured her.

Jitsu huffed. She wasn't a dog, she was a warg. Clearly superior.

"That is not a dog," Ashi protested, echoing Jitsu's feelings as she studied her. "She might be a wolf, but a dog – no."

Jitsu flattened her ears. She wasn't a wolf either. Warg! Why was this confusing?

"She would like it to be known that she is actually a warg," Takeshi relayed dutifully. "And better than a dog."

"Certainly *more* than a dog," Ashi laughed, hesitantly reaching out a hand. "This is a Caron-sized creature. Wait, what do ye mean, 'would like it t' be known'?"

He shrugged. "She can communicate with me to some degree. It's not with words, but feelings, mostly." He watched as Jitsu helpfully pressed her head up to Ashi's hand. "She likes having her ears scratched."

"Well, no wonder ye count her among the combatants," Ashi said after a moment. "I'd run, if I saw her comin' after me."

Jitsu wagged her tail.

"Wizard!" came a happy screech.

Takeshi turned to see Salisha and Desha both tumble from the mess. They stopped short upon seeing Jitsu, who stared back placidly. "Oooh, is that the dog?" one of them cooed.

Jitsu sneezed. Still not a dog.

"Warg," Takeshi corrected absently. "Her name is Jitsu."

"'Ow the hell did we miss that coming aboard?" the other sister laughed.

"She is soooo fluffy!" the first one squealed, sidling closer. "Oh, can I pet her? Can I, can I?"

"Well, that's that. Desha loves dogs," Salisha chuckled.

Takeshi nodded. "She likes being petted and especially having her ears scratched."

Desha practically threw herself at Jitsu, running her hands through the white fur. Jitsu eyed Takeshi – this was how wargs should be treated. They were special, after all.

"Don is probably going t' love her too," Salisha reflected after a moment. "I'm glad she's friendly. Oh! We almost forgot!"

Desha blinked at her sister. "We did?"

"We did!" Salisha nodded enthusiastically. "Wizard! The other wizard be out-wizarding ye!"

Takeshi stared at her. He had hoped he would have fewer problems understanding them this time around, but that was not to be, apparently. "Pardon?"

"Oh, yeah!" Desha exclaimed. "Yeah, the other wizard! He be doing... something! In the mess."

"Seems more impressive than what ye usually do," Salisha finished.

Jitsu leaned into a particularly good scratch. Yes, the tall-white priest was just inside. He was doing something with paper; she hadn't been interested enough to find out what.

Ander was doing something with paper? Something involving magic, if Takeshi was picking up on context clues correctly. Curious despite himself, he left Jitsu with the women and slipped into the mess.

He almost walked right back out again.

Strips of paper covered in glyphs were strewn about the room. Some were crumpled, others relatively flat, a few burned. Ander was at the table, hovering over another piece of paper with a pen, finishing another series of glyphs. He paused, then touched the paper carefully.

Nothing happened.

With an annoyed twist of his lips, Ander tossed the paper aside and grabbed a blank piece, starting to draw more glyphs.

"What... what are you doing?" Takeshi asked, picking up a discarded attempt at whatever this was and revising his earlier assumption that Ander had gone to his cabin. He must have come here to work on this. He studied the glyph in the center of the pattern, recognizing it as the glyph for vision, and realized what this was as Ander answered.

"I am trying to figure out how the array on the Truth Seekers' blindfolds works," he snapped, frustration clear in his voice. "I got a good look at maybe a third of the glyphs, those on the left side of the blindfold. If we assume it is symmetrical, that leaves us with just the glyphs on the tails to be determined, if there even are glyphs on the tails. I've managed several possibilities that balance, but no matter what I do the array never triggers when I power it."

:Oh dear,: Hades whispered in his mind. *:He has found A Project.:*

Takeshi didn't need to ask what that meant. He could see it. "Have you considered using a pencil, so you can erase the incorrect attempts and not waste so much paper?" When had he even created all of these blindfold-shaped sheets? Where had he gotten the paper from?

"What?" Ander asked absently as he drew another glyph on his current attempt.

:Yeah, that's probably a lost cause, unless you can switch out the pen without him noticing.:

Takeshi hummed thoughtfully, watching the glyphs go down. "How certain are you of the glyphs you saw?"

:Oh, oh no. Not you too…:

"Very."

He nodded as the twins snuck their way back inside, giving him a mischievous look. "See?" one whispered. "Actual wizard things!"

He shook his head at them, then returned his attention to Ander's neat bridging lines. "The glyphs on the blindfolds aren't nearly as neat as yours. Perhaps it affects the balance somehow?"

Ander paused. "Are you suggesting I try a subpar attempt?"

Takeshi shrugged. "Here, this is what I remember…" He took one of the strips of paper as Ander handed him the pen. He thought back to the press conference he had seen long ago in Charve and the Truth Seeker who had spoken. Slowly he started with the vision glyph, elongating it so it took up the entire width of the strip. The actual glyph for balance looked to have overlaid it – also strange, as normally glyphs weren't crowded together that way – and he thought he had seen illusion's dots in this part, and mirrored over here...

When he was done, he considered it compared to Ander's previous attempt. They were very close. "Do you think this is a balance line, or the glyph for increase? It could have been either from the angle I saw it at."

Ander's eyes narrowed. "I thought it was just a balance line, but if it is the increase glyph, then wouldn't it mirror as decrease? They would cancel each other out."

"What the hell happened in here?!"

Marjori and Jamirh had just come down the stairs and were looking around in a combination of horror and fascination. Marjori's ears were twitching in a decidedly downward direction.

"Shhh!!! They're doing magic things!" the twin on the right whispered.

"Do they have t' do it right here?" Marjori asked, exasperated.

"Is this what you wanted all that paper and the scissors for?" Jamirh asked curiously.

Takeshi paused, then slowly turned to look at Ander. Jamirh hadn't just been stealing food in Bariza. "What?"

"I needed the paper!" the other priest justified.

There was a tired sigh in the back of his mind. It sounded a lot like Hades.

"A pencil! You could have used a pencil!" Takeshi argued.

"Why so many?" Marjori also sounded tired. "What's even happening?"

Ander turned to face her. "The Truth Seekers use a non-circular array on their blindfolds, which should be impossible. We are trying to discover what it does by re-creating it."

"But... it's a blindfold," she said slowly.

"Yes, that is what I said." Ander waved her away. "We need to figure out if the tails are important, or–"

"Isn't a blindfold itself a circle? Like, around your head?" Jamirh interrupted.

Silence.

Takeshi felt like a complete idiot. He cleared his throat. "The glyphs are rotated ninety degrees outward, then." That made so much more sense than a rectangular pattern. Still odd, but less impossible.

He felt Jitsu press against his back. She still thought he was the best Human.

"Or inward I suppose, but that is the most likely explanation for the structure," Ander agreed. He picked up Takeshi's strip of paper and brought the ends together to form a ring. "I think we can assume the tails are not important."

Takeshi watched, but nothing happened. He frowned. "Perhaps the glyphs are still wrong, then."

"Yes, but I think we are on the right track," Ander murmured. "This could be just a balance line, then..."

"Is this what learned magic is?" Jamirh asked. "Some strange guessing game of symbols and circles?"

"Don't be ridiculous," Ander snapped. "It is a careful balancing of intent and nature, an application of will focused and guided by the glyphs, which are carefully balanced to prevent accidents or unintended results."

Marjori pursed her lips. "That sounds a lot like 'things could explode'."

"Things could explode," Takeshi agreed absently as he reconsidered the pattern he had drawn. "Hopefully not, but the possibility exists."

"*What?*"

"Well, probably not with these glyphs," he clarified. "Illusion, vision, and balance are definitely in the forefront. Vision makes sense – somehow, the Seekers must be using the blindfold to see, or perceive, or something related – but illusion? Balance?"

"I didn't see anything that could be one of the more destructive glyphs, either," Ander agreed. "This is safe. Probably."

"Probably?" Marjori repeated as her ears lowered further.

"Magic doesn't work in absolutes." Ander waved her concern away.

Takeshi was mostly absorbed in trying to remember which glyphs made up the pattern and so almost missed it when Jamirh said, "Oh, yeah – I can probably take this off now."

Ander made a sound of agreement.

It took a moment for Takeshi to catch up to those words. His head snapped up in time to see Jamirh removing the pendant Jak had given him and his hair return to its deep red color.

It was a mistake. He saw Marjori's face pale.

Of course another Avari would recognize Jamirh's colors. And Marjori, who wanted to know all relevant information ahead of time, was not going to be pleased Takeshi hadn't mentioned this.

Desperately, he shook his head at her. Her eyes narrowed, but Jamirh didn't seem to notice anything was amiss. "Never thought I'd miss the red," he commented, eyes still on the pattern Ander was attempting to recreate. He slid the pendant into his pocket.

Takeshi glanced around the room. The sisters didn't seem to have noticed anything, completely enthralled with what Ander was doing. No one else had come in. Not that it mattered; the damage was done.

Marjori slid close to Takeshi. "Shuurai..." she hissed, voice threatening.

"It's not for me to tell," he hissed back. "Leave it be."

"And what would ya know o' it?" she all but growled before turning and storming from the room.

Right. Because Jamirh was important to the Avari.

:I'm sure that's fine,: Hades said with forced cheer as the blue-haired Avari disappeared. *:Maybe not ideal, but not horrible either.:*

It occurred to Takeshi that while Hades couldn't lie, she could be overly optimistic. Still, he found himself hoping she was right; while he didn't think Marjori could or would cause the mission any harm, the harm she could cause Jamirh – intentionally or not – was another matter entirely.

Chapter Twenty-Four

J amirh stared out over the rapidly moving waves. He had never been on the open ocean before. Lyndiniam was a port city, sure, but Jamirh had never had the opportunity to be on a boat.

He loved it.

Everything about the ship was cool – from how all the rooms fit together to optimize space, to the tech used to keep track of where they were, to how such a large structure made of metal and plaster managed to stay afloat on the open ocean, to the *Sea Spirit's* crew. Hell, the Human captain of the ship was *married* to the Avari doctor.

A Human. Was married. To an Avari.

Jamirh was trying not to think about it, because every time he did his mind was blown all over again.

It was all amazing and new and fascinating, and a huge upgrade from having been in the Empire again.

He wasn't salty about having to pose as a Human's servant; he really wasn't. He had utilized similar disguises in the past – hell, he had been pretending to be a servant of sorts when he had met Jeri that first time in the casino.

It was just... that he had seen another possibility of how life could be in Romanii, and going back to seeing Avari being treated as second-class citizens didn't sit right. Hell, nothing about the whole mess sat right. The encounter with the Truth Seeker in Alenci had shown him how everyone, not just Avari, lived in some sort of fear – Jamirh had never noticed it before, or cared, but the Humans had been just as unsettled and afraid of the dark-clad officer. Avari definitely had it worse, but something was deeply wrong with how the Empire operated.

Was change possible at this point? Jamirh wasn't sure. This was how the Empire had been for decades, if not centuries. Even if they succeeded in destroying the factory creating the bionics, even if they then managed to track down each remaining Abomination – what would change? The Empire had existed before the bionics, and it would almost certainly continue to exist after them. Jamirh, Hero reborn or not, could not change that. No one person could.

But out here, on the sea?

Freedom.

He could see it in the way the pirates interacted with each other and with their passengers. A carefreeness that Jamirh hadn't even seen in Romanii. He envied that. He didn't think he had it in him to be like that, but he wanted it.

At least he was a little more free. Jeri was too sick to continue hovering over him like she had been. He felt bad for taking advantage of how she was feeling, but... for gods' sake, she'd tried to get him to sit next to her on the bus. That would *never* happen in the Empire, and he knew she knew it. That hadn't even been a particularly dangerous part of the mission. What was going to happen when they were actually on the base? At this rate, was she even going to let him participate? He had to, otherwise what was the point of coming along?

Was he going to be able to do this at all?

"Jamirh?"

He looked back at the sound of Marjori's voice, ears twitching up. He hadn't seen her at all since the first day. She had offered to let him watch them set out from the bridge, and then they'd gone down to the mess to see Takeshi and Ander's disaster of paper and lines. Then she had disappeared. He thought they'd gotten along pretty well in that brief period of time, but now she looked uncertain. Jamirh wondered why. "Hey, what's up?"

Her mouth twisted into something like a smile, then she rolled her eyes and joined him in leaning on the rail. "I got t' ask... what, exactly, be going on with yar group?"

"What do you mean?" Even the way the pirates spoke was cool.

She was silent for a long moment. "Ya know... Humans see an Avari with red hair and silver eyes, and they think nothing o' it. Our colors mean nothing t' them. But we Avari know." Deliberately, she met his eyes. "And now the wizard brings ya ont' our ship, looking fer passage t' the Nyphoren t' destroy some sort o' factory-meets-mad-scientist-lab. It makes a gal wonder, is all."

Jamirh felt his ears and stomach sink as reached for his key. He should have known. He shrugged, looking out over the ocean, rubbing the cool metal between his fingers. "Sounds like you have a pretty good picture of the whole mess."

"Never thought I'd get t' meet a legend. Not a real one, at least." Marjori stared off into the distance.

Jamirh fought down a wave of shame as his earlier thoughts circled back. "Sorry to be a disappointment." Was he a disappointment to Jeri?

"That's not..." She drifted off with a frown before shaking her head. "Ya know, the wizard told us ya were a skilled swordsman," she said instead.

"Really?" That was a pleasant surprise. Takeshi thought he qualified as "skilled"?

She raised an eyebrow. "I don't see a sword."

"Oh, yeah." Good point. "Jeri has all our weaponry." He looked down at the water.

"I'd been wondering where the wizard's sword be," she mused. "Y'all are allowed t' have yer weapons on the ship."

"Not really my call to make," he admitted. "But I'll mention it to Takeshi."

"Why's he in command?" she asked, eyes narrowing.

Jamirh tilted his head in confusion. "Who else?"

Marjori gestured at him as though it were the most obvious thing in the world.

"Me?" He laughed. As though any of them would follow him. "Oh no, definitely not. I'm just here to help out, really."

"Not gonna lie, that feels like a bit o' a waste, t' have a hero around just t' help out." She sounded completely unimpressed.

Jamirh shrugged. "I'm not really a hero though, am I? I haven't done anything even remotely heroic. Even if you subscribe to the idea that I was a hero in a former life, does that make me a hero?" He looked away, thinking of Jeri and her obvious doubt. His grip tightened around the key. "I don't feel like a hero."

"Doesn't really matter," came the surprisingly blunt reply. He found himself looking back up at her. "I don't know what it be like where yar from, but all the Avari I know grew up on tales o' Ebryn. He was able t' do things no one thought was possible." She paused, looking thoughtful. "An' that... that's what matters, ya know? What ya have or have not done won't change what people think upon seeing ya. Like it or not, ya've already made a first impression. Whether or not ya be Ebryn doesn't even matter – only the colors do."

"I can't change things," he whispered, ears sinking. "I've always known what people wanted from me. The 'promise' they see when they look at me. But I can't deliver on that. It's not fair to expect it of one person."

She shrugged, pushing off from the railing. "Maybe, maybe not. One person might not be able t' change things on their own, but sometimes all it takes is one person t' rally many. And many people... many people can get stuff done." She started to walk away. "But if ya be involved in ending those things from being made, then certainly that be the gods' work, and maybe that's enough fer one person, hm?"

He watched her go, considering. Not that he particularly wanted to put himself in harm's way, but she had a point. Hel, who was a god, wanted him to help end the threat of the Abominations. It was other Avari who seemed to think he could make their lives better the other way.

He looked down at the worn gold metal in his hand. Aether had tried to avoid pressuring him, but Jamirh knew his friend had believed that he was destined for "great things."

Aether would have been ecstatic to see Jamirh now.

Jamirh didn't think he deserved that.

He slid the key back under his shirt. Maybe he should just focus on surviving this whole mess and try to ignore what other people thought of him. Or at least put it off for later; not that he would be rallying anyone to any cause. Besides, he had the pendant Jak had given him, and while he didn't particularly care for the orange it did give him a sense of anonymity he'd never had before. Maybe, after all this was over, he could use it to melt back into obscurity and leave everyone else's judgements behind him.

Except... that wasn't really what Takeshi had meant when he talked about personal responsibility, was it?

It was several days later when the *Sea Spirit* came within range of Crescent Island.

Tension was thick in the air. The island's waters were regularly patrolled by military vessels. The routes had been observed by the priest they were meeting on the island and she had passed the information on to Ander and Takeshi. After some discussion, it was decided that the *Sea Spirit* would have to approach in the dead of night with the ship running as silently as possible in order to drop off its passengers safely.

It was now or never.

The captain was overseeing the lowering of the rowboats, keeping an eye on the gathering clouds above them. There was a storm brewing and everyone wanted to be done before it broke, though they were taking advantage of how black the night had become.

Jamirh was nervous. Not so much at the boats, but at the fact that they were essentially entering enemy territory. From now on they would have to be extremely careful to avoid detection, and then... then they would be actually attempting to take out the factory.

His stomach did a flip at the thought. Maybe it wasn't too late to stay on the *Sea Spirit*. What had he gotten himself into?

Ryn's thoughts floated through his. *Eh, it's not so bad. Can even be kind of fun, though... uh... maybe not with your group. Then again, maybe? The warg looks like fun! We didn't have a dog. And she's super friendly.*

Jamirh looked over to where Jitsu was sniffing at one of the small boats with interest, white fur visible even in the dark. *Most wargs are, I've found. Do you think she'll make a difference?*

Who knows? There are a lot of things your party has over mine, including three priests of Hades. Three! *I think you're good to go, honestly.*

That was a good point. Even if he hadn't met the third priest yet, he knew Takeshi and Ander were both capable. Jeri, too – he remembered how she had beheaded that Truth Seeker long ago in Sturlow.

Right! And we are going to help provide information on where to go. We should be able to start offering up real information as we get closer.

"Jamirh?" Takeshi called softly, snapping him out of his thoughts. "You are with Jitsu, Ander, and me."

Jamirh climbed carefully into the boat. Don waved at him cheerfully.

"Mara is waiting for us on the shore," Ander said as he settled down opposite Jamirh. "We should hurry."

Everyone glanced up at the clouds.

"For that reason too, I suppose," Ander finished.

Takeshi stepped in. Jitsu jumped in after him, settling to fill the bottom of the boat.

"We'll be nearby. The gals have a radio if ye need us, and we'll pick ye up again when ye be done with it," Caron rumbled at Takeshi.

"Thank you for everything you've done," the shinobi responded quietly.

"'Tis not over yet." Caron chuckled quietly. "Twins be with ye. Straight there and back," he said with a nod at Don as he tapped the side of the boat. Don nodded back.

Then they were descending.

The boat hit the water with a quiet splash. Don disconnected them from the *Sea Spirit* and began rowing them towards the shore. Jamirh wasn't sure how far sound carried over water, but since everyone else was being as quiet as possible, he figured he should follow suit. He looked up at the dark clouds overhead, wondering how long they had before they got wet.

It both felt like forever and like no time at all had passed before the bottom of the boat ran aground. "All right, out y'all go," Don murmured. "Maybe I can still make it back to the ship before this breaks." He winced as a raindrop landed on him.

"Thanks for the ride," Jamirh offered sympathetically as he stepped out of the boat and into the water. It wasn't deep, but his feet were instantly soaked.

And... there was a strange pull, coming from somewhere inland. Jamirh squinted off into the dark, trying to parse that, but it felt like something wanted him to go that way. Perhaps that was where the base was?

It is, Ryn murmured a little uneasily. *This wasn't exactly what I meant, though. It doesn't feel like that to me.*

Takeshi gracefully leapt into the water, followed by Jitsu, who wasted no time in getting herself onto the shore proper. "Indeed, thank you very much," the shinobi echoed Jamirh's earlier statement.

Ander snorted as he got out. "Row fast," he suggested as another drop hit him.

Takeshi shook his head and shoved the boat free, giving it the push it needed to return to deeper water. "Safe travels."

Don nodded and began rowing with a cheerful wave goodbye. Another rowboat carrying Jeri, Salisha, Desha, and Benjen was rapidly approaching in his place.

Jamirh decided that joining Jitsu on dry land was a good idea. He was still pondering the odd feeling. The warg was vigorously shaking herself as he approached, but gave up as the rain finally began to pour from the skies. Jamirh sighed, ears sinking as he was instantly soaked. Jitsu huffed in his direction, then went to splash in the surf.

Jamirh watched as the others attempted to hurry up in a flurry of activity. He didn't feel compelled to walk off into the dark, but it did feel like something wanted him to go in that direction. Maybe because Ryn already had the proper feeling of the base, it felt different to him? Maybe it was the start of knowing how the base was laid out?

But then why did it feel like something wanted him to go there?

Maybe Jeri was right. Maybe he couldn't do this.

He shook his head to clear it, deciding he could ask Takeshi and Ander about the odd feeling after they were someplace dry. Maybe they would have an idea. They were good at the whole magic thing.

Trying to ignore the sensation, Jamirh looked around. He wasn't sure what he should be doing. It wasn't like he could help bring the boat in faster; surely the pirates knew how to do that. He wasn't sure what Takeshi and Ander were doing; it was hard to tell in the dark through the rain, but Jitsu was definitely playing. The boat looked like it was almost to the shore.

He pushed his bangs out of his face. He could wring his hair out, it was so saturated. Jamirh wiped some of the moisture out of his eyes, then blinked as he realized that while he was soaked, he wasn't getting any wetter. Which was odd, as he could still see the rain falling – it just looked like it was falling about a foot away.

"Wow, that looks miserable," a voice said conversationally from right behind him.

Jamirh jumped nearly out of his skin, whirling around.

A tall Avari woman with bright-blue eyes and excessively long dark-blue hair in a ponytail smiled at him. She was also perfectly dry despite being dressed as though she were going to a party instead of a beach, her short, dark-blue dress, black tights, and high-heeled boots untouched by the weather or sand. A violet crystal shaped like a hound hung from a decorative rope around her upper thigh.

"Oops, sorry," she laughed, backing away with her hands up. "Didn't mean to scare you. I'm Mara, the person you're meeting here. Hel – Hel? – Hel says hi!" The woman grinned.

She reminded him of Hel. If he had known she was a god before he met Ander, this was the kind of person he would imagine being her priest. They had the same energy. "Hi," he greeted her belatedly. "I'm Jamirh."

"I know," she chirped. "It is nice to meet you, though. I'm glad you all made it! Well, almost."

Jamirh turned to see a very green-looking Jeri stumble out of the boat and practically scurry onto the beach, brushing off Takeshi's attempt to help her. She collapsed into a ball on the sand, ignoring Jitsu as the warg wandered over to sniff her.

"She probably should have stayed in the coffin," Mara snorted. "Come on, let's go make sure she's all right."

"There's a lot of stuff in the coffin," Jamirh tried to explain as he followed the blue-haired woman. He tried to stay close; the rain seemed to avoid the area immediately around her. "Not a lot of room for Jeri." It sounded weak even as he said it. He felt a twinge of guilt over taking advantage of her health to enjoy himself on the *Sea Spirit.*

Mara shot him an unimpressed look over her shoulder. "Nothing that could have been carried?" she asked pointedly.

Jamirh thought of the Crystal Light Blade and said nothing, looking down.

The blue-haired priest plopped herself down on the sand next to the Vampire. "Hey there; how are we doing?"

Jeri made an unhappy sound. Jitsu licked her face.

"Well, the good news is you made it," Mara continued as the rest of the group joined them in the protective bubble. She rolled up a billowing sleeve and pulled off one of her gloves. "The bad news is eventually you'll have to go back. But at least that's not now! Here, have a snack."

And with a dagger Jamirh hadn't seen her holding, Mara cut a thin line above her wrist. Blood began to well up, ruby red even in the dark. Jeri moved with a speed Jamirh hadn't seen since she beheaded the Truth Seeker in Sturlow and attached herself to Mara's wrist.

Jamirh took a step back, shocked. Sure, Jeri was a Vampire, but she never... he'd never seen... none of the Vampires he had interacted with had acted, well, like Vampires. They drank blood, yeah, but out of glasses, not from people. Half the time he thought it was wine. Seeing Jeri drink from Mara like this was...

...but then again, Mara herself looked completely unfazed. And clearly she had done that on purpose, so... it must be all right?

"Oooooh, look at that!" one of the sisters stage-whispered. Jamirh couldn't tell them apart. "A Vampire being a Vampire!"

"What an astute observation." Ander rolled his eyes.

"Isn't it?" the other sister giggled, unaffected by Ander's sarcasm.

"Desperate times call for desperate measures," Takeshi noted.

"And Jeri was very desperate," Mara agreed. "Honestly, bringing a Vampire across the ocean. Was this really the best we could do?"

"It was the Lady's call," Ander snapped.

"I'm okay," Jeri whispered, pulling herself off Mara's wrist. She ignored the incredulous looks being shot her way. "I'll be fine in a bit. Thank you." Jamirh wasn't sure if it was a trick of the light, or lack thereof, but Jeri's eyes seemed to be glowing red.

Mara smiled. "You. Are. Welcome!" Each word was cheerfully emphasized as she stood, brushing the sand from her clothes. Then she turned to face Ander, opening her arms up wide.

Ander took a step back, almost leaving the protective bubble around Mara.

"Come on, little brother! My once-per-century hug!" she whined. "It's been so long since we saw each other!"

"I'm wet," he tried. "Do you really want to hug me while I'm wet?"

"A little water never hurt anyone," she wheedled.

Ander sighed, shoulders slumping as he caved. "One," he warned. "You get one hug."

With a happy squeal, Mara threw herself at him in a crushing hug, almost sending them both crashing to the ground.

"Is this really the time?" Takeshi asked. "We need to be moving. You have secured a space for us?"

"Shush. I get one hug a century from Ander; I need to make it count," Mara said, tightening her hold on the other priest. "But yes, I've got a place, no worries. It's in the city."

Jeri pulled herself to her feet, looking unsteady. "We should head out, then."

There was a long, awkward pause while everyone waited for Mara to let go of Ander. Finally, the woman reluctantly pried herself off him. "Well, I suppose we should get off the beach, at least," she said with a sigh. "Wouldn't want to be accidentally spotted by any bad guys."

Jamirh stared at her, deciding that yes, this woman was exactly like Hel – completely oblivious to the fact it was her own actions that were keeping them here longer.

"And don't think I've forgotten about you and your hug, either," Mara declared, pointing at Takeshi.

The shinobi blinked at her, barely visible in the dark. Jamirh thought it was brave of him not to step away the way Ander had.

"But that can wait until we get under a roof. Let's see, how many of us are there?" She did a quick count, pointing at each of them briefly.

"Six of us plus a warg, not including yourself," Jamirh offered.

Mara nodded definitively. "Yup! Alrighty then, might be a hair tight, but we'll be fine. Let's get going, gang!"

The twins giggled quietly as they followed the priest without complaint into the dark trees, followed by the shadows of Takeshi and Jitsu. Ander shook his head as he too slipped into the trees with more skill than Jamirh would have expected of a doctor or scientist. He glanced back at Jeri as the rain began to fall on them once more.

"I'm fine," she reiterated, visibly pulling herself together. "Stay close – I'll be able to follow her even if she gets a little too far ahead. She's just... a little enthusiastic."

And they were right back to where they'd been before the *Sea Spirit*. Jamirh looked down, fingering the crystal that once again hung around his neck. "She reminds me of Hel."

"Is that a good thing, or a bad thing?" Jeri asked after a pause, sounding uncertain.

Jamirh didn't know how to answer her.

Rhode evenly met the eyes of the shinobi guarding the door. "I did make an appointment."

"Of course," the shinobi replied smoothly. "The Lady is ready for you. Your companions will have to stay out here today, I'm afraid."

Rhode saw Cole's mouth twist before her expression smoothed back out. She glanced at Madine, who remained as impassive as ever, before looking back to Rhode. She visibly struggled with what to say for a second before deciding on, "Good luck, sir."

It wasn't what she wanted to say; he knew that. Cole had already had a lot to say to him about this idea. She thought the Duchess of Ni Fon was dangerous and didn't like the fact that Rhode wanted to ask her for information, but the truth of the matter was that Kobayashi was likely the most well-informed person on the continent. Why the other dukes and duchesses allowed her to keep that information to herself was something Rhode would likely never understand. As part of the Empire, shouldn't she be required to share her information with the military? It wasn't as though it were a secret that Kobayashi had spies everywhere. Perhaps they just assumed that she would share information if she thought it was relevant or important enough?

Or maybe they just lacked the ability to force her into line. Maybe she had information on them; Rhode wouldn't be surprised.

He kept his face impassive as he stepped into Kobayashi's office, glad she was still in Gallia for the time being. She looked as perfect as ever, black sequined gown revealing a surprising amount of skin and red lips ever so slightly stretched into a smile Rhode didn't believe. Two shinobi flanked her, masked faces impassive. "Colonel. What is it you absolutely had to discuss with me?"

"I'm looking for any information regarding the concept of 'magic shaped like an Avari'," he began, respecting her desire to get straight to the point.

She didn't allow him to get any further. "Ah yes, it is almost as though wiping out all information about magic might not have been the greatest play for the Rose, hmm? But magic shaped like an Avari... explain. No, don't – this is in regards to the disaster at the Charve base." Her mouth formed a slight frown. "I've already told you that the traitor had nothing to do with me, and that he is dead by now besides."

He shook his head. "I'm not interested in him, I'm trying to get more information on the woman he freed."

"You said she wasn't actually Avari in the meeting," Kobayashi mused, "though everyone else ignored you. You think she was some sort of... sentient magic? Such a thing does not exist. Magic is a tool, to be used by those who can touch it. It does not use itself. Where did you come up with such a preposterous idea?" Her voice turned amused.

And here was the bit Cole had not wanted him to share with Kobayashi, but if he wanted information he would have to give some in return. "The Truth Seekers responsible for guarding her told me."

Kobayashi actually let out a short laugh. "And you thought–" She cut herself off abruptly, all amusement wiped from her face. "The Truth Seekers told you this?" she asked.

Rhode nodded, suddenly uncertain.

"To be clear – the Truth Seekers guarding this woman told you she was magic shaped like an Avari? Those exact words?"

He frowned and struggled to remember. "Yes, I believe so."

She stood and turned to the large window behind her, looking out over Alenci. "Interesting," she said after a moment. "Tell me, Colonel – what do you think of my shinobi?"

Thrown by the non sequitur, Rhode found himself looking at the two shinobi. They looked back impassively. He shrugged. "I don't think much of anything about them, I suppose. I'm sure they are effective guards." He tried to be charitable.

"Guards," she repeated absently. "They are so much more than that. And sometimes, they succeed at the impossible despite such odds that even I am impressed. How did this prisoner of yours escape your Seekers, I wonder? Your elite troops?" She turned back to Rhode, ignoring his confusion. "Thank you for this information, Colonel. In return, I'm afraid all I can do is reiterate this – there is no such thing as magic in the form of a person of any sort. Magic does not work that way."

"What about the death goddess?" he tried, feeling this opportunity slipping from him. "The prisoner was a follower of Hades. Perhaps something involving–"

Kobayashi shook her head, eyes pitying. "You are looking down the wrong path, misguided by that which has been put before you. The Silent Goddess is not your true enemy here, for all that she comes for us all in the end. But as I do not wish to meet her yet myself, I do believe I will be leaving post-haste to return to Ni Fon. Good luck to you, Colonel."

Without waiting for a response, she strode from the room through a side door, followed closely by the two shinobi, leaving a confused and frustrated Rhode standing by himself in an empty room.

Chapter Twenty-Five

Ander's fish had been at the mercy of Jak's idea of care for three weeks.

:I keep telling you, they are fine*,:* the Lady soothed. *:None of them look even a little stressed. They are going to make it until you return, I promise.:*

He supposed if anyone was going to be able to tell him that with any degree of accuracy, it was the Goddess of Death, but still... *:Jak doesn't like my fish. He doesn't understand how fragile that ecosystem is.:*

:Oh, I think he likes them just fine,: came the wry response. *:Don't worry – the logs may not be filled out to your exact standards, but you won't lose any fish or coral while he is watching them.:*

Something about the way She inflected "to your exact standards" made Ander wonder if the logs were being filled out at all, but there was little he could do about that from here. At least She seemed certain that everything was going to remain alive, even if She had not directly responded to his second point.

Luckily, everything so far was moving along a little ahead of Takeshi's original estimates, so maybe his fish would not have to suffer for as long as previously thought. They had managed to save over a week getting to Star Light City, and with Mara and the twin pirates helping Takeshi it was looking like they would be ready to strike at Tilden Base sooner than expected.

And then, gods willing, they would all be able to go home.

To his fish.

Who would hopefully not be dead.

He fought hard to squash the feeling that coming here had been a mistake.

:Beloved....: came the exasperated sigh, but She did not continue the thought.

"Why does Hades feel so... put out?" Takeshi asked tiredly as he settled into the armchair next to the couch. Ander had missed him come in; the shinobi had been out scouting for most of the night. He nodded at the glyph-covered paper strip Ander was fiddling with. "Surely it's not because of that?"

"No, it's his fish," Mara called from the kitchen where she was throwing some eggs into a pan. "He's worried Jak is going to kill them. The Lady keeps trying to tell him the fish are fine, but he's very stuck in the belief they are not."

Takeshi raised an eyebrow as Ander shot an annoyed look Mara's way. "The Lady cannot lie, though?"

Ander grimaced. "No, but Jak is Jak. I do not trust him with my fish."

"Ander, honey, you don't trust *anyone* with your fish." Mara laughed.

Not true. He would trust Mara with them. For a short time. Like a day or so.

"But honestly, don't worry – Jak knows how important they are to you!" she continued. "I'm sure he's putting in the effort."

Ander scowled at the glyphs in his hands. He wasn't sure Jak put effort into anything.

Takeshi coughed. "Still no luck on the blindfolds, either?"

The half-Avari frowned. "Not a single permutation I have tried has been even remotely successful by any metric."

The shinobi hummed thoughtfully. "Depending on how this goes, maybe we can get our hands on one of the actual blindfolds. There must be a missing piece."

:*Please don't prioritize that.*:

Ander ignored Her. "There are definitely Truth Seekers on the base, then?"

Takeshi nodded. "I don't know why there aren't any in the city, but there are at least four in Tilden."

Takeshi and Mara had been focusing their reconnaissance efforts on the base itself, while the twins had been scouting the city. Unlike what Takeshi had experienced with Charve, Star Light City was not under a lockdown, making it much easier to get around.

Still...

"Then why do I have to stay here?" Jamirh whined from where he was slumped over the table in the kitchen, waiting for Mara to finish breakfast.

Though the apartment Mara had brought them to was nice, it was cramped for seven people and one warg, who was currently taking up the floor under the coffee table. They were making it work, but Ander found himself agreeing with Jamirh – too much longer in such tight quarters, and someone was going to snap.

"Because there is no reason not to be overly cautious," Takeshi responded calmly. "I would rather not have you go out and end up running into a Truth Seeker we missed. No one goes out unless they have to." His tone of voice did not leave any room for argument. "Do you still feel that… pull?"

Jamirh's head moved in a nod without lifting from the table. "Yeah. Still weird. Ryn thinks I have to be on the actual base for it to work right," came the muffled reply.

"That's not anything we hadn't already guessed," Jeri pointed out. She was leaning back, balancing her weight on the back two legs of her chair while she shuffled a deck of cards. "Which is why we need to be as sure as possible of what we are walking into before we do it. We don't want to risk… any more than we have to."

Jamirh muttered something that might have been a "sure, whatever," and his hand went to that old key he wore.

"I think our current plan still has good odds of success," Takeshi mused. "If Ryn is correct, Jamirh should be able to help us avoid people on the base long enough to plant the explosives. Then we get out, and everything gets destroyed. Simple and elegant."

"And if Ryn isn't correct?" Ander had to point out the possibility.

"Then we go about it the old-fashioned way," the shinobi said with a shrug. "While Jamirh could make our lives easier, it's not a hard necessity. However, considering what Ryn, Jamirh, and Hades have had to say about it, I think we can consider it likely to work."

:Yes,: was the incredibly short acknowledgement.

"Have you been attuning yourself to the paper for the fire bombs?" Takeshi asked.

Ander nodded. "Yes, though it is... odd."

Mara made an angry sound as she attacked the eggs in the pan with a spatula. "No."

"She tried," Ander explained with a wince, saying a silent prayer for their breakfast. Mara's cooking could charitably be described as "non-toxic" at the best of times. "While the paper does attune to her, she can't seem to connect to the glyph after it is drawn."

"Stupid fire," she hissed, stabbing at the pan.

Takeshi hummed thoughtfully. "It's not surprising that you struggle with trying to connect to an element opposed to your own, though it is disappointing. Salisha and Desha have been creating the more conventional kind of bomb; you will have to plant those around the docks."

"Fine," she muttered darkly, glaring at the food before taking the pan off the stove and starting to distribute eggs onto the waiting plates.

"Where are Salisha and Desha, anyway?" Jamirh asked, lifting his head to look around.

"They already went to scout around the city for today. They said they'd grab something to eat while they were out," Jeri explained as she expertly bridged the cards together.

Jamirh put his head back down with a disgusted sound.

"Breakfast is almost ready," Jeri tried sympathetically. "Food. You like food."

Jitsu huffed from under the table.

Ander shook his head and decided to ignore that mess for the good of his sanity. He looked back to Takeshi. "How successful have your attempts to manifest your soul crystal been?"

He could see the grimace on Takeshi's face even with the mask. "It could be going better, I'm sure. I've managed to convince it to show itself briefly, but it is... so horribly uncomfortable that I lose it almost immediately."

"'Convince it to...'? I don't think that's the right way to think about it." It made his head hurt. "It should just manifest, no convincing necessary."

"I think it likes being where it is," came the dry reply. "Where it belongs."

"No wonder you aren't getting far with that attitude," Ander snorted, putting the paper blindfold down.

"Don't be rude, Ander," Mara scolded as she placed a plate of mostly unburnt eggs by each of them. A single piece of unmelted cheese rested on top.

Takeshi shrugged as he picked up a piece of bread that had gone right past toast straight into char. "To be fair, attitude matters with magic. He's not wrong."

"There's still a nice way and a not-nice way to say things," Mara pointed out. "You have the not-nice way down pat; you need to work on the nice way."

Takeshi inclined his head in acknowledgement, while Ander frowned. "Truth is truth. It shouldn't matter how you say it."

"But it definitely does," Mara chirped. "That's how society manages to hold itself together instead of devolving into chaos."

"Truth might be truth, but how it is said can be used to deceive." Takeshi pulled his mask down and took a bite of once-toast. His voice was thoughtful. "This is also how society manages to hold itself together. There is no such thing as absolutes."

Ander expected Hades to have something to say about that, but She remained silent.

Mara sighed in disgust and moved back into the kitchen, where Jeri was dealing cards to herself and Jamirh. Jamirh looked to have already devoured his breakfast.

"What attitude then would you recommend?"

Ander took a moment to rewind the conversation to figure out what Takeshi was referencing. "It just is." He held out a hand, and his own soul crystal manifested instantly. He considered it a moment, but he had been summoning it for so long that the discomfort barely even registered at this point.

Takeshi studied it with narrowed eyes as he took another bite. He chewed slowly, staring with startling intensity at Ander's soul crystal, and then at Ander himself. He held his own hand out, almost glaring at it, and the crystal blinked into view, taking a few tries to reach stability. It held for just a moment as Takeshi's face twisted, then disappeared again as Takeshi shook his hand out as if it had been stung.

"It is just a matter of keeping it present at this point," Ander offered. "Practice should help with that."

"He already knows that, Ander," Mara laughed with a roll of her eyes. She shoved a forkful of eggs into her mouth. "He needs different help than that."

"If I have to be nice with my word choice, you have to finish chewing before you talk," he suggested.

Mara grinned. "Deal."

Ander heaved a sigh, feeling like he had just been played somehow. He returned his attention to Takeshi and tried again. "You have to accept that part of you is not where it should be."

The shinobi tilted his head. "Hmm?"

"You were correct earlier, when you said that it belongs inside you. It doesn't think – that's you, the thinking part – but it is still a vital part of you. That's why we call it the soul crystal. Normal people who lose it become comatose. Some part of them that should be there no longer is."

"This supports my theory that it is an odd choice for a weapon. Or armor," Takeshi observed.

"We are different," Ander denied with a shake of his head. "As priests of Hades, we are capable of more. What is the soul, if not that which moves on when the body dies?" He considered that a moment. "We are the guardians of such, and to us are given abilities that pertain to this. So our souls and our bodies are able to act... more independently of each other than might otherwise be expected. And since sentient beings are what they are, we've discovered how to use it offensively."

"And this extends to the Vampires, too?" Takeshi questioned.

Mara nodded. "As Her children, yes. It extends to them too. Remember – they have already died, so technically this bit is a little easier for them."

"Their souls have already separated from their bodies, they've just been convinced to continue inhabiting them," Ander continued.

"I see," Takeshi murmured. "So I should... pretend to be dead?"

Ander could feel Hades trying not to laugh. "No. We are not dead. None of us have ever been dead, and we can die, it just takes a lot to get to that point. But you do have to find a way to convince yourself that your soul can be outside your body, and that is fine."

Takeshi squinted at him. "I might be too tired for this conversation. I wasn't expecting to return to existential philosophy."

"Why don't you get some sleep, then? The puzzle will still be waiting for you when you wake up!" Mara reassured him. "And it's not like you have to learn it by a specific date, either."

"Thankfully, I do not," Takeshi agreed, though something about the way he said it sounded not quite right to Ander. "Good night, then." He stood among a chorus of responses and disappeared into one of the two bedrooms, Jitsu following close behind.

The rest of the day was spent much the same as the previous four. Ander spent some time attuning paper to his magical signature the way Takeshi had shown them, and he contemplated the blindfold puzzle he had yet to solve, allowing it to distract him from how very not in Tarvishte he was. Jeri appeared to be teaching Jamirh every card game she knew in an attempt to distract him from how stuck he was, to some degree of success. Mara went out at one point after glaring at another failed attempt at one of Takeshi's fire bombs, declaring that she needed to pick up groceries. Takeshi slept.

Ander wasn't made for this sort of monotony. He was going to go out of his mind at this rate without some sort of challenge. He was still working on the blindfold glyphs, but felt he may have come up against a wall on that for now. At home he usually had three or four projects going simultaneously. He needed to move forward, make progress, discover *something*.

And a part of him just wanted to call it quits entirely and go home. Why had he agreed to this again?

Still, he wasn't quite desperate enough to join the card games. He forced himself to refocus on the blindfolds, taking his time as he drew another one out. Perhaps if this glyph was rotated ten degrees this way...

It was late afternoon when everyone began congregating again. Takeshi had dragged himself out of bed and was marking up a drawing of the base. Jitsu had joined Jamirh and Jeri in the kitchen, sniffing at what they were doing. Mara had apparently met up with the twins at some point, and the three women were chatting animatedly as they came in.

"Oh, oh! Guess what!" one of the twins cooed as she sidled up to Takeshi. Goddess, they didn't even dress differently. Why was he expected to tell them apart?

"What?" Takeshi asked blandly, eyes still focused on his map.

"We got Mara t' buy some spam!" the other twin exclaimed.

The first one was practically wiggling in excitement. "Dinner's going t' be sooooo good!"

"I have no idea what that is," Takeshi replied in exactly the same tone as before.

Ander could see the displeasure at the lack of a reaction. He glanced over at where Mara was unloading her shopping bag and was unsurprised at her enthusiastic nodding as she placed two cans of spam on the countertop. "It is a type of canned, pre-cooked pork," he explained. "It also lacks any sort of nutritional value."

"Ah. I see," Takeshi murmured.

Maybe someone else should be in charge of meals. Unfortunately, Mara was the only one that had offered, and her cooking skills were... well. She was over eight hundred years old. How could one last that long and not know how to feed themself? But the alternative was that Mara did know how to cook and was purposefully doing a bad job just to mess with them. She wouldn't do that, surely.

No, she wouldn't. Ander held on to that. Somehow, she had just never learned how to cook.

Maybe he could find a way to convince Jeri to cook? She tried to hide it, but she also looked disturbed every time Mara served something to her.

He supposed he could cook, but... no. The thought of cooking for a group of people made his stomach feel queasy. He hadn't cooked for anyone but himself since he'd left Elbe.

Had Alice cooked for Fredrik after Ander had left?

The twins glanced at each other, then at Ander. Something predatory gleamed in their eyes. "So, Ander," one twin purred happily.

"We were thinking," the other continued.

"O' the two o' us..." Goddess, why wouldn't they speak like normal people?

"Which be more yer type?" they finished together.

Mara winced. "Oh no, maybe don't–"

Ander was unimpressed. And maybe it was the reminder of what he'd lost, but... "First of all, neither of you are 'my type.' Second of all, you are both exactly the same by definition. You are identical twins, split from the same fertilized egg into two individuals, meaning that you share the same genetic code. You are duplicates of each other, indistinguishable and interchangeable."

Mara groaned and hid her face in her hands.

The twin on the right looked downright scandalized at this even though it was simply the truth of how their genetics worked, while the one on the left made an annoyed sound. She planted her hands firmly on her hips. "This is why we usually do this with Ben." Her gaze slid consideringly towards Takeshi, who was determinedly ignoring the conversation. "Hey, what about–"

"YES!" She was cut off by Jamirh's cry of victory startling everyone in the vicinity. He also looked surprised to find himself the center of attention as everyone's head swung in his direction. "Uh... I win?" he stammered, dropping his cards onto the table.

The twins were immediately distracted. Ander shook his head. His fish had longer attention spans than that.

"Not your type?"

Ander glanced over at Takeshi, who had picked up one of the paper blindfolds and was studying it carefully. "Absolutely not," he affirmed. He purposefully did not think of...

"Hmm." Takeshi's eyes slid towards him. "They're not mine, either."

"Whose type *would* they be?" he muttered. Some sort of masochist? A psychopath?

Takeshi snorted in agreement, returning his attention to the paper glyphs.

It was three days later when Takeshi called everyone together to go over the data they had collected. The shinobi was sitting in the armchair, papers spread over the coffee table in front of him. Mara perched behind him on the back of his chair. Jamirh and Jeri had taken the couch and were looking at the documents with varying degrees of interest. One twin was sitting on the floor, Jitsu's head in her lap, while the other sat on the arm of the couch. Ander himself was leaning against the far wall, not interested in crowding together with everyone else.

"Barring some sort of legendarily good luck, we've gathered all the intel we can," Takeshi began. "Most of our suspicions have been confirmed regarding Tilden Base, thanks to the combined efforts of many of us here."

Ander noticed Jitsu's tail wag.

"But there are still a number of uncertainties that we are going to have to deal with as they come up. The largest of these is the Avari who are being held here – we don't have any solid information on how many there are, where they are, or what state they are in," Takeshi continued.

Mara frowned. "We have a likely location – it's this building over here" – she pointed on the map – "but other than that…"

Jamirh was frowning. "Ryn says there's no saving them."

That earned him everyone's attention. "No?" Ander asked.

"He says…" Jamirh paused, ears sinking as his face twisted. "He says we should count them as already dead, even if they are alive. Trying to save some of them was part of the reason his own group failed. They won't be able to get out on their own."

Takeshi nodded after a moment. "I see. That makes sense."

"We don't know how long they've been here, or what they have suffered since they were taken by the military," Ander said with a frown. "We did consider this possibility back in Romanii."

"We will see when we get there." Mara's eyes shaded into violet as Hades spoke through her. "If they ask for death, we will grant it and send them on. Three of us will be present. It will be fast."

"Right, since the three of us should be able to… ah… warp the area," Takeshi agreed.

Ander nodded. "We won't be able to dedicate the area fully to Hades, but the three of us should be able to allow Her power to flood the area. Hopefully, this will not immediately cause the Abominations to explode, though if it does, it will be an easy success."

:It won't,: the Lady assured them. *:The first thing I did when I fought the Abomination by the Waste was flood the area with my power, and there was no instantaneous explosion. And you flooded the one you fought in Tarvishte.:*

:I did less of a flood and more of a trickle,: Ander disagreed. *:Scale could be important.:*

:Believe me, I flooded.*:*

Ander disregarded the brief feeling of disappointment. "Regardless, the effects of an almost-sacred ground will give us the advantage. They won't be able to rely on their tech, even though we won't be able to cut power to the base itself."

"Static," Takeshi muttered with a grimace. "So we start in a triangle just after midnight. Mara at the docks; myself, Salisha, and Desha to the north; and Ander, Jeri, and Jamirh to the south. Yes, you are with me," he assured Jitsu as her head whipped in his direction. "Once we are in position, we flood the area."

"Oh, then it's time for the bombs!" one of the twins giggled. "Bomb time is always fun."

"Not quite," Takeshi corrected. "Then my group and Ander's group need to meet up here." He pointed to an area just outside the base to the east. "That way, all of us except Mara can take advantage of Jamirh and Ryn's base-walking ability."

"Base-walking?" Jamirh asked, confused.

"That's what I'm calling it for now," Takeshi said with a shrug. "The military will know something is wrong because their tech will be acting up, so the *Sea Spirit* will be running interference with Mara's help to draw their attention away."

The twin on the arm of the couch held up her radio. "The Cap'n's all ready t' help out!"

"They're pretty close by," the other pitched in as she rubbed Jitsu's ears. "Just waiting on the word!"

"And also kinda excited t' see what they can do with a wizard," the first one laughed.

"Now that we be *expecting* a wizard's help," the other concluded teasingly.

"Right." Takeshi coughed. "So Mara will quickly place her bombs around the dock, then go help the *Sea Spirit*."

Mara gave a thumbs-up. "You got it!"

Takeshi nodded. "When the docks explode, we go in, taking advantage of the confusion. There's a lot of empty ground between the forest's edge and the complex, but at that time of night there will be shadows everywhere. With Ander's help, I will shadowstep all of us except for Jeri...?"

The Vampire nodded. "I'll be able to use the shadows to remain hidden on my own. I'll be close by the whole time, though, even if you can't see me."

"Then it's bomb time?" one of the sisters asked hopefully.

Takeshi gave another nod. "Yes, then it is bomb time. We make use of Jamirh's base-walking to avoid large groups of combatants while placing bombs in these key places." He marked nine spots on the map with a red pen. "Remember that we need to be fast – get in, get out. That means avoiding all possible confrontation. A battle will only slow us down."

Jeri leaned back against the couch, arms folded, though her eyes darted towards Jamirh. "It seems overly optimistic to expect to avoid both Truth Seekers and bionics."

Ander frowned, his eyebrows drawing together as he considered that. He thought back to his notes. "Do the Truth Seekers actually fight *with* the bionics? Seekers are mages. Surely they must be able to feel the Abomination as well."

Takeshi shrugged. "They did not exactly fight with each other when I came upon them in Charve. It was more like they took turns. And the Seekers did not seem pleased when a second Abomination stabbed Hades. Maybe because it was their 'turn,' so to speak?"

"But with both Truth Seekers and bionics as confirmed presences on the base, is it wise to bring so many non-mages?" Jeri looked concerned.

"The presence of non-mages on our side might actually be critical," Takeshi admitted. "When Hades and I were fighting the bionic in Charve, it was able to disrupt our magic with some sort of ability. I didn't notice an explosion, just the buildup of sound, and then every spell we had going shattered. It was difficult to pull together enough control to use magic in the immediate aftermath. If that should happen again, non-mages will be of vital importance." He looked at Jeri. "I don't know how it will affect you, if at all." He glanced at Jamirh. "And I don't know how it will affect inherents."

Jamirh looked thoughtful. "Ryn doesn't remember anything like that happening, so either they didn't try it or it didn't work."

"Impossible to guess, then," Ander declared.

Jeri shrugged. "We will find out when we find out. We've been warned it's a possibility, so we won't be blindsided, at least. And these ladies" – she indicated the twins – "won't be affected regardless."

The two women nodded. "We'll be ready," they chorused.

:My explosion was better than their not-explosion,: Hades muttered.

Ander saw Takeshi twitch, but he didn't address it. "And Jeri, about the bionics' UV rays...?" the shinobi asked instead.

The Vampire grimaced. "Yeah, I'm going to take a bath in sun lotion just before we head out, and Mara is working on a spell crystal that should cover anything the lotion doesn't."

Mara nodded forcefully. "Yup, will do!"

"Then, if we are in agreement?" Takeshi asked, looking around at each individual. His eyes met Ander's last. "We take tomorrow as a rest day to gather our strength. Then we strike the night after next."

Ander nodded along with the others, ignoring the cheering at Takeshi's proclamation. Still, something niggled at the back of his mind, an echo of the feeling he'd had back in Tarvishte. He found himself frowning in Jamirh's direction.

They were still missing something. And it had to do with the Blade.

Chapter Twenty-Six

Jamirh felt a shiver travel down his spine that had nothing to do with the balmy Nyphoren weather, though he couldn't tell if it was caused by what they were about to do or by whatever Ander was trying to do now.

The priest was on one knee, one hand on the ground and head bowed. They were about a hundred feet away from the tree line, though as dark as it was all Jamirh could see were lights from the base filtering through the trees. He hoped whatever the three priests were going to do wasn't going to involve lights – that would definitely give away their position. As it was, every time they heard someone patrolling near the tree line Jamirh had to fight down panic, though Jeri, Ander, and Ryn all told him they were fine.

He had the Crystal Light Blade in its sheath on his hip as well. He wasn't sure if it was making him feel better or worse. He knew he would be fighting for his life tonight, no matter what Takeshi said about trying to avoid battle. Hopefully the inherent power of the Blade and his own abilities would be enough to see him and everyone else through.

Now that they were close to the base, the pull he felt was even stronger, and he was beginning to doubt it had to do with the other sense he had of people just outside of his perception. What was there? What was calling for him?

His hand lifted, but he forced it down before it could find his key. Best it stay where it was against his chest for tonight.

Ander had been holding that pose for a while. What were they waiting for? Were Takeshi and Mara all right? What if something had gone wrong already? What if this whole thing was cursed–

The weight of the air suddenly changed around him, becoming instantly heavier, and for a moment it was difficult to breathe. Jamirh felt a primal fear well up within him, though of what he couldn't say – just that something was wrong, something was different, something was here that *should not be here.*

And then he could breathe again.

It was still there, the feeling of wrongness, but he wasn't overwhelmed by it anymore. He felt himself shudder again, this time unable to stop himself from resting his hand against where his key lay.

Ander stood, brushing dirt off his pants. "That should do it." Green eyes tinged with violet studied him for a moment before falling on the Blade. The priest frowned. "Give yourself a moment to adjust. Mortals don't often do well with too much of the Lady's power."

"It felt like... like something was, something was stalking me. No, something was waiting for me," Jamirh realized as he said it.

Ander nodded. "Death comes for us all in time. Mortals don't like to be reminded of it. Worry if you start hearing hounds baying; that means your death is near and Hades is about to come for you personally."

"As opposed to...?" Jamirh asked, confused. His ears twitched.

"One of Her spirit helpers – Valkyrie, we call them. Hades reserves Herself for special cases. Most people find the Valkyrie more comforting. Maybe it was different, in a time when people would treat death as an old friend, but in recent eras everyone fears Her." Ander glanced towards the base, where there was definitely increased activity, though Jamirh couldn't tell what kind. "Let's go. We need to meet with Takeshi's group."

It was a silent walk through the woods, no one feeling much like speaking. Jamirh could feel Jeri's worried gaze on his back, but he didn't know how to reassure her, or even if he should. He himself did not feel very reassured.

So focused on trying not to be scared, Jamirh nearly jumped out of his skin when Takeshi, Salisha, and Desha materialized out of the dark. Only Jeri's hand on his shoulder kept him from making a sound.

Takeshi nodded at Ander. "This is interesting."

The other priest shrugged. "It's not something we can do very well on our own, but with three of us involved... we can warp far more than just the area immediately around each of us."

"I can feel the ambient power in the area. I know you said our spells will be more potent, but this..." His voice trailed off. "This is something else. Hades did this, I think, in Charve."

"Don't get lost in it," Ander warned. "It's *Her* power, remember. It can overwhelm us too if we are not careful."

The twin on the left shuddered. "It felt real bad there, fer a minute."

"Are you going to be able to continue?" Jeri asked, sounding worried.

"Oh yeah," the other twin answered. "'Twas just fer a moment. It's nothing we can't handle."

Takeshi nodded. "Very well, then. Mara is just about done; she's just waiting for–"

He was cut off by the sound of multiple explosions going off in the direction of the base. If the weird thing the priests had done hadn't alerted them to danger, that definitely had.

"She mistimed it a bit." Takeshi's voice sounded strained. "But she says she's fine. She's rendezvousing with the *Sea Spirit* now. Remember, speed above all else. Let's go!"

And then they were off.

They didn't have far to go to reach the tree line. The base fence was about a hundred feet away across very lit, very empty ground. But Takeshi had been correct – there were shadows on the other side of the fence, as well as lots of people running around.

Jamirh felt his stomach flip, ears sinking. How were they going to do this?

We've got this, Ryn soothed. *Just wait for it!*

Wait for what?

Takeshi was watching the movement on the base very carefully. "Everyone coming with me, grab ahold of each other."

Jamirh found his hand being grabbed by one of the twins. He looked at her and found her smiling reassuringly at him. She gave his hand a squeeze. "Salisha," she whispered with a wink as her sister grabbed her other hand.

He found himself smiling back, even if it was a little wobbly.

Takeshi glanced back to make sure everyone was connected. "Jeri–"

"I'll be fine," she interrupted him, though her eyes were glued to Jamirh. "Go!"

Jamirh had just enough time to notice Jitsu pressing against him firmly before everything went completely dark. It felt like he'd tripped, even though he hadn't moved. He could still feel Salisha's hand in his and the warg against his side for a moment–

And then they were on the base.

And. Everything. Was. Moving.

Suddenly, the confused mess he had tried to draw back in Tarvishte made complete sense. He could practically see the layout of the base through where the people were and what they were doing, how they were moving. The awareness was completely alien and yet completely correct at the same time, similar to how he felt when he was able to correctly tap into his inherent, and yet... he knew this wasn't him, not really. Somehow, this was Ryn's awareness.

And the pull hadn't gone away.

People were moving, moving, moving...

"This way!" he hissed, darting quickly towards the nearest point he remembered as a bomb spot. They could do this; they would have to be fast though, so very fast, avoid the people, avoid that group, *there,* and then that one...

The others were following closely; he could feel them, too. That was good; he wouldn't lose them this way, and they couldn't lose him. No one questioned him. He could still feel Salisha holding his hand.

They ran up to a building. Takeshi did something to the door, and then they were in.

It was odd, he reflected as he stumbled to a stop at the point he had been heading to. He knew where everything was, but he didn't know *what* everything was. Why was this spot important? Takeshi and Ander were placing their paper explosives by Salisha and Desha's more powerful ones, so this was important, but why?

"Jamirh?"

He met Takeshi's eyes and nodded. He reached out, focused for a moment, and then he was leading them off again.

Something still pulled.

Jamirh... something doesn't feel right. I don't feel well.

We need to finish.

...Yeah. Keep going.

They had successfully placed bombs in two more places, weaving through the complex with unnatural awareness, before Jamirh realized that something wrong was heading towards them. Something even more unnatural.

He didn't need Ryn's warning. He'd seen them before.

Jitsu began to growl.

"Bionic, incoming!" he hissed. He considered trying to redirect, but the things were fast, and he was realizing there were a lot of them on the base. Better to go through one than many.

"Overwhelm it!" Takeshi snapped. "Go for the joints, then the core!"

Jamirh dodged out of the way as it came around the corner, finding it incredibly easy with his increased awareness. Ander stood back, a green shield coming up around him and the sisters. Jeri and Takeshi attacked without pause, lightning crackling ominously from Takeshi's katana as Jeri's shadows reached up to pin the thing in place. As horrifying as the things were, one was no match for the combined might of a Vampire and a shinobi who knew what they were dealing with.

One down...

Oh gods.

Many, *many* to go.

How many bionics had they made?

Focus!

Jamirh fought down the combined nausea of himself and Ryn and saw the route they had to take. "This way," he said, turning and heading for another door.

"Any Truth Seekers?" Ander asked as Takeshi opened it.

Jamirh considered. "I can't really tell," he admitted. "I can tell where there are people, but only the bionics feel different." And there were people and bionics *everywhere*.

"Keep going," Takeshi ordered, practically shoving Jamirh through the door.

Ryn had gone silent.

That was okay; Jamirh still had his awareness of the base. Ryn would be fine. Technically, he was in the least danger out of all of them, existing inside Jamirh as he did. They could do this.

As more bombs were placed, Jamirh shuddered, ears twitching down. "They're coming," he warned. "Four bionics, headed this way!"

Ander swung around and a green wall filled the doorway. "We can't waste time with four."

"I have an idea," Takeshi said. "Hide, and on my mark run for the door. Jamirh, which way are we heading?"

"Right out the door, then left at the end of the hallway," he replied. They were halfway; surely they could finish it.

"After the left turn, regroup," Takeshi ordered. "Hide!"

Everyone scattered about the room, and Ander's shield fell.

It was quiet, except for the scream of alarms Jamirh hadn't noticed before, so focused he had been on trying to keep track of the location of every individual on the base. He was still doing that, but without having to worry about moving he found he was able to take in his actual surroundings more clearly.

He could still feel that pull, though.

It felt closer.

He tried to put it out of his mind. They just needed to place... five more bombs.

He could hear *and* feel the bionics in the hallway now, clicks of metal against metal as they came steadily closer. There was a pause, then one entered the doorway, red light from its mechanical eye sweeping the room.

Two hundred and fifty pounds of electrified, snarling warg threw herself at it.

Warg and bionic crashed into the Abominations still in the corridor, and then Takeshi was shouting "*Now!*" and Jamirh was running, feeling the others do the same.

He passed by Jitsu, fur still sparking as she ripped into the thing's exposed spine with her teeth. The electricity was visibly traveling into the bionic's systems, and Jamirh didn't think that one was going to make it. Even as he thought it, he could feel his awareness of it dimming, but one of the other ones was doing... something. Something loud.

"RUN!"

Jamirh didn't hesitate at Takeshi's shout, skidding around the corner as something broke in the air. It didn't feel like how Takeshi had described it. Jamirh still felt weirdly hyper-aware of everything, but he could tell that something had changed. He turned to help, drawing the Blade, but...

...it was right there. Whatever it was.

Everything seemed to fade as Jamirh realized that whatever the pull was, it was in the next room over. He lowered the Blade, though he kept it in hand as he frowned at the shadowed alcove that sheltered the door. He took a step closer.

"*Stop.*"

Jamirh blinked. Someone was standing in the way. The figure was male, wearing old-fashioned leather armor. He had long red hair pulled back into a ponytail. Silver eyes gazed at Jamirh, impossibly sad.

"Don't go that way."

Jamirh felt tangible rage build up in him as the ghost of Ebryn Stormlight barred his way.

"How *dare* you," he began, barely even able to get the words out. "How dare you, *you*, tell me what to do–"

"I haven't been able to spare you much, but I would spare you this. Go back," Ebryn urged. *"That room is not for us."*

"Not for us?!" Jamirh snarled. He lifted the Blade. "But *this* is? What, are you the only one of us that gets a say in what we do? How dare you come to me now, and demand I do or not do something, *when my whole life has been dictated by your shadow!"*

Ebryn's eyes closed, and his form faded from view.

Jamirh strangled down an enraged scream. That... that *coward!* Even dead, he wouldn't face him! And to give Jamirh orders! *Orders!* Like he cared even slightly what that miserable excuse for an Avari thought he should do! Don't go in? There was *nothing* Jamirh had ever been more sure he was going to do. He was going to find out what that pull was, and then they were going to finish this godforsaken mission, and he was going to be able to put all of this behind him forever!

With a strength he did not know he possessed, Jamirh shoved the door open, looking around for whatever it was that was calling to him.

He froze.

The room had six large, cylindrical tanks against one wall, filled with a pale-green liquid. In them were bodies, or pieces of bodies. Some had more parts than others. This one had half a torso and a leg, that one only limbs, the next a spine floating between two arms.

In the next one–

He suddenly understood why he had to be on the base in order to understand it.

Ryn's severed head stared back at him, silver eyes unseeing.

"He remained here to give you a chance, though the Lady blessedly took his memory of the particulars. Don't waste it."

Jamirh turned to the side and heaved.

"Jamirh! What in the–" Jeri's voice cut out in horror. "Oh Goddess," she whispered.

And then Takeshi was standing between Jamirh and the tanks. Forcibly, he spun Jamirh around. "Salisha, if we have any bombs to spare..."

"Yeah, we've... got a few. This is a good spot."

Jamirh was pushed past Ander, who was looking at a data pad left on one of the tables.

"Jamirh!" Takeshi had his hands on his shoulders. He shook him. "Jamirh! Come on! Focus! Now is not the time!"

Jamirh shuddered. Right. One... one last thing to do. They had... what were they doing? Right, bombs. They had to place more bombs. He tried to focus on where everyone was.

All he could see was Ryn's face. He keened.

Slap!

Jamirh's head whipped to the side, cheek burning. The pain helped, gave him something else to focus on. He blinked to clear his eyes, saw Jeri with her hand still in the air. Green eyes met silver.

"We need to keep going," she whispered. "I know it's hard, and I know it's bad, but now is not... now is not the time. We need you to keep it together, Jamirh, or we are all going to die here. Just like... just like him." Her voice broke, and she paused for a moment. "We have to do better. *You are not alone.*"

That's right. People... people were relying on him. Relying on him to get them out of here alive. He had to... he had to do this for them.

He could do this for them.

He closed his eyes and took a deep breath, forcibly putting the image out of his mind. By sheer strength of will, he brought back up the awareness of the base, purposefully ignoring the silence where Ryn had been. Purposefully ignoring the feeling that still pulled at him.

There were fewer people than there had been before.

That was... good, he hoped.

He took another deep breath. "This way," he managed to say, pushing himself away from the wall. He ignored Jeri's look of concern, mirrored by the sisters, and Takeshi's steely resolve. Ander's face was blank, but Jitsu made sure to press up against him, giving his hand a small lick.

Five bombs to go.

There were so many of the bionics. It was okay, they could go this way – it would take a bit longer, but they would avoid the vast majority of the ones swarming in this direction. Absently, he wondered if they were like the Truth Seekers, connected in some way. That would make sense. All of them, connected into one big family of horror and despair. Did they feel despair?

This way, now. He almost crashed into Desha as he switched direction. "There are two this way, but it's better than all the other ways," he informed the group woodenly.

"Bionics?" Takeshi asked.

Jamirh nodded as they ran.

Takeshi, Jitsu, and Jeri managed to clear the way, but Jamirh noticed everyone was beginning to flag. How long had they been here? It didn't seem like a long time, but Jamirh was also fairly certain his perception of most things was a little skewed right now. Had they been here five minutes? Thirty? Surely not more than that, though it felt like both forever and a blink of an eye. Takeshi said they had to be fast, had to hurry hurry hurry...

"Jamirh?"

He looked at Jeri. "I'm okay."

"You're not," she refuted quietly. "But that is, itself, okay."

He considered the area, heart beginning to sink. "How many more do we have left?"

"Four," she answered. "Is that bad?"

"It's not good," he muttered as he reviewed possibilities. "Takeshi, we are running out of options."

The shinobi studied him carefully, then nodded. "How many more do you think we can pull off?"

If they went this way, around that group... "Maybe one." And even then...

He could see Takeshi's frown through the mask. "Maybe?"

He shrugged. "My head is… a weird place right now." He felt a hysterical laugh bubble up. "For a whole bunch of reasons."

The shinobi inclined his head, eyes grim. "All right. We'll have to make do with only one more. Then we get out."

Ander frowned. "That might not be enough."

"We can't afford to waste any more time. Jamirh?" Takeshi indicated the corridor.

And they were off again.

It wasn't possible to skirt around all the bionics anymore. The best Jamirh could do was herd them into the smaller groups, but each battle took more and more of a toll. Twice more Takeshi had to do something big with lightning to stop a bionic from doing whatever it was they did that messed with the mages, and each time Takeshi looked more run-down. Ander had started stepping in to help, and Jamirh was pretty sure that was a bad sign. The sisters were low on ammo, and Jeri seemed to be moving more slowly.

He still hadn't used the Blade.

"Don't use it. What good is it anyway?"

"Shut up," he whispered, a hint of anger returning. "Don't tell me what to do."

"Jamirh?" Jeri was looking at him with that concerned look again.

"It's nothing," he said with a shake of his head. "Sorry." He consulted his mental map again. Routes with even a small likelihood of safety were rapidly disappearing. "This way."

They fought through another group of three bionics and placed the last set of bombs. Jamirh searched for the best route out, ears sinking.

Takeshi looked around. "Our only goal now is to get out by any means necessary. Fight only as much as you have to in order to get past, and then run. Does everyone understand?"

Nods answered him, except for Jamirh, who was starting to feel the cold creep of panic for the first time since entering the base. "I don't... there's no good way to go," he admitted, sensing the number of bionics closing in around them.

"Are they only Abominations?" Ander asked.

Jamirh considered, then nodded.

"No Truth Seekers still, or even ordinary soldiers. Why?" The priest was frowning. His gaze fell on the Blade. "Something... we are missing something."

"Not our problem right now," Takeshi snapped. "If there isn't a good way, we make one. Go!"

Jamirh led them left. If nothing else, it was the shortest path to the outside, though what they would do at that point, he had no idea.

He swung around a corner, knowing what was coming. "Here; six!"

He brought the Blade up.

The Crystal Light Blade screamed to life, multi-colored light illuminating the area. A bionic slashed at him with the blade in its right arm, finding him too close, but his training paid off.

Dodge; strike.

Something rang hollow and wrong as the Blade met the Abomination.

Jamirh jumped back as a bolt of lightning shot past him into the thing's face, followed closely by Jitsu. Jeri and Ander were engaging another, and the sisters were providing what support they could from the back. Takeshi slammed a dagger into the bionic's non-mechanical eye. It staggered.

Jitsu finished it off, and then they were moving on to the next.

That odd sound was building up again. Jamirh looked around, trying to pinpoint which one was preparing the anti-magic blast.

There!

He shot forward, trying very hard not to think about what he was doing. The bionic saw him coming and shot at him. He moved, fast fast *faster*, got right in front of it. Jamirh dropped and rolled to get behind, then swung at the arm with the gun.

The Blade made a sound like a broken bell, and the limb crashed to the floor.

"That doesn't sound right!"

Panic, but now it was doubled by panic not his own.

He couldn't disengage. The bionic brought its blade around to meet his, and he met it in a flurry of blows and slashes. The light of the Blade almost made it difficult to see, but he found he didn't need to – the skill was there, and he moved with instinct.

Each time the Blade connected, the sound repeated.

"Jamirh!"

He wasn't sure who had shouted it and he couldn't look, though he could hear the alarm in their voice. The sound was almost at its peak, if he could just–

There!

He ducked around a swing and came up inside the Abomination's guard, plunging the Blade into its chest where the sound seemed to be coming from. The Blade screamed.

The sound cut out, and the bionic twitched to a halt.

Movement, to the right–

Jamirh pulled the Blade free, swinging to meet the next attack, knowing that if he stopped now he was dead, so very dead.

"Jamirh!"

The Blade met the blade of the bionic.

And shattered.

Chapter Twenty-Seven

Takeshi could pinpoint the exact moment things went from "bad, but workable" to "catastrophic."

Hades was still screaming in his mind as he tried to get past the two bionics between him and Jamirh, who was standing frozen as he stared at the hilt of the Blade. The Avari's eyes were wide in shock, which was understandable, but he wasn't moving and the bionic that had shattered the Blade was not bothered by the sudden destruction of a near-holy weapon. Jitsu managed to streak past, shouldering Jamirh out of harm's way as she went for the bionic still threatening him.

:NOT the Abomination; the Blade! Get away from the Blade, all of you!:

Even with Hades' power flooding the complex and the stored power in the *crystallus*, Takeshi was tiring. This much sustained casting in a short amount of time was difficult to maintain, Hades' power or no. He had started to feel the exhaustion some time ago, could feel each movement he made get a little slower. He wasn't going to be able to get to Jamirh in time, even as he tried to alert Jitsu that something was wrong.

Jitsu understood, but she didn't dare turn her back on the evil-metal-not-Avari as it slashed at her. She would distract it; someone else would have to get the helpful-red two-foot.

A shadow skated across the ground and then Jeri was between Jamirh and yet another bionic as it slashed down with two blades. Jeri twisted in a way Takeshi was sure was unnatural. One of her cutlasses went flying, shattering into ethereal crystal before reforming in its sheath. Takeshi thought he might have seen blood, but it couldn't have been that bad because then she was pulling Jamirh away from the bionic. But she didn't know about the Blade, couldn't hear Hades. Takeshi opened his mouth to try to warn her that something Bad was going to happen.

:Bad Bad Bad DANGER STOP IT–:

Ander grabbed the remains of the hilt from Jamirh's hands as Takeshi dodged another attack. The white-haired man threw it back towards the remains of the Blade itself, blue crystal scattered across the ground, except it wasn't just blue. Takeshi realized the shards were still glowing, and in fact they seemed to be getting brighter, not dimmer. Ander shouted something and Jitsu retreated as a violet shield snapped into place around the remains, threads of magic weaving together over and over again, creating layers of protection.

The first pulse of yellow light was contained by Ander's shield, but the sound caused everything present to stagger. Even the bionics stopped and turned to face the violet dome.

The second pulse of blue light made the floor shift like liquid under his feet and Takeshi almost slid sideways.

The third pulse, green, caused cracks to travel around Ander's shield as the floor shook, and Takeshi saw him pale as the threads of magic tried to repair the damage. Sensing how much Ander was pouring into the weave, Takeshi threw himself into the pattern, tried to strengthen the threads with his own magic and pulling from the remnants of what remained in his *crystallus.*

A red blast shattered the dome. Takeshi was thrown back into a wall, and he felt the pain of the impact in addition to the heat of the blast. Jitsu cried out for him as she too went flying. Desperately, he tried to throw up another shield in case the Blade wasn't done with them yet, but he was disoriented and there was...

Oh gods, there was *too much magic.* Far too much magic; it was everywhere, and not like Hades' magic which had felt protective and watchful, this *hurt,* pure elemental energy surging to escape that which had contained it for so very long it felt like he was breathing it–

Hades shrieked in rage, and then there was silence. Cool, blissful silence.

Takeshi tried to reorient himself. They were still in danger here. He pushed himself up, blinking to clear his vision. There was dust in the air. Debris was everywhere. The hallway was mostly intact but warped, metal twisted and singed. He saw something twitch just in his field of vision and he shifted to face it, but it was the charred and melted remains of a bionic, red light dying even as he watched.

Jitsu whimpered, but she was already pushing herself to her feet before he could so much as turn in her direction. She was fine, she insisted. She hurt, but in a will-get-better way, not a that's-very-bad way. She shook herself vigorously.

:Ander? Takeshi?: Mara's voice echoed worriedly. *:We felt that from out here, the ambient magic went completely insane. What happened?:*

Takeshi glanced around, doing a head count. He paused upon seeing the ethereal shadows of Hades floating above where Ander had tried to contain the Blade. *:There's been a complication,:* he informed Mara shortly.

Everyone was slowly getting to their feet, though Ander was leaning heavily on one of the sisters and the other sister was limping. The women were talking quietly to Ander, who was shaking his head, hurt and angry. Jamirh almost looked catatonic.

It was awful – he'd done so much better than they could have hoped. He'd guided them with considerable accuracy, and though he had suffered a horrible shock at coming upon the body of his predecessor, he'd been handling it as well as could be expected – not great, but he'd been functional after Jeri had snapped him out of his panic.

But then the *Blade* had failed, not the wielder.

This was why Takeshi disliked magical artifacts. People always put far too much faith in something that could never be fully understood. Hades had known something was wrong the first moment that odd sound had rung out. Jamirh had withdrawn, and Takeshi had thought he'd realized it too. But then Jamirh had moved to intercept the one about to do its anti-magic blast, and that was when Hades had started screaming.

There were too many bionics. Neither Takeshi nor Ander had been able to get to him in time.

Certain that Jeri was helping Jamirh now, Takeshi turned to Hades' shade. She was examining the space where the Blade had been, wisps of shadow flickering around her. Her gaze was cool, dispassionate, as violet eyes flickered to him.

:I smothered the elemental magic with my own, but the price of this...: She trailed off, but Takeshi could already feel it happening, could feel himself weakening as her magic faded from his reach. Without the added pool of magic to draw from, his own reserves sank from low to dangerously low. *:This was not truly consecrated ground, and I fear I have... overreached.:* Her shadowy form began to fade as well. *:Don't give up; keep going. I can no longer act directly, but we may yet have one more play.:*

"The tech in the Abomination," Ander spat. Despite his anger, his face was drawn and gray, and he was still leaning heavily on one of the twins. Takeshi could feel how drained he was. "We should have realized that would be an issue. The Blade was completely magic, meant to fight Abomination, but the tech – Goddess, tech didn't even exist when She forged the Blade, magic and tech have never mixed well, we should have known there would be complications..."

Despite the rant, Takeshi could tell Ander was losing focus. *:Take the* Sea Spirit *and go,:* he ordered Mara.

:What about all of you?:

:We are also going to run,: he reassured her. *:Go! We will contact you when it is safe.:*

She hesitated but then sent a feeling of acknowledgement. He felt her withdraw.

Takeshi took a deep breath and recalled the map of the base he had managed to put together, considering how large and labyrinthian it was. Jamirh was in no shape to guide them, but they just needed to reach the closest exit at this point and get out. They were losing what advantage the death of the Blade had given them the longer they stayed here, though at least it had taken care of the nearby bionic problem.

They weren't anywhere near an exit.

Grimly, Takeshi revised the situation. The narrow hallways did not allow them much room to move, but they hampered the bionics as well. They couldn't seem to aim their ranged weaponry well in the confined space, which up to this point had favored their small group's speed and magic. But now he doubted any of them had much left to give, given the soot-streaked faces and tired eyes regarding him quietly.

Jitsu bumped her head against his arm. They should go.

He nodded. No matter where this would lead, they had to try. "This way."

And now it was his turn to lead them through the base. He didn't dare show how he too was beginning to flag, especially without the aid of Hades' magic flooding the area. His *crystallus* was drained. For the second time in four months he found himself courting magicore exhaustion. Muscles screamed with fatigue and pain from when he had been thrown, but bruises seemed to be the worst of what he had suffered from the explosion. The same couldn't be said for everyone in their party. He took Ander from the twin and allowed her to help her sister, who had a significant limp. Jeri was pulling Jamirh along. Jamirh hadn't been terribly present throughout most of this mission, something Takeshi attributed to the Avari's attention being taken up by trying to keep track of every living thing on the base, but now he was nearly unresponsive. Takeshi also noted freely bleeding gashes down his hand and arm from where shards of the Blade had cut him. Jeri herself looked okay, though her eyes were shading red every time she looked back at Jamirh and there was something odd about her left arm Takeshi couldn't pinpoint.

It didn't matter. They just needed to get out. Everything else could come after.

Where were all the people who were not bionics? They had not been challenged by either soldiers or Truth Seekers, though the *Sea Spirit* had led some of the military vessels on a chase according to Mara. They hadn't even come across any non-combatants, scientists or contractors or even a janitor. Where were all the people? Had the flooding somehow caused most of them to flee in panic? He had seen how Salisha and Desha had reacted when it was first put in place, and they had been just outside the area. Perhaps a stronger reaction had occurred within?

What was going on? Had they somehow known they were going to be attacked? But even if they had, this response of only bionics still felt strange. How were they even being controlled?

Where was everyone?

:People are dying here,: Hades whispered darkly.

He considered Jamirh for a moment as they ran. The Avari still looked unwell, but Takeshi couldn't afford to let it go. "Jamirh," he called.

He blinked at him, silver eyes a bit unfocused. "Hmm?"

"When we first came here – could you tell approximately how many people were on the base?"

Silver eyes blinked at him blankly, but there was real hurt buried in there. He looked like he was trying very hard not to be upset. "A lot. It's hard to guess exact numbers, since it's like being aware of everyone's existence simultaneously." His voice wavered.

"But there were people besides the bionics?" Takeshi pressed.

Jamirh nodded. "Yeah, a bunch. There's a lot less, now. I don't know what happened, but the numbers of non-bionics are definitely getting lower." He wiped at his eyes, leaving smears of blood on his face. "I think the number of bionics is lower too, but it's harder to tell. There's still a lot of them."

That was not great.

"Where are they all coming from?" one of the sisters breathed. "I know this is like a factory for them, but by the love o' the Twins this is insane."

They had known they were going to be fighting Abominations, but this was far more than Takeshi had hoped. Jamirh had been correct when he warned them about the Empire's ability to produce. Maybe they were twenty years too late, and everything they were doing here was futile, a temporary stopgap at best.

:No! You can't think like that!: Hades interrupted his thoughts desperately. *:We have to keep going! Abomination CANNOT win!:*

:Yet it does appear to be winning,: he thought at her bleakly as they rounded another corner and found... far too many for them to fight in their current condition.

"Back!" Takeshi barked, spinning himself and Ander down another hallway, ignoring the priest's reflexive protest at being man-handled. He threw up a weak shield, hoping that would at least delay the bionics from following them. They needed more time to get out.

Jamirh shuddered and nearly fell. Only Jeri's quick reflexes stopped him. He stumbled to a stop, and when Jeri tried to pull him with her he broke free. Takeshi slowed, wondering if he needed help. "We're being surrounded," the Avari informed them despondently.

Takeshi closed his eyes for a moment, leaning Ander against the wall. He was so tired.

Jitsu rubbed against him like a cat, letting him soak in her warmth to help ground him. They weren't dead yet, so they still had options!

He mentally thanked her for her optimism, even if he wasn't sure he shared it. Something would have to change if they were to actually succeed in escaping at this point.

"Takeshi–" Jamirh started.

"Have you come here to die?" A cool female voice cut him off, just a hint of interest coloring it.

A Truth Seeker stood not ten feet from them, blindfolded head cocked to the side ever so slightly. Short blonde hair cut at a severe angle framed her face.

Takeshi stepped forward, katana drawn, but words aside she wasn't threatening them. Her sword was sheathed, her gun holstered. Her hands hung empty at her sides. Takeshi couldn't even feel any magic gathering around her. While her words were aggressive, her tone was almost curious.

He remembered, back in Charve, a Truth Seeker telling him to go.

And he knew she was in far better condition than any of them.

So, as Jeri and Ander both moved to intercept, he held up his other hand, ordering, "Wait!"

Jeri danced back to stand between Jamirh and the Seeker, but Ander frowned at him. *:Are you insane?:*

Jitsu sniffed in the blind-one's direction. She didn't seem to be challenging them.

Takeshi decided to roll with it. It wasn't like they really had much left to lose. He eyed the Seeker. "No. Have you?"

Her head tilted a little more. "Yes."

Well then.

He could feel the confusion beginning to set in as she and the group faced off. "That's a little defeatist," he finally said, not at all sure where this was going.

"You came here too early," she accused in response.

"My apologies; were we coordinating?" he questioned.

Ander was slowly turning to look at him, a look of utter bafflement crossing his face. Takeshi didn't dare look at the others' responses.

She continued to stare in their direction, and he felt an odd shiver travel down his spine, as though he were being studied far more closely than he was comfortable with. "We know you," she said after a moment. "Would you see the Truth we see?" Moving slowly, she pulled off one of her gloves and held out her hand to him.

Hades said nothing, but Takeshi could feel her wary attention.

"What truth would that be?" he asked, not moving.

"There is only ever one Truth, though it may be wielded in different ways, shaded to fit one perspective over another. See what we see," she urged, a hint of emotion entering her voice.

"I think we should probably go, actually," he deflected. "There's a number of bionics heading this way, I believe."

"There is very little time left, yes, but the corrupted ones will find it difficult to reach us. This will take but a moment."

The corrupted ones?

Ander managed to dredge up a feeling of tired pleasure. *:I was correct; they don't like the Abomination.:*

It was oddly – amusing? Exasperating? – that Ander felt the need to be correct even in this situation.

"We would offer you understanding, before our end," she continued.

What did that mean?

Takeshi turned his head so he could see the group without taking his eyes fully off the Seeker in front of them. Jamirh was still mostly hidden behind Jeri, who looked grim. The sisters had completely lost expressions on their faces, looking back and forth between Takeshi and the Seeker. Ander had his eyes closed, still mildly pleased with himself. Jitsu was sitting right next to Takeshi, eyes firmly glued to the Seeker, clearly uncertain what to make of her.

He had to try. For them.

He took off one of his own gloves and reached out.

As soon as they connected, he knew he'd made a mistake.

In fact, he knew *far too much*. Several thousand minds, existing in harmony with each other, but all of them trying to impart information to him. It wasn't malicious, he realized instantly, it was just what they were, and what they were was too much for him alone, for him to be alone, he was slipping, joining–

Shields slammed up around his mind, cutting him off from their collective and allowing him to just be him again. *:No!:* Hades radiated defiance as he pulled his hand away as though burned.

But he had seen what she had wanted him to. Both things, actually, amidst the deluge of information. The far more relevant of which was that they were going to absolutely destroy this place in mere moments. This Truth Seeker, and the three others who had stalked and murdered throughout the night, were meant to be sacrificed to ensure the total destruction of this base.

He paled as she hummed. "I told you: you came here too early. Unfortunate, that the one who signaled it was our time must be sacrificed along with us, but with the death of the Blade, perhaps it is time for him to rest." She indicated Jamirh.

Before he could do anything, Takeshi felt the flex of power activate the pattern they had drawn under the base itself, giving their own life energy to fuel it. "Wait!" he shouted, well aware there was absolutely nothing he could do to counter this. Desperately he tried to summon his soul crystal, hoping against hope he could use it to offer some protection to their little group, but the damn thing *still wouldn't come*, even now, and he could feel Hades cry out–

Spell crystals bloomed into existence around them, pale-blue and violet offsetting the uncanny red slowly suffusing the air. They were huge for spell crystals, several feet high, forming a rough circle around their group. Jak appeared in the air above them, black wings forming even as Takeshi watched, holding a long black staff with a soul crystal at the end of it. Hades hovered behind him, ethereal as always, actions mirroring Jak's as he held the staff high. The soul crystal glowed like a star as violet lines of power began to twist into a sphere around them.

Takeshi felt his stomach drop as he lifted off the ground and reality warped.

Then they were all crashing to the floor. It was easier to breathe, and Takeshi took in several gulps of air, not having realized that in those last few moments the air had become so heavy that he had been struggling to get oxygen. There had just been so much else to deal with, as well as the information from the Truth Seekers that even now was making it a bit difficult to focus. He shook his head, trying to clear it, and pushed himself up to do yet another check.

They were scattered about, but everyone was accounted for. Salisha and Desha were slowly getting up, looking around with wide eyes. Ander had managed a sitting position, but Takeshi could tell he was going to need medical help soon. Jamirh also needed to get those cuts seen to, but he seemed responsive as Jeri helped him stand. There was still something about her arm that was bothering Takeshi, but he couldn't figure it out.

Jitsu flopped down at her Human's feet. They were home now. She was going to nap.

Takeshi blinked and finally took in their surroundings.

They were in Hades' temple in Tarvishte.

How... how had Jak... had he gated them all the way back? *How?*

Takeshi saw Jak crumpled on the floor off to the side, and he felt a spike of alarm. The man looked like he was struggling to push himself up. Takeshi felt a growing horror as he darted as quickly as he could to Jak's side. This close, he should be able to feel some echo of magic, proof of life, but Jak had none. To Takeshi, Jak felt like a corpse.

But he was still moving, face full of pained determination.

"Ander!" Takeshi called, beginning to panic. He reached for his own failing reserves, hoping beyond hope that they could at least stabilize Jak before–

"No, don't do that, kid," Jak coughed, pushing Takeshi's hands away even as Ander stumbled over. "Don't waste your time or energy. You need it more than I do at this point. You, either," he warned in Ander's direction.

Takeshi met Ander's eyes and found them equally horrified. He looked up, and Takeshi followed his gaze.

Hades was still present, watching Jak quietly.

"You must choose," she said soothingly. "To all living beings – the right to choose."

Somehow, Takeshi didn't think she meant the Choice to become her priest.

Jak met her eyes defiantly. "No." He paused to cough again, radiating pain. "I do *not* choose death."

What?

She nodded, unfazed. "Sleep, then. You've done well. The world will still be here when you awaken, beloved."

Jak closed his eyes.

And with that, she began to sing.

Ripples of power in the air formed threads of magic that danced to the music of her voice. Takeshi could feel the music in the air directing the magic, felt a surprising pull, like the magic wanted him to join her in the song. He shook his head, confused, as the music lifted Jak away from him and Ander. Eddies of power began to swell in the air, saturating the area with magic as little crystals began to form around the threads. Jak began to glow with a pale blue-lavender color, and his soul crystal appeared before him. It pulsed brightly once, and Jak began to turn translucent.

He was turning to crystal.

Hades continued to sing as the transformation took place. The crystal spread outward from his chest, forming whimsical and geometric shapes around him, not unlike the explosion of spell crystal that had heralded Jak's arrival at Tilden Base but in a much smaller area.

And then it was over.

A perfect crystal statue of Jak stood in Hades' sanctuary, surrounded by the bruised and broken people he had saved.

Rhode was upset.

Every avenue he followed led to either a dead end or more questions. How was Hel really connected with the cult of Hades? Was she even actually connected to Romanii? What was "magic shaped like an Avari," and how was it able to break free of the prism sphere? Who and what was the Witch of the High Tide? Why had Kobayashi Rikona, a woman who feared nothing, fled the mainland in favor of her backwater province?

Why had the priest called Hel a distraction?

Was all of it connected, or none of it?

Someone, somewhere, had to know *something* about this Avari! She couldn't have just popped into existence moments before the arrest of Ebryn. She had to have traveled from the Wall. There had to be some real trace of her somewhere in the Empire! Why couldn't he find it?

The radio on his hip crackled to life, but he turned it off. Maybe, if he went over what they had one more time, something would stand out, something he could follow.

Cole fell into step beside him. "Did you just turn your radio off, sir?"

"It's a distraction right now. The answer has to be here somewhere," he snapped.

"Yes, sir," she agreed, looking back over her shoulder at the Truth Seeker keeping pace behind them. "Madine?"

"Some success, some failure," the blindfolded woman answered. "As expected."

"No, not as expected," he disagreed. "Expecting failure is how one suffers failure. We know the information is out there somewhere, we just have to find it."

"Yes, sir," Cole repeated again after a pause. She adjusted her glasses.

Rhode stopped suddenly, head whipping around. "Did you hear that?"

Both women tensed, looking around, but they were alone in the hallway just outside his office. "Hear what?" Cole asked.

"I thought I heard dogs barking," he said, puzzled. None of the research in Charve involved dogs. "Odd." Actually, where was everyone? The offices weren't usually this deserted until later at night.

"No, sir. I didn't hear any dogs," Cole said after a moment, glancing back at Madine again.

"There are no dogs on this base that I am aware of," the Truth Seeker affirmed. "But it is time." Her hand hovered over her gun.

"Time for what?" Rhode asked absently. He opened his office door, already making a mental list of material to review as he entered. He took several steps into the room before he froze.

Inside, sitting on *his desk*, was the white-haired Avari witch herself, wearing a long black dress that seemed to disappear into the shadows of the room. Strangely, he could see through her. He could hear dogs barking again.

Hel smiled.

"Change," Madine answered him dispassionately.

The door swinging shut coincided with the sound of a single gunshot.

Epilogue

Jamirh didn't know what to do with himself anymore.

The Blade was broken. Did that make him free? Release him from Ebryn's promise to Hades?

He didn't know.

Neither Ebryn nor Ryn had spoken to him since they'd returned to Tarvishte, no matter how much he'd called, begged, or threatened. He didn't know why. Did they blame him for the loss of the Crystal Light Blade? Was it somehow his fault? Ander had said it was because magic and tech didn't mix well, but what if it was because of him, something he did or didn't do? Had the Blade itself been part of what made them talking to him possible? What if Ryn was upset after having seen... after having seen...

Jamirh forcibly pushed the image away as his stomach rolled. It was gone now. It didn't exist. He didn't have to think about it ever again. Especially not when he caught a glance of himself in a mirror.

There'd been a whirlwind of activity surrounding the Temple after Jak had become a statue, so Jamirh didn't feel comfortable going there and trying to confront Hel, either. Takeshi and Ander had been pulled into a bunch of meetings with Vlad and Prim and other important people about all the things that had happened. Even Jeri...

They'd all been rushed to the hospital following their sudden reappearance in Tarvishte. Jeri had checked in on him, made sure his hand and arm had been treated, but since then he'd barely seen her. He hoped it was because she was one of the important people who needed to be at the meetings, and not because she was avoiding him. Was she mad at him because of the Blade? He hoped not. He could remember her helping him through the shock of the loss of the Blade, so maybe it was just because she was very busy.

He was definitely not one of the important people. Not anymore, not without the Blade.

He'd been sleeping a lot since they returned. He was just so tired.

And being awake meant there was a possibility of seeing a mirror.

But still, Jeri had been hovering to an almost obnoxious degree before they'd left to go on the mission. And even during the mission.

Now she was nowhere to be found.

He might have felt abandoned, if not for one thing. Well, two things. Two people.

"But how does all this work?" Desha asked, poking at his television screen.

"The connectors and things don't look anything like they do at home," Salisha agreed, stretching to look at the back.

"Everything looks old," the first twin snorted.

"And wide! Look how wide it is," the other said, gesturing with her hands.

"Boilers and steam," Jamirh explained with a shrug. "I really haven't thought too much about it."

Salisha squinted at him. "Why not?"

"Uh..." How was he supposed to answer that?

"Well, we've got some time t' work on it," Desha shrugged.

Her sister nodded cheerfully. "The Wizard said that Mara said that Cap'n said it'll take two t' three weeks t' get here."

"Don'll love it!" Desha squealed.

Jamirh winced as Salisha pulled a screwdriver out from a pocket. "Please don't take anything important apart."

"Anythin' we take apart..."

"...We can put back together again."

"That's why Cap'n keeps us around!" Salisha finished with a huge grin.

"Uh huh." Jamirh hoped this was okay, but he also didn't think he could stop them. The twins were like a force of nature. But they were keeping him from dwelling on how badly everything had gone, and for that, he was thankful. Absently, he rubbed his right hand. The bandages itched.

The mirror on the wall across the room caught his eye and he shuddered, gripping his key tightly.

Maybe he could cover them?

Takeshi watched the recording. Despite the poor quality, the events that played out were difficult to deny.

Two Truth Seekers, beheading the Emperor during a speech in front of thousands of people.

"It lines up with what I could understand of their thoughts," he informed Vlad, who looked grim. "When she touched me, I could hear and feel all of them, simultaneously. They wanted me to know that our deaths wouldn't be in vain, since they were also trying to destroy the bionics, and breaking free of the Empire simultaneously." He considered the flood of information he had been privy to for that one moment before Hades cut him off. "I think this might have already happened by then."

Vlad nodded. "Based on the timing, then yes. This took place during your assault in the Nyphoren." He heaved a deep sigh. "This is going to make things interesting."

Takeshi petted the top of Jitsu's head absently. "Interesting" was one word for it. "Has there been any word about the Em– the Duchess of Ni Fon?"

"She hasn't made an official announcement just yet, but you might as well call her Empress," Prim said with a grimace.

"Without a clear heir, the Rose Empire will almost certainly fracture as the dukes and duchesses all vie for power," Elena agreed.

Vlad looked thoughtful. "Most of them may try to avoid all-out war, but Kobayashi has no reason not to simply declare her independence. Ni Fon's distance will ensure it breaks away cleanly. The others won't have what's necessary to keep her in line."

"Especially without support from the Truth Seekers," Prim agreed.

Well, then. Takeshi supposed his original mission had been successful after all. But who could have guessed the rebellion he'd been sent to find would be the Empire's own elite troops? He didn't think the Empress had known. He liked to think she would have told him if that were the case.

"The Empire now lacks any true magical support," Elena mused. "That'll make things even more interesting."

"It's good for us," Takeshi pointed out. "Since we aren't done yet."

Hades agreed wordlessly in the back of his mind.

Vlad brought a hand up to rub at his eyes. "Do we know how many other plants there are? Or which ones the Truth Seekers targeted?"

Takeshi hummed. "I believe that was the only facility that was putting out finished bionics, so that was a heavy blow to production. But if I am understanding this information correctly – and I might not be – I think there are a number of other facilities that were in charge of specific parts. I don't know how many of those remain. And there are still bionics left out there, though Hades can't tell how many."

"Does the Lady expect you to hunt down each remaining Abomination?" Elena asked with a frown.

"She won't tolerate their existence," he agreed, feeling Hades seethe at the thought. But how were they going to do that?

And where did he stand with her?

He was deeply disappointed at his failure to summon his soul crystal when they had needed it most. Jak had been forced to step in and sacrifice himself to make up for Takeshi's failure.

:That is absolutely not what happened.:

But it was, wasn't it? If Takeshi had been able to shield them, Jak wouldn't have had to save them.

:Nothing short of an aegis would have protected you from the Truth Seekers' spell. Death was woven into the very fabric of it. It's possible they even accidentally piggy-backed off the flooding to make it stronger,: Hades tried to reassure him. *:Using one's soul crystal is something that takes time to get right.:*

Takeshi shook his head, knowing that was how she saw it, but it wasn't the truth.

And why could he still hear the music Hades had sung, whispering through everything?

Ander leveled an unimpressed look at Jeri. "So you'll just... not tell him?"

She wouldn't meet his eyes. "He doesn't have to know." Her left arm wavered as the shadows it consisted of wandered before she could rein them back in.

He raised one eyebrow. "He will if it keeps doing *that*."

"It won't!" she denied quickly. "I just need more practice keeping it in place."

Ander rolled his eyes as he turned back to his papers, shuffling them into the proper folders since the exam was over. "You're a Vampire. It'll grow back in a decade or so. The charade is completely unnecessary."

"You don't understand – he'll blame himself," she insisted. "And it wasn't his fault. None of it was! So if I can–"

"Sure, using your shadows to replace an arm – something that will increase your required blood intake by about seventy percent and require almost constant concentration to keep them in the proper shape – is much easier than simply admitting that you *lost it in a battle with Abomination*," he snapped. "But fine – do it your way. There's no way this could go wrong later when he finds out, because no matter what you think you will not be able to keep this up as long as you'll need to."

She whirled and stormed out of his office without another word.

Ander sighed, suddenly feeling very tired in a way not even coffee could help. The loss of the Blade was... well. It had been a symbol people had relied on, and many people – Ander himself included – had sacrificed much to ensure it would reach an Ebryn. With it gone, where did that leave them? Even knowing that the Blade had not been their only route to success didn't ease the shock and sting of its loss.

Had it all been for nothing? This mission, the previous Ebryn's death, the catastrophe of three hundred years ago... had any of it meant anything, in the end?

Alice had almost died because of that damned Blade. Had died, in fact, before Ander and Hades had managed to bring her back.

And now it was gone, and Jak with it. A bitter, mirrored echo of when the Blade had come into Ander's possession. There would be no miracle to bring Jak back.

He gave Jeri a few more moments to leave, then entered into the sanctuary proper himself, heading to where Jak stood, and would likely stand for some time.

:How long?: he asked Her again, knowing the answer wasn't going to change.

:Five years, fifty, five thousand… it's impossible to know.: There was sympathy in Her voice. *:But he will return to us when he is ready.:*

Ander shuddered. How did one recover from that? Jak didn't have magic. It felt like he had used his life force instead, and by the time Ander had gotten to him, it felt like he'd had none left. But he'd still been moving and talking, so… somehow he'd held on.

:He did not choose to die.:

Could it really be that simple?

There were so many places they had gone wrong, and Jak had paid for it. Hell, he'd known they were missing something. If he had realized earlier that the Blade wouldn't be able to deal with the tech in the bionics–

:It's difficult to predict the exact ways magic and tech will react.:

And if he hadn't used up so much power to contain the Blade's energy when it broke–

:Then everyone would have died in the resulting explosion of elemental energy that had been contained for over a thousand years.:

Then maybe he could have helped Takeshi shield them when the Truth Seekers destroyed the base–

:Which would have required an aegis, which none of you have ever cast.:

And then Jak wouldn't be dead.

:Jak is not dead. He is healing. It will take time, but he isn't gone.: Hades' voice was calmly reassuring.

:Semantics,: he retorted bitterly.

:There is no fault here that belongs to any of you,: She insisted. *:It is what it is. Hear me – Jak is not dead.:*

Perspective made it so truth varied from person to person, Ander reflected.

How would Siva see it, when she arrived?

Sherri Cole remembered the day her sister had been taken away.

Their parents hadn't called it that, of course – they'd said she was going to become a strong soldier for the Empire, so they had to say goodbye – but five-year-old Sherri had been deeply affected by the fear in nine-year-old Madine's eyes as the two strange adults in blindfolds had led her away. Sherri had been scared of them too.

So when she realized that plants would do things if she wanted them to, she kept that information to herself. It was a quiet thing. No one noticed.

Madine would later tell her the word for what she was – "dryad." A type of "inherent" magic that was difficult to sense and easy to hide.

She joined the military herself, when she was older. If Madine had become a soldier, then so could Sherri. She'd find her on her own terms.

And one day she had.

Madine was different than she remembered, because Madine was now one of many, but she was still Sherri's sister, and Sherri still loved her. And really, Sherri was more like the Truth Seekers than the rest of the military with her magic anyway. They understood when Sherri told them how unsettled she felt after seeing that first bionic in action, how dirty the air around it had seemed. Madine had explained how the bionics were some sort of corruption of the natural world and only mages seemed to realize how terrible they really were. She told Sherri their desire to be free and she agreed to help instantly.

They waited for Ebryn to appear, for the god to appear with him. They decided on plans and contingencies.

Ebryn appeared, but he fled north before anything could be confirmed. A woman was captured who might have been a god. It was hard to tell; gods had not walked the earth in centuries. They had to be sure. When she flaunted the rules of magic, they decided that was a good sign. When the god died at the side of a person who was not Ebryn, they hesitated, but then Ebryn had resurfaced again – with the Blade, no less – clearly attempting to destroy the bionics. He was even with the shinobi who had attempted to free the god. The Seekers agreed that was the sign they had been waiting for, even if they hadn't finished putting everything into place. And they acted.

Successfully, for the most part. Losses were within projected totals. There was still work to do – the Seekers weren't safe by any means, and many of the bionics still existed – but today had been a good start. Most people responsible for the creation of the bionics were dead, and the death of the Emperor would keep the remaining military from striking back as one.

Sherri deeply regretted having to kill Rhode. She had liked him as a commander. But he wouldn't have understood the world they wanted to bring about.

Magic wasn't something you could stomp out.

Magic was something that *lived*.

Jak is gone. The Blade is shattered. Truth Seekers have killed the Emperor. Abomination is still present in the world at large, and we have – to all intents and purposes – failed.

Thus I have done my best to record these recent events. Though they ended fairly catastrophically, with the (I am assured temporary) loss of the head of my order, words have power – and I am certain you have an opinion on the story so far. So perhaps you might be convinced to leave proof that these words have been read, maybe on Goodreads or Amazon? Or wherever you found them. Maybe it will make a difference. It certainly will to the author, even if we ourselves are doomed, anyway.

In the meantime, I have important work to get back to.

- Ander 3/1/27

Acknowledgements

Two books down! And more to go... so many more to go. I am always thankful to those who have given my their unwavering support and time as I work my way through these projects.

Thank you:

To Jessy Jacobs, who gave me tons of early feedback and was always chomping at the bit for more content. To Lydia Troiano, who is always down for an in-depth conversation about character and characters. To Angel Moisés Cruz, whose excitement over new plot revelations was always inspiring. To Bill Millette, whose medical expertise did come in handy for this book.

To my brother John Sauco, who still hasn't finished the first book but still lets me ramble. To Sarah LaFontaine, only ever a text away with infinite support and commiseration.

To my editorial team, Breyonna Jordan, Naomi Munts, and Jane Spencer, all who had to deal with my interesting choices in punctuation and formatting.

To others who gave feedback and support along the way: Josh Hornoff, Ashley McKhann, Joe Millette, and Andrew LaFontaine.

To Jessy (again) and Jen Jacobs, who continue to bring my book to life through audio.

And finally, to my parents, for many childhood trips to Barnes and Noble and Borders.

About the Author

Liz Sauco is an author from Rhode Island who enjoys a host of nerdy pastimes, such as crocheting cute animal plushies and playing video games. After graduation from the University of Rhode Island with a degree in Classics, she spent several years teaching Latin to high school students while working on her first manuscript. You can find her on Facebook, Discord, and Tiktok, and read her blog at lizsauco.com.

Free Short Story

Want to stay up to date on the latest news?

Join my newsletter, and receive a free short story "Another Beginning", set twenty years before *Lost Blades*. Be among the first to get news about new releases, giveaways, events, and promotions!

Want more from the world of Gaia?

Can't get enough? Want to really dive deep into the lore? Check out Campfire, where you can get character profiles, art, maps, timelines, location info, bonus short stories, and more for all of my stories!

But... maybe you are interested in being *spoiled*? Ream is a new subscription platform - like Patreon, but for authors - and having one allows me to spoil readers with tons of extra content! Sneak peeks, art works-in-progress, name in the acknowledgements of books, polls, direct access to me, and

more are all offered at different tiers. You can even give me a follow for free to get a monthly update!

Also By Liz Sauco

Coming May 12, 2024

Coming September 12, 2024

Blades of the Goddess book 3, *Blades Reforged,* and *Colors of Magic,* a short story anthology looking at the lives of nine characters before the events of *Lost Blades* are both now available for preorder.

Blades Reforged Preview

Jamirh stared at the fancy drink Salisha plopped on the table in front of him. Silver eyes took in the thick, pale pink liquid in a tall glass, topped with a swirl of whipped cream and a strawberry. A red and white-striped straw stuck out next to some thin curls of white chocolate. A strawberry milkshake. Probably spiked with some sort of alcohol, if he knew the twins at all. They added it to everything. Twice in the past month they had added it to soup, and once to a sandwich. He still wasn't sure about the salad.

Desha grinned at him from where she lounged in her chair, feet up on the café table. Her green eyes sparkled with mischief. "Ohh! That one looks good!"

"It is," her sister confirmed, putting two more milkshakes on the table and dropping into a third chair. She leaned so that the umbrella hid her face from the sun, ending up practically laying on Desha, who pushed her sister's sun-bleached blonde hair out of her face.

Jamirh cringed internally, seeing the disapproving glances of the other patrons, but obediently tried a sip. "It's good," he agreed, taking another sip to savor the creamy strawberry flavor. There was definitely alcohol in here. And also little crumbs of cake, maybe? "Very, uh, strawberry." He tried to muster up some excitement for them, tugging on his short ruby-red ponytail as his long ears twitched.

The way the sisters glanced at each other made him think he wasn't successful. "Well, o' course!" Salisha laughed, stretching awkwardly to grab her milkshake while keeping her eyes out of the sun. The weather was warm for late March, and the sun was obnoxiously bright. "It be a strawberry shortcake milkshake! With rum."

That made him pause. "They have rum here?" It was a little café overlooking Tarvishte's port. They served little cakes and pastries, and a selection of teas and other sweet beverages. He hadn't actually thought they had alcohol at all.

In his Life Before Hel, he never would have believed that this would be possible – an Avari, hanging out with two Humans. In Lyndiniam, the city he had lived in for his whole life, such a thing was practically unheard of. But here, in Vampire-ruled Tarvishte, the only thing that made them stand out was the disrespect Desha was showing the café furniture by putting her shoes on the table.

Hel had changed everything when she broke him out of that jail.

"No." Salisha didn't even have the grace to look sheepish as she answered his question. "I supplied it."

Jamirh decided that wasn't his problem as the sisters high-fived each other. They *were* pirates, and the milkshake *was* good. And they'd been trying so hard to cheer him up over the past month. He looked down at his right hand, and the angry red lines still present, spiraling up his arm. Marcus had removed the stitches two weeks ago, but the wounds caused by exploding magical artifacts took longer to heal, apparently.

Everything that could have gone wrong in their raid of Tilden Base had. Bionics had followed them everywhere. The ghost of Ebryn Stormlight had appeared. The Crystal Light Blade had shattered. Truth Seekers had magically blown up the base. It was a miracle any of them were still alive – a miracle Jak, Hades' first high priest, had paid for with his own life.

Despite the sisters' efforts, Jamirh felt lost. Takeshi and Ander had been busy doing something priest-related, since another priest was supposed to be arriving soon. Jeri, who'd been by his side since Hel had broken him out, was busy as a member of Romanii's defensive force trying to determine if the Emperor's death was going to cause problems for Romanii. Many of the other friends he'd made here were also members of the Black Watch. Everyone was trying to figure out how to track down the remaining bionic Abominations, since Hel had been clear that some still existed somewhere and they had to be destroyed.

Everyone except Jamirh, it felt like.